Stories of Crime & Detection
Volume Twelve

She Got What She Asked For

James Ronald

Edited by Chris Verner

Moonstone Press

This edition published in 2024 by Moonstone Press
www.moonstonepress.co.uk

Introduction and About the Author © 2023 Chris Verner

She Got What She Asked For originally published in 1941 by *J.B. Lippincott*

Stories of Crime and Detection, Vol XII She Got What She Asked For © 2025 the Estate of James Ronald.

The right of James Ronald to be identified as author of this work has been asserted in accordance with the Copyright, Designs and Patents Act 1988

ISBN 978-1-899000-98-2
eISBN 978-1-899000-99-9

A CIP catalogue record for this book is available from the British Library
Text designed and typeset by Moonstone Press
Cover illustration by Jason Anscomb

Royalties from the sale of this book will be donated to MND Scotland, who fund ground-breaking MND (motor neurone disease) research and world-class clinical trials to combat an uncommon condition that affects the brain and nerves, and causes weakness that gets worse over time, eventually resulting in death.

Contents

INTRODUCTION	7
ABOUT THE AUTHOR	9
SHE GOT WHAT SHE ASKED FOR	15
THE LONELY MAN	251

INTRODUCTION

This twelfth and final volume of James Ronald, Stories of Crime and Detection, contains a full-length novel *She Got What She Asked For*, a swift moving American story of detection set mainly in New York, and a novella, *The Lonely Man*, set in Scotland.

Claire, the woman Nick Abbott married, was beautiful. She was so beautiful she hurt your eyes. She also hurt your pocketbook. In fact, she was so beautiful she could take the gold out of your teeth and get away with it. At least for a while... Then, quite suddenly, she got what she asked for—a bullet through her heart!

Nick, ragged and penniless, was caught standing drunkenly over her, his fingerprints on the gun—enough evidence and motive to send him to the electric chair. But Nick's favourite bartender, Barney, an ugly, pugnacious ex-prizefighter, and two fair and capable young women (who realise that if they succeed their client once more becomes first class matrimonial bait!) organize their own detective team and set out to prove him innocent—by fair means or foul!

Here is an expertly written mystery by an author at the top of his game, the culmination of several years of experience creating mystery thrillers. With a refreshingly new angle, a sinister and baffling plot, plenty of pulse-quickening action and plenty of twists and turns leading to a surprise finish, this is a fine example of James Ronald's ability to maintain pace while simultaneously creating real characters.

She Got What She Asked For was published by J. B. Lippincott

Company, Philadelphia, 1941. A Handi-Book version, No 8, 1942 Paperback, Kingston, NY: Quinn Publishing Co., is severely abridged. To my knowledge this story was not published in the UK.

She Got What She Asked For is the last of the Crime and Detection stories written by James Ronald before he embarked on the first of his mainstream novels; *Old Soldiers Never Die*, published by J. B. Lippincott Company, Philadelphia in 1942 and that same year released in the UK as *Medal for The General* published by Hodder and Stoughton.

The Lonely Man is a novella set in Scotland that has never before been published in hardback, paperback or pulp format. In 1957, the story was serialised over 36 days, a chapter a day, in various United States newspapers as written by James Ronald. Like his earlier story *Trial by Jury*, *The Lonely Man* was distributed by King Features Syndicate, a unit of Hearst Holdings Inc. The story was written in Scotland. It is a return to his Stories of Crime & Detection roots, after leaving Fairfield in Connecticut where he lived in the U.S. and wrote his mainstream novels.

Deborah Vail, an actress unengaged at the moment, is driving from London to Garnock, in Scotland to visit a married cousin. During a late evening storm, a flat tyre stops her on a lonely stretch of road. Lacking tools with which to change the tyre, she sloshes ahead to locate a telephone. Upon finding a house and knocking repeatedly, she is confronted at the door by a man who greets her angrily: 'You're all the same— What do you think I am—a bloody peep show? By God, —I ought to welcome you with a gun!' Thus, she meets with mysterious artist Andrew Garvin, a man shunned by a whole community who suspect him of murdering his wife. Deborah finds herself enmeshed in a thrill packed mystery of prejudice and intrigue which changes her life forever.

ABOUT THE AUTHOR

James Jack Ronald, to give his full name, was born 11 May 1905, in North Kelvinside, Glasgow, Scotland. He was the son of James Jack Ronald, a Chartered Public Accountant, and Katherine Hamilton Ronald. He was educated at Hillhead High School, Glasgow, established in 1885.

Until he was five, James Ronald says he was chubby, happy, and irresponsible; but in 1911, his sixth year, he was run over by an automobile causing a very real morbidity to creep in. For ten years following the accident he suffered recurrent dreams about a wheel that became larger and larger as it turned faster and faster. He was invalided over a long period during which, with his mother Catherine's encouragement, he enjoyed a prodigious amount of reading. He later claimed he owed his literary gift and resultant career to this near-fatal automobile accident, which caused him to change from a sunny little extrovert to a cloudy introvert.

When he was fourteen he wrote an account of the accident, setting down all the details in a somewhat light vein, not forgetting to note that the candy he had purchased with such delight on that foggy morning was found sticking to the wheels of the car as he was being carried off. The piece won him first prize for composition and congratulations from the masters at the school and even the headmaster wished him well, but that did not prevent corporal punishment for his appalling handwriting. He was called into the headmaster's office, but kept waiting so that everybody knew that he, James Ronald, was going to receive a beating from the headmaster. This injustice obviously affected him very deeply, because it remained with him all his life, and crops up in interview after interview:

> After all, I taught myself to read before going to school and could see no reason for accepting a beating because they failed to teach me how to write, so I bolted.

In a spirit of rebellion against repeated punishments for bad handwriting for compositions for which he invariably got an 'A', Ronald came home from school one day announcing he would never return. It was time to leave. His mother Catherine was understandably distressed, concerned her elder son leaving school at such a young age would diminish his career prospects. Aware of the scarcity of jobs just then in Glasgow, she told him he could only stay away from school if he remained active in some useful employment, making it clear she would not condone an idler in the family.

Within three days James Ronald was an errand boy for the *Glasgow Evening News*, a paper into which he had smuggled a poem some months earlier. But there was 'no writing, nothing editorial' in his set up and he thoroughly disliked it and lost the job. He found another post immediately with the *Glasgow Sunday Mail* and kept this one until he printed his own rival paper on the office mimeograph. He broke the machine and, failing to cover his tracks by leaving a sheet in the copier, he was fired. Then came a dozen jobs, including one with an art dealer for whom he gilded statues and washed windows. His mother told him, 'It is no disgrace to wash windows, James, but it is a disgrace to wash them like that.'

By the age of seventeen, James Ronald had run through all prospective employers in Glasgow, including every newspaper.

He felt the need of open space—'a lot of it'—and after various and sundry abortive departures, finally won grudging permission to seek his fortune in the New World.

For some reason, Chicago stuck in the mind of the young Ronald as a magic word. He became determined to travel to the United States of America. The main method of crossing the Atlantic Ocean in the 1920s was by steamship and ocean liner. The passengers aboard the *SS Saturnia* included seventeen-year-old James Ronald, who arrived at his destination on 6 December 1922, at the Port of Québec, an inland port located in Québec, Canada. From there he continued his journey across the Great Lakes to Chicago, Illinois, United States. He managed to survive in Chicago; the fastest-growing city in world history, with a flourishing economy approaching three million people, attracting huge numbers of new immigrants from Eastern and Central Europe. Ronald stayed in Chicago for five years, wanting to write, but unable to afford the time because he was forced to earn money to live. He was taken on and fired from a variety of jobs with monotonous regularity. Like his experiences in Glasgow, he exhausted all potential employers, dabbling in some forty jobs ranging from short-order cook and dishwasher to muslin salesman; from dance promoter and theatre manager to washing dishes again in a Greek restaurant. He edited ten trade journals at one time for a Chicago publisher; and gave new life to a women's religious magazine. A chain-smoker, he confessed slyly to have worked for the Anti-Cigarette League, his excuse being 'a man must eat don't you know'—at that time eating being the only philosophy he could afford to practise. It was in the Windy City that he learned about life.

Working in the U.S. as 'a visitor' to avoid immigration may have caught up with Ronald because, in 1927, he returned to Britain on a more permanent basis, and secured a well-paid job with an English newspaper chain, and a promise of future advancement. However, during his first holiday in the job, a car accident disrupted this promising career trajectory. Whilst driving a small open two-seater Rover 8, Ronald was struck by a two-ton truck and thrown out against the radiator of another vehicle. Left with a broken hip and temporarily crippled (and without the newly acquired job), he settled down to write.

Ronald's writing developed in three stages. First, he hammered out serializations and short stories which were syndicated in newspapers, both at home and abroad; and a number were also published in obscure pulp magazines. Some stories then became lost and forgotten and this has unfortunately contributed to a lack of recognition for an impressive body of work. These early narratives were very difficult to track down, but searching has provided me with an enjoyable and rewarding task—a treasure hunt for lost tales. This was not made any easier because many of these stories were published under pseudonyms; Peter Gale, Mark Ellison, Kenneth Streeter, Alan Napier, and even women; Cynthia Priestley and Norah Banning—in addition to known pseudonyms Michael Crombie and Kirk Wales. Those I have discovered have all been gathered together for republication in this series.

A second writing stage followed; the full-length mystery stories which have made him so popular with Golden Age of Detection aficionados. They are out-of-print, elusive to find, and first editions are very expensive.

Finally, late in life, James Ronald embarked on his Dickensian-style life drama novels. He received enthusiastic praise for his ingenuity, freshness, and sharp sense of humour by many critics and writers of the time, such as August Derleth. Orville Prescott, the main book reviewer for *The New York Times* for 24 years, called James Ronald 'a born novelist', and that he 'has in full measure the two basic drives which inspire a writer of fiction—the urge to create characters and to tell stories about them. Mr. Ronald does both naturally, directly and well.' His work received praise and has been compared to William de Morgan, H. G. Wells, Rudyard Kipling, J. M. Barrie, and Somerset Maugham.

James Ronald is a writer who has not gained the long-term recognition he deserves. His work has received high praise for his ingenuity, freshness, and sharp sense of humour by many critics and writers of the time and current enthusiasts, highlighting him as one of the leading storytellers of the day, yet barely anything has been republished since his death in 1972. I hope the reader will enjoy these imaginative and entertainingly written stories as much as I have collecting them.

Chris Verner
Berkhamsted, Buckinghamshire, UK
April 2023

SHE GOT WHAT SHE ASKED FOR

Chapter 1

It was past noon when Mrs. Cleary marched into Nick Abbott's room without knocking. Although he had been half awake for hours, Nick was pretending to be asleep. It was not Mrs. Cleary he wanted to fool—but himself. Life had become a creditor he was trying to dodge and only when asleep or drunk could he do it. So, his days had fallen into a shiftless routine: as long as possible he kept his eyes screwed tight, his face buried in the pillow and the blankets pulled over his head; and when he could no longer kid even himself, he went out and pawned something and got plastered.

Mrs. Cleary had no time to play games. She did not trouble to go through the motions of waking him. When she spoke, her voice was a file rasping over metal.

"Woman wants you on the phone. Says she's your wife."

Keeping his face on the pillow, Nick grunted, "Tell her I'm out."

"Tell her yourself. I've no time to bandy words with her."

Nick rolled over on his back, pulling the bedclothes up about his neck. His eyes had trouble with the bright noon sun. He made no move to rise because, under sheet and blankets, he was naked. Without being told, Mrs. Cleary knew that he was not wearing pyjamas; he had none to wear.

"Here," she said, taking his raincoat from a hook and tossing it to him.

She looked the other way and Nick slid out of bed. He went out to the hall and picked up the telephone receiver, which dangled at the end of its cord. He moistened his lips but did not speak. Nick had nothing to say to the woman at the other end of the wire, the woman who was his wife. The sound of her voice would start his nerves jumping with pain. Without saying anything, he hung up and went back to his room, avoiding the scornful gaze of Mrs. Cleary, standing just inside the door.

The telephone bell shrilled again. Mrs. Cleary went to answer it.

"He don't live here no more," she said flatly; and banged down the receiver. She came back into the room.

"You heard what I said? Well, I meant it. I've waited six weeks for my rent, that's long enough. You're getting out right now. Call back for your things when you've got my money."

For weeks Nick had expected her to tell him to go, so it was no surprise. In a way, it was a relief; one unpleasant experience he need no longer dread. Mrs. Cleary eyed him as if requiring him to go that instant, just as he was, in birthday suit and soiled raincoat.

"Mind if I shave first?"

Ignoring the sarcastic inflexion in his voice, she said, "Go ahead and shave."

He waited for her to leave the room but she stood there as firmly as if she had taken root.

"Last time I let a deadbeat shave before he went, he put on two suits and all his shirts when my back was turned. That don't happen to me twice."

So, Nick washed and shaved under her eye. It was like being a child again and having his mother stand over him to see that he made a thorough job of neck and ears. There were no clean shirts in the drawer and he could not remember whether he had worn the one that lay over a chair five days or only four. He asked if his laundry had come.

"Sure, it came. It came yesterday when you were out. The man wanted ninety-six cents and I wasn't laying out my own good money, so he took it away again."

Nick put on the shirt that lay across the chair. "I'm sorry about the money I owe you. You'll get it one day."

"Yeah, one day—judgment day."

"Thanks, anyway, for letting me stay so long."

"I didn't let you stay because I wanted to be kind to you. I got my hands too full making a living to waste pity on a bum. I let you stay because I thought I'd get my money. You looked like you were on the level when you first come but you're no good and now it's showing in your face. I never saw a man run to seed so fast."

She was saying nothing that Nick's conscience did not tell him when he was neither asleep nor drunk, so he tried not to listen. He could not talk back—like his conscience, she knew all the answers. When dressed, he started for the door but Mrs. Cleary put one of her large hands on his chest and held the other under his nose: "I'll take my key."

Nick produced his keyring. At one time a lot of keys had dangled from it but he had given up those to his desk and office when his partners forced him out; and the key to his safe-deposit box when there was nothing left in it; and the key to his car when the loan company claimed it; and the key to the apartment when Claire told him she was through; and now there was only Mrs. Cleary's front door key and three others which had been on the ring as long as he could remember, which he had not used for years, whose use he had long ago forgotten.

His hands were shaking so that he could not detach Mrs. Cleary's key. He handed her the ring and went down the stairs. Without a thing in the world to lock or unlock, what did he want with a keyring? There was a letter for him on a table in the hall. He put it in his pocket and went out of the house, shutting the door behind him. It was a lovely day but Nick was not in the mood for it. Rain would have suited him better. Blue skies and a brassy sun were like personal insults. Fifth Avenue may have been bright and sparkling but West Twenty-Ninth Street was only hot and dusty. Chipped railings. Crumbling stone. Rotting wood. In the strong light the houses looked like wrinkled hags.

There were plenty of bars in the neighbourhood and Nick was sweating for a drink but he walked all the way uptown to Poli's. In the past, Nick had spent a lot of money in the place and he hoped Poli would remember it and trust him for a couple of drinks. That would make four, for he had enough in his pocket to pay for two; and four drinks was about the number he needed these days to make him feel almost human.

His empty stomach was flapping against his backbone and the warm smells from the restaurants he passed made him light-headed with desire for food but he kept going until he arrived at Poli's. There he spun his last fifty cents on the bar and ordered two shots of rye. After downing the first at a gulp, he took his time over the other, trying to frame words with which to ask for credit. He took out his letter and tore open the envelope.

Dear Nick,
"What do you mean by disappearing and making me hunt all over town for you? If what I hear is true and you're in trouble, why haven't you got in touch with me? I'm at my place in Connecticut and I'll be good and sore if you don't join me there as soon as you get this. Make it a good long stay; it seems an age since we saw anything of each other. On the off chance that it may be of use to you, I'm enclosing a check. I'll be expecting you soon. No excuses.

Julian

The check was for two hundred dollars. Nick hesitated before tearing it up. It was good of Julian—especially good since Julian regarded money as slightly more precious than his life's blood—but Nick had not reached the point of taking money from his friends. He could owe money to a landlady; get drunk on credit; but there were still things he could not do. It might be a queer kind of pride but it was all he had left. He shredded the letter and dropped the pieces into an ashtray.

Henry, one of the barmen, came over to him and said curtly, "You're wanted on the phone. It's your wife." Henry had patent-leather hair and was reputed to be the politest barman in town but he had stopped wasting politeness on Nick about the time Nick pawned his gold watch.

"Tell her I'm not here."

"I already told her you are."

"Then tell her I don't want to talk to her."

Henry went away but in a few minutes he came back. "She's going to keep phoning until you answer."

"Well, it's her phone and her time."

"Maybe so," said Henry, with a bleak up-and-down stare that made Nick itch to pull his nose, "but it's the boss's phone at this end. You better talk to her. The boss will get sore if she keeps calling."

The telephone was fixed to a wall in a corner and to reach it Nick had to squeeze past a table at which sat three men. He recognized two of them: Big Eddie Grogan and his manager. The talk around Poli's was that Big Eddie was a coming heavyweight champion. If having the ugliest face that ever appeared in a ring would help, Nick decided it ought to be a cinch for Eddie.

When Claire's voice came to him over the wire he felt as he had known he would feel. She was poison and he knew it but his bones melted. The sound of her voice conjured up the image of her body. Moon-white. Velvet-soft. So beautiful, it almost broke your heart. Holding it in your arms, you choked with awe that anything could be so lovely. You knew you were not the first, or the tenth, but under her spell you did not care. That was about all there was to Claire; a body. Her brain was little and scheming. In the year of their married life Nick had never had the smallest reason to suppose she had a heart.

"I want to see you. Come up to the apartment at four this afternoon."

"Look," said Nick, "we're through. I like it that way. Why don't you leave me alone?"

"You flatter yourself. I only want to talk to you."

"We've nothing to talk about."

"I think we have."

"Just what?"

"I want to talk to you about a divorce."

"We don't need to talk about that. You can go to Reno any time you like."

"I don't want a Reno divorce. I want a New York one."

"I get it. I'm supposed to provide evidence?"

"That isn't it at all," she retorted impatiently. "I'll provide the evidence."

"Let's get this straight," said Nick. "Who divorces who?"

"You guessed it. You divorce me."

That one almost floored him. It was the essence of Claire's racket always to be the injured party. None of the mud she stirred up ever stuck to her.

"What about your reputation?" he asked, with a sour laugh.

But Claire did not think that was so funny.

"Who's up there with you?" Nick said.

"What makes you think there's someone with me?" she stalled.

"I don't know. I just have a feeling. It's a man, of course. You don't know any women. It wouldn't be worth your while."

"It won't pay you to talk like that," she said angrily. "Be nice and there's five hundred dollars in this for you."

"You bitch," Nick said; and hung up on her. As he pushed past Grogan's table the prize-fighter caught his eye.

"That's no way to talk to a lady," he said, grinning.

Nick gave him a look that wiped off the grin. "Pull in your ears and button your lip."

Eddie Grogan bobbed up as if stuck with a pin and made for Nick, his huge hands clenched. Nick stood waiting for him but Grogan's manager jumped between them.

"No, no, Eddie," he cried, gripping the big man's arm. "You break your hand on this mug and where'll we be Saturday night?"

"The guy insulted me," protested Grogan. The other man who had been sitting at the table was helping the manager to hold him.

"I couldn't insult you," Nick sneered. "There aren't words."

What had got into him, Nick did not know. It was not what the fighter had said, or the way he had said it. Nick bore him no grudge; he was just a big cocky kid trying to be funny. But Nick wanted Grogan to hit him and, before the fighter knocked him out, Nick wanted to plant a fist in the middle of Grogan's ugly face. Inside Nick there was an insane desire to hurt—and to be hurt.

"The guy's a screwball, Eddie," said the manager. "Don't pay him no heed."

"Sure, sure, he's crazy," agreed the third man. "You don't want to waste your time on a crazy guy."

"Look me up some day, Grogan," Nick said, "when your nursemaids aren't around."

There was not going to be a fight, so he turned and walked away. Mike, the bouncer, had appeared and he walked behind Nick, breathing on his neck, as far as the door. Nick could have had a fight with Mike without even trying but the finish of a scrap with a bouncer is always ludicrous and he had made a big enough fool of himself already.

He wanted another drink, he wanted a lot more drinks, so

he went downtown to Muldoon's Tavern on Twenty-Eighth Street. Barney, the bartender there, was a friend of his. Nick had done him a good turn which was not forgotten. It was like this: late one night Barney had addressed a few reproving words to a drunk and the drunk had not liked it. Barney had been tactful but this drunk did not know tact When he saw it. He pulled a knife. Barney had turned to serve another customer and the knife was within an inch of his back when Nick kicked the drunk's legs from under him. After they threw the drunk into the street Barney bought Nick a drink and said that Nick had saved his life.

So now Nick was going to scrounge more drinks from Barney on the strength of it.

That was the kind of heel Claire had made of him.

Chapter 2

In the lull after the midday rush at Muldoon's, Old Doc Learie took from behind the kitchen door a broom almost as bald as himself and began to ply it lethargically. From the front he worked in past the cigarette-machine and the beer-slopped bar. Behind the bar, above the cash register, hung a framed dollar bill, the first money the place had taken when it opened and Old Doc Learie never passed near it without larceny in his heart. He had dreams in which no one was looking and he jerked the framed bill from the wall and stowed it under his coat.

While sweeping, he kept up an angry grumbling below his breath, most of it in Latin, much of it profane. He was telling the cock-eyed world where it got off. He did that often when Muldoon's was empty; never when there were customers at the bar. Those he greeted with pulpy, ingratiating smiles, for a customer represented a possible free beer and the acquisition of free beers had become the motivation of his life. For a free beer he would have stood on his ancient hairless dome or sold his fully mortgaged soul. The butt of many a crude and pointless jest, he took them with moist grins. Behind their backs, he told his tormentors what they were in a dead language long void of any other use for him.

Every bone showed through his flesh, for a dozen men would buy him a drink—and make him clown for it—for one who would buy him a meal. Face, neck and hands wrinkled as prunes, yellow as old ivory; rheumy blue eyes with swollen veins crisscrossed like road maps; a scattering of decaying teeth, resembling the rotting posts of a collapsed fence; wispy white hair fringing the bare crown of his head; a tobacco-stained moustache drooping raggedly over his slack mouth. A suit of black worsted, green at the seams, beer-stained in front, shiny behind, hung loosely on his shrunken frame. About once a week his battered derby was knocked from his head and used as a football. His shirt and high stiff collar were as dirty as garments can become and yet be recognizable as once-white. His tie was a length of black tape, with a chewed appearance, tied in a bow. He had cut his shoes in several places to make room for his bunions.

Why he was allowed to hang out in Muldoon's was a mystery lost in the cluttered past. He was there all day and most of the night, dozing in one of the booths when weariness overtook his aged bones. At closing time Barney usually tossed him a coin for a bed in a flophouse. When the coin was not forthcoming Old Doc Learie slumbered through chill early morning hours wrapped in newspaper in a packing-case at the rear of a nearby fur-warehouse and the policeman on the beat let him be.

Two or three times a day the old man would shuffle from one end of the place to the other, going through motions with this all but hairless broom. Now and then he made a great show of carrying out a cuspidor and bringing it back after a short absence but he always brought it back in the same condition as he had taken it away. It would have been as easy to empty it as to make a pretence of doing so but this small chicanery gave him a feeling of independence. Such dust as insisted on clinging to the broom he thrust, when Barney was not looking, into a dark corner behind the jukebox or in one of the booths.

Between two rows of tables lay a grey cat of aloof and malignant personality, whose yellow eyes stared at the old man through slit-like lids with insolent dislike. This was the only living being to whom Old Doc Learie could transfer some of the abuse visited on him and between them flourished a feud of long standing.

They looked their hatred at each other and then, with unsurpassable marksmanship, Old Doc Learie spat in the cat's eye.

"Scat," he hissed, "go on—git," jabbing the broom at the arching feline. The cat disappeared under a table—routed without a fight—and Old Doc Learie felt for a moment warm with victory.

Putting away the broom, he shuffled over to the bar and stood waiting. Barney finished mopping the slopped mahogany with a damp cloth, drew a glass of beer, and set it before the old man. With brightening eyes Old Doc Learie looked at the creamy head, the golden-brown body and his tongue stole out and licked his lips.

"Yessir," he said. He nodded his head sagely, as if he had made a remark well worthy of note. "Yessir," he said again, with a different intonation, as if adding to his previous utterance a thought pointing its significance. Picking up the glass, he bore it to a booth at the rear, there to sip it preciously and then, in weariness of soul and spirit and body, to sleep.

Barney watched him go. "Crummy old bum," he muttered to himself. "I'd like to know why I put up wit' him."

Leaning on the bar, Barney sipped a small beer and conned the sports pages of the Journal-American. Barney was in the late forties; of average height; and his body bulged front and rear. His mouth was large enough to have sucked in a pudding basin and from a wart on the crown of his bald head his brow sloped to a wart on the left nostril of his long nose. He wore a pale-blue shirt, a navy-blue bow tie with white polka dots, and washable white trousers with black stripes. Around his bulging middle was an apron white on Mondays and progressively piebald the rest of the week.

Looking up at the sound of footsteps, he saw Nick Abbott and reached for a bottle of rye.

"I ought to tell you," said Nick, sliding on to a stool, "I'm broke."

"Did I, ask?" growled Barney, pouring a drink, and flanking it with a water chaser.

"You're a good friend, Barney.

"Don't fool yourself on that. A guy who stakes you to a drink when you're broke ain't no friend. At the best he's a bad influence, at the woist he's an enemy. I'll be right back. Got to phone Sam the Bookie. Just got a hot tip on a horse."

Barney went into the telephone booth, closing the door firmly behind him; dropped a nickel in the slot; dialled a number. When the call was answered, he said, "Miss Bannerman? This is Barney. You-know-who just walked in."

The answering voice was that of a girl and sounded eager, almost excited. "I'll come right over. Can you keep him until I get there?"

"He won't go away. I left a bottle of rye at his elbow."

Hanging up, Barney walked back to the bar. "When did you eat last?"

"I'm not hungry."

"That ain't what I asked you."

"I had a big breakfast."

"How many days ago?"

"You'd be a good guy, Barney," said Nick irritably, "if it weren't that the mother keeps cropping out in you."

"I ain't et yet. How's about havin' a bite wit' me?"

"I'm putting the bite on you for a couple of drinks. Isn't that enough?"

"We'll sit over there in the foist booth," said Barney placidly. He turned his head and shouted, "Hey, Joe."

A dark sweat-beaded face with glistening black hair appeared in the open hatch leading to the kitchen. "Wharra you want?"

"Two double hamburgers wit' onions and french fried. Make it snappy."

"Comin' up." The face disappeared.

Carrying the bottle of rye, Barney came out from behind

the bar. He put a slug in the jukebox and punched a button. Emptied glass in hand, Nick followed him into a booth and they sat facing each other. The juke-box started to play 'Melancholy Baby' and Barney's eyes brightened. That was his favourite tune but he rarely had a chance to play it for his customers had heard it so often they always groaned in unison at the opening bars.

When the hamburgers appeared, sizzling hot and oozing juice, Nick realised how hungry he was. He sat for a moment poised over the food, knife and fork in hand, stomach rumbling with impatience and then he started to eat—very slowly, for there was a lump in his throat. After the meal had fulfilled its destiny, Barney took a pack of cigarettes from his pocket, put one in his mouth and pushed the rest across the table. Nick helped himself and took a light from a match Barney struck.

"Put those in your pocket. I got plenty more."

"Thanks," said Nick—but he left the pack on the table. He put out a hand and gripped the rye bottle by the neck. Barney was holding it by the base but he let Nick take it from him.

"I never been one to tell other guys what to do—"

"That's what I like about you, Barney," said Nick, pouring himself a drink.

"—and I don't intend to start—"

"I'm glad to hear it."

"Okay, okay. But if I was goin' to start, I'd start right now. I'd say to you, 'Nick,' I'd say, 'snap out of it. You ain't no crummy bum like Old Doc Learie. You got youth and brains; you could put yourself on top of the heap again.' That's what I'd say to you."

"And maybe I'd say to you, 'Barney, you old goat, why the hell don't you mind your own business?'"

"Okay, Pal, okay. I only thought maybe—"

"Sure, I knew. But if I won't listen to myself—"

"Maybe you been listenin' to yourself too long," said Barney, rising and stacking the dishes. He reached for the bottle of rye but, on second thought, left it where it was; at Nick's elbow. After taking the dishes to the kitchen he went straight to the bar and buried his long nose in his newspaper.

With a clicker of tiny high heels on the linoleum a girl came in, moving as lightly as if her feet had wings. She had fine, clear skin; soft, curling hair of a striking bronze-red; dark eyebrows and lashes; candid blue eyes; and a small nose with a slight tip-tilt, which was rather charming. She wore a tailored fawn suit which made the most of a figure well worth observing; and a tiny hat, pert, gay, absurd. There was about her a quality making her more than only pretty, combining zest for living, a frank inherent friendliness and a sense of humour that would make her laugh at good and bad breaks alike. At first glance one did more than merely admire her; one liked her.

"What'll it be?" asked Barney, when she paused at the bar. Out of a corner of his huge mouth, he whispered, "He's in the foist booth—but in no mood to listen."

"Rye highball," said Kay Bannerman, breaking her own rule against drinking before the sun went down. In a low voice, she added, "Barney, we've got to snap him out of it."

"If he won't snap out of it for you"—Barney's eyes paid wistful homage to her shapely figure—"we might as well give up."

"I'll never give up"—Kay's face was grim with determination—"never."

Glass in hand, she rounded the corner of the bar, went toward the row of booths against a wall. Oblivious of her approach, Nick stared unseeingly at a point in midair. His eyes had a faraway expression.

"Hello, Nick," she said softly, sitting down opposite him.

With a start, Nick shortened his gaze. He looked at her for a moment without speaking and then he said, "Hello, Kay."

The girl forced a smile. "Long time no see."

"Maybe that was a break for you. What brings you here?"

"Oh," she tried to speak casually, "I happened to be passing."

"You happened to be passing," he repeated with flat disbelief. "I get it. You're Barney's horse."

"Barney's horse?"

"The one he was in a hurry to phone about when I came in." Nick poured himself another drink. "You used to consider yourself my conscience, Kay. I thought that was all over when I stopped needing a secretary."

The girl was silent. Without being so obvious as to stare, she looked him over and was sad at what she saw. His soiled collar and cuffs, his need of a haircut, were only details in an unhappy picture. It was the drawn pallor of his face, the bitter twist to his mouth, the haunted misery staring out of his eyes, that made her acutely wretched. In the four years she had worked for Nick Abbott he had come to mean much more to her than merely an employer.

Their eyes met. Kay was the first to look away.

"Go on," said Nick roughly. "Say it. You might as well say it as sit there looking it."

"What shall I say? Would it matter if I said it breaks my heart to see you looking like this? Or have you reached the point where nothing makes any difference?"

"Words don't matter a lot any more, if that's what you mean. I've called myself all the names there are and names have lost their sting. Amazing how easily you get to be a bum, Kay."

"Only, you haven't got there yet. Bums don't hate themselves, Nick—and you do."

"Let's change the subject, shall we? How's the firm of Grainger & Dunn making out since it got rid of Abbott?"

"I wouldn't know. I don't work there anymore."

"Oh." Nick raised his brows. "Better job?"

"Just at present I'm not working."

"Don't tell me they fired you? Why, you know more about the business than Grainger and Dunn put together."

Nick was not the only one who thought so. His former partners agreed with him. They had offered to double Kay's salary if she would stay.

"I quit. I wanted a change."

"It won't be easy to find as good a job."

"Oh, I don't know," she replied, studying her glass. "I may have found one already. It rather depends on you."

"On me?" Nick stared at her. "What do you mean?"

Drawing a deep breath, Kay said all in one mouthful, "Nick, there's a place for you in Otto Kramer's office. He'll pay you a hundred a week to start. You'll need a secretary —that's where I come in."

"Kramer wouldn't want any part of me. He knows what I think of him and his whole setup."

"He happens to need you, Nick. He has a chance to get the contract for that town-planning job on Long Island."

"The Soundview job? Grainger and Dunn have it sewn up."

"It came unstitched when they eased you out of the firm. Maybe getting rid of you wasn't as smart a move as they thought."

"I begin to see the picture. It was my job in the early stages. Kramer figures he can hire me to steal it for him from Grainger & Dunn."

"They didn't consider you when they took advantage of a clause in the partnership agreement to throw you into the street. Why should you consider them?"

"I don't think that way, Kay. Never could. You can tell Kramer—"

"Let's forget Kramer. If you don't want to work for him, go

after the Soundview job yourself. Grainger & Dunn have lost it. You won't be poaching on their preserves."

"Ask them about that and see what they say. Besides, I couldn't land a contract to design an outhouse. An architect needs an office, a place to work, equipment. I can't pluck 'em out of a hat."

"You can have all you need, if you say the word."

"Just how?"

In a small voice, Kay said, "I have over two thousand dollars saved up. That's enough to start on."

Watching his face anxiously, she added, "Don't go up in the air, Nick. Think it over. It would be a good investment for me."

Putting out a hand, Nick pressed her cool slim fingers.

"I'm not sore, Kay. It's swell of you to make the offer. But—keep your money in the bank. You'd be backing a loser. I couldn't make good for you; there's nothing left in me that even wants to try." He laughed unsteadily, harshly. "Funny. This is the second time today I've been offered money by a woman."

"Who was the other woman?" Kay's attempt at indifference was not successful.

"My wife. She wanted to give me five hundred dollars."

"And you turned her down? After all she's had out of you. Nick, you must be mad."

"If she hadn't had so much from me the gesture might have been less infuriating. Like stealing an apple and tossing back the core."

"She's not the type to part with even fifty cents for nothing."

"No. She wanted me to divorce her."

"You got that wrong. She meant it the other way round."

"That's what I thought. But I was right the first time. She wanted me to divorce her for infidelity and offered to provide the evidence."

"There's something phony about the proposal," said Kay, wrinkling her nose. "But why not take her up on it? What can you lose?"

As if he were speaking to himself, with an anger that shook him, Nick said, "I don't want to see her. I couldn't bear to look at her. I think I'd kill her with my bare hands."

"You're talking like a fool," said Kay furiously. "She isn't worth killing and you know it. Get rid of her the easy way, by divorcing her or letting her divorce you. You'll never amount to anything until you get her out of your system."

"Perhaps she's too deeply rooted for me ever to get her out. And perhaps I don't care whether I ever amount to anything or not."

"And now you're talking like a damned fool." Kay drained her glass and lit a cigarette. "Order me another drink, please. I need it."

Nick walked to the bar and ordered a rye highball. "Pretend I'm paying for this," he whispered to Barney. "I don't want her to know I'm broke."

Barney nodded comprehendingly. When he placed the highball on the bar they touched hands, pretending to transfer a bill. Barney rang up the price of the drink on the cash-register and counted four ones and some silver into Nick's hand.

"What's this?" asked Nick, staring at the money.

"Your change, Pal. You gave me a five-spot."

"Nothing doing," whispered Nick fiercely. "I owe you enough already."

"You gimme five bucks," repeated Barney, looking him in the eye. "How many times must I tell you?"

"I'll see you about this later," muttered Nick, walking away from the bar with the glass and the money in his hand.

Setting the drink in front of Kay, he let her see him putting the bills in a vest pocket, the coins in a trouser pocket. They sat in silence for a while, neither of them looking at the other.

"You could at least see her," remarked Kay, at last.

"Whatever this spell is that she's put upon you, it might lose its power if you saw her again."

"And if it didn't?"

"Then you'd know where you stand." In a spurt of irritation, she added, "If you're the kind of spineless, gutless idiot you're making yourself out to be, you fooled me for four years. I won't believe it until you go and see her and come back and tell me with your own lips that you still aren't cured of your obsession."

"It's no obsession. I know what she does to me, what she's always done to me."

"Maybe you'll find out that she doesn't do it any more, that her magic, or whatever it is, is gone. Nick, you've got to see her. She's still under your skin. You've got to set yourself free."

"And then?"

"And then," Kay said vehemently, "you can start all over again at the foot of the ladder—you can dig ditches or wash dishes—it won't matter what you do, you'll be your own man again."

"Women are all alike," said Nick, with a solemnity of manner derived from too much rye. "Never content to leave a man alone. Always wanting to make something of him."

"I couldn't make the sucker of you your wife made. Maybe you've got it right, Nick. Maybe you're not worth bothering with. Maybe all you're good for is to drink and scrounge and feel sorry for yourself. If that's the way you want it, go to it. See if I care."

"No need to cry."

"I'm not crying," she gasped, dabbing her eyes. "I—I'm just too damn mad to see straight."

Nick stood up. "All right," he said, swaying a little in disengaging himself from the booth. "I'll see Claire, if it'll make you happy. And if I ever have a secretary again it'll be one with a drunken husband and six no-good brothers and a father in the penitentiary, so she'll have enough menfolk of her own to worry about without picking on me."

After he had gone Kay sat in the booth and wept silently for a while. Drying her tears, she applied powder, lipstick, eyebrow pencil. In an effort to compose herself she lit a cigarette and finished the high-ball. Barney came over and stood looking down at her with an embarrassed air of sympathy.

"Make me another high-ball, Barney," she said, with a wan smile. "I feel like chewed string."

"You had two, that's plenty. It's no good drinkin' to forget your worries, you only wind up with more worries."

"Barney, what are we going to do about him?"

"It's up to Nick to do somethin' about himself. Maybe the guy just hasn't got the stuff."

"He's got everything it takes, Barney. I can't be wrong about that. I've known him too long. He's told me things about himself, about his origin, his fight to make his way in the world. He started from scratch, Barney. His mother died when he was nine and his father thought all you need do for a kid was keep him from starving, buy him new pants when his rear end showed through the old ones and cuff him now and then to keep him in line.

"Nick ran errands, mowed lawns, tended furnaces, to pay his way while he went to High School. He put himself through college in Indiana the same way, working hard after classes and in vacations. He told me once he didn't have a whole day off for ten years. After graduating, he came East with fifty dollars and took architecture at Yale. For two years he washed cars ten hours a night in a New Haven garage, studied by day—and ate and slept when he could. When he qualified, he came to New York, got a job in a drafting room, worked hard and saved his money. He saw a chance to join two other young men starting for themselves, and he took it. His brains, his guts, his initiative built up the firm of Abbott, Grainger & Dunn to where it amounted to something. He's got the stuff, all right. He couldn't have come up from ragged, half-starved kid without it."

"He certainly made the return trip to half-starved kid in record time," said Barney.

"He can go back up just as fast when he finds himself again."

"You don't exactly hate the guy, do you?"

"No, Barney, I don't exactly hate the guy. But when Nick looked at me, all he ever saw was a secretary. He met Claire and she took him for a sleigh ride. It didn't worry me—at first. He'd never known anything but hard work; he had a right to play. I thought he'd have fun and maybe learn a few useful lessons. I never dreamt he'd be dumb enough to marry her."

"How come you let her get away wit' it?"

"I guess she must have something I haven't got."

Barney's eyes rested approvingly on the girl. "Lady," he said lingeringly, "I don't see what it could be."

Chapter 3

While he walked east to a Fifth Avenue bus stop, the rye began to assert itself and Nick became more than a little drunk. He was angry, too: angry with Kay for interfering and for being so confoundedly right; angry with Claire for all she had done to him; angry with himself for behaving like a hurt and sulky child; angry with the sun for shining, the world for existing. He was in the blind mood in which a boy kicks the stone that trips him—and bruises his toes.

In this mood he took the wrong bus and was carried several blocks down Fifty-Seventh Street before realising his mistake. He bawled out the unoffending conductor and was crushingly bawled out in return. He forgot to ask for a transfer and had to pay another dime to continue his journey in the right direction. At Eighty-Eighth Street he alighted and walked east to Park Avenue. At the ornate building in which Claire lived he went into the elevator and said, "Eighteenth floor." The boy in uniform looked at him politely but uncompromisingly. "You have to be announced, sir. If you'll give your name to the clerk—"

"It's all right," said Nick curtly (every slight impediment was a major annoyance), "I'm calling on my wife."

"Even so, sir, it's, one of our strict rules—"

"Damn your rules," said Nick but he wavered out of the elevator and over to the desk.

The clerk, a young man with permanently waved hair and a slave bracelet, gave him a supercilious glance. "I'm sorry, Mrs. Abbott is out."

"When did she go?"

"I really couldn't say," simpered the young man, patting his back hair languidly. "I only just came on."

"Then how do you know she's out?"

With a disdainful moue, the clerk said, "I'll be terribly, terribly frank. Mrs. Abbott is always out—to you. There's nothing I can do about it, really there isn't."

"Listen, my lovely one," said Nick angrily—the young man lowered his eyes—"Mrs. Abbott just phoned me to come and see her."

The clerk looked as if he thought Nick was telling a naughty fib but condescended to lift a rose-pink telephone and enquire.

"Mrs. Abbott says she told you to come at four," he said reprovingly, after a short conversation on the telephone.

"Tell her I'll see her now or not at all."

"My, my," remarked the clerk. He repeated Nick's ultimatum into the mouthpiece.

"Mrs. Abbott says you may go right up," he said, replacing the rose-pink instrument on its cradle.

The sensation of being hollow inside came back to Nick when he stood at the door of Claire's apartment. Already he could feel her cold perceptive gaze on his rumpled suit, his soiled shirt, the betraying pouches under his eyes. One appraising glance and Claire would know all there was to know about his life since she had told him they were through. She would make him feel like dirt beneath her shoes. There was in Claire no gentleness, no pity, for the beaten or the weak.

His flesh goosed as he rang the bell. There was no answer. After a longish pause, he rang again. What was she trying to do? Keep him waiting, to humble him still further? Make him angry, knowing that he was always at a disadvantage when he lost his temper? His uneasiness made the wait seem longer. After a while, he knocked loudly, the sound echoing down the corridor. In mounting irritation, he rattled the doorhandle; and the door opened. Pushing it wider, he walked in.

Nick hardly felt the blow someone behind the door landed squarely on the back of his head. He lost consciousness as suddenly as the flame of a candle yields to a snuffer.

When he came to, he was not sure what had happened: whether he had been hit or had slipped and struck his head. The bright sunlight from a window opposite the door hurt his eyes. For a while he lay where he was, sick, squeamish, dizzy. He felt as one feels when, having drunk too much, one lays a weary head on the pillow and has to lift it quickly. His stomach sent warning shudders through his body.

With an effort, he staggered up and looked about him. He was alone in the entrance hall of the apartment and the door by which he had come in was shut. Muddled and annoyed, he lurched into the living-room. No one was there. He held on to a chair for a moment, trying to rally his faculties, then wobbled into Claire's bedroom.

It was large and the walls were painted in graded shades of mauve, gradually deepening from ceiling to floor. Woodwork and mouldings were off-white. The ceiling was pale-grey, the same colour being repeated in looped curtains of heavy silk framing two long windows. A blood-red carpet, tailored to the dimensions of the room, covered the floor, with white rugs—oval and round and triangular—arranged upon it to form an arresting pattern. The bed, so large it could comfortably have accommodated five or six people, had head-and-foot rests of quilted white satin. Beside it stood a tall table with a square glass top on which lay a copy of Vogue and a silver cigarette-box beneath a lamp with a shade of pleated white silk, whose cylindrical porcelain standard rose from a round porcelain base.

In the middle of the room was a low, glass-topped table with chromium legs on which were one or two magazines, a book unhandled except for the purpose of dusting, a statuette of a naked girl, some yellow tulips in a tall glass vase, a large glass ashtray, another silver box containing cigarettes; and a silver lighter. Beyond this table stood a chaise longue upholstered in quilted white satin to match the bed.

On her knees beside the chaise longue knelt Claire.

Her slender arms were braced against the seat; her head was bent, making her slim smooth neck seem incredibly long; her silky golden hair hung down over her face. She had on a black silk housecoat, trimmed with gold brocade, clinging to her lovely figure and revealing her shapely bare legs. One foot wore a gold harem slipper. The other foot was naked and its slipper lay half across the room. Around her left ankle was a thin chain of platinum links.

"Supposing you tell me what the game is," said Nick gruffly, "and I'll play, too."

Claire did not answer. Claire did not stir.

Her handbag lay on the chaise longue, most of its contents—money, handkerchief, lipstick, compact, key, notebook, gold pencil, cigarette case, lighter—strewn haphazardly across the seat. A few things had dropped to the floor. One of Claire's hands clasped something tightly but Nick could not see what it was. He felt stupid and ill-at-ease, standing there staring in semi-drunken bewilderment at the beautiful kneeling figure.

The utter immobility of the pose set him wondering. His brain was not sufficiently clear to make sense of the thoughts stirring in it but he began to be afraid.

"Claire," he said; and his voice was thick, his palms were moist. "Claire."

Still she did not answer. Still she did not move.

Feeling a reluctance he did not quite understand, Nick touched her shoulder. Claire fell sideways in a sort of slide and lay sprawled on the floor, arms and legs extended, one hand still clutching something Nick could not identify. There was a crimson patch on the front of her housecoat at a level with her heart and the white satin of the chaise longue had a similar red stain where her body had pressed against it.

Claire's eyes were wide open, staring up at him emptily. Nick had no need to touch her again to know that she was dead.

In that moment his bitterness and rancour against her drained out of him, leaving a dull wonder that one could be dead and yet remain so heartbreakingly lovely, so like a sleeping child.

For the first time he noticed a silver-plated revolver with a mother-of-pearl handle lying on the floor a few feet from the body. Almost at once he realised that it was his own gun. Before he fully grasped the implications of that fact, a voice behind him said, "Don't move or I'll let you have it."

Something grim and convincing about the voice froze Nick where he stood. He tried to speak but his tongue would not frame words.

"Turn around," said the voice harshly. "Keep your hands in sight."

With empty hands outstretched, Nick obeyed.

There was a uniformed policeman in the doorway, with a large revolver in his hand. Behind him hovered the reception clerk, looking ready to swoon, and the elevator boy, open-mouthed, goggle-eyed. The policeman's gun pointed directly at Nick's middle, his finger tight on the trigger. A slight increase in pressure would have sent a bullet thudding into Nick's body.

"For God's sake be careful," said Nick, "or that damned thing will go off."

"If you're not damned careful," said the policeman, "it sure will."

"I knew something like this would happen," cried the clerk shrilly. "I told Edward this man looked like murder when he walked in. Isn't that what I told you, Edward? Didn't I say he looked like murder?"

"Yeah," said the elevator boy, gaping at the body, "and—man, oh, man! —you certainly called it."

"Get headquarters on the phone," said the policeman, watching Nick warily. "Let me talk to 'em."

"I can't," wailed the clerk. "I just can't move. This is too, too awful. There's never been a scandal in the building, never, never, never. I think I'm going to faint."

The elevator boy dialled the number the policeman gave him and handed over the phone when the connection was made.

"Sergeant? This is Kozinsky. A woman's been murdered in an apartment at Eighty-Ninth and Park and"—a note of triumph infused the policeman's tone—"and I've got the guy that done it right here."

Chapter 4

When the cell door clanged behind him Nick turned and gripped the bars, staring out at the puffy plump face of the jailer. "Listen, this is important. I've got to—"

"Don't tell me," said the jailer stolidly, turning the key in the lock, "let me guess. I know, you got to phone your lawyer."

"I've a right to, haven't I?"

"I wouldn't know about your rights. In my job a man ain't supposed to know from nothing. All I do is look after the canaries in these here cages."

"Be a good guy and phone him for me."

"Well, I'll tell you how it is. I like to eat regular. I got a wife and three kids and they like to eat regular. We got my sister and my wife's mother living with us and they got to eat regular, too, or—boy, oh, boy!—do I know all about it. You're one of Inspector Gort's cases and when Gort says, 'Lock him up and don't let him talk to nobody,' that's the way it has to be—or else. If I was to phone for you—"

"Skip it," said Nick wearily. "Got a cigarette?"

"Always the same with you guys. First you want to phone, then you bum a smoke." While he grumbled the jailor took a flattened Camel 38 from a crumpled pack and handed it through the bars. Striking a match, he held it while Nick took a light.

"Thanks," said Nick. "Inspector Gort. That the fat man who brought me in?"

"Big, fat—and mean? No, that's Sergeant Mayo, he works with Gort. The inspector is tall, stringy—and mean. You'll meet up with him pretty soon."

"It's quiet as a tomb down here."

"If you want to sing songs and liven it up, go ahead. You

won't disturb nobody. You got the place to yourself right now. This ain't no regular can. We only hold you here while you're waiting for questioning."

On flat, spreading feet the jailer plodded away, his huge keyring jingling at his waist. Nick stood grasping the bars, looking out at the grey cement passage. He drew the cigarette smoke deep into his lungs, inhaling each steel-blue wisp until the disintegrating stump scorched his lips.

Built of cement blocks, like those lining the passage, the cell contained a wooden bench—or bed—about six feet long and two feet wide, a washbasin with a single faucet, and a johnny. Beyond arm's reach was a small barred window whose dirty opaque glass soiled the meagre daylight that filtered through. The cell stank: the sweat and misery of all the men who had occupied it had seeped into the walls, rendering them forever malodorous.

Nick was cold sober now. And scared. A hollow feeling in the pit of his stomach went all the way down to his knees.

This looked like the start of a tortuous process which would take him to the electric chair for a crime he had not committed. Lest he be tempted to hang himself, the police had taken his belt and necktie. They had searched him, confiscating his penknife and the few coins in his trousers but they had missed the four folded bills in his vest pocket. He sat on the bench and tucked the dollar bills into his sock, pushing them down until they reposed under the sole of his foot.

When he tried to think his brain was a frightened rabbit bolting helter-skelter through the tangle of a warren made unfamiliar by fear. He shied from every thought as if it had fangs. Rising, he paced the floor, his footsteps sounding loud and hollow in his ears. He had an insane impulse to hurl himself against the door. The feeling of being trapped was acutely unbearable. Sitting down, he tried to compose himself but almost at once he jumped up and went on walking jerkily to and fro. Four paces from wall to door. Four paces from door to wall. His footsteps spoke to him: you can't get out; you can't get out; you can't get out.

He kept reaching into his pocket the way you do when you're a chain-smoker, each time renewing his sense of frustration when he brought his hand out empty.

Except for the slow fading of the dim light from the window he had no way of marking the passage of time. He only knew that the dragging period which elapsed before he heard the returning step of the jailer was the most agonising time of waiting he had ever known.

A key grated in the lock. The door swung open. The jailer beckoned him out. Nick did not know where he was going but he was glad to be going anywhere.

"Smoke ?" suggested the inspector. With a smile in which his eyes played no part, he pushed cigarettes across the desk.

"Thanks." Nick had to tussle with the pack, for his hand was all thumbs.

His smile a coy replica of his superior's, Sergeant Mayo struck a match and offered a light. The police officers resembled two wolves endeavouring to reassure the sheep that was to be their dinner.

Nick said, "I'd like to call an attorney."

"Well, I guess that can be arranged," replied Inspector Gort pleasantly, "a little later."

"But not right now?"

"No,", said the inspector, "not right now. Right now, we're going to have a sort of informal talk. You look kinda shot. Maybe you'd like a drink. Give him a drink, Mayo."

The sergeant opened a drawer and produced a bottle but Nick shook his head.

"Thanks, I guess not."

"It's up to you. I know how you feel. You were sore as hell

when you shot her. Who wouldn't be?—after a run-around like she gave you. Nine men out of ten would say she had it coming."

"Sure," said Sergeant Mayo. "She got what she asked for."

"But, now it's over, you're feeling kinda low. You can see what a spot you got yourself into—you're beginning to think of yourself, where before all you could think of was how sore you were at her."

"You're quite a psychologist," said Nick, with a shaky laugh.

"In a modest way, perhaps," agreed Inspector Gort, with a deprecatory wave of his hand. "In my job you've got to be."

"The only thing wrong with your reasoning is that I didn't kill her."

Leaning forward, the inspector eyed Nick reproachfully. "Don't be like that. We've got you cold, boy. Where's it going to get you to play dumb?"

"Sure," said Mayo, shaking his head like a kindly but reproving uncle. "Where's it going to get you?"

"She was dead when I found her."

"Wait a minute," said the inspector to a third police officer, in the background, who was taking all this down. "Let's give the boy a chance to think. Let's not rush him into a story that won't stand up, that he'll be stuck with later."

He put his fingertips together, resting his elbows on the arms of his chair and gave Nick a paternal look. "I know how it is, son. You've been sitting in that cell with your head in your hands, wondering how to get out of the mess that a shot fired in anger landed you in. You can't deny you were caught right there in the room with her, that her body was still warm, that your own gun was lying on the carpet where you dropped it. You got brains enough to know that all the facts pin the rap squarely on you—but, sitting down there in the cell, you were too panicky to use your brains. The only thought running through your head was that you mustn't admit you did it. So, you got the dumb idea of cooking up a story about finding her dead. Well, all that's going to get you is a load of grief. You can't get around the facts."

"That's right," said Sergeant Mayo, "you gotta face the facts, Nick."

"Before you say another word, son, I'll tell you something for your own good. There are two ways to do this. You can play ball with us and we'll go easy on you; or you can hold out on us and we'll do it the hard way.

"For instance, there are two answers to this killing. Maybe you went up to see her to talk things over; maybe she wouldn't listen to reason and an argument started that developed into a fight; maybe you only threatened her with the gun to quieten her—and in the heat of the moment it went off and killed her. Well, that would make it unpremeditated and the worst you'd get would be ten or fifteen years."

"Maybe less," said Sergeant Mayo, sucking a hollow tooth. "A clean-cut young fellow like you would have the parole board eating out of his hand."

"Looking at it the other way," said Inspector Gort darkly, "maybe you went up there on purpose to kill her. Maybe you never gave the poor kid a break; maybe you blasted her before she opened her mouth. That would make it premeditated murder and, boy, you'd get the chair."

"Sure," said Mayo placidly, "you'd fry, kid."

"You see how it is—it all depends on how the case is shaped up in the first place. Now, you're a smart young fellow. You can figure the percentages as well as anyone else. You can see that acting dumb won't get you anywhere. Why not get together with us on this thing?"

"If I confess, I shot her during a scuffle, you'll be satisfied to build your case that way?" asked Nick. His restless fingers pinched out the glowing end of his cigarette and tore it to shreds.

"Now you're getting bright. A man with your brains doesn't go on for long butting his head against a brick wall. You spill the whole story, son, and I'll see you get all the breaks."

Leaning back, Inspector Gort motioned to the police officer armed with notebook and pencil, who readied himself to take down Nick's confession.

Nick said slowly, "I wasn't up there long enough to have an argument with her that developed into a fight—and you know it. You must have checked the time I walked into the building and you know it was only a few minutes later I was caught in her bedroom with the body at my feet. In other words, if I killed her, I must have gone there to do it. You want me to confess to killing her in a fight because you can prove there wasn't a fight. The confession would sew me up tight in a first-degree murder rap. Well, I'm not confessing to anything. I went there to talk to her and when I rang the bell there was no answer. Tired of waiting, I tried the handle and the door opened and I walked in. Someone hit me and I passed out. When I came to, I wandered to the bedroom and found her kneeling beside the chaise longue. I didn't know she was dead until I touched her and she fell over."

"A child of five wouldn't believe that story."

"It's still the truth."

His hand trembling slightly, Nick took another cigarette from the pack on the desk, put it between his lips, fumbled for a match. With a sudden movement, Sergeant Mayo struck it out of his mouth, leaving the stinging imprint of fingers on Nick's cheek.

"We tried to be nice—now we'll do it the hard way."

"You killed her, Abbott," said Inspector Gort, "and we've got you cold, even if you're too goddam dumb to see it. The clerk at the apartment says you were drunk and in an ugly mood when you arrived there. Your wife was alive when he announced you. A few minutes later you were caught beside the body. The gun that shot her is registered in your name. She didn't kill herself; there were no powder burns around the wound. How does it add up?"

"I'd been drinking. I wasn't drunk. I was in an impatient mood, not an ugly one. As for the gun, I hadn't seen it for months until I saw it lying near the body. I think I left it at the apartment when I cleared out."

"Handy when you came to kill her," sneered Sergeant Mayo.

Nick's eyes narrowed. "How did it happen that the policeman arrived so quickly?"

"A tenant phoned the reception desk, saying he'd heard a shot. Otherwise, you might have had time to blow."

"If a tenant said he heard a shot, he was lying," said Nick. "That building is soundproof. He could only have heard it in my wife's apartment. Don't you see?—he knocked me out, shot her and then gave the alarm to make sure that I'd be caught."

"Now tell us the one about the Three Bears," grunted Sergeant Mayo.

"What did you do with the key?" demanded Inspector Gort.

"What key?"

"The key to your wife's safe-deposit box. Her maid tells us she always wore it on a chain around her neck. Her throat is scratched where you yanked it off, chain and all. What did you do with it?"

"I never saw it. If I'd taken it, they'd have found it on me when they searched me."

"You cached it some place before you was pinched," said Mayo. "Don't fool yourself—we'll find it."

"Where was the maid this afternoon?" asked Nick.

"Your wife never had her around in the afternoons," answered Gort impatiently. "Don't pretend you didn't know that."

With a wry laugh, Nick said, "You'd be surprised how much I didn't know about my wife."

"We're getting nowheres fast," said Mayo, a peevish look on his red fat face. Exchanging a meaning glance with his superior officer, he turned, with a gesture of one of his podgy hands, to the police stenographer. "Scram for now, buddy. We'll give you a ring when we want you."

After the stenographer had gone out Inspector Gort switched on a bright light on his desk, turning the blinding beam on the chair in which Nick sat. Sergeant Mayo put out the other lights, leaving the rest of the room in darkness. He took something from a drawer and came toward Nick.

"Get on your feet."

When Nick obeyed the sergeant thrust into his hand the article he had taken from the drawer.

"We'll play I'm your wife. Show us how you shot her." Looking down, Nick saw that the thing in his hand was the gun that killed Claire. He placed it on the desk.

"I didn't shoot her. She was dead when I found her."

"That ain't the answer," rasped Mayo, striking him across the face with the flat of his hand.

Nick started forward; his fists clenched. The sergeant knocked him into his chair with a punch to the jaw.

"He attacked me," said Mayo to Gort, in a tone of mock amazement. "You saw it, chief. He came at me. I hadda clip him in self-defence."

"Quit clowning," retorted Gort. Wrapping Nick's revolver in a paper towel, he replaced it in the drawer.

Rising suddenly, Nick started across the room. Sergeant Mayo made a move to stop him but stood back when he saw the greenish pallor of the prisoner's face. Bent over a washbasin in a corner of the room, Nick was violently sick. When he straightened up, he was shaken and perspiring. It was all he could do to stumble back to his chair.

Bunching Nick's lapels under his chin in a large fist, Sergeant Mayo shook him and said, "Be smart, Abbott. We know the answers we want. We're gonna get 'em if we spend the rest of the night working on you."

For the moment unable to speak, Nick shook his head numbly. Sergeant Mayo raised his fist threateningly.

"Don't mark him," warned Inspector Gort. "Remember what the Commissioner said."

"I got to make him talk, don't I?"

"Sure. But there's no need to mark him up. He's got to look good when we call in the reporters."

Nick sat staring at the light, which sent stabs of painful brilliance through his eyeballs. When he turned his head away Sergeant Mayo jerked it back. The two detectives volleyed questions at him but he was not prepared to give the only answers they would accept.

"Come on, quit stalling."

"Come clean, Abbott, we know you did it."

"It was your gun, wasn't it?"

"She was alive when you went up, wasn't she?"

"You killed her, all right. What did you do with the key."

"Take your time, if that's the way you want it. There's no hurry. We got all night."

"She took you for every cent you had, then gave you the air. You were broke and plenty sore."

"That's why you shot her. You were sore and you went up there and shot her."

"Don't give us that squawk about being framed. We've heard it till we're sick. Come on, make it the truth for a change."

"Use your brains, Abbott. You're licked now. Where's the sense of holding out any longer?"

"You're gonna spill your guts before we finish with you."

The telephone rang shrilly and, with a grunt of exasperation, Inspector Gort answered it. His manner underwent a sudden change. He became purringly respectful. After a brief conversation—subdued and submissive on his part—he hung up and rose to his feet.

"I'll be back as soon as I can. The Chief wants a report on this case. He's getting impatient."

"Maybe he'd like to handle the dumb bastard himself," grumbled Sergeant Mayo. "He'd get impatient, all right, all right."

"Better call in one of the boys to help you with Abbott while I'm gone."

"I'll take care of him. I'll take care of him good.",

When the inspector left the room, Sergeant Mayo jerked up Nick's head and glared into his eyes. For a time, they looked at each other: one weak but still defiant; the other ugly with the lust to torture.

"It's you and me now, sweetheart. You and me—and you're gonna talk, see? I'm through playing. Now I'm gonna get results. I'll give you one more chance to come clean before I go to town."

"You win," said Nick dejectedly. "Give me a cigarette and I'll talk all you want."

"That's better. Now you're getting sense."

Taking his fists from Nick's throat, the sergeant reached into a pocket. At that instant, Nick struck. He put every ounce of fading strength into a blow to Mayo's jaw and the fat man staggered but did not go down. With the desperate knowledge that he had burned his boats, Nick snatched up a desk calendar and hit the sergeant on the head with the heavy base of it. A look of incredulous horror that was very funny came into Mayo's eyes and his mouth fell open. Nick hit him again; and stood back as the fat man dropped forward onto the floor and lay still.

Rolling him over, Nick made sure he was unconscious. He

had to struggle with himself to keep from bashing in the detective's skull. His hand trembled as it put down the desk calendar. Going on his knees beside the limp figure, he removed the sergeant's belt and necktie. He put them on himself, making a new hole in the belt to adapt it to his less protuberant abdomen.

He dared not try to find a way out through the building. Throwing up the window, he looked down into the darkness. Thirty feet below ran an alley connecting two streets; he could see the glare from lampposts and electric signs at both ends. The drop from the window was too great—it was an odds-on bet he would break a leg if he tried it—but, within reach, a drainpipe hugged the wall from roof to ground. He climbed on to the window ledge, grasped the pipe with his right hand, swung himself over to it and began to inch his way down.

Passing an open window on a lower floor, from which came light and a hum of voices, his scalp prickled with fear that those within would hear, the scrape of his feet, the suction of his hands, the labouring of his lungs. Reaching the ground, he went up the alley at a stumbling run in the opposite direction to the street on which the police station was located. Coming from the dark into a glow of light, he hailed an empty taxi.

"Drive north," he said, climbing in. "I'll let you know when to stop."

A few blocks from the One Hundred Twenty-Fifth Street Station, he halted the cab and paid the driver. He waited until the vehicle was out of sight before walking toward the station. His new-found luck held: when he reached the northbound platform a New Haven train was slowing down at it.

Chapter 5

Up an incline from the wayside station of Stonefield, Connecticut, he plodded to the road and the cars of belated commuters swished past him in both directions, bound for homes at the beach and homes among the green hills. Turning his back on the lights of the little town, he followed the winding inland route through the night-hushed woods of a bird sanctuary and between fields whose next crop would be little houses. The road was made for those who go on wheels, not feet. His step beat crisply on the hard surface.

An aloof and haughty moon wore the night like a spangled cape. Small furry creatures darted under his feet, seeming to have awaited his coming before venturing across the road and to be scared out of their wits by their own daring. Dried leaves beneath the hedges rustled with living things, in the long grass an insect orchestra harped without pause on a single note and frogs in baleful chorus croaked in a marshy hollow. A mile from the station he trudged past the first human dwellings he had seen since leaving the small town behind: pretentious houses with windows ablaze, grouped together as if lacking courage to inflict themselves singly on the rural scene.

Beyond them stretched fields and meadows doomed to lie fallow while a shrewd farmer waited for land prices to go up and the speculative builders waited for them to come down. The road dipped and rose and, as it wound deeper into the hills, the climb from each successive dip became steeper. He crossed a stone bridge over a chattering stream and took a narrow-rutted road branching from the main one and cleaving into the heart of a coppice of straight-backed pine and gnarled oak.

Following this road for almost two miles, he came to a clearing of about ten acres in which stood a farmhouse that had seen the redcoats pass when America was only a name in the hearts of men. A crude stone wall, level with his breast, bounded the place. He entered through an opening once made for horse and cart and went up a gently curving drive, gravel crunching under his heels. Much of the clearing was waist-high in grass but as he neared the house, he saw through the dark the smooth slope of a shaven lawn. Stepping off the gravel on to the turf he approached the house stealthily, skirting trim flowerbeds and a sunken garden walled and paved with slabs of stone in which the plants and flowers that love rock grew from every crevice. A muted tinkling came to him from the far end of the garden, where a brook danced over pebbles to swell the placid waters of a moonlit pool.

The house was in darkness. Behind a bush, Nick halted and hooted like an owl. After a pause, he repeated the cry. Before he had expected it, a ground floor window glowed yellow and then a side door opened, throwing a slanting splash of light across the clipped turf. In the doorway appeared a man of about thirty, in slacks and sweater, who peered right and left.

Leaving the shelter of the bush, Nick darted to the house and slipped in; and the man who had opened the door closed it softly behind them.

"When I heard our old signal," said the man, in a startled whisper, "I couldn't believe it was you. I can hardly believe it yet. I heard on the radio the police were holding you for murder."

"They were."

"But they let you go? I can't tell you how glad I am."

"They didn't let me go, Julian. I saw a chance to escape."

With an apprehensive glance over his shoulder at the stairs, Julian Deering motioned to Nick to lower his voice.

"Go into the living-room. I'll be with you in a moment. I'll make sure the Hodges are asleep."

Nick entered a room panelled with wood the colour of ancient leather, polished so that its grain shone like figured satin. Most of the panelling was as old as the house, that which was recent being so exquisitely faked it could hardly be detected. There was a huge fireplace of wrought native stone; and on the naked beams of the ceiling one could identify the cuts of the axe with which they had been hewn.

A door to one side of the room stood ajar. Nick walked to it and looked into the large closet. Julian used as a darkroom. Long strips of narrow camera film hung from clips on the near wall, gleaming darkly in the light of a red bulb. On a shelf lay some shallow enamelled pans, filled with liquid; and another strip of developed negative. Idly, Nick picked it up and carried it to the brighter illumination of the living-room. Holding it in front of a shaded lamp, he saw that one of the little pictures was of a very fat woman. A hand came over his shoulder and took the negative from him.

"One of my failures," said Julian. "I don't know what went wrong. Perhaps the film was faulty."

Putting a lighted match to the strip, he tossed it, blazing, into the fireplace. He looked annoyed. Too late, Nick remembered that Julian hated people intruding on his dark-room.

"The Hodges are asleep. I let them go to bed early. I had some work to do."

For the first time, Julian looked Nick full in the face and he brought out a question that apparently had faltered on his lips from the start.

"Good God, Nick, why did you do it? Damn it, man, you didn't have to kill her. There were other ways of getting rid of her."

"Et tu, Brute," quoted Nick, his lips twisting bitterly. "I didn't kill her, Julian. I walked into the room in which she lay dead in time to take the blame."

"From the radio bulletin it looks black for you?'

"Black as night."

Julian ran long slender fingers through his sleek yellow hair. He had a pale sensitive face, lined beyond his years, with patrician features. His lean alert body suggested a grey-hound.

Nick was almost the only close friend Julian had. They had roomed together throughout Nick's post-graduate years at Yale and, although the two men could hardly have been more dissimilar, they had never had a serious disagreement. Born to wealth and position, Julian Deering had been given the fright of his life when his father died insolvent in the first year of the depression, leaving him only the income from an insignificant trust fund. His horror of being poor and all that it entailed had made money the nearest thing to a god that Julian had. He had resolved to be rich again, at whatever cost. At Yale he set himself to live with monastic simplicity and Nick, out of a vast experience of poverty, was able to teach him to stretch the inelastic penny. Quite soon the pupil was astounding the teacher with economies so niggling that no one of less inflexible purpose could have bothered with them. Julian once said to Nick: "You don't know what it is to be poor." Nick laughed and answered, "I've been poor all my life"; and Julian retorted, "That's just it. Only when one has been rich and become poor can one know what poverty is."

Now Julian was society's favourite photographer, with an income in five figures—and a legacy from an aunt had given him a comfortable independence—but he still lived sparsely, as if afraid that by some strange alchemy his fortune might vanish. For several years he had occupied this Connecticut farmhouse with only an elderly couple, who had served his father before him and whom he grossly underpaid, to keep him company. Claire could not have sucked Julian dry, as she had done to Nick. Julian would never be the kind of fool to sacrifice his all on the altar of love.

"I know I shouldn't have come here," said Nick. "I've no right to involve you."

Punching him lightly on the chest, Julian said, "For heaven's sake, don't talk like a fool. I'd be a poor thing if my best friend couldn't turn to me in trouble. You say you didn't kill her. I believe you, of course, and I'm glad of it—but you ought to know it wouldn't matter a damn if you were guilty; I'd stand by you just the same. You can count on me to the limit, Nick."

"I knew I could"—there was a dryness in Nick's throat —"you're a better friend than I deserve, Julian."

"Don't be an ass, you ass. You must be hungry. I'll raid the icebox."

"No, thanks."

"A drink, then?"

Julian moved to a table on which stood a bottle of scotch, a siphon of soda and glasses. Bottle in hand, he glanced enquiringly at Nick, raising his eyebrows in surprise when Nick shook his head.

"Do you good," he urged.

"I'm not drinking, Julian."

"Maybe you're right—but you look all in."

"I am; absolutely all in. And, Julian, I'm scared. Honest-to-God scared. I wouldn't admit it to anyone else."

"You're going to be all right, old man. You can lie low here until the police uncover the real murderer."

"They won't even look for him," said Nick jerkily. "They've tagged me. As far as they're concerned, I'm 'it.' "

"Then I'll hide you until we find a way to get you out of the country. We can rely on the Hodges. They'd do anything under the sun for me, anything."

"We'd never get away with it. Too many people know that you're my friend. Before long the police will be here looking for me."

With a frown, Julian nodded his head. "I'm afraid you're right. We'll have to think of something else."

Almost as though the words were being forced out of him against his will, Nick said, "I'm, going to need money."

"Of course. That's where I come in, old man."

"I tore up the check you sent me. At the time I felt I couldn't take it, even from you."

"I've about five hundred dollars in the house, if that will help." Probably Nick was the only living person who could have asked Julian for funds with any prospect of success. "When you're holed-up somewhere you can write me and I'll send you more."

"I can't thank you."

"Don't try."

Julian went out of the room and returned shortly with the money. He gave it to Nick, who put it in an inside pocket.

"I wish there were more I could do."

"There isn't. There's no sense in your getting mixed up in this."

"I'd risk it, if it would do any good." Julian hesitated for a moment and added, "and if I had only myself to consider. Did you know I'm probably going to be married? She's very wealthy"—he said it as if that explained everything—"and altogether charming. Maybe you knew her, she comes from the little town in Indiana where you were born. No, I guess you wouldn't."

"Most of the people I knew in that town were poor as church mice."

With the sort of futile little gesture people make when aware of the inadequacy of words, Julian said, "Nick, I can't let you walk out of here to be hunted like an animal. Where will you go? What will you do?"

"I haven't the slightest idea," replied Nick truthfully. "Stay for the night, at least."

"It wouldn't be safe, old man."

"No, I suppose not. But, darn it—"

They heard the sound of a car on the road and stood in silence, waiting for it to pass but it did not pass; they heard it turning into the drive and coming toward the house, the tires scuffing the gravel. Julian went to a window and peered out. He turned back as brakes squealed at the front door and his face was white.

"It's a police car. God knows how they traced you here so soon. You'll have to run for it. Quick—out that window. I'll do my best to stall them."

As the doorbell rang through the silent house, Nick threw up a side window, unhooked the screen, and clambered out. He started running at the split second his soles met the springy turf. Barely had he reached the limits of the lawn when a fusillade of shots rang out behind him and, as if dealt a crippling punch in the back, he was thrown headlong into the tall grass. He lay still for a moment. Something warm and sticky trickled down his arm and he knew he had been shot. The wound seemed to be in his left shoulder; that side of his body was numb.

Bullets whistled over the place where he lay and from the vicinity of the house came the shouts of men, high-pitched with excitement. On knees and one arm he stumbled deeper into the long grass like some lamed and shambling beast. When he reached a tree, he clung to it and painfully drew himself up, using the stout trunk for cover while he looked back. The police car was being turned so that its lights shone across the garden and men were running toward him through the twin beams. Dropping to his knees again, he wormed his way at an angle to the far end of the clearing and the wall flanking the road. He lay there and watched the pursuers beating the grass around the place where he had fallen. They were weaving back and forth in a widening arc. It could only be a matter of minutes before they reached the spot where now he crouched. He set his teeth, for the bullet wound was beginning to hurt. With the aid of a tree that rose beside it, he mounted the wall, dropping down quickly on the other side. There was another burst of shots but none came in his direction. The police were firing at shadows among the trees at the edge of the clearing.

He saw the bobbing headlights of an approaching car and huddled down, trying to make himself small, afraid that it was bringing more police. When it drew near it slowed and he was able to see that the driver was a woman. Letting the car slacken speed to a crawl, she stared out of the window at the house—lit now from attic to kitchen—and at the men who ran about shouting with flashlights and guns in their hands.

As the car passed him Nick ran behind it, his body bent double, and jumped on to the offside running-board. Uttering a startled gasp, the woman at the wheel turned her head to stare at him. She was alone. Nick thrust through the open window a pocket of his coat with his fingers bunched inside to make it look as if he was holding a gun.

"Keep going," he ordered. After a frightened glance at his grim face, the woman obeyed.

She trod on the accelerator and they went past the entrance to the drive. Nick looked back to see if they were being followed but the police were still frantically busy near the house. He clung to the car door; his feet braced on the running-board. The woman gripped the steering wheel tightly, her eyes intent on the bumpy winding road. Neither of them spoke.

About a mile from Julian's house, they neared a bend sharp even for that part of the country. Without so much warning as a flicker of her eyes, the woman swung the car at a tree, brushing it with the fenders. The tree scraped Nick neatly from his perch and, as the ground rose dizzily to meet him, his brain was mercifully blacked out.

Chapter 6

Although for a time nothing that followed was quite clear in his mind, he had a dim impression of a car drawing up beside him, of being rolled on to his back, of having a strong light flashed on his face, of someone bending over him, tugging at his arm. A voice with authority kept urging him to rise and, in dismayed acceptance of the end of his futile run for freedom, he tried to obey. He brought one knee up and then the other, wincing with pain when he attempted to brace himself on his wounded arm. He kept losing and regaining an awareness misty and incomplete.

Someone helped him to his feet, kept him from crumpling to the ground again. Feeling himself being pushed into a seat, he relaxed with shut eyes against cushions smelling of leather, and two hands tucked in his feet and legs. The hands went exploring into his pockets. He tried to say that he had not a gun but could not bring the words out. A door beside him slammed; an engine came to life. He must have fainted as the car started, for the next he knew was raising his head and finding himself in the motionless vehicle between concrete walls. Probably, he thought weakly, the walls of a garage in the basement of a police station.

The car door at his side opened and, turning his head limply, he looked into a woman's face. A good face: the kind young mothers should have; and hospital nurses; and the wives of great men; all those who are sources of strength to others. The eyes had more than beauty, they had depth and warmth. The mouth was resolute, yet kind. Thick waving raven hair, brushed back from brow and ears, was softly bunched at the back of the head. An odd moment for Nick to reflect that if you took out a few clips it would cascade like a black waterfall on her white rounded shoulders.

"How do you feel?" Her voice had a charming lilt.

"A strange question," he said, after a pause, "coming from you, who almost ended my capacity for feeling."

"Brushing you against the tree. was the only way I could think of to dislodge you from my car. I had to get rid of you. For all I knew you were an armed desperado."

"First you brush me off, then you come back and pick me up. Isn't that carrying feminine contrariness a little far?"

"Not at all. I came back to make sure I hadn't killed you."

"I hope you weren't upset to find me still breathing."

The woman made a little gesture of impatience. She was younger than Nick at first had thought. With her lovely skin and features she could have made herself look still younger but he had an idea she would scorn the aspiration. Her evening gown and sable wrap had an exquisite simplicity suggesting Mainbocher or Molyneux and she wore them with the unstudied elegance the designer had intended.

"I hate to seem inquisitive," said Nick, "but shouldn't the police be here in force?"

"Perhaps they should—but I wanted to have a talk with you. You see, I recognized you when I turned my light on your face."

"That explains everything," said Nick, his head spinning a little. "I don't get it."

"That's because you've forgotten."

"I forget so many things. Which of them are we talking about?"

"For one thing, you've forgotten that you once drenched me with a garden hose." Before Nick had quite digested that, she added, "Do you think you could walk, with my help?"

"I could try."

"I want to take you upstairs. We could go to the house but I'd rather my aunt and the servants knew nothing about this. There are rooms for a chauffeur above the garage and, as I've no chauffeur at present, they're empty. Don't be afraid to lean on me. I'm pretty strong."

They paused at the foot of the stairs while she turned off the garage light, then she helped him up a long flight into darkness relieved only by grey squares that were windows. He held himself up by gripping the back of a chair while she drew down the shades and switched on the light. He blinked around him at a large room with a divan bed, a carpet, some comfortable chairs and a radio. Through a partly open door he glimpsed the tiles of a bathroom.

Stumbling to the bed, he sat down heavily, hanging his head as a wave of nausea came over him. For the first time, the woman noticed the streaks on the back of his left hand.

"You're bleeding. I didn't know."

"It's nothing much. A flesh wound. One cop was a better shot than the others."

"I'll call a doctor."

"And have him call the police?"

"If the wound isn't treated you may lose the arm."

"I prefer that to losing my life."

"How long do you expect to stay out of the hands of the police?"

"Lady," said Nick wearily, "just as long as I can."

"But it's so stupid, running away. It's making you look guilty, when all the time you're innocent."

"Say that again," said Nick, staring at her.

"I said, it's stupid, running away."

"No, the last part. The part about me being innocent. It sounded like music. What makes you think so?"

"I know so. You aren't the type to kill. When I read of your arrest in the evening papers, I knew the police had made a mistake. I wanted to go to you and offer my services. I'm an attorney; I thought I might be able to help."

"What makes you think I'm not the type to kill—if there is a type?"

"I know you too well."

"I'd swear we never met before. I couldn't forget a woman like you. What was it you said about a garden hose?"

"It was a long time ago."

"Wait a minute," said Nick suddenly. "No. That couldn't be you. That was a little girl with skinny legs and pigtails. Her aunt was the richest woman in town—in the county—and the grimmest old lady I ever knew. I worked on the place two afternoons a week and the little girl kept tagging after me, talking a blue streak. Asking questions—Lord, could she ask questions!"

"You used to answer some of them. That's how I know so much about you."

"Althea Archer," said Nick, thinking hard. "That was the little girl's name. I thought it a lovely name—but it didn't fit. It belonged to a regal lady, tall and beautiful like—like—" He glanced at the woman, then quickly looked away. "Well, it didn't belong to a skinny, freckled kid."

"It's unkind to bring up the freckles. There isn't a last one left."

"The old lady told the gardener to fire me if I didn't keep away from her precious niece—but the brat wouldn't keep away from me. One day I got sore and turned the hose on her; and lost my job."

"I wept all night," said Althea Archer. "Not because of the drenching, not even because of the spanking my aunt gave me—but because I'd got the brown-skinned boy into trouble."

"Those two afternoons a week meant a couple of dollars to me. In those days, I could eat for a week on two dollars."

"A skinny little girl in pigtails couldn't be expected to realize that."

"No. And you were so very rich. To the rich, eating is a habit, not a problem. And now you've grown into a very lovely woman—and, of all things, an attorney. The two don't seem to fit."

"Is it so strange that I grew tired of simply existing, like an expensively tended plant; that I wanted to make use of my brain?"

"With your connections you won't lack cases."

"They wouldn't be the kind I'd care about. My last client was a pushcart pedlar, arrested for not having a licence. The fee was a melon."

"And now the heiress turned attorney would like the thrill of a murder trial. It should make swell headlines."

"You're being crude and unkind. I know I could help you, Mr. Abbott, if you'd let me."

"That's the first time you ever called me 'Mr. Abbott.' It used to be 'Nick.' When I told you my name you said, 'Abbott rhymes with rabbit'—and when you wanted to get my goat you ran after me, shouting, 'Ole Nicholas Rabbit, Ole Nicholas Rabbit!'"

"We were both very young," said Althea, almost primly. "First, Mr. Abbott, you'd have to tell me the facts as you know them. After that, I'd drive you in to New York and surrender you to the District Attorney."

"And that," said Nick flatly, "is where our points of view part company. Thanks very much, I'd better get me another lawyer."

"You can't run away from the law for ever. Don't you see, you're only making it blacker for yourself?"

"It was good and black this afternoon when two police officers punctuated their questions with blows."

"They won't dare do that when you have legal counsel."

"I wish I were as sure of that as you are. You see Justice holding scales; I see her armed with a length of rubber hose."

"Nevertheless, you've got to face the charge against you."

"And be tried, convicted and electrocuted by due process of law?"

"It's a matter of proving your innocence."

"Who's going to do that? I'm the little man the police want

to see in the electric chair. If the real murderer cried, 'Yoo-hoo!' they wouldn't even bother to chase him."

"I'll hire detectives. Nick, I'll do everything for you that's humanly possible."

"Will you hold my hand when they turn on the juice?"

"It won't come to that."

"If it doesn't, I know a sergeant and an inspector who are going to be bitterly disappointed."

"Let's talk it over in the morning, shall we? Things may look different then. You can spend the night here. Promise, you'll stay until we have another talk?"

"What if the police come?"

"That isn't likely. You're all of fifteen miles from where I found you. Promise you'll stay?"

"I promise," said. Nick, keeping his fingers crossed.

"Now we've got to do something about your wound. We ought to have attended to it before. I've had Red Cross training. Let me look at it."

Laying aside her fur wrap, Althea helped Nick off with his coat and shirt. A grim look at the blood-crusted puncture in his shoulder and she went up to the house for her first-aid kit. When she returned, she was wearing a simple morning frock. Nick could not help admiring the calm, efficient way in which she went to work with warm water and bandages.

"The bullet ought to be extracted but if you won't have a doctor—"

"No, thanks."

"Well, that's another thing we'll talk about in the morning. You ought to be fairly comfortable for the present. I brought you a pack of cigarettes and some matches, in case you care to smoke."

"Thanks," said Nick. "Thanks for everything. You're a pretty swell person."

Left alone, he shed his trousers, turned off the light, lay down to nap for a few hours. With his eyes shut, he murmured the name "Althea Archer." His eyes opened again. How did he know her name was still "Archer"? Was it likely so charming a person would be allowed to remain single? Well, she had spoken of an aunt and of servants; but not of a husband.

And then he remembered words Julian Deering had spoken: "Did you know I'm probably going to be married? She's very wealthy and altogether charming. Maybe you knew her, she comes from the little town in Indiana where you were born."

Althea. And Julian Deering. This little world, knit closely by coincidence.

He sank drowsily into slumber and when he awoke with a start it was daylight. It took him a second or two to realise where he was. The wound in his shoulder was throbbing but he had no intention of being hampered by that. He rose and dashed cold water on his face.

Hanging in a closet, he found a chauffeur's uniform, complete even to the cap. He put on his own trousers and the uniform coat and cap and went downstairs, carrying his own coat. There were two cars in the garage, an impressive limousine and the smaller one Althea had driven the night before. He laid his coat on the driving seat of the limousine.

Finding a stub of pencil on a workbench and a scrap of wrapping paper on the floor, he wrote a note to Althea: "Never trust the promise of a man running for his life. If I reach New York, I'll leave your car parked somewhere."

He opened the garage doors and backed the limousine out and down the drive to the road. He drove several miles along winding back roads and found his way to the Merritt Parkway. He was doing the prescribed fifty miles an hour when a policeman on a motor-cycle overtook him. Nick's heart thumped quicker in his breast. The policeman kept level with him for a while, glancing at the peaked cap and silver-buttoned jacket.

"You're out early, buddy. Ain't that Miss Archer's car?"

"Dio posente, dio d'amor, nel la sciareil patrio suol," shouted Nick, using in desperation the only Italian he knew—the words of a song from "Faust."

"A wop, huh? It's a wonder those rich dames wouldn't hire Americans, instead of giving work to foreigners."

With a disapproving glance at Nick's black hair, the policeman put on speed and left the limousine behind.

Chapter 7

All day Nick hid in a dingy room in a cheap Eighth Avenue hotel for men only. At times, in desperation, he paced the threadbare carpet but mostly he lay on his back on a mattress hilled and hollowed as a contour map, staring at a cracked and cobwebbed ceiling. His wound throbbed in rhythm with the beat of his heart. Now and then it stabbed him with pain so fierce he had to clench his fists and bite his lip to keep from crying out. He chain-smoked cigarettes until the pack was empty. Waking from a stupor, his empty stomach clamoured for food. His jangled nerves demanded the anaesthesia of drink. There was nothing he could do about that. Nothing except suffer. He dared not go out in daylight and it would have been as dangerous to allow a bellboy a look at his face—if this shabby dive boasted a bellboy. By this time his picture, under screaming headlines, must be in all the papers.

Rust-red blots on the walls marked the spots where the hands of previous tenants had squashed bugs. In places the stained wallpaper hung down in ragged strips, showing still dirtier, more ancient paper underneath. The torn window shade dangled at a rakish angle, with the effect of a mocking leer. Above a rickety chest of drawers hung a mirror which made faces if one looked into it.

Time lagged like an old man going up a hill. He tried to sleep but failed to find a position in which he could be comfortable. Toward evening he fell into a state akin to delirium in which the happenings of the past thirty-six hours made a jumble in his mind, like a motion picture cut and spliced by an idiot, with the end at the beginning, the beginning in the middle and one shot superimposed crazily on another. Murder and a bottle of rye and a frowning landlady and a tree rushing to greet him with a kiss. He sat up with a jerk and fought back to reality, for the path his brain wandered led to madness.

Outside his window an electric sign with some bulbs missing winked on and off, alternately lighting up the room and plunging it in darkness. Walking over, he looked down at the street, from its sluggish tempo judging the time to be about ten. The women on the steps of a tenement across the way sat withdrawn into themselves, slack against the stone, in tired apathy. The youngest child in a group at the corner was all of eight years old; the smaller ones had been dragged, wailing, to bed or to their mothers' sagging laps. He watched the entrance of a cheap movie theatre and for several minutes no one came out or went in; the first show was over, the second under way. Yes, it was about ten and he had two hours to kill before venturing out to do something about the aching hole in his shoulder.

He dared not lie down lest he fall again into the nightmare state from which he had delivered himself. Imagining a pack of cards, he played mental solitaire for a while. Wearying of the pastime, he designed in his mind a tall building and built it the same way, starting with the foundations and even picturing the gaping faces of those leaning on the railing watching the piledriver at work. He wrote a letter which could not be sent on a typewriter which had no existence. These things he did to keep himself from going mad and, as he settled to chess on a make-believe board with an imaginary opponent, it struck him that perhaps he had already gone mad.

After a while it had to be midnight, whether it was or not. He could wait on time no longer.

Leaving the drab room, become as hateful as a prison, he went quietly down the stairs. On the second floor landing he halted abruptly, for the sound of a gruff voice had come up to him from the lobby. Hanging over the banisters, he peered down the stair well. Two men in plain clothes, looking more like policemen than they would have done in uniform, were questioning the night clerk. The clerk was explaining that he had just come on duty and knew nothing of the guests checked in earlier, except the meagre details the register supplied.

"Most of our people are regulars, though. We don't get much transient business."

One of the burly men grunted something Nick could not catch and the clerk bent over the register.

"The one in 514 is a new name to me. The guy in 410 don't sound familiar."

Nick's heart skipped a beat. Four hundred and ten was the room he had just left. "Let's have your passkey. We'll take a look at those birds."

Turning, Nick went swiftly up a flight of stairs and followed a series of red arrows, painted on the walls, which pointed the way to the fire-escape. Round a bend in the corridor a final arrow indicated a window, the lower half of which he eased up gingerly. As he put a leg through, he heard heavy footsteps and laboured breathing on the stairs and a surly voice bemoaning the lack of an elevator. Climbing out on the skeleton structure of rusting iron, he went down on tiptoe. The lowest section hung, balanced by weights, parallel with the ground. It swung down with a clatter when he set foot on it. Nick did not wait to ascertain whether the noise had betrayed him. He ran to the ground and along an alley cluttered with garbage cans and empty crates.

Reaching the street, he slowed to a brisk walk, assuming a purposeful air and looking neither to left nor right, which, he had learned, was the best way to avoid attracting attention. Momentarily he expected to hear a shout or a shot and he breathed more easily when, unchallenged, he rounded a corner into a street of warehouse buildings, deserted but for an occasional prowling watchman.

He made his way south. and east, quelling the impulse to take to his heels when a car went by or a pedestrian looked into his face. There were few people about when he turned into Twenty-Eighth Street at the block where the red neon sign of Muldoon's Tavern punctuated a gloomy huddle of loft buildings. As this hour there would still be a handful of drinkers at the bar near the front door but there was a rarely-used way in by means of which he could avoid them. He went into the building adjoining Muldoon's and tried the handle of a door to the rear of a dimly lit hall. It opened and he slipped through into the back of the tavern, where the booths and tables were. From the bar came a clinking of glasses and murmur of voices but an angle of the wall hid him from those standing there. He slid into the first booth, flattening himself against the partition.

It was then he became aware of a policeman in uniform sitting behind a pillar with a glass in his hand. The policeman stared hard at Nick, then rose ponderously and walked over to him. The moment of his approach seemed unending; his eyes never strayed from Nick's face. Nick could almost feel the coldness of handcuffs on his wrists. The policeman leaned over him with an anxious frown.

"Would you look outside, buddy, and see if my sergeant is nosing about? I got to get back on my beat and I t'ink the son of a bitch is laying for me."

"Sure," said Nick, swallowing hard. "Sure."

He went back to the street the way he had come, drew a deep breath, waited until his hands stopped trembling, then walked in again.

"Not a soul in sight."

"Thanks, buddy," said the policeman, making a hasty exit.

Lying back in the booth, Nick listened to the thudding of his heart. He was alone in that part of the tavern, except for Old Doc Learie, dozing in the end booth, aged head on bony hands. No light showed through the kitchen hatch: the cook and his helper had ceased work and gone home. The voices at the bar went on and on and on. Occasionally Nick heard the swish and thud of the front door as someone came in or went out. A Man lurched past, heading for the lavatory but did not spare Nick a glance on his hurried passage or on his blundering return. After what seemed a long time the hum of activity at the front of the place slackened. Nick put a coin in the jukebox and pressed the button that made it play 'Melancholy Baby.' That fetched Barney. Nick knew it would.

When he looked into the booth, the barman said, "Judas Priest," in a strangled voice and glanced back quickly over his shoulder to make sure no one had followed him.

"You got your noive, comin' here," he whispered fiercely, turning again to Nick. "What d'you wanna do? Get me in wrong wit' the cops?"

"I'm hurt, Barney. There's a bullet in my shoulder."

"What gives you the right to come to me? Where'll I be if the cops find you here? What did you have to kill her for, anyway? You crazy?"

"I didn't kill her, Barney."

"Don't give me that. What kind of a dumb chick d'you think I am? You killed her, all right. The papers say the cops even found your prints on the gun."

"Listen," said Nick earnestly, "I went up' to see her, to talk to her—"

"Don't tell me. I don't want to hear about it."

"I'll go," said Nick, rising clumsily.

His forehead was bathed in sweat. His eyes mirrored the pain and tension under which he laboured. Putting a large hand on his chest, Barney pushed him—not roughly—back on to the seat.

"What d'you wanna do? Faint on my doorstep? That would fix everythin' up just swell." Barney's sloping brow was wrinkled with thought. "Jeez," he said plaintively, "everythin' happens to me."

Rubbing his long nose with a stubby finger, he said, "How bad is your wound?"

"Pretty bad."

"You'll need a sawbones. If it was still prohibition I'd know where to find a dozen we could trust—but these days I don't know one that wouldn't turn you in."

He took another swift look at the drinkers at the bar, then jerked his thumb toward the darkened kitchen.

"Get out there and lie low. I'll brush off the barflies as soon as I can—then we'll see."

Stumbling up, Nick threaded his way unsteadily between the tables to the kitchen. Barney returned to the bar and started a campaign to ease his customers out without damage to their feelings. When the last one had gone, he locked the door, let down the shades with a rattle and switched off the neon sign. He went into the telephone booth and called Kay Bannerman.

"This is Barney," he said, when her sleep-drugged voice answered. "You-know-who is here wit' me. He's hoit pretty bad."

He heard a gasp from the other end of the wire and when Kay spoke again, she was very wide awake. "I'll come as soon as I can. It might take a while. The police may be watching my apartment. They questioned me for two hours today and I'm almost sure I was followed when they let me go."

"Don't go bringin' any cops wit' you."

"I won't."

Going out to the kitchen, Barney turned on a light and leant over Nick, who was sitting limply on a table, his head lolling on his chest. "Let's have a look at the wound."

Between them they stripped off Nick's coat and laid open his shirt. Barney's lips tightened as he looked at the swollen and discoloured shoulder.

"It's pretty bad, alright. How do you feel?"

"Lousy."

"Hold on to yourself a while longer."

Switching off the light, Barney went out and seated himself in the end booth, facing the old man slumbering there. For a time, he looked at the skinny shoulders, the shrunken neck, the filthy, claw-like hands; and then he reached over and shook the sleeper until his greenish derby fell off. Old Doc Learie raised his head with a bewildered air, his bloodshot eyes blinking in the light. He ran his fingers through the wispy hair fringing his skull and stretched himself with a shiver. Thinking that he was being turned out for the night, he rose uncomplainingly and rescued his hat from the dusty floor.

"Sit down," said Barney, "and tell me straight: what kind of a doctor were you?"

Old Doc Learie considered the question for a while. It was a long time since anyone had been interested in his past. "I was a goddam good goddam doctor."

"You were an honest-to-God doctor for sick people? You weren't some kind of a vet?"

"A few of the women I helped to bring babies into the world were cows," said the old man irritably, "but that doesn't make me a vet."

"This is on the level? It ain't a pipe dream you cooked up. "

Peering dubiously at Barney, the old man took more time to marshal his thoughts. He had become unused to thinking and the process was slow. He seemed not to relish some of the memories it brought back.

"If it was a pipe dream, it lasted a hell of a long time. Eight years of college and medical school, two years walking a hospital, pretty nearly twenty years of general practice. That would be some pipe dream."

"If you could bring a baby into the world, I'll bet you could take a bullet out of a man just like that"—Barney snapped his fingers.

Old Doc Learie searched Barney's face for a clue to what lay behind all this.

"It would depend on where the bullet was lodged."

"Say it was in his arm. It wouldn't be much of a trick getting it out?"

"Hell, I could do it with a hairpin."

"Then you got yourself a patient."

The old man's jaw dropped. "You mean, you're serious about this? You weren't just talking?"

"Your patient's out in the kitchen, half-crazy wit' pain. The wound is all swollen and red and puffy. Looks like somethin' better be done about it pretty quick."

"Who shot him?" asked Old Doc Learie in a fearful whisper, with an awed glance over his shoulder.

"What do you care? All you got to do is get the bullet out and keep your mouth shut afterwards."

The old man's head began shaking like a pendulum, as if it would never stop. "I've got to think about this."

"There's nothin' to think about. Can you do it or not?"

"I don't know," said Old Doc Learie in a frightened tone, "I don't know."

Their eyes met squarely and the old man's gaze was apologetic. "I need a drink."

"Sure. Come over to the bar."

They walked the length of the place and Barney took a glass from a zinc tray, reached for the handle of the beer pump.

"I don't mean beer," said Old Doc Learie, "I mean a real drink."

"What'll it be? Scotch or rye?"

"Brandy."

Barney poured a stiff drink and the old man downed it at a gulp. He looked at his hands with a frightened expression on his thin, wrinkled face.

"You were kidding me," he said pleadingly, with a weak smile. "No one's going to ask an old has-been like me to operate on a man."

"I'm not kiddin'."

"It doesn't make sense. I haven't practised in years. Look, let's forget it. Get someone else."

"There's no one else. I done plenty for you. If you won't help me, there's the door. Get out and stay out."

"Wait a minute, Barney. There's more to, this than you think. I'd need instruments. I'd need scalpels and probes and forceps and surgical gut and—and—"

"Hell, if I had all those, I'd yank it out myself. You said you could do it wit' a hairpin."

"That was a figure of speech."

"Hell wit' you and your figures of speech. Could you do it if you had the tools?"

Old Doc Learie looked at his hands again. "Maybe. I wouldn't know until I held a scalpel in my hand."

"I'll get you the tools," said Barney, taking off his apron and putting on his coat. "And you better be sober when I come back wit' them."

He went out by the front door, rattling it behind him to make sure it locked. Old Doc Learie stood at the bar looking at his hands.

The night man at a garage a few blocks away was spraying a car when Barney came in. He put down the hose and rubbed a sponge over the car's gleaming flank.

"Hi, Barney," he mumbled awkwardly, his eyes turned down, "I been meaning to come and see you."

"Don't give me that. You ain't been in the joint for months. How's about the dough you owe me?"

"I'll tell you the truth, Barney, I ain't got it. The wife's been sick and—"

"That's the story you told when you tapped me."

"It's still the way things are. Can I help it if she's always sick?"

"Sure, I know—you have all the bad luck."

"On the level, Barney, I'd pay you if I could."

"You got some nice cars on the floor," remarked Barney, looking about him. "One or two of 'em belong to doctors, don't they?"

"Yeah—that one over there; and the blue Buick in the corner." The garage man's eyes became wary. "So what?"

"So maybe you don't have to worry about that dough. You go on wit' your washin' and I'll walk around for a spell."

"Nothing doing, Barney. You take something from one of those cars and I'll be fired."

"Who's to know if I borrow somethin'? I'll bring it back. That's on the level, kid."

"Nix, Barney. I couldn't take the chance."

"Suit yourself," said Barney, turning as if to go. "See you on payday, kid—and you'll hand the dough over wit' a smile or find yourself behind the eight ball."

The garage hand looked dejectedly at the barman. "You win," he said, picking up the hose.

Barney crossed the concrete floor to the blue Buick. The garage hand concentrated on the car he was washing and did not even look up to see what Barney was carrying when he walked out.

* * * * *

"Never mind your hands. Take a look at the kit."

Old Doc Learie dipped into the black bag standing open on the bar. "I've never seen a more beautiful set of instruments. Where did you get them at this time of the night?"

"There's sure a lot of careless people in this world," said Barney virtuously. "Imagine a guy leavin' a layout like that in his car. I was worried you might not be here when I got back."

"I almost ran out on you. I don't think I could tell you why I stayed."

"It's good enough for me that you did. Muldoon is in hospital wit' stomach ulcers and his apartment upstairs is empty. You can do the job there. Here's the key. Go on up and I'll bring my friend."

"We'll need a bottle of brandy," said the old man. Barney gave him a cold stare. "For what?"

"I can't give your friend an anaesthetic without qualified assistance. We'll have to get him drunk before I operate."

"Yeah, I get it. Help yourself."

Old Doc Learie went up the gloomy staircase of the adjoining building with a bottle of brandy in one hand and the black bag in the other. Setting down the bag, he unlocked the door of Muldoon's apartment with the key Barney had given him. Switching on the light, he retrieved the bag and went in.

In the kitchen of the tavern Barney found Nick half-lying on the table with his eyes shut. He was not asleep, or unconscious, but in an in-between, soporific state. Murmuring under his breath, as if reassuring a child, Barney took him on his shoulder with a fireman's lift and carried him upstairs. The instrument bag and the brandy bottle stood on a chair in the living-room of the apartment but Old Doc Learie was not in sight.

Barney carried Nick into Muldoon's bedroom and laid him on the bed. The shabby garments of Old Doc Learie were strewn about the floor; Barney followed the sound of running water to the bathroom and found the old man standing there, stark naked, skinny as a newborn sparrow, and indescribably dirty.

"What the hell are you doing?"

"I'm about to take a bath."

"You picked a nice time for it. If you could do wit'out one for ten years—"

With simple but impressive dignity, Old Doc Learie drew himself up and gave Barney a look that put him in his place—at the foot of the class. He had become, in some strange way, an entirely different man from the shuffling bum the barman had known.

"What kind of ignorant bastard are you? Don't you realise that in my present state of filth I'd infect the patient with every variety of germ?"

"Sorry, Doc," said Barney, almost humbly, staring curiously at the old man. "Yeah, I guess you're right about that. "I didn't think."

When the temperature of the bath was just too hot for comfort, Old. Doc Learie, stepped into it, hopping from one foot to the other and began to lather himself with brown laundry soap.

"Don't stand there gaping at me. I'm no Greek athlete. Put water on to boil. Take off your friend's clothes and give him a stiff shot of brandy. Find me some clean things to wear. A Shirt and pyjama pants will do. And scrub your grubby paws—you may have to help me."

In somewhat of a daze, Barney obeyed. Returning to the bedroom, he kicked the old man's sour-smelling clothes into a corner. With clumsy gentleness, he undressed Nick, who swore at him feebly when he jarred the injured shoulder. Half-filling a' tumbler with brandy, Barney put it to Nick's lips, coaxing him to drink. "This'll do you good, boy. Hold your head up. That's it. Now swallow." When the last drop had trickled down Nick's throat, Barney let the patient relax while he washed his hands at the kitchen sink. He was in the bedroom, rummaging in a drawer, when Old Doc Learie came out of his bath.

"Try these on," he said, handing over a starched white shirt, and gaudy pyjama trousers belonging to Muldoon.

In these, the old man looked at first as if he was in a tent with his head sticking out of the top. He rolled up sleeves and legs, tucked the shirt well in and wound the waist of the trousers twice round his narrow hips, tightly knotting the cord.

When Barney gathered up the wounded man's clothes to put them out of the way, the money Julian Deering had given Nick fell out of a pocket. The barman stared at it.

"Judas Priest! Where did he ever get a roll like that?" He picked up the money and laid it on the dresser. "If he croaks, I'll split it wit' you," he mumbled, meeting Old Doc Learie's gaze.

In the kitchen Old Doc Learie boiled a handful of surgical instruments in an aluminium pan. He filled another pan with warm water and disinfectant.

"How's the brandy taking hold?"

"He's beginnin' to mutter kinda crazy, Doc."

"Give him some more. The drunker he is, the less he'll feel."

Before the start of the operation, Old Doc Learie painted all-round the wound with a strong disinfectant. He repeated the process three times, letting each coat dry before applying the next. He talked to Nick in a calm, assured way while he did so. Nick did not grasp what he said but something about the old man inspired confidence and he lay still.

Old Doc Learie soaked his hands in the pan of disinfectant and hot water. With a pair of silver tongs, he fished a probe out of the other pan. He motioned to Barney to hold Nick down.

The wounded man was balanced as by a hair on the brink of

unconsciousness but at the first touch of the probe he uttered a shrill cry of pain and started threshing his arms and legs. The old man stood back with a harassed frown and let Barney struggle with him. Beads of sweat came out on Nick's forehead as if squeezed from a sponge. Barney drew back a little and, when Nick's head came up, dealt him one swift hard punch on the angle of the jaw. Nick's eyes rolled up and he fell limply back.

"Okay," said Barney hoarsely. "There's your anaesthetic. For Christ's sake get it over quick."

Snatching up the brandy bottle, he took a long drink. He needed it. Old Doc Learie bent over his patient, working methodically with a glittering instrument, and Barney averted his eyes. He could not look. In a little while, the old man dropped a misshapen piece of lead into one of the pans. He threaded a long curved needle with surgical gut. His twig-like fingers were amazingly deft.

Afterwards he went over the drugs in the bag one by one. He paused with a tall slim bottle of white powder in his hand.

"Sulfathiazole. There's been a lot about that in the papers lately."

"I didn't know you ever read the papers."

"A few things, I read." There was a wry twist to the old man's lips. "This stuff is like high explosive in the war on germs. They use it to cure pneumonia and even gonorrhoea. Maybe it's worth using in this case. There's a danger the wound will turn septic. If I only knew how to give it to him; whether to inject it, or give it through the mouth, or dust it on the wound."

"Why not try all three?"

After some further deliberation, the old man dusted some of the powder into the wound and injected some in solution.

"You done a beautiful job," said Barney, gazing admiringly at the stitched hole while the old man prepared bandages.

"You may not think so, later, if he has to lose the arm."

"He won't lose the arm. I tell you, you done a beautiful

job. You're one swell sawbones. How come they ever took your licence away?"

A faraway look came into Old Doc Learie's eyes. "There was a girl. She was sick and broke and scared— Oh, what the hell do you care how I came to lose my licence?"

Cocking his head on one side, with a disconcerting resemblance to a parrot, Barney listened intently. Someone was knocking insistently on the door of the tavern. He went down and peered out, then opened the door to admit Kay Bannerman.

"It took me longer than I thought," she said breathlessly. "When I came out a detective followed me so I bought some aspirin at the drugstore and went back to my apartment. I turned out the lights as if I'd gone to bed and walked up the stairs to the roof, over two other roofs, and reached the street by the side door of another building. I had my taxi drive all over town to make sure no one was following before I came here. Where's Nick? Is he all, right?"

"He's upstairs," replied Barney non-committally. "I'll show you the way."

When they entered the bedroom in which Nick lay, Old Doc Learie was putting on his filthy high collar. He already wore the trousers of his ragged suit and the shoes that were cut to make room for his bunions.

Kay dropped on her knees beside the bed. "What have you done to him? He looks awful."

"He'll be all right," said Barney. "He was taken care of by one damned fine doctor."

Taking some money from the wad of bills on the dresser, Barney turned to give it to Old Doc Learie but the old man had donned the rest of his ancient garments and departed. Barney heard the door of the apartment shutting and footsteps receding down the stairs. He ran out to the landing and whispered, "Hey!

Come back here," but the old man went on without replying.

In the alley behind a nearby fur-warehouse, in one of the big packing-cases in which he had often dozed through the chill early morning hours, Old Doc Learie lay down and composed himself as if to sleep. He was very tired. His eyelids drooped but his inner eye—the eye of what men call the soul—was wide open. With pitiless clarity he saw himself and his life in all their ugly squalor and wanted no more of either. With a surgical blade he had filched from the black bag, he severed the veins of one frail wrist and then the other. There was not much blood in his puny body. The life he despised ebbed out of him quite soon.

Chapter 8

The last thing Old Doc Learie had done for his patient was to give him two pellets of phenobarbital and Nick had sunk into a deep sleep. Kay leant over the bed, straightening the sheets, smoothing the pillow, putting a cushion under the bandaged shoulder. Wearing an apron, Barney moved about the place, clearing up. Going into the bathroom, he exclaimed "Judas Priest!" at sight of the black ring round the tub. "That was one bath that certainly was overdue," he grumbled, attacking the dirt with rag and cleaner.

On her knees beside the bed, Kay stroked Nick's hair gently, gazing with wonder at his face, ironed smooth by sleep. He looked so young, so pale, so defenceless. Impossible to think of him as a killer. It did not fit with the picture of him she had carried so long in her heart, or the one that now she saw.

"Barney," she said, "why did he do it?"

"Huh?" Barney came out of the bathroom, rag in hand.

"Why did he kill her? She was going to divorce him. Surely getting rid of her would have been enough?"

"Maybe it griped him to think of another man havin' her. He was crazy about her once. Maybe he still was. Maybe he figured if he couldn't have her no one else would."

"That doesn't sound like Nick. He isn't the dog-in-the-manger kind."

"Okay, okay. You tell me why he did it."

It did not occur to either of them that Nick might be innocent. They had both read the day's newspapers.

"Could be he got sore when he thought what a sucker she'd made of him," said Barney. "Or maybe she said some of the things a woman says when she's tryin' to hoit your feelin's and he shot her wit'out stoppin' to think. I dunno. It don't matter why he done it. I guess she asked for it, one way and another." He looked forebodingly at the girl. "You know what'll happen if we're caught helpin' him?"

Kay made an impatient gesture. "I don't care about that. Do you?"

"Sure, I care. A stretch in jail is no picnic."

"But you're taking the risk?"

"A guy like Nick gets under your skin," said Barney, apologetically. "What can you do but help him? If I wind up in a cell, I'll ask the prison doctor to examine my head. Maybe I'm nuts."

"If you are, Barney," said Kay, putting a hand on his arm, "you're the most lovable screwball I ever knew. That's an elegant belt you're wearing. Who did you steal it from?"

"I didn't swipe it. My sister give it to me."

"Why the initial 'D' on the buckle?"

Barney looked uncomfortable. "A guy can have more than one name, can't he?"

"Of course he can. What does the 'D' stand for? Daniel? Dennis? David?"

"You mind your own business what it stands for. That's somethin' I don't never tell nobody. I dropped me foist name as soon as I could talk—but that's the way my sister is. No consideration for other people's feelin's. Pervoise —like all dames."

"Come on, Barney, what is it? Desmond? Dugal?"

With' a furtive glance over his shoulder, as if afraid someone might overhear, Barney said, "You won't ever bring it up again?"

"Cross my heart."

"It's Dorian." Merely speaking the hated name made him squeamish with disgust. "How do you like that? Dorian. For a guy like me. Wouldn't you think me old lady would have had more sense? Boy, I tell you, if you want to get me hoppin' mad, just call me Dorian. Wit' me, it's a fightin' woid." He glanced at his watch. "Holy Mary, it's after four. I gotta get along home. My old man will give me hell."

"Don't tell me he sits up for you?"

"He don't sit up. He wakes up. And if it's after three when I come in, he knows I've been up to somethin' besides woikin'—and it's the rough edge of his tongue for me."

"I'll stay and look after Nick."

"Keep the shades drawn. The cop on the beat knows that Muldoon's away. If he sees a light, he'll come nosin' round."

After Barney's departure, Kay bolted the door of the apartment, switched off all the lights and settled in a chair beside the bed. There were cigarettes and matches in her handbag but she was afraid to smoke lest the fumes disturb the sleeping man. She tried to nap in the chair but concern for Nick's welfare kept her awake. Half a dozen times she rose and bent over the bed to draw the covers up or ease the injured arm into a more comfortable position. When the sky was greying, Nick began to mutter and toss. He rolled over and would have fallen out had she not caught him and pushed him gently back. He did not waken but the things he mumbled became more and more incoherent and he hardly lay still for a moment. Kay had to watch him with uneasy vigilance for he kept sprawling from one edge of the bed to the other.

Kicking off her shoes, she lay down beside him, one slender arm under his head, the other over his chest. She held him close and he relaxed; his subconscious mind seemed more at peace; with a sigh he snuggled to her and the delirious muttering ceased. Kay put her lips softly on his forehead. It was the first kiss that had passed between them. At long last she fell asleep.

When she wakened, hours later, her arms were numb. She disengaged herself gingerly from the sleeping man. Nick did not stir when she stole from his side. In those hours, with the strength and vigour of her own body, she had given him comfort and strength.

Glimpsing herself in the mirror above the dresser, Kay made a wry grimace. Only after a wash and a brisk hair-combing could she bear the sight of herself. There was no food in the apartment and she took the risk of leaving the door unlocked while she ran down to Eighth Avenue for oranges, bread, milk and eggs. Passing a corner stand, she saw Nick's photograph staring at her from the front page of a newspaper. An accurate likeness, it spread over three columns. Above it, a headline two inches high proclaimed:

"ESCAPED SUSPECT STILL AT LARGE."

Buying a copy, she hurried back to the apartment, her arms full of bundles.

Nick was awake. His eyes opened wider when he saw her in the bedroom doorway. "Kay! You're the last person on earth I expected to see."

"I spent the night watching over you."

"I've been trying to imagine where I can be."

"You're in an apartment over Muldoon's. Barney brought you here and a friend of his took the bullet out of your arm."

"I must have passed out in the tavern. I don't remember a thing—except some appalling nightmares."

"They're over, now, Nick—the nightmares."

"Or are they only just beginning?" murmured Nick, a shadow passing over his face.

"Don't think, Nick," cried Kay shakily, "for God's sake, Nick, try not to think."

It was all she herself could do to keep out of her mind a perpetual image of the electric chair. Nick noticed the paper under her arm.

She Got What She Asked For 91

"May I see it?"

"Do you think you ought?"

"I'm all right, Kay. I feel fine."

His eyes were reassuringly clear and the hand held out for the paper was quite steady. Still, it was with reluctance that she gave it to him. Going to the kitchen, she started to prepare breakfast. After a while she returned bearing a tray laden with glasses of orange juice, tall glasses of milk, some dry toast and four soft boiled eggs. Placing the tray on the dresser, she went to the bed to make Nick comfortable for the effort of eating.

Nick stared at her. "It says here—"

"Let's not worry about it now, Nick," said Kay hastily, taking the paper from him. "Let's eat first."

"But it says they found my fingerprints on the gun. That isn't possible. I never touched the gun."

"You never touched the gun?" Kay repeated, staring at him open-mouthed.

"No. It was lying on the floor near the body—"

"Nick!" Kay almost choked. "Oh, Nick—she was dead when you got there."

"Of course." And then, "I see. You, too, thought I shot her."

"I tried not to think so. I couldn't see you doing it. But the stories in the papers— And you weren't yourself when you went to see her. I've been hating myself for making you go. Nick, I don't know what to say."

"You thought I killed her, yet you played guardian angel to me all night?"

"Let's eat," said Kay huskily, turning for the tray.

Placing it on the bed between them, she watched him like an anxious mother to make sure he ate his share. Afterwards, she darkened the room, made him lie down flat, begged him to sleep. Bedclothes tucked under his chin, a meek expression on his face, Nick said, "Shall I tell you something? You're the most wonderful girl I've ever known."

Holding the ravaged tray, Kay looked at him sceptically. "I might believe that if you hadn't babbled another girl's name half the night."

"I did? What name?"

"Althea," said Kay, in no gracious tone. "You kept raving about Althea and her long raven hair." With a little noise remarkably like a sniff, she added, "Sounds like something out of Godey's Lady's Book for 1893."

"You wouldn't be jealous?"

"Jealous? Me? That's funny. That's really very funny."

But Kay did not laugh very heartily. The big dumbbell, she thought, he has to have a bullet in the shoulder before he realises that I'm not a piece of office furniture.

In the middle of the morning, she taxied home, re-entering her apartment by the round-about way in which she had left it. She was barely in when the doorbell rang. She answered the summons and Inspector Gort and another police officer came in without waiting to be invited.

"You again," said Kay, leaving the door ajar. "I thought you exhausted my conversational charms in our two-hour interview yesterday."

The man who came in with the inspector shut the door with a backward kick of his heel. He was younger than Gort's usual companion, Sergeant Mayo. The sergeant had temporarily been relieved of duty as the immediate result of Nick Abbott's escape.

"You didn't tell us much in those two hours," retorted Inspector Gort, his eyes roving over the room.

"I thought I made it plain I had nothing to tell. After all, I was Mr. Abbott's secretary—not his keeper. My job with him ended months ago. I haven't seen him since."

"That's what you say," murmured Gort, opening a door and peering into her bedroom.

"If you're looking for the johnny," said Kay, "it's that door on the right."

"You were on pretty friendly terms with Abbott," accused the inspector, lowering bushy brows at her. "He used to take you to dinner."

"Sure," agreed Kay, lighting a cigarette. "We'd scramble through a sandwich at Childs and hurry back to the office—to work."

"Yeah? A pretty girl like you—"

"You're a smarter detective than I thought," said Kay, blowing a smoke ring. "At least, you have eyes in your head. As far as I was concerned, Mr. Abbott was blind."

"Still and all, you must know quite a bit about his friends —the places he hung out at when he wasn't at the office—his habits in general."

"The last few months I worked for him, when he wasn't at the office, we used to try all the bars. I wouldn't know about his friends. He used to talk about a Mr. Kramer—a Mr. Otto Kramer."

"Make a note of that name," said Gort to his assistant. To Kay, he added, "Someone's helping Abbott to hide out. We'd have nailed him long ago if he was on his own."

"I don't think Mr. Kramer would do a thing like that," answered Kay, looking shocked.

"You never know. You'd be surprised, the chances people will take for a friend. We'll soon find out when we put this Kramer on the grill."

"Isn't it against the law to help a wanted man?"

"Lady," said Inspector Gort with feeling, "when we nail the guy who's helping Abbott, he'll get ten years. I'll see to that personally?"

"By the way," said Kay, with an ingenuous air, "I have a lot of shopping to do this afternoon. Would it be all right to ask the detective who's shadowing me to carry some of the parcels?"

Inspector Gort gave her a long, calculating look. "Better get someone else," he grunted. "I'm taking that guy off your tail."

When she was alone, Kay telephoned Muldoon's and asked Barney how a certain party was keeping.

"He's makin' out okay. I went up for a look at him when I came to woik. He was sleepin' like a baby."

"That's fine. I'd better stay away for a while, Barney. The police say I won't be shadowed any more but it's safer to take no chances."

"I get your point. He better be quiet for a while, anyway, while he catches up on his sleep. I brought a cold roast chicken from home. That'll feed him for a couple days. The cops been here askin' questions—but not about him. Seems Old Doc Learie committed suicide oily this mornin'."

"How awful."

"Yeah. Tough, ain't it? I'm keepin' the news from you-know-who. If he thought he was responsible it might prey on his mind."

"Why did he ever do such a thing?"

"Well, I'll tell you. I read a book once. It said somethin' I never forgot. Seems like a man's life is a sort of diary in which he means to write one story—and winds up writin' another. The way I figure it, Old Doc Learie got a glimpse last night of the story he meant to write—and it made him sick and sore wit' the story he had written. Me and some of the boys will give him a decent burial. A few drinks under their belts and my regulars would buy a funeral for an alley-cat. Muldoon's chippin' in, too—only, Muldoon don't know it."

Two full days elapsed before Kay returned to visit Nick, taking care not to be followed. She brought bandages to dress his wound and an armful of magazines and paper-bound books to keep him amused. Nick was sitting up, in a faded green dressing-gown belonging to Muldoon, playing solitaire with a greasy deck on a tray balanced on his knees. He was flatteringly pleased to see her. He had been alone almost all of the time, for Barney, fearful of attracting attention to the apartment, had made his visits few.

When she removed the bandages, Old Doc Learie had applied, Kay was relieved to see how cleanly the wound was healing. The old man's swansong had been a beautiful piece of work. Kay redressed the wound and burned the used bandages. She showed Nick a clipping from The World-Telegram. It was of an advertisement which had appeared in three or four other newspapers as well.

"Nick. Yours is still the wrong way. Please get in touch with me. Skinny."

When he read it, Nick could not help smiling.

"Who's 'Skinny'?" asked Kay, watching his face.

"That's a sort of joke between Althea and me," replied Nick absently.

"Oh," said Kay. The murmur was subdued.

"I saw her the night I escaped. Althea's an attorney and believes in doing things in strict accordance with the law. She wanted me to give myself up and trust a jury to believe in my innocence."

"No jury would. At least, not until it can be proved."

"That's what I said. If I gave myself up, I'd be whisked into court before I could turn round and sentenced to death while Althea and her private detectives were still making fluttering motions with their hands: All the evidence the police have points to my guilt—and that's all the evidence they care about."

"Nick, we've got to prove you didn't do it."

"How?" asked Nick, with a hopeless gesture.

"I don't know. Somehow. I'll find a way. Meanwhile, we've got to get you out of here, away from New York. It would be terrible if the police found you too soon."

"I'm all for running away, myself. But how? Where?"

"I don't know that, either. I'm going down to talk to, Barney."

When Kay entered Muldoon's there was a sprinkling of customers at the bar and Barney was in heated argument with one of them, who kept jabbing a soiled forefinger at a newspaper page. Kay ordered a highball and perched herself on a stool. The drinkers were silent for a few moments after her entrance and then the one who had been arguing told Barney frankly, man to man, that he was crazy.

"Okay," said Barney with false affability, "so you're the only one that's sane. So why waste your time talkin' to a screwball like me?"

"I tell you, I seen the guy right here at this very bar. A dozen times, I seen him." The man passed the newspaper page among his friends and Kay glimpsed the picture over which they were pouring: one of Nick. "Look, fellows, ain't you seen this guy in here? He used to drink rye."

"Johnny drinks rye," jeered Barney. "Maybe Johnny's the guy they're lookin' for."

A roar of laughter went up from the group and the man who had passed round the picture jumped up and down with rage.

"A wiseguy," he spluttered. "A comedian. Maybe you oughta be clowning on the radio, 'steada Jack Benny. I tell you, I seen him a hundred times. In here. At this very bar."

"I know the guy you're thinkin' of," said Barney, eyeing the picture critically. "He's got more hair than that and his nose ain't so straight. Sure, I know who you mean. He looks kinda like this fellow the cops are after, at that—only, he ain't as tall as it says here. He drives a truck for Oppenheimer's. Yeah, he was in for a shot of rye this mornin'."

"Go tell a cop, Augie," scoffed one of the other men. "Have the guy hauled off his truck."

"So maybe I'm wrong," snarled Augie. "Can't a guy make a mistake?"

"We wouldn't know it was you, Augie," said Barney, "if you ever made anythin' else."

"Aw, nerts to the lot of ya."

Snatching his paper, the irate man stamped out, followed by another gust of laughter. Barney looked at Kay, then glanced briefly, meaningly, at the row of booths. Taking the hint, Kay rose unhurriedly and carried her highball to one of them. In a little while Barney came over and wiped the table in front of her with a damp cloth.

"We've got to get him out of here, Barney," she said, in a whisper.

"Sure. Out of the country."

Barney put a slug in the jukebox, which began to play his favourite tune, causing the men at the bar to hold their noses expressively.

"Have you any ideas?" murmured Kay, under the cover of the music, which Barney had turned up loud.

"I been talkin' to Nick. Him and another kid used to monkey wit' a short wave sendin' set when he was at college. He ain't no wireless operator but he can take and send messages in Morris code. That gives me an idea, for a guy I know has connections wit' a crummy shippin' line between here and South America. I had a few woids with this guy and there's a tub sailin' for Honduras tomorrow night. This tub is supposed to carry two radio operators but it's carried only one for half a dozen trips. Could be the operator would find a way to fill the spare boith wit' Nick—if his palm was greased. It'll cost about two hundred smackers, counting phony identification papers for Nick."

"I'll bring you the money this afternoon," said Kay swiftly.

Barney shook his head. "The money end is fixed. Nick's got half a grand."

"Are you sure you can fix the rest?"

Barney straightened up. "Come around about eleven o'clock tomorrow night," he said, "and say goodbye to Nick." He walked back to the bar and started drawing beer for his impatient patrons.

Chapter 9

The taxi trickled to a halt and the driver turned his head and said, "This is it." Beyond a barrier a row of hooded lights cast white pools on crates and packing-cases and on the sides of a ship bound to the dock with ropes. Between the bright pools the shadows lay in slabs; a slate-grey sky pressed heavily down, calking with darkness each unlit, corner. Of about three thousand tons, squat and unlovely, her butt broad like a woman's, the ship had an appearance of neglect betraying fly-by-night ownership. Her paint was dingy; in places, scabrous with rust. Her name and South American port of registry were lettered in faded gilt on her stern.

On dock and ship men stripped to undershirts sweated and heaved in a bedlam of rattling chains, groaning winches, wheezing donkey engines, hoarse-shouted profanity. Men on the deck, grotesque as gorillas against the backdrop of night. Men swarming like ants on the dock, pigmy in the light, giant in the dark. Black men with glistening skins and gleaming white teeth. White men with damp curling hair on chests and in armpits. Only one stood remote from the bustle to load the ship and speed her on her way: a government inspector, bored, blase, indifferent, leaning on a box, hat tipped over brow, yawning and scratching the back of his neck.

In the taxi, looking out of the window at the wretched little ship, Kay held on to Nick's hand, unaware that her grip was so tight it hurt.

"It won't be for long," she said, trying as much to convince herself as him. "Barney and I will be working for you every hour, every minute. One day you'll be able to come back, Nick—one day soon."

"Sure," said Nick, with false heartiness. "Sure. I'll be back."

He was wearing a new suit and belted raincoat, neat but inconspicuous, bought for him in the ready-to-wear department of a large store. The high collar of the coat was turned up about his ears, the brim of his hat drawn low on his forehead. Barney had bought him shoes with lifts that made him a good two inches taller. He had on rimless spectacles, serving to broaden his face and lend it added maturity and a slight studiousness. In a small bag he carried shirts, socks, underwear, shaving-kit and toothbrush.

"Where's that guy keepin' himself?" fumed Barney. "He said he'd meet us here."

"He'll be along," said Kay. "There's no hurry."

"What d'you mean, there's no hurry? Every second we hang around here makes it more likely someone will start askin' questions."

In a few minutes a man appeared at the window of the taxi, although watching the dock keenly they had not seen him approaching. He could not have been more than forty but his shaggy hair was quite white. He wore a shabby blue uniform and a soiled white shirt and was obviously a little drunk. Looking in at them with a sardonic gleam on his lean face, he wavered slightly on his feet.

"You're dead on time," he said, with a hiccup.

"More than I can say for you, Hayden," hissed Barney. He jerked a thumb at Nick. "This is the Mr. Smith I told you about."

His eyes on Kay, Hayden nodded perfunctorily to Nick. "How d'you do, Mr.—Smith. In a moment I'll walk down the dock to that dark patch at the end. You count up to ten, then follow me. Keep out of sight. There's plenty of cover you can use."

"I thought you had everythin' fixed?" grunted Barney.

Hayden turned a bleak face on the barman. "Certainly, everything's fixed. Only, the government man and the owners don't know it." His eyes shifted again to Kay. "You're very pretty," he said.

As mysteriously as he had appeared, he disappeared.

"Here," said Barney awkwardly, thrusting a farewell gift, a

carton of cigarettes, at Nick. Into their handshake the two men put a warmth they could not otherwise express. Nick offered his hand to Kay but she threw her arms round him and kissed him on the mouth. He let the bag slip from his fingers; his arms came up and held her tightly; his lips returned the eager pressure. All too soon, Barney parted them, thrusting the bag into Nick's hand and pushing him out of the cab. Even then, Nick stood numbly at the window, staring at the girl, who looked at him with a smile struggling against tears.

"Get goin'," called Barney to the driver; and the taxi rolled away.

Avoiding the glare of the lights, taking advantage of every concealing stack of cargo, Nick went stealthily along the dock in the direction Hayden had indicated. They came together in a dark place and Hayden, with a jerk of his head, motioned to Nick to follow him up a rope ladder. Across the deck they picked their way, over hawsers, between hatches, to a door which Hayden opened, pushing Nick through into unrelieved gloom. Shutting the door behind them, Hayden switched on a light and Nick blinked about him at a small cabin with curtains drawn over the portholes, in which radio equipment occupied the greater part of the space.

Another door, opposite the first, stood ajar. Hayden went through, beckoning to Nick to follow. Obeying, Nick found himself in an inner cabin containing two bunks, one above the other, a washbasin, a chest of drawers, a tin trunk standing on end and two rickety wicker chairs. Disorder and confusion everywhere; personal belongings strewn on the bunks, chest of drawers and chairs; pipes, hairbrushes, dirty socks, tattered books, ties, tins of tobacco, empty bottles, rusty razor blades, nicked strop, scissors, pillbox, old magazines, soiled tumblers, letters in torn envelopes, matchbooks, a watch-chain, a pyjama coat, a bottle of aspirin, a whiskered comb... Hayden cleared the upper berth, dumping the debris on the cluttered lower one.

"You sleep up top. You can put your stuff in one of those drawers. Most of 'em are empty. Never use 'em myself. They complicate life so." He took a half-full bottle of whisky from under his bunk, slopped some of it into an unwashed tumbler and drank. "Help yourself," he said, offering the bottle to Nick.

"I don't drink."

"If you don't, you'll find this a lousy trip. By the way, you're my cousin, making the voyage for your health and paying your passage by helping me. I made it right with the Old Man—the bloodsucker took half of what your friend paid me—but the less anyone else knows the better. What's your name again? Jones?"

"Smith."

"Oh, yes, Smith." The radio operator ran a cynical eye over Nick from head to foot. "Fine old name, Smith. Some of the best people have used it."

Emptying a chair by tilting it so that everything on it slid off on to the floor, he sat down and replenished his glass. He put his feet on the other chair and lay back. Outside, the hubbub of activity went on. Rattling chains. Shouting voices. Creaking derricks. Thud of cargo in the hold.

"What are you running away from?" asked Hayden, without the smallest genuine interest in his voice. "Rob a bank?"

"Maybe."

"No." The bleak eyes became shrewd. "That suit came off a peg at Macy's. If you paid more than twenty bucks you were robbed. Absconding cashiers dress better—at first. Well, we're all running away from something. I'm running away, too. Been running away for years. From myself, in case you want to know. Sounds silly, doesn't it, running away from yourself—when a man's condemned to take himself wherever he goes? But, sometimes, for a little while, I manage to leave myself behind." He patted the bottle. "It only takes enough of this. You should try it."

"I have."

"Yeah, I guess you have, at that. Sit down. Go on, sit down. You make me nervous, standing there. Relax. You'll be on this rotten tub a long time—longer than you'll care about. She's so slow, before we touch port you'll want to get off and walk. It'll be a good half hour before we sail. You have to lie low until then."

Nick sat on the lower berth without troubling to clear it of litter. He removed the spectacles, laying them beside him while he rubbed his eyes. Hayden picked them up and glanced through them.

"Plain glass. Funny how you fellows always wear them when trying to disguise yourselves. Don't look at me like that. I don't care who you are or what you've done. You're worth a hundred bucks to me; fifty quarts of cheap whisky; that's the extent of my interest."

"For a fellow who isn't interested, you talk a lot."

"Hell, I like to talk to a man like you who's had no better luck than myself. It makes me feel good. If you know anything about psychology, you'll understand that. I've seen a lot like you in my time. All of 'em running away from something or other and, whatever they're running from, they always take it with them. If they're running from the Law, it's never more than a step behind. They can feel its hot breath on their necks. Even when they get way down below the Equator, it's still right on their tail. Most people think they'll be safe in one of the banana republics—but it isn't so. You can be extradited from every one of them nowadays."

"I begin to understand why you're running away from yourself," said Nick. "I don't blame you."

Hayden threw back his head and laughed.

Nick took the bottle from him.

"You've got clean habits," said Hayden, watching Nick rinsing a tumbler, "but you'll lose 'em, boy—you'll lose 'em."

"Maybe," replied Nick, pouring himself a drink.

He refilled the glass the radio operator silently held out and laid the bottle on the floor within reach. Although they went through none of the palaver of touching glasses and mouthing high-sounding phrases, when they drank it was a toast—damnation to memory.

"Perhaps you think you'll go back one day," droned Hayden, his eyes shut. "That's a pipe dream they all have. Well, they go back in handcuffs or not at all. They keep drifting a little further into the interior, away from the ports where American ships drop anchor. They steer clear of the whites and the natives don't want 'em—"

"Look, cousin," said Nick curtly, "let's talk about something else."

"Certainly, cousin," replied Hayden, with mock courtesy. "What shall it be? Shall we discuss the charms of the fair damsel you left behind?"

"We'll avoid that topic also—unless you want your skull split with this bottle."

"Not while there's still whisky in the bottle," said Hayden quickly. "That's one of my sacred principles, cousin—perhaps my only one."

The rivet-studded walls began to reverberate to the labouring of the engines, a slow uneven rhythm faltering then quickening as the screws churned the water. Every timber straining, every plate complaining, with a shaking and a quaking, with a clanking and a groaning, the ship backed and filled into the Hudson. She made as much fuss about it as an old Irish woman boarding a jaunting car. "Ever been sea-sick, cousin?"

"No, cousin, never."

"You'll be sea-sick this trip, cousin."

Hayden reached for the bottle and filled Nick's glass and his own.

"How did you leave Uncle Herman and Aunt Emma and all our revolting little kinfolk, cousin?"

"The same as you left them, cousin. Weeping into their beer."

"You're a wag, cousin."

"You're a wit, cousin."

"We're a pair of no-goods, cousin," said Hayden, taking a long drink. "Feel that shaking and thumping? That's little old New York shaking us off. She doesn't want us. No decent place on earth does."

"You're becoming morose, cousin. Have another drink."

"I'll have another drink, cousin—but I'll still be morose. At this point, it is my custom to shed a few tears."

"A maudlin habit, cousin."

"Old age and remorse, cousin."

"You should look on the bright side, cousin."

"How right you are, cousin. After all, maybe our luck is about to change. Perhaps the damned old, washtub will sink. She's overdue in Davy Jones's locker. Pass the bottle, cousin. I drink my whisky straight, diluted only by my tears.

"They heard the outer door opening; footsteps in the radio cabin; and a thick-waisted man with the face of a disgruntled bulldog, in stained uniform and navy-blue sweater, looked in at them.

"How about a drink?"

"Help yourself," said Hayden, handing him the bottle.

The newcomer wiped the neck of the bottle with a grubby hand, put it to his lips and took a long swallow.

"This person of elegance and charm," said Hayden, with a wave of his hand, "is Mr. Hennessey, our first mate. Hennessey, meet Mr. Smith, my new assistant."

"Pleased to meetcha," said Hennessey, giving Nick a hard stare. "Ain't I seen you somewheres? Your face is familiar."

"Mr. Smith's manners are even more familiar, when you get to know' him," remarked Hayden. "He's almost finished the scotch."

"Yeah, I seen your face somewheres," grunted Hennessey. "Smith, eh? What was your name before it was Smith?"

"Smythe," replied Hayden. "He's the democratic type, so he changed it."

"What ships you work on before?"

"Their names would mean nothing to you," said Hayden. "He's new to this coast. Used to ship out of San Francisco."

"Let the guy speak for himself. He's got a tongue, ain't he?"

"Certainly, he's got a tongue," agreed Hayden, in a tone of sweet reasonableness. "Open your mouth and show it to him, cousin. The trouble is—and I regret to say it—Mr. Smith is drunk."

"You mean, you're drunk," said Hennessey. "You're never anything else. Maybe with an assistant you'll get a few messages straight, for a change." To Nick, he added, "You play poker?"

"No," lied Nick. He wanted to reach his destination with funds intact.

"Here's your, chance to learn. A bunch of us play every night. Helps pass the time."

"And keep me broke," said Hayden.

"I don't learn games quickly," said Nick.

"There's plenty of time," said Hennessey. "The going is slow on this barnacled mud-scow. See you guys later. I got work to do."

After both doors had closed behind Hennessey, Hayden sat up and looked solemnly at Nick. He was much less drunk than he had appeared to be.

"Steer clear of that man, cousin. He's poison."

Chapter 10

"Miss Archer will see you now," said a bespectacled woman secretary with a mannish haircut; and Kay followed a severely tailored back and two beanpole legs into a private office where Althea Archer sat at a desk.

"Miss Kay Bannerman," the secretary announced primly and withdrew, shutting the door behind her.

Kay's first impression of Althea was of a charming personality, assured but unassuming. Prepared to dislike her at sight, she was faintly piqued to find no obvious reason for doing so. This tall gracious woman with skin of an incredible whiteness had breeding as well as good looks. In her presence, Kay felt like an immature girl, a sensation which Althea's evident desire to set her at ease did nothing to lessen.

"Do sit down. I think you'll find that chair comfortable."

"Thank you," said Kay, perching on the edge of it.

"My secretary said you preferred not to tell her the nature of your business. I'll be happy to do anything I can for you, Miss"—the woman attorney glanced at a slip on her desk—"Miss Bannerman."

"I'll come straight to the point. It's about Nick—I mean, Mr. Abbott."

Althea looked Kay straight in the eyes, then she lifted an inter-office telephone and said briskly into it, "Miss Cleaver, please see that I am not disturbed until I ring." Replacing the instrument, she looked again at Kay.

"What do you wish to say to me about Mr. Abbott? Is it possible he sent you to me?"

"It was my own idea to come. I got the address of your New York office out of the phone book."

"But you've seen him lately? Otherwise, you wouldn't know

that Mr. Abbott and I are acquainted. Until the other night he had forgotten our early friendship."

"Perhaps he hadn't altogether forgotten," replied Kay, being honest, although she grudged the other woman such satisfaction as her words might offer. "Perhaps you were always in the back of his mind. This I know: in delirium it was your name he kept repeating."

"He's ill?" cried Althea in dismay.

"No, he's all right now. As right as a man can be with a murder charge hanging over him."

"He ought to face it. By hiding he is only delaying the inevitable."

"He said you told him that. Frankly, I'm all for the delay. At least he won't be railroaded to the electric chair before his friends have a chance to prove his innocence."

"Where is he now?"

"I'd rather not say."

"I can understand that. You've seen him lately, so he's probably in New York. How long do you think he can stay at large with every policeman in the city looking for him?"

"He has left New York, I'll tell you that, much."

"Even so"—Althea spread her hands in an expressive gesture—"isn't it inevitable that he'll be caught? Doesn't he see that to give himself up would create a favourable impression?"

"A favourable impression isn't enough. Proof of his innocence is more important."

"You're sure of his innocence," said Althea gently.

"Aren't you?"

"I was"—Althea's slim hands toyed with a platinum chain around her neck—"but now I'm not quite. The evidence against him is strong. His fingerprints on the revolver are all but damning. And I've found out things about him I never knew before.

Perhaps you don't know them either. Did you know, for instance, that at college he almost killed a man in a fight over a girl?"

"I didn't know it—and I don't believe it."

"I'm afraid it is true. It sheds an unpleasant light on his character."

"Nick's a dear, fine person. If you want light on his character, ask me. I've known him for four years and I shan't believe a word against him. As to the fingerprints on the gun, Nick swore he never touched it. He wasn't lying. I'd stake my life on that. He wasn't lying."

"Fingerprints cannot be faked. I've gone into that possibility."

"Those were."

"But how?"

"I don't know. But I'll find out."

"If you could, it would make a great difference. Those fingerprints are the most important evidence against him."

"If I find a way to prove they're false, will you help me prove his innocence?"

"But how could you ever prove such a thing?"

"If I can, will you help me?"

"Do that," said Althea firmly, "and I'll stop at nothing to help. Nick has another good friend who will also do everything he can. Between the three of us, we'll turn this case upside down."

"If we do, a choice rat will fall out. Whoever killed Claire deliberately framed Nick."

"Won't you tell me where Nick is? You can trust me. That's easy to say, I know—but it's the solemn truth."

Hesitating, Kay studied Althea's face, finding there no hint of insincerity. "He's on a boat bound for South America. It's up to us to make it possible for him to come back."

After leaving the woman attorney's office, Kay telephoned to Barney. "You have a lot of friends on the police force," she said. "Can you find out something about the men on the Homicide Squad?"

"Just what d'you wanna know?"

Kay explained what was in her mind and the barman said, "I get it. You want a cop close to Nick's case who ain't too bright. Well, they's plenty of dumb clucks on the force. It's only a matter of locatin' the right one. I'll see what I can do."

"It has to be one who doesn't know me," said Kay. "Don't forget, I was questioned at headquarters."

"Sure, sure. I'll bear that in mind. How did you make out with the dame you went to see?"

"She was charming and lovely and friendly," replied Kay sourly. "And I hate her guts," she added, after she hung up.

In the late afternoon Barney gave her a ring at her apartment. "I think Sergeant Mayo's the guy you want. The boys tell me he's as dumb as they're made. He ain't one of the cops that questioned you, is he?"

"Mayo?" Kay wrinkled her nose. "No, I'm quite sure he isn't. I was questioned by Inspector Gort and another man—but the other man's name wasn't Mayo."

"Well, he's the dope that let Nick slip through his fingers, so maybe the Commissioner put him on ice. They tell me dames and liquor are his weaknesses."

"What does he look like?"

"More like a chimpanzee than anythin' human. One of the boys had a snapshot of a group wit' Mayo in it, taken at a clambake. I borrowed it when the guy wasn't lookin'. You can pick it up here."

* * * * *

In avid pursuit of a girl who had given him the eye in Herald Square, Sergeant Mayo paused briefly at a window with a long mirror, straightening his tie and cocking his white fedora at a jauntier angle. He was glad to be wearing his new chocolate-brown suit with the broad white stripes; it seemed to belittle the bulge of his abdomen. And although his buckskin shoes were torturing his corns and bunions, he had to admit they made him look like a million dollars. Pink shirt. White tie. Pink silk handkerchief, coyly peeping. Fawn socks. Pearl pin. Fresh from barber and manicurist, his nails a bright pink, his ruddy complexion heightened by a facial and toned down by a mask of powder, Sergeant Mayo felt complacently that he was looking his best. A pity, though, about that frontal bulge. Perhaps one of those rubber belts would help. He would have to find out.

He went after the girl, his eyes slightly popping, the tip of his tongue moistening his full red lips. She had more with which to tantalize a man than most janes who gave you the eye on the street. A cute little fanny. A swell pair of gams. Hair of a shade between gold and red, under a funny little hat. Frontal contours that must look great in one of those tight sweaters. In every way, a tasty dish.

She walked south on Broadway, not so quickly as to make him think he must have got his signals mixed, not so slowly as to seem an easy pick-up. And she wasn't out to make just any guy. Most of the men she passed turned their heads admiringly but she ignored them all. It made Sergeant Mayo feel pretty good to know he was the one in whom she had shown interest. It proved she had taste and judgment, he had to admit that.

At Thirty-First Street he was a couple of yards behind her. At Thirtieth, he drew level and raised his hat. "Haven't I met you somewheres?"

With a coquettish glance from under long dark lashes, the girl said, "Your face is familiar."

"Yours, too," said Mayo, falling into step with her. "Yeah, I'm pretty sure we met some place. Maybe at the Copacabana or Leon & Eddie's?"

"I've been to the Copacabana."

"Yeah? That's where it must have been. How you been keeping, Miss—Miss—"

Her big blue eyes reproached him. "So, you've forgotten my name? I'm sure I must have told you the first time we met. I even have an idea I gave you my phone number—but you never called me, you naughty man."

"You can give me them again," said Mayo, taking her arm, "and this time, baby, I'll write 'em down. Where you going? You ain't got a date?"

"No, I'm all alone this evening."

"Not any more, you ain't."

"I was on my way to a cosy bar I know of for a weeny drink before going back to nay apartment."

"Sounds pretty good. Let's make it a couple of drinks—and then we'll both go back to your apartment."

"You're an awful fast worker, Mr.—Mr.—"

"You're as bad as me, you forgot, too. The name's Mayo—but just call me Leonard."

"I will, if you'll call me Rosie."

"Try and stop me. That's a pretty name—Rosie."

"I like yours, too—Lennie."

"Is that all you like about me, my name?"

"Now you're fishing. What broad shoulders you have."

"You should feel my muscles," said Sergeant Mayo, pulling in his stomach and going a shade redder with the effort.

They went through the door under the neon sign of Muldoon's Tavern and walked past the bar to a booth.

"This don't seem much of a place to me," said Maya, guiding the girl into the seat and squeezing in beside her.

"How's about having just one drink here, then taking a cab to one of the classy spots uptown?"

"They're all so crowded, Lennie, and I don't feel like crowds."

"Me, neither, baby," said the sergeant, pressing his flabby bulk against her.

Barney appeared; his long face dolorous. "What'll it be?"

"I'll have a rye highball," said the girl, powdering her nose.

"Me, too," said Mayo. "And let us taste the rye, buddy."

"Give the man some money to put in the jukebox, Lennie. Rosie craves music."

"I'll put the coin in myself," replied Mayo, extricating his bulge with difficulty from the booth. "This guy don't look like he'd know one toon from another." Frowning, he studied the names of the records. "This junk is all pretty old. I guess I'll play, 'I Met a Dream'; that's kinda appropriate. And 'Scrub Me, Mama, With a Boogie Beat'—that's a pretty hot number."

"I've got an awful funny record at my apartment. It's called, 'Who Slapped Annie on the Fanny With a Flounder?' If you're good, I'll play it to you. You'll die laughing."

"'Who Slapped Annie on the Fanny With a Flounder?' Say, that's a hot one, all right, all right."

When the highballs came Sergeant Mayo sipped his suspiciously before paying for them. He smacked his lips; his face cleared.

"Not bad at all, buddy. It's got a real kick." To the girl, he added: "You got to watch these guys, or they'll give you a thimble of rye in a tumbler of ginger ale. How's yours, baby? It don't look dark enough to me. Better let me taste it.

"It's just right, Lennie-boy. Rosie doesn't like her drinks too strong. Liquor goes to Rosie's head awful fast. If Rosie drinks too much, Lennie-boy will have to carry her out."

"Rosie better have another, quick, if that's the way it'll be," said Mayo with clumsy gallantry. "Listen, buddy, bring us two more in about ten minutes."

She Got What She Asked For 113

"Okay," replied Barney, looking as if he was about to throw up.

His hand playing the piccolo up and down the girl's leg, Sergeant Mayo said huskily, "Look, baby, you don't live with your mother, or anything like that?"

"I live all alone, Lennie-boy. Isn't it too bad about poor lonely little me?"

"Baby, from now on lonely is the one thing you ain't ever gonna be." He tried to kiss her but, with a light laugh, she evaded him.

"Not now, Lennie-boy. Be good."

"I can wait," said Mayo, sitting up a little straighter. "Care for a smoke, baby? Finish your drink like a good little girl, the guy will be along with another in a minute. See—mine's all gone already."

They lit cigarettes and talked about nothing in particular and giggled and drank three highballs in twenty minutes. Sergeant Mayo began to wonder if the barman had not taken too literally his expressed desire to taste the rye. He could not remember when three drinks had taken hold of him so quickly or so thoroughly. Nor could he remember drinking in such delightful company. This girl had what it took to get a guy wound up. It gave him a kick to see the rapt admiration in her big blue eyes.

"What you thinking about, baby?"

"You, Lennie-boy. You're so big, so strong, so manly. I'll bet you're a success in your line of business—a big shot."

"Aw, I dunno."

"Now, Lennie-boy, no false modesty. By the way, what is your business?"

"I'm on the force, baby."

"A detective?" The blue eyes opened wide with wonder. "How thrilling. What do you do? Do you track down gangsters and all like that?"

"I'm a—an inspector on the Homicide Squad, baby. They ain't many gangsters, no more."

"I'll bet you shot them all, Lennie-boy."

"Some of 'em, babe. Some of 'em."

"I'll bet it keeps you awful busy, running down murderers."

"Not so busy I won't have plenty of time to spend with you, baby."

"You're so sweet, Lennie-boy. Tell me about some of your cases."

"Well, lemme see." Sergeant Mayo tried to focus his eyes on his fourth highball, which seemed to be twins. That struck him as funny. Very, very funny. He had to laugh. It took him a moment to remember what they had been talking about. "Aw, you don't wanna hear about my cases, baby. Let's talk about you."

"Tell me about that awful man who killed his wife, Lennie-boy."

"Which one? Guys are killing their wives alla time."

"That brute, that Abbott man, Lennie-boy."

"Oh, him." Sergeant Mayo's face darkened. Because of Nick Abbott's escape from his custody, he was on suspension without pay.

"Yes, tell me about him. Are you working on that case, Lennie-boy?"

"I work on all the big cases. It was me that pinned the rap on Abbott. He got away—but I'll nail him."

"It couldn't have been very hard, proving Abbott guilty. After all, he was caught bending over his wife's body. The papers say you even found his fingerprints on the gun."

"Yeah, we found his prints on the gun. Aw, forget it, baby. Let's talk about something else."

"I don't see where you were so smart, Lennie-boy. It looks more to me as if Abbott was dumb."

"There's a lot of things you don't know, baby."

"Such as?"

"Well—there's all kinds of angles to detecting."

"You're just trying to put me off, Lennie-boy."

"No, I ain't, baby. Honest, I ain't. It's only that—look, can you keep a secret?"

The girl went through the motions of crossing her heart and cutting her throat.

"Well, now, baby, supposing we hadn't found Abbott's prints on the gun. Supposing we knew goddam well he done it—but needed that last little bit of proof to convince a jury."

"But the papers said, —"

"The papers don't know everything, baby. There were no prints on that gun. I don't know how Abbott prevented them—he didn't wear gloves, he hadn't even a handkerchief to wipe 'em off on."

"But won't it come out in court that there aren't any fingerprints on the gun?"

"That's where brains come in, baby. His prints are on the gun now, alright, alright. I got a bright idea while we were questioning him. I stuck the gun in his hand and said, 'Show us how you shot her.' Abbott didn't want to play that way so he laid the gun down and we wrapped it up quick and put it away—with a beautiful set of his prints on it."

"Why, how clever of you, Lennie-boy?'

"Aw, it was nothing," said Mayo modestly. "Only an inspiration, baby—only an inspiration. But keep your mouth shut about what I just told you. There's a lot the public don't understand about police methods—and it ain't always wise to enlighten 'em."

"Let me out," said the girl, rising.

"Where you going?"

"I'll be back."

After she squeezed past him, Sergeant Mayo settled back and watched her trim figure going to the rear of the place. When she returned, he reflected pleasurably, they would have one more highball and take a bottle to her apartment. Boy, the fun they would have. Thinking of it, his popping eyes glistened.

He expected her back shortly but a quarter of an hour passed and he was still sitting alone. In five minutes more he was thoroughly uneasy. He told himself that so amiable a girl would not run out on him; but he was not convinced. Barney came to the booth, gathered the empty glasses, wiped the table with a damp cloth.

"That girl who was with me," said Mayo jerkily. "You happen to see where she went?"

"Where would a lady go after a few drinks?" said Barney reprovingly.

"She's been a damned long time. She said she'd be back."

"Did she say what year?"

With an angry snort, Sergeant Mayo squirmed out of the seat and lumbered clumsily in the direction the girl had taken. He knocked on a door chastely inscribed 'Ladies'. "You all right, Rosie? It's me, Lennie-boy." There was no answer. Yanking the door open, he looked in.

The only occupant was an enormous fluffy blonde who looked up at him and said affably, "Come on in, girlie. I'll be through here in a minute."

After Sergeant Mayo had searched the deserted kitchen, finding the back door unlocked, and stamped out of the tavern in drunken and frustrated fury, Barney went quietly to the booth in which the girl and the detective had sat and unhooked a small microphone from the underside of the table. He wound in a length of wire running from the booth to a Dictaphone in a closet. He took a record from the machine, placed it in a cardboard container and put it in Muldoon's heavy iron safe. After that he went to the telephone and dialled Kay's number.

There was no reply. Kay was in the bathtub, scrubbing herself vigorously to cleanse away the clammy touch of Mayo's fumbling hands.

Chapter 11

The morning started badly for Lieutenant Hull of the Homicide Bureau with a press conference at which he was ribbed unmercifully over Nick Abbott's continued freedom; a painful interview on the same subject with the Commissioner, who passed on the Mayor's blistering comments on police inefficiency, adding a few of his own; a stormy ten minutes with Inspector Gort, who had many excuses but no fresh plan for finding the badly wanted man. A few minutes before noon, in the sanctuary of his private office, the lieutenant frowningly studied a map of New York City which covered one wall.

Strips of red cellophane, pasted to the map, marked the ground covered by a body of detectives who, in pairs, were investigating hotels and rooming-houses. Blue pins denoted the approximate positions of policemen in cars equipped with machine guns, tear gas and short-wave sending sets, who prowled the streets hunting for Nick Abbott. Green pins plotted roughly the areas in which other special officers in plain clothes covered a few blocks each, on foot, scrutinizing every pedestrian.

At strategic points riot cars stood, manned and armed, awaiting the signal to take off if Abbott was located in circumstances requiring their use. They had sped through the streets three times in twenty-four hours, sirens wailing like banshees—Nick had been 'seen' going into a midtown movie, theatre; was reported hiding in an uptown hotel; was 'positively known' to be working under an assumed name at a garage in Washington Heights—but each time their errand had turned out to be a wild-goose chase. Although Lieutenant Hull was a man of exceptional patience, his nerves were stretched now like taut elastic.

His clipped iron-grey moustache, air of authority, lean

alertness, suggested an army general. He wore grey Harris tweeds and a hand-blocked foulard tie, and his shoes were a little browner than his seamed face; owed to a sunlamp in his bedroom. On his desk he kept two briar pipes and a jar of tobacco flavoured with Latakia, although he had yet to outgrow an early preference for five-cent cigars.

A desk-worker poked his head into the office and, in a tone of apology, said, "Those dames are still waiting."

"Tell them I'm busy," said Hull impatiently.

"I've told them twice already," replied the man, coming into the room. "Maybe you better see them, Lieutenant."

"Damn it, man, be firm."

"It ain't easy to be firm when the tall one looks right through you. You know what I think, Lieutenant? I think she's getting sore."

"Oh, she is, is she?"

"And I think maybe she's Somebody. She certainly acts like it."

"Oh, she does, does she?" His nerves at breaking point, the lieutenant rose and stalked across the room. "We'll see about that."

Opening the door, he marched to a railing dividing the outer office in half and gazed wrathfully at Althea Archer and Kay Bannerman, sitting on an oaken bench against the far wall.

"Madam," he said, addressing Althea, "my assistant has told you I am too busy to be disturbed. You persist in disturbing me, nevertheless. I can add nothing to what he has said, except good-day, madam—a most emphatic good-day."

"We have something of importance to discuss with you," replied Althea imperturbably, "and mean to discuss it."

"My good woman, do you realise that—"

"I am not your good woman," retorted Althea glacially. "Perhaps it would be better if I asked my cousin, Mr. Peter Courtney, to telephone the Commissioner for an appointment."

The lieutenant looked sad and weary. He had not risen from

a beat to his present eminence without playing politics every step of the way and he could smell when to play with great wariness. This was apparently one of the times. Sighing, he swung open a wicket gate and said, "Come in."

They preceded him into his office, Kay carrying a black leather case. Lieutenant Hull made haste to bring forward chairs.

"I had no idea you were related to Mr. Courtney. You ought to have said so in the first place."

"It ought not to have been necessary to say so."

"Ordinarily, it probably would not have been. I'm not so inaccessible as I seem. Believe me, I see a score of people without appointments every day, many of them cranks and crackpots. But, today of all days"—he ran his fingers through his thinning grey hair—"well, today I'm snowed under with work. However, if your business is important, I shall have to make time for it."

"I gave my card to your assistant."

"Yes, of course. I have it somewhere." Hull looked about for the pasteboard oblong, his eyes carefully avoiding the wastebasket, into which he had dropped it. "You're a lawyer or something, Miss—Mrs.—"

"Miss Archer. This is Miss Bannerman."

"Bannerman," repeated the lieutenant sharply. "The Miss Kay Bannerman who was Nick Abbott's secretary?"

"Yes," said Althea. "The Abbott case is what we've come to see you about."

"Are you Abbott's counsel?"

"He may retain me."

"Where is he?" asked Lieutenant Hull quickly, his hand hovering over a button on his desk.

"I'm afraid I don't know."

"You're sure of that? If you do, it's your duty to turn him in. You know that, don't you?"

"I am aware of the duties of a citizen and the special obligations of an attorney. I repeat, I don't know where Mr. Abbott is."

Lieutenant Hull shot a hard look at Kay. "And you, Miss Bannerman? Someone is helping Abbott, or he'd have been recaptured long ago. You wouldn't by any chance be in on it?"

"If I were, would I come here?"

"You might, to throw us off. I don't understand this setup. Exactly why are you ladies here?"

"We're convinced of Mr. Abbott's innocence," replied Althea, "and are searching for proof of it. We came to ask the cooperation of the police. We'd like access to your records of the case."

"That's out, Miss Archer. I don't care who you're related to, that's out. Abbott is guilty. I won't have you standing my department on its head in a futile effort to prove otherwise."

"Before you make up your mind," said Althea quietly, "we'd like you to listen to something. Will you please play the record to Lieutenant Hull, Miss Bannerman?"

"It will be a pleasure," said Kay, placing the black leather case on the desk.

"I've no time to listen to music."

"I hardly think this will be music to your ears," replied Althea, "but I'm sure you will be interested."

Something in her expression made the official shrug his shoulders in resignation. He said, "Oh, well . . ." with a sigh and slumped down in his chair until his head rested on his haunched shoulders. But he sat up with a jerk when a gruff inebriated voice came from the transmitter. He knew that voice. Beyond all possible doubt, he knew it. The unmelodious voice of Sergeant Mayo: and the things Mayo was saying at the prompting of another voice, a girlish voice, made Hull's flesh crawl, his blood run cold.

"Why, the lying rat—"

"I don't think he's lying," interposed Althea coolly, "and

I don't imagine a jury would. Sergeant Mayo is admitting to manufacturing evidence—you can hear that for yourself—and the fact that he'd been drinking when the record was made won't help you. This won't do your cherished department any good, Lieutenant. I think you said something about standing it on its head? The phrase seems appropriate."

Lieutenant Hull leant forward and took the record off the machine.

"How did you get this?"

"Does that matter? I'll take it, please."

In silence he looked at her, remembering the agonies he had gone through during the last departmental shake-up—a nerve-racking ordeal with some of the worst features of the French Revolution. The thing he held in his hand was sufficiently akin to high explosive to blast him with a score of subordinates right out of the force. Frowning, he reached out as if to give it to Althea. Within inches of her outstretched hand, the record slipped from his fingers. It lay, cracked, on the floor and, in pretence of hastening to retrieve it, he put a foot on it, grinding it into black dust.

"Clumsy of you," said Althea, with undisturbed poise, "and rather obvious, Lieutenant. Fortunately, I took the precaution of having a duplicate made before bringing the original here."

They crossed glances, like fencers crossing rapiers.

"I'll play ball," said Lieutenant Hull, with a sickly smile. "What do you want?"

"In the first place, a letter on official paper, signed by you, to the effect that no fingerprints were found on the gun that killed Claire Abbott."

"You'll get it. If those fingerprints were faked—and I guess they were—I had no hand in it. I've never framed a man in my life and I don't intend to start. What else do you want?"

"You have a policeman guarding the apartment in which the

murder was committed. I'd like written authority to examine the apartment. I'd like to see the photographs your experts took before the body was removed. I'd like to see everything the police removed from the flat."

"You don't want much, do you? Well, I said I'd play ball with you and I will. For your part, you'll forget what's on that record?"

"I shan't forget it—but I'll suppress it."

"I have your word for that?"

"My solemn promise."

"You're a lady. I can trust you to keep that promise."

"You can."

"And you?" He glanced at Kay.

"I'm no lady but I don't welsh on a promise either. "I can't remember a word Sergeant Mayo said."

Lieutenant Hull touched a button on his desk and his office assistant came in. The lieutenant dictated the two documents Althea had outlined and gave instructions that they were to be typed and brought to him without delay.

"Find Duffy," he added, "and tell him I want him."

When the desk-man went out, Lieutenant Hull leant toward Kay and Althea and said, "You're wasting time trying to help Abbott. He's guilty. I've had a lot of experience and I know. Wait, please, let me finish; I know what you're going to say. You still intend to have a whack at finding a substitute murderer. Well, it's your time, if you want to waste it. I can understand your sympathy for Abbott, even if my job prevents me from sharing it. All in all, I guess his wife got no more than she asked for. Did you know she was arrested about four years ago in Kansas City for operating a badger game? She was Claire Jansen, then."

"What on earth is a badger game?" asked Althea.

The lieutenant chuckled. "Well, you don't play it with cards. It works like this: a good-looking girl picks up some man she thinks is rich and dumb and takes him to her hotel room or goes to his. After she's had time to get him into a compromising situation, a man rushes in with a gun and says he's her husband. Between fear of the gun and fear of scandal, the victim usually parts with all the money he has on him—and perhaps a fat check as well."

"So, Claire had been married before she met Nick Abbott? I wonder if she ever bothered to get a divorce."

"I didn't say she was married. I said a man would rush in, claiming to be her husband. There's a difference. Hundreds of teams have worked that racket and few of them ever stood up together in front of a parson. Claire beat the charge because the victim, dreading publicity, refused to prosecute. But she cooled her heels in jail for a couple of weeks while they tried to find a charge against her that would stick. According to the reports I've had, she was good and mad at her partner, who ran out on her just before the police came in, leaving her to face the rap alone. I have his description here." The lieutenant flipped open a folder on his desk and extracted a paper.

"'Name, Arthur Jansen—that's probably an alias. Age, about twenty-eight—he'd be thirty-two, now. Hair, dark brown. Eyes, dark brown. Height, approximately five feet, eight inches. Weight, about a hundred and forty pounds. Clean-shaven. No scars or other identifying marks.'" Replacing the paper, Hull added, "You could walk out on the street and count off ten men answering to that description in a single city block, so it isn't surprising that the police never found Jansen."

"You think Claire may have been working some kind of a badger game in New York and was shot when something went wrong?" asked Kay.

"Nick Abbott shot her, replied Hull flatly. "But since you insist on trying to prove otherwise, I'm offering you a lead, for what it's worth."

The desk-man came in, laid some typed sheets on the desk and went out again. After careful perusal of the papers, the lieutenant signed them and handed them to Althea. She read them also, nodded approval, and put them in her handbag.

There was a knock on the door and another hatless man looked in. "You wanted me, Lieutenant?"

"Yes, Duffy, come in. Ladies, this is Duffy. He's in charge of the exhibits you wish to see. Duffy, meet Miss Archer and Miss Bannerman. I want you to show them everything we have on the Abbott case."

The newcomer looked surprised but said he would be happy to oblige. After saying goodbye to the lieutenant, who appeared not at all sorry to see them go, Althea and Kay went out of the office with Duffy.

Lieutenant Hull picked up a telephone. "Get me Mayo," he said, after a pause. "Yes, I know he's under suspension. Find him for me. How should I know where he'll be? Have 'em search the bars and brothels—but find him. I have something terribly, terribly important to tell him—and I just can't wait to do it."

Following Duffy's shiny serge and bald head down a long corridor, Kay whispered to Althea, "I thought I'd die when he dropped the record. It was clever of you to think of having a duplicate made."

"I didn't," murmured Althea placidly. "That was a monumental piece of bluff. I don't approve of such methods but, in the circumstances, I felt justified."

"And how!" breathed Kay, regarding her companion with a new respect.

Duffy took them into a large room lined with cupboards and filing-cabinets: In the middle of the room there was a long table and some chairs. "If you'll sit down, bring you all I can find on the case of the glamourous Claire Abbott. Can one of you ladies tell me why women victims of murder are always beautiful? If they have buck teeth and turn-up noses, even if they hail from the Bronx, let them be shot or stabbed or strangled and they're raving beauties."

"Perhaps women in search of looks ought to have their throats cut instead of their faces lifted," remarked Kay lightly.

"You got an idea there," said Duffy, opening a drawer. "I wish you'd tell it to my wife. Still and all, I guess the Abbott woman had a lot on the ball even before she was croaked."

He laid before them photographs, taken from every angle, of the room in which Claire had been found dead. Her body, sprawled on its back on the floor, featured in most of them.

"Here's one the boys took of the position in which Abbott claims he found her," he said, showing them one of the body on its knees beside the chaise longue. "Did you ever see anything less likely?"

"Why shouldn't a woman die on her knees?"

"Maybe it was appropriate for this woman, at that," conceded Duffy. "First time she'd been on her knees in years. Only, she wasn't shot in that position. The boys found the bullet imbedded in the wall at an angle that showed she was standing up when she was shot. She didn't even fall where she was lying when Abbott was found bending over the body. Blood spots on the carpet show where she fell—a good two yards from the chaise longue. I can't figure why Abbott dragged her to a different part of the room. He must have had a reason—but only God and Abbott know it."

"Why couldn't she have crawled on her hands and knees from the spot where she first fell to the chaise longue?" asked Kay.

"I suppose she could—but why should she?"

"Look," said Kay, pointing to a photograph. "All the things from her handbag are scattered over the seat and floor."

"Sure," said Duffy, "and you can bet your life Abbott did that, looking for something."

"Why Abbott? Why not Claire? Perhaps there was something in the bag that would point to the man who killed her. Perhaps, after shooting her, he left the room, thinking that she was dead. Perhaps she had strength enough to try to find the thing that would indicate the killer's identity. I can see her struggling on her knees to the chaise longue; fumbling desperately through her handbag; turning it out on the seat; dying there, on her knees."

Duffy laid an assortment of small articles on the table. "These are the things that lay on the chaise longue and the floor. All the junk a woman carries; nothing of any special importance."

"Scattered in her haste to find something before she died," murmured Kay. "I wonder what?"

"This was in her hand," said Duffy, extricating an object from the pile of small things. "The boys had quite a time getting it away from her."

It was a cheap combination compact and lipstick.

"She'd hardly be in a hurry to powder her nose when she was dying," remarked Althea disappointedly.

"You can't ever tell what a woman will do," replied Duffy, with a sigh heavy with experience. "Maybe she wanted to look good for the press photographers."

"Will you let us see any of her personal papers that were removed from the apartment?"

"I'm sorry, ma'am. There wasn't a scrap of writing in the place. No letters, no documents, not even a scribbled phone number or a signed photograph. I guess Claire Abbott liked privacy and kept all her papers in her safe-deposit box. We haven't located that, yet. She used to wear the key on a chain round her neck. I guess Abbott snatched it after he killed her—although it wasn't on him when he was searched."

"She must have led a peculiar life," said Althea thoughtfully, "to take such care to keep her affairs secret."

"I guess she did. You'd be surprised how little her maid knew about her."

"How can we find the maid?"

"She gave the boys the address of her rooming-house. I'll write it down for you."

Taking out pencil and notebook, Althea made a list of the things that had been strewn on the floor and chaise longue in the dead woman's apartment. She pored over the pictures of the scene of the crime, as if imprinting them on her memory; and copied the detailed measurements attached to them.

"What was that?" asked Kay suddenly.

The others looked at her questioningly.

"I thought I heard a knock," she explained.

Duffy went to the door and looked out. "No one there now," he said.

"I must have been mistaken."

"Yeah, I guess you must. If you ladies would like to see the body, we're still keeping it in cold storage. I'll take you down and show it to you, if you wish."

Although neither of them had the morbidity which craves to look on death, both Althea and Kay decided to view the body. It was a disagreeable duty but not to be avoided if they were to help Nick. To their surprise, the corpse was neither awing nor unsightly. It had been kept in an excellent state of preservation.

"I'm ignorant about such things," said Kay, in a subdued tone. "I suppose she's been embalmed or something?"

"No, she hasn't been touched, except to be lifted into the death wagon and brought here. It's being kept good and cold that's preserved her so well. After the autopsy she'll be embalmed and buried. The Chief delayed the autopsy for some reason or other."

When they came out in the sunlight at last, Kay said to Althea, "Did anything strike you about the corpse?"

"Only that she must have been very lovely. Ought I to have seen anything else?"

"Her lips were made up as if for a party."

"Well, after all, she had a lipstick in her hand when she was found dead."

"That's the point. The stuff on her lips had a slight orange tint. It had been applied with the lipstick lying on the chaise longue. The lipstick in her hand was a garish red."

"Perhaps she was going to change the colour of her mouth," said Althea, with a confused air.

"I don't believe it. No woman caring for her appearance as Claire Abbott did would use so cheap and obvious a colour. By the way, let's call her Claire Jansen for a change."

"Oh, yes, let's," said Althea quickly. "I hate to be continually reminded that the woman was Nick Abbott's wife."

"You hate to be reminded," said Kay sourly—but only to herself.

Althea said, "I'm afraid I'm not very observant. I failed to take a good look at the compact and lipstick found in her hand."

"Take a good look at it now," said Kay, giving it to her. Althea stared. "How did you get it?"

"I borrowed it when Duffy went to investigate the knock I pretended to hear. I'm going to try to buy one exactly like it and then I'll return this one and say I carried it away by mistake."

"Why so much trouble and risk for an article worth about ten cents?"

"Mostly because that is all it's worth. I have an idea it's the most important clue in the case."

"I can't imagine why." Althea turned it over in her hand. "A worthless trifle of painted tin, containing cheap and nasty cosmetics. Where does its importance come in?"

"Yes," agreed Kay, "it's cheap and nasty. So inferior in every way I doubt if even the five-and-ten would bother to have it on sale. Will you tell me what a woman like Claire Jansen, who surrounded herself with silver and platinum and gold, was doing with it?"

Chapter 12

Althea belonged to a club that had no listing in the telephone book or in any other work of reference, no sign or nameplate at the front door of its grey stone building in the East Fifties. She took Kay to its rose-pink and silver-grey dining-room for luncheon. Over a grilled sole, a half-bottle of excellent claret and a souffle so light that it could almost have floated on air, they discussed the morning's developments.

"I think you put a finger on something," said Kay thoughtfully, "when you suggested she might have been married before she ever met Nick; and that she might not have troubled about a divorce."

"If she was," said Althea, "we would have at least one suspect to work on—the man to whom she was married."

"Two suspects, counting the Arthur Jansen involved with her in that badger game, four years ago."

"Yes, two—unless Arthur Jansen was also the husband."

"How can we find out if she was married?"

"It means delving into her past and examining the marriage records of every place in which she lived. Even then, we can't be sure. She might have gone somewhere for a few hours for the express purpose of getting married. I'll put a firm of private detectives on that job. It'll be a lengthy business—but, in any case, we ought to know all we can about her."

"I suggested that Claire might have been working some kind of badger game when she was shot," said Kay, offering Althea a cigarette and lighting one herself. "Lieutenant Hull pooh-poohed the idea but it still looks good to me. On the day of the murder, she asked Nick over the phone to divorce her."

"Nick was mistaken. She couldn't have meant that. She meant that she was going to divorce him."

"That's what I thought. That's what Nick thought—at first. But she made him understand quite plainly that she wanted him to get the divorce on grounds of infidelity and that she would provide the evidence."

"I don't understand."

"Neither did I—but perhaps I do, now. Nick told me he thought there was a man with Claire when he phoned. He couldn't say why he thought so, it was just an impression he had. Couldn't it be that Claire was working a variation of this badger game on some man—threatening to have Nick name him in a divorce action if he didn't pay her handsomely?"

"Why, of course, that's possible. It explains why she wanted Nick to divorce her, instead of doing it the other way round."

"Perhaps this man couldn't afford the scandal that would be stirred up if his affair with Claire was aired in court. Perhaps she was using the divorce as a threat to extort money. Perhaps she phoned Nick in this man's presence to make him see that she was in earnest."

"It fits perfectly," said Althea eagerly.

"Of course, it does. And perhaps her intended victim silenced her with a shot instead of a handful of cash."

"Do you know, I think you've hit upon the answer to our whole problem. All that remains is to find the man."

"That's all—but something tells me it isn't going to be easy. Where do we start?"

"At Claire's apartment, of course. By the way"—Althea studied her lovely hands with an air of indecision—"you're a stenographer, aren't you, Miss Bannerman? I've been thinking that there might be an opening for you in my office, if you'd care to take it."

"Thanks; but I intend to give all my time to this case until it is solved."

"That's what I mean. I am eager to solve it too, and I can see your help is going to be invaluable. And—forgive me if I put it abruptly—you have your living to earn, do you not? A position in my office would take care of that and leave you free to work on the case."

"Thanks again—but my savings are enough to carry me for a long time."

"It's a pity to eat into your savings."

"Look," said Kay bluntly, "I was an eighteen-dollar-a-week typist when I went to work for Nick Abbott. At the start I couldn't even do the work he required but he was patient while I learned. It almost doubled his own work but he put up with that to help a green kid. I never had to ask him for a raise, he always paid me a bit more than I was honestly worth. And he never made a pass at me. For Nick Abbott I'd spend my last dime—and scrub floors on my knees into the bargain."

"You leave me nothing to say," replied Althea gently, after a pause. "I hope I didn't hurt your feelings."

"I don't bruise that easily."

"You—you don't like me very much, do you?"

"I'd like anyone who helped me clear Nick Abbott."

"Yes, of course—but, apart from that, you just don't care for me?"

"I don't think we'll ever be spiritual affinities, if that's what you mean."

"And why not? I find you a very likable person."

"You asked for it," said Kay, "and you're going to get it, straight from the shoulder. I ate my heart out when Claire grabbed off Nick. I've a feeling I'm going to have to stand by and watch another grab when he's in 'the clear."

"You mean— Oh, but that's absurd. Why, until the night of his escape, I hadn't seen Nick for all of fifteen years. Even when I did know him, he was only a boy who worked about the place."

"And the boy who worked about the place had changed a lot in those fifteen years; but you knew him as soon as you flashed a light on his face."

Althea reddened a little. "My dear Miss Bannerman, I'm practically engaged to be married."

"All 'practically engaged' means is an option on a property which you may want if no more desirable property comes on the market."

"In any case, wouldn't Nick himself have a say in the matter?"

"Not much of a say," replied Kay practically. "A man never does, if an attractive woman decides to marry him."

"You are rather attractive yourself."

"Thanks for the bouquet, but I know my limitations. You have beauty, pedigree, poise, position. I can't match all those. Besides, it was your name he kept muttering in delirium."

"I didn't expect you to be quite so frank. I hardly know what to say."

"You won't say that you wouldn't marry Nick if he asked you to?"

Althea considered the point for a moment. "No, I won't say that."

"I thought not. Well, if women were waiting in line to marry Nick when he's cleared, I'd still do my best to clear him. But I'd feel no obligation to like the women."

"My dear Miss Bannerman, I'm not lined up to marry Nick. I don't expect to make a grab at him. In fact, the whole conversation strikes me as rather absurd. Let's forget it, shall we?" Althea held out her hand. "As we're to be partners, if not friends, I'm going to call you Kay, if you don't violently object?"

"I don't object," said Kay but there was little warmth in her handshake.

"And you'll call me Althea?"

"If you wish it."

"And now, let's see what we can find out at the dead woman's apartment."

The reception clerk was proud of his well-kept hands. He kept patting his marcelled hair with them while answering questions.

"No, I'm afraid I can't tell you which tenant gave the alarm the day Mrs. Abbott was killed. It was a man, that's all I know."

"But surely," objected Althea, "it would be the natural thing for him to say: 'This is Mr. So-and-so. I've just heard a shot.'"

"I suppose it would. But that isn't how it happened. The phone rang and when I answered, a voice said, 'just heard a shot from Mrs. Abbott's apartment.' That was absolutely all. He hung up right away. I sent out for a policeman at once. I just knew something terrible had happened. Mr. Abbott looked so vicious when he went up."

"Why didn't you go up and find out what had happened before calling the police?"

"Me?" The clerk looked shocked. "Go up there? With someone firing shots? Well, really."

"Surely the switchboard showed the origin of the call," said Althea.

"Yes, of course," agreed the clerk. "But I was so flustered when I heard about shooting in Mrs. Abbott's apartment that it completely escaped my notice at the time."

"How long was it after Mr. Abbott went up before the phone rang?"

"Oh, not more than three or four minutes."

"It must have taken Nick a minute or two to go up in the elevator, knock at the door and wait to be admitted," said Kay. Changing the line of questioning, she asked, "I suppose Mrs. Abbott had quite a lot of visitors?"

"Oh, dear me, no," said the clerk, arching plucked eyebrows. "None at all—with the rare exception of Mr. Abbott."

"You mean, never?"

"Not a single visitor, ever. I used to wonder at it, I must admit."

"What about phone calls?"

"Oh, she got those quite often. Never from women, though. There were three different men who each phoned her about once a week or so." The clerk looked arch. "I can tell you something rather funny about that."

"Go on," said Kay, "don't keep us in suspense."

"Well, you know I have to ask the caller's name before I can put a call through to an apartment? There was something rather peculiar about the names these three men gave. They were all the names of colours. Mr. Brown, Mr. White—and Mr. Green."

"That's odd," said Althea.

"It adds up," remarked Kay; but she did not explain what she meant. "And none of those men ever came here? They just phoned once a week or so?"

"Precisely."

"Can you come upstairs with us to examine the apartment?"

"Well, I can leave the desk and switchboard in charge of the janitor—but there's an awful brute of a policeman guarding the apartment."

"We have a paper that will take care of him."

"In that case, I'll be charmed to come."

The policeman read the letter of authority rather slowly, as if spelling it out word by word. He turned it over and tried to read the blank side. He held it up to the light, suspiciously scrutinising Lieutenant Hull's signature.

"I guess this is okay," he said grudgingly, at last. He opened the door of the apartment and followed them in. "You unnerstand, I got to be careful. I got my orders."

Althea and Kay went over the apartment minutely, looking

into every drawer and cupboard. Clothes and toilet necessities and a few trinkets were all of the dead woman's belongings that they found. The place was as impersonal as a hotel room. Only the decorations offered a clue to Claire's personality and they had obviously been designed for her by an interior decorator.

"How cold and unliveable it seems," said Althea, glancing, round the bedroom.

"A package designer's dream," said Kay, looking at the colour scheme.

"This is where she was lying when the policeman and I came in," remarked the clerk, pointing to the carpet with a little shudder of delicious horror. "If you like, I'll lie down, and show you how she was."

"Thanks, sweetie," said Kay, "but we've seen photographs. You wouldn't do the part justice."

The clerk looked at Kay as if he thought she was horrid. Kay knocked on a wall. "Sounds solid."

"It's as solid as—as can be," declared the clerk peevishly. "The whole building is completely soundproof throughout."

"Then how could the shot have been heard?"

"I—I really can't imagine. Perhaps it isn't quite, quite soundproof—although the engineers claim it is."

"In any case," said Kay, "the shot could probably only have been heard in the apartment above, the apartment below, or the adjoining one."

"There's no apartment above," replied the clerk, giving Kay a disdainful pout. "This is the top floor, as for the one below, Mrs. Peters has that. I talked to her about the murder and she told me—but definitely—that she hadn't heard the shot and that no one had made the call from her apartment."

"Which leaves," said Kay, "the one next door."

"Mr. Black's," said the clerk.

"Mr. Who?"

"Mr. Black. B-L-A-C-K. Mr. Black."

"Some relative, no doubt, of the gentlemen who used to phone Mrs. Abbott?"

"Why," stammered the clerk, opening his eyes wide. "Why, I hadn't thought of that. Mr. Brown, Mr. White, Mr. Green—and Mr. Black. Quite a coincidence, isn't it?"

"Quite a coincidence," Kay agreed. "I think we'd better have a word with Mr. Black."

"I don't think he's home. At least, I haven't seen him all day."

"Did you see him going out this morning?"

"Why, no. But then, we never see a great deal of Mr. Black. I'm sure I haven't laid eyes on him in a week."

"Have you seen him since the murder?"

"Well, really, now you come to mention it, I don't believe I have."

"Let's see if he's in now," said Kay.

In a little procession, the two women, the clerk and the policeman trooped out to the hall. The clerk tapped timidly on the door of the adjoining apartment (there were only two on that floor). There was no answer.

"Have you a passkey?" asked Kay.

The clerk plucked nervously at his fingertips. "I hardly like to—"

"Go on, open it," said the policeman roughly. "I wanna know more about this Mr. Black myself. He ain't shown up as long as I've been on duty."

"Well, if you insist—" his hands still fluttering like frightened birds, the clerk produced a key and opened the door.

They crowded in and looked about them. The apartment was furnished in simple and impersonal style but there was no other sign of occupation. No shirts or underwear in the bedroom drawers. No suits or shoes in the closets. No soap or towel or toothbrush in the bathroom; not so much as a magazine lying by a chair in the living-room; not even a crust of bread or a tin of sardines in the kitchen. Althea drew back the bedclothes and felt the sheets. They were clammy and had obviously not been aired for a long time.

"Do you notice the peculiar smell of the place?" cried Kay. "The smell an apartment gets when it's been empty for months. Musty. Stuffy. I'll bet it's an age since the windows were opened."

"But—but—" The clerk gaped around him in wonder. "This is uncanny. I simply can't understand it. Mr. Black came here, regularly three or four times a week."

"And went straight into Mrs. Abbott's apartment," said Kay, "without even looking in on his own."

"Do you really think so? But how awful. The management would never approve of such an arrangement."

"It's perfectly plain to me," said Kay, "that he only kept this place as a blind to cover his visits to Mrs. Abbott. What did he look like?"

"Well, he always wore a long dark coat with the collar turned up and a rather wide-brimmed hat with the brim turned down. Oh, and tinted glasses and he had a moustache and—and—"

"You're describing props, not a man," interrupted Kay. "He can't have worn this long dark coat always—on hot days, for instance?"

"Oh, but he did—always. I used to think he must be some sort of an invalid. He was always so muffled up from head to foot."

"Surely you can tell us more about him than that? Was he tall or short? Fat or thin?"

"Well—" The clerk made more nervous flutterings with his hands. "He was about average height, I think. And about average weight."

"Just a very average sort of man in a long dark coat and tinted glasses," said Kay bitterly. "What a help you turned out to be."

"I am doing my best," replied the clerk stiffly. "Perhaps Edward can tell you more. I'll ring for him."

In a few minutes the clerk ushered in the elevator boy. "This is Edward," he said, in a deeply wounded tone.

"Well, I'll tell you," said Edward, "I think this Mr. Black was some kind of a crank. He was always wrapped up in a—"

"—a long dark coat," said Kay, throwing up her hands.

"Yeah, a long dark coat. He had a sorta scrubby moustache that came down over his mouth. I don't know as I could tell you an awful lot more than that."

"He had a nose, I suppose?" said Kay sarcastically, "and eyes?"

"Oh, sure," said Edward, doing his best to be helpful, "he had a nose. I guess everybody does, don't they? I couldn't see his eyes very well. You see, he wore—"

"Tinted glasses," snapped Kay. "How old would you say he was?"

"I dunno. Middle-aged, I suppose."

"Oh, Edward, he was not," exclaimed the clerk. "I'm sure he couldn't have been more than thirty-five."

"Sure," said the boy, shrugging his shoulders. "Middle-aged. Ain't that what I said?"

"Why, Edward, a man isn't middle-aged in his thirties. Why, I'll be thirty soon."

"So, you'll be middle-aged," said Edward phlegmatically.

"You must know more about this Mr. Black than you've told," remarked Althea, to the clerk. "There must be a record of him in the renting-office. One can't take an apartment without some formalities, can one?"

"He took the apartment six months ago, by letter," replied the clerk, "and paid six months' rent in cash when he signed the lease. He didn't go to the office to sign. it. I had it on my desk, waiting for him, when he came to take possession of the apartment and he signed it there and then. Now I come to think of it, his letter was on Waldorf-Astoria stationery and we sent our reply there. If he was only a transient guest, they'd hardly remember much about him after all this time."

"He gave references, surely?"

"Oh, dear me, yes. We always insist on references."

"That's a help," said Kay. "To whom did he refer you?"

The clerk looked a little taken aback. "Oh, my. Oh, my goodness. I've just remembered: he gave us one of the other tenants as a reference."

"Claire Abbott," said Kay, unhappily.

"How did you know?"

"I'm becoming clairvoyant," said Kay, in a disgusted tone.

Going to the back door of the apartment, she unlocked it but left it shut. She stationed the clerk in the kitchen, the elevator boy in the bedroom. and Althea in the living-room of the obscure Mr. Black's apartment. With the policeman at her heels she returned to the apartment occupied until death by Claire Abbott. She asked the policeman if he had a reliable watch. With an emphatic nod, he pulled out one almost as large as an alarm clock.

"Lend me your revolver."

"What kind of a dope do you think I am?" he demanded, giving her a hard look.

"You can take the bullets out."

He shook his head several times but yielded reluctantly when she persisted. "Well, okay. But no funny business."

Emptying the cartridge chambers, he handed the heavy gun to her.

"Now go outside. Ring the bell a couple of times. Knock at the door. Turn the handle and walk in."

"Yeah? And what will you be doing?"

"I'll be waiting to bop you on the head." His eyes bulged at that and Kay hastily added, "Don't be silly. I'll only pretend to do it. Oh, and look at your watch before you ring. I want you to time all this."

"Seems pretty screwy to me," grumbled the policeman but he went out and, a moment later, the bell rang. It rang twice, followed by a loud knock at the door. Turning the handle, the policeman re-entered warily, on the alert lest Kay forget that the blow on the head was to be imaginary. Kay made a pretence of striking him, then hurried through the living-room to the bedroom, the policeman breathing on her neck every step of the way.

Pointing the gun at an imaginary victim, Kay pulled the trigger and there was a roaring explosion and a flash of flame.

"Jeez!" roared the policeman, "I coulda swore I emptied that gun."

"That was a blank," replied Kay coolly. "I brought blanks of three different calibres, to make sure I'd have some to fit your gun."

She fired three more noisy shots and the policeman covered his ears, making agonized faces at her.

"Have a heart, lady. It sounds like a cannon going off. I'll have a headick all afternoon."

Without answering, Kay hurried to the kitchen, opened the back door and crossed a narrow landing to the rear of the adjoining apartment. She went in, followed by the policeman and went through kitchen and bedroom to the living-room. The others crowded round her while she picked up the telephone, pressing her finger on the cradle to keep the wire dead.

"I just heard a shot from Mrs. Abbott's apartment," she said; and replaced the instrument.

She glanced enquiringly at the policeman, who consulted his enormous watch.

"Just over a minute and a half, lady," he said.

"Did any of youse hear the shots?" he asked, looking at the clerk, the elevator boy and Althea.

Shaking their heads, they returned his stare wonderingly.

"I fired several blank cartridges of heavy calibre in the dead woman's apartment," Kay explained. "If you didn't hear those, no one outside the apartment could have heard the shot that killed her. Don't you see what that means? The man who gave the alarm must have been in Claire's apartment when she was killed. He knocked out Nick, shot Claire—and gave the alarm to make sure Nick would be caught on the scene of the crime."

"The things some people will do," said the clerk.

* * * * *

The driver of the taxi at the head of the stand round the corner from the apartment building dropped his newspaper and threw away a cigarette butt when he saw Althea and Kay approaching. With a hopeful look, he touched his cap and put a hand back to open the door of his cab.

"We want you to take us somewhere," said Althea, "but first we'd like to ask you one or two questions."

"I guess I know the ones you mean," said the driver wearily. "Yes, ma'am, I'm a careful driver. No, ma'am, I never speed. Yes, ma'am, I'm sober. You can smell my breath, if you like. You wouldn't be the first dame to go that far."

"Those aren't the questions," said Kay, laughing. She took a five-dollar bill from her bag and put it in his hand. "Try this one: did you by any chance know Mrs. Claire Abbott?"

"The dame that was shot? I'll say I knew her. She used to take my cab alla time."

"Where did she go?"

"Oh, places. Shows. Night clubs. You know, places."

"Alone?"

"Yeah, mostly alone. I guess she met friends where she went. The only times she ever had anyone in the cab with her would be once in a while in the late afternoon."

"Where did she go then?"

"Well, I'll tell you. It was kinda funny, at that. She'd get in alone and tell me to take her driving in Central Park. We'd drive around for a while and near one of the gates she'd tell me to stop and we'd pick up some guy that was waiting about. I'd drive some more and in maybe five minutes the guy would get out and go about his business and Mrs. Abbott would tell me to take her home."

"Was it always the same man?"

"The one that got into the cab? No, there was two or three different guys that used to do that. One at a time, though—on different afternoons."

"Mr. Brown, Mr. White and Mr. Green," said Kay.

"Huh? I don't get you."

"What did they talk about, Mrs. Abbott and the men who got in with her?"

"I'm a monkey's uncle if I know. She always made me close the partition, so I couldn't hear a thing."

"You could see them in the mirror, though? Perhaps they held hands."

"Now you mention it, sometimes they did."

"They held hands," said Kay thoughtfully. "Or perhaps they only pretended to, while the men gave something to Mrs. Abbott?"

"Could be. I wouldn't know."

"You wouldn't happen to know any of the men?" asked Kay.

The driver looked uneasy. "I might know one of them—but not for no five bucks. I'd get my ears pinned back if this certain party ever thought I was poking my nose into his affairs."

"We'll make it ten dollars."

The driver shook his head. "Lady, this guy is dynamite."

"We'll give you twenty dollars for his name," said Althea, opening her handbag. "Or would you prefer to talk to the head of the Homicide Bureau?"

"For twenty dollars, lady, I'll talk to you. Only, if anything comes out of it, I didn't tell you nuttin'. If you get me mixed up with the cops, I'll swear blind I didn't say a word. Get this, because I'm only going to say it once: one of the guys Mrs. Abbott used to pick up in Central Park was Morrie Stern."

"Morrie Stern?" repeated Althea.

"One of the ex-racketeers who smell so sweet since Dewey cleaned them up," Kay explained. "He runs a night club—the Hoot Owl."

"I didn't tell you nuttin'," reiterated the taxi-driver, 1 grabbing the twenty-dollar bill.

Giving him the address Duffy at Police Headquarters had written down for her, Althea climbed into the taxi, followed by Kay.

* * * * *

In the gloomy lounge of a rooming-house in Brooklyn, they interviewed the dead woman's maid, who had little to tell them.

"Mrs. Abbott never let me know anything about her affairs and I always had to put the apartment in order and be out of it by three in the afternoon. If I stayed a minute after that, she'd almost throw me out."

"Did you ever admit any callers?"

"Not a one. Anyone who visited her came after I left."

"What about the day of the murder? We've reason to think someone was with her at noon that day."

"I don't know anything about it. On the day of the murder, she told me to leave soon after eleven. I guess there was a man who came to see her pretty regularly. Some mornings the ashtrays would be full of cigarette ends, more than half of them a different brand from the kind she smoked. Those wouldn't have any lipstick on them and hers always did. Besides, on those mornings I'd find that someone had been using the shower. Mrs. Abbott never used it. She loved a warm tub. She'd soak in it for hours."

"No wonder Mr. Black didn't keep soap in his own bathroom," said Kay.

"I beg your pardon?"

"It that all you can tell us?" asked Althea.

"I'm 'afraid so—except that I wasn't any too sorry when I heard she was killed. I guess that sounds heartless—but she was always awful mean to me."

* * * * *

"It only surprises me that Claire wasn't murdered sooner," remarked Kay, as she and Althea came down the steps of the rooming-house in Brooklyn. "Hers was a dangerous profession."

"I'm afraid I haven't formed an idea of her profession, unless it was the oldest in the world."

"Nothing so crude, although crude enough. Reason it out for yourself: nothing in writing at her apartment, where it might go astray; phone calls from gentlemen giving obviously false names; clandestine meetings in a taxi in Central Park. It all adds up to just one thing: blackmail. Do you wonder she was murdered?"

Chapter 13

If such a thing is possible, the snub-nosed freighter was allergic to the sea. In an ocean smooth as a mirror, she rolled and groaned. With the gentlest of following winds, she lurched like a drunken sailor. A dimple in the water made her tremble like a bride. Battling the slightest of waves, she panicked and faltered; dropped her nose between each with a sickening shudder; quaked in the trough, her engines labouring as though every gasp would be their last; rose, shivering, to meet the next with bump and wallow. Every time it was lifted, dripping, out of the sea, the screw at her stern made earnest endeavour to thump itself loose, as if anxious to desert so unseaworthy a craft.

A crust of barnacles on her bottom, thicker than her plates, slowed her to a dreary six or seven knots an hour. The seagulls, wheeling and dipping above her squat and ugly hull, screamed at her in shrill derision, like street urchins at a shambling crone.

In taut misery, Nick lay on his bunk for hours at a time, feeling in every queasy organ each jarring buck and heave. This was no ship but a fugitive from a fairground, a nightmare fusion of Ferris wheel, merry-go-round, whip and bumping car, haunted house and wall of death, with all of their slap-happy gyrations but none of their gaiety. Nick ate little at the meals served to him and to Hayden in the wireless room and what he did eat he generally deposited over the rail soon after.

At first, he could not even compose himself to read but, becoming accustomed, if not reconciled, to the old tub's hysterical way of life, he began at last to dip into the paper-bound books that littered the sleeping-cabin. Thumb-marked, dog-eared, they gave him a curious insight into Hayden's character. There was no trash in Hayden's library; it was all literature.

Norman Douglas's South Wind. Wilde's Salome, in the original French. Walt Whitman's Leaves of Grass. Pierre Loti's Life of Christ. Hardy's Tess of the D'Urbervilles. Galsworthy's Man of Property. Willa Cather's The Lost Lady. Dreiser's An American Tragedy. Stevenson's Kidnapped. Mary Webb's Precious Bane. There were others, all soiled, all much handled, all good.

On the second afternoon out from New York, Hennessey came in and found Nick reading. He took the book from Nick, glancing contemptuously at the title. It was Maeterlinck's The Story of a Bee.

"What d'you wanna waste your time on this junk for? Where's it gonna get you?"

"You wouldn't know, Hennessey," said Hayden, over the rim of a glass. "I don't suppose you ever read a book in your life!"

"Not all the way through, I didn't." The first mate said it as a boast. "I always had sumpin' better to do. Is this what you need an assistant for—to help you swill scotch and read crummy books?"

"I do the swilling," replied Hayden, with undisturbed calm, "Cousin Smith attends to the books."

"He drank plenty when he first came on board."

Nick rarely went on deck during the day, for Hayden had advised him to lie low. At night he walked, or rather, staggered, from one end of the tramp to the other. Almost always he could see pinpricks of light far off to starboard, for they were sailing a course that seldom took them many miles from the shore. After four days at sea the Delaware coast was a dim smudge on the horizon. At this rate of progress, it would be four days more before the creaking, swaying freighter was out of United States territorial waters.

When Nick came in from his nocturnal perambulations the first mate and Hayden and a couple of other men were usually playing cards at a small table cluttered with chips and glasses, with a bottle of scotch in reach. Nick would put on earphones and listen to news broadcasts from land or the spaced dots and dashes of ship talking to ship; or he would go straight to the inner room and stretch himself on his bunk to read. When the wireless was untended it was kept tuned to the ship's waveband and Nick was expected to take messages which came through during the poker session. Apart from that, Hayden let him do as he pleased. But Hennessey, generally the winner at poker, never stopped trying to lure Nick into the game.

It would be three or four in the morning before Hayden stumbled to bed. Nick would be asleep with the light on and an open book lying on his chest. Dog-tired and far from sober, Hayden always fell into his birth with his clothes on and the dawn, stealing in through the porthole, would pale the still-burning light.

At about ten in the morning, Hayden dragged himself up, tugged a damp comb through his mane of white hair and breakfasted on whisky and water and aspirin tablets. He had always a tale of woe to pour into Nick's ear. The cards had wronged him the night before: bad hands had been his all but continual lot; the good ones had seduced him into staking more than they were worth, only to betray him at the showdown.

"I lose my pay to Hennessey every voyage. A lot of good the hundred bucks I got for smuggling you aboard has done me—that wound up in Hennessey's pocket, too."

"You're no poker-player. Why don't you quit?"

"And give up my chance to win it all back? What do you think I am—a sap?"

"Yes," said Nick. "You're a sap."

"Oh, well, hell. There's nothing else to do on this lousy washtub. How about lending me a ten-spot? I've a hunch my luck is about to change."

"It won't change. But I'll lend you five bucks."

"Thanks, cousin."

"And that's all you get. Don't come asking me for more in the morning."

"I wouldn't think of it, cousin. In the morning you can have this fin back. Tonight's my night to hold four aces."

"And Hennessey will hold a straight flush."

"I thought you didn't play poker, cousin?"

"I've been around, cousin," said Nick curtly.

On the fifth night out, Nick paused to watch the game when he came in from walking the deck. He was beginning to get his sea-legs but never expected to walk straight on this rolling, lurching tramp. He stood behind Hennessey's chair and the first mate kept glancing sideways at him and fidgeting. Pretending to lose interest, Nick sat at the wireless table, flipping over the pages of a book. Out of the corners of his eyes he watched Hennessey and soon understood why close surveillance made the man uneasy; and why he so consistently won.

Although his hands were large and calloused, there was nothing clumsy about the way in which Hennessey handled the greasy deck when it was his turn to deal. It was fascinating to watch him, when you knew what he was doing. Nick had seen cardsharps at work before and none of them could palm a card more deftly or deal from the bottom more neatly than the first mate. Nick tried to catch Hayden's eye but the wireless operator was intent on his own hand.

Taking two coins from his pocket, Nick began to clink them together. He made long and short taps with one on the other, repeating over and over the ship's wireless call signal. After a time, Hayden looked up and their eyes met. Nick made the coins clink a message in Morse code and, listening to it, Hayden's mouth tightened. He glared across the table at Hennessey. The first mate's dour face reddened.

"What's the matter with you?"

For a moment, Hayden stared at him and then, throwing down his cards, he stood up.

"I don't feel like playing anymore."

"What's eating you? You never broke up a game before."

Hayden said bitterly, "Maybe I never got wise before."

"Meaning?" asked Hennessey, rising slowly to his feet, his eyes glittering and hard.

In the background, Nick took a firm grip of an empty bottle. But Hayden backed down. "What would I mean? I'm tired, that's all."

The other two players threw in their hands, one of them remarking that his luck was dead out, anyway, and the game ended. With a bleak look at Nick, the first mate followed them out.

When they were alone in the wireless cabin, Hayden looked at Nick. "You're dead sure about the message you tapped out? Hennessey was cheating?"

"He was dealing the cards from all over the deck."

"My bad luck made me wonder about him a couple of times. I watched him one night but didn't see a move that looked phony."

"You wouldn't, unless you knew what to look for."

"When I think of all the dough I've lost to him—"

"Don't think of it. Don't lose any more, that's all." Nick opened the cabin door, pausing on the threshold. "I'm going along to the galley for a cup of coffee. Shall I bring some back for you?"

"No; thanks. Guess I'll go to bed."

Nick shut the door behind him and walked across the deck. In the dark, a burly figure stepped out from behind a foghorn.

"I happen to know the Morse code, too—wise guy," snarled Hennessey, shooting out his fist.

The blow landed squarely on Nick's nose and he staggered back against a hatch, tasting his own blood. The first mate came after him, sure-footed on the pitching deck. Bracing his back against the hatch, Nick brought up both feet with all the power of his legs behind them and planted them in his adversary's abdomen. Hands clasping his stomach, Hennessey doubled up with a groan. Nick straightened him out with a fist to the chin. The back of Hennessey's head hit the deck with a thud and the first mate gave a spasmodic quiver and lay still. Nick bent anxiously over him. The prostrate man looked very dead.

Hayden was still up when Nick stumbled back into the wireless cabin.

"What the devil have you been doing with your face?" he demanded, staring.

"I think I've killed Hennessey."

"Where is he?" asked Hayden quietly.

"On deck. He was laying for me."

"I'll take a look at him."

They went outside and the wireless operator knelt beside the prone body of the first mate.

"He hit his head when he went down," Nick explained.

Hayden looked up. "He'll be alright in a minute. You can't kill his thick-headed breed. Fetch a bucket of water."

Nick obeyed and Hayden sluiced the water over the unconscious man, drenching him from head to heels.

The first mate stirred with a groan. One of his hands came up and groped in midair.

"What'll we do with him?"

"Let him do something with himself when he comes to," replied Hayden indifferently.

They returned to the wireless cabin and Hayden refilled his glass. He offered the bottle to Nick, who shook his head.

"No, thanks. I'm off that stuff."

"Smart boy. You're going to need your wits about you for the rest of the trip. Hennessey will be stalking you—and next time he won't give you a chance. If you reach Honduras in one piece it will be a miracle. You ought to see your nose. It's spread all over your face. You must have stopped a beauty."

"I did," Nick agreed, touching his nose gingerly and wincing with the pain of it.

A chattering of Morse code came from the wireless receiver. Hayden sat at the table and reached for pencil and pad to take down the message.

The cabin door swung back on its hinges and Hennessey stood, dripping and scowling ferociously, on the threshold. In one hand he held a short iron spike. His eyes burned into Nick's face. Nick reached for a bottle, pausing with a chill, empty feeling, when he heard the message that was coming in over the air. Hayden started to take it down but, halfway through, dropped his pencil and turned his head to gape at Nick. The first mate was also listening intently. His lips curled back from his teeth in an ugly grin.

"It's you they mean, Mister Smith. The description fits you like a glove, even to the wounded shoulder— I saw the bandage when you were washing. Nick Abbott, eh? Wanted for murdering his wife. Believed to be on a freighter bound for South America. That's you, alright. Boy, this is one message that's going to reach the captain in an awful hurry. I'll be back with a couple of men, Mister Smith, to put you in irons until we can turn you over to the cops."

He went out in a hurry and the door swung shut behind him.

"Why didn't you hit him with that bottle?" cried Hayden, staring at Nick. "Why didn't you stop him?"

"What good would that do?"

"None, I suppose. I'd have suppressed the message if I could, though—if he hadn't heard it."

"I guess you would, at that. I hope this doesn't get you into trouble."

"Forget it." Hayden eyed Nick curiously. "You don't look like a murderer."

"I'm not—but that won't help when they sit me on the electric chair. I was a fool to think I could escape by boat. Once you're on a boat you're in a trap—you can't get off."

Hayden stood up. "How well can you swim?"

"I did a mile once."

Hayden sat down again. "We're about four miles from shore. You'd never make it."

"I can try," said Nick. "If I fail, there are worse ways of dying."

Tearing off, his coat, kicking off his shoes, he snatched open the door and ran across the deck. For a moment he poised himself on the rail before diving out and down into the swirling black water. When he hit the sea with a splash it gripped him and whirled him round, sucking him toward the churning blades at the stern of the battered tramp. He went down so far that he thought he would never come up, helpless as a piece of flotsam in the plucking grasp of the freighter's wash. It used him as a toy, turning him upside down and almost inside out, twisting him this way and that, with a roaring in his ears and a pounding in his lungs. It dragged him along twenty feet below the surface at a speed far greater than that at which the rusty old ship was steaming south. He could not think. He could not breathe. He could not even go through the motions of trying to swim.

Half-suffocated, he bobbed up at last and took a great gulp of air before going under again. The second time it was easier to strike up to the surface. Treading water, he looked about him at the swelling breast of the ocean and had no idea in which direction land lay. And then he glimpsed the lights of the ship, quite tiny, and seeming far off and knew roughly which way he must try to go. He put his head down and started to swim. Against the imperturbability of the ocean it was difficult to make headway. It rebuffed him blandly: there was no wave of any consequence to fight but at every stroke a gentle swell relentlessly carried him back. He became lost to everything but the effort to make progress, be it ever so little. He had no way of knowing whether or not he was advancing, for the shore was distant and obscured by night.

When, at last, he paused and trod water to look about him again, the freighter was not in sight. He was alone, beneath a placid and indifferent sky, in a grey infinity of salt water. And he knew not which way to shape his next futile thrust.

Chapter 14

"One thing is certain," remarked Julian Deering, lying back in his chair until reposing on his spine, "in normal life the mysterious Mr. Black doesn't in the least resemble the description of him given by the clerk and the elevator boy. We can be sure he has no moustache. He doesn't wear tinted glasses. By this time, he'll even have disposed of the long dark coat. When he visited the apartment building, he probably put on his disguise in a nearby telephone booth or even in his car, before going in." Julian tapped his pipe idly on the knee of his crossed leg. "Clever of him, in a way, to provide the clerk and the elevator boy with a ready-made and altogether inaccurate description. He ought to have assumed a limp as well. That would have been a neat touch."

"I lent Mr. Deering our letter of authority to inspect the dead woman's apartment," said Althea to Kay. "I thought as he is going to help us, he ought to be familiar with the scene of the crime."

"I can think of no more suitable, setting for a 'Love Nest' shooting," smiled Julian, smoothing his sleek yellow hair, "than that awful mauve and red and grey and white bedroom. I never met Claire Abbott—Nick always put me off when I suggested he ought to present me to his wife—but, from all I've heard of the lady, the room admirably expresses her somewhat shallow personality."

The society photographer looked in turn at each of the other people sitting in Althea Archer's Madison Avenue office. Althea herself, at the desk, cool and lovely in a suit of grey flannel; Kay Bannerman, almost like a school girl in a simple print frock and very much in earnest about the purpose of this meeting; Barney, red-faced and perspiring in high collar and Sunday best and

She Got What She Asked For 155

at a loss what to do with his hands. Studying each face with eyes trained to read character, Julian's own face became grave.

"I suppose we all realise what a man-sized job we're taking on in setting ourselves to clear Nick?"

"It's a large undertaking," said Kay, "but by no means impossible, if the four of us give our minds and energy to it."

"I think we are already off to a good start," declared Althea.

"I agree," said Julian. "You and Miss Bannerman have worked wonders. By the way, this is going to cost money. I'd like to take care of that part. To help Nick, I'd gladly spend my last cent. I owe him a lot. He practically raised me by hand at Yale."

"I think we all feel that way about Nick," said Althea.

"Yeah," responded Barney. "There's something about the guy that gets you."

Kay was silent. She had no intention of declaring the depth of her feeling for Nick. From a drawer of the desk, Althea produced a folder containing papers.

"After our interview with Lieutenant Hull the other day," she said, looking at Kay, "I hired a detective agency to investigate Claire Ab—Jansen's past. I have here the agency's first report. Already they've uncovered one or two interesting facts about her. About four years ago, under the name of Claire Day, she toured the Middle West with a third-rate theatrical company in a farce called You Can't Fool Margie. One of the other members of the cast was a young man named Arnold James. People who change their names often take new ones with the same initials as the old—or so I've heard—so it seems not unlikely that Arnold James was the Arthur Jansen later involved with Claire in the badger game."

"Did your agency get a description of this Arnold James?" asked Kay.

"No; but I've instructed them to try and find him. By the

way, the show, was stranded in St. Louis and the company broke up. St. Louis is a fairly short distance from Kansas City, where Claire was arrested soon after. The detective agency discovered something else about Claire. She was a striptease performer for a while three years ago."

"If her life was short," murmured Julian, filling his pipe, "it was also crowded."

Closing the folder, Althea placed her clasped hands on it and looked at Kay. "What luck did you have in your search for a compact similar to the one in Claire's hand when she was found dead?"

"I tried drugstores and five-and-tens all over town. None of them had one like it in stock; even the girls in Woolworth's turned up their noses at it. The cheapest compact I could find was definitely superior."

"I can't for the life of me imagine how she ever came to own the thing."

"I racked my brains for the answer to that. As you know, my theory was that, after the shooting, at the very point of death, she turned out her handbag to find it, hoping it would leave a clue to her murderer."

"No man would give a woman so worthless a present."

"No, of course not. At least, not as a serious offering. And yet, I felt sure that some man had given it to her. It wasn't the sort of thing she'd buy for herself."

"I don't get it," grunted Barney, scratching his bald head. "If a man wouldn't buy it for her— If she wouldn't buy it for herself— I don't get it."

"Supposing she was at a fair or carnival with a man," suggested Kay. "Supposing he put a ring round the compact in a hoopla booth. No matter how cheap it was, wouldn't it be natural for the man to hand it to her with a laugh—and wouldn't she laugh also and put it in her handbag?"

"Of course, he would—and, of course, she would," cried Julian, sitting up with a jerk. "Clever of you to think of that, Miss Bannerman."

Kay took two compacts from her handbag and placed them, side by side, on the desk. They were identical in every respect. One of them was the compact Claire had held tightly in death.

"I bought a copy of 'The Billboard,' which had several advertisements of firms who supply trash like this to carnival folk. The third one I tried sells these compacts to concessionaires at Coney Island, and places like that for two dollars a gross."

With a sudden exclamation, Althea opened her folder again.

"A detail I stupidly neglected to mention is that Claire did her striptease at Coney Island."

"That was three years ago," objected Julian. "She'd never keep a cheap tin trifle all that time."

"No, of course not," agreed Kay, "but couldn't she have visited Coney Island recently with a man?"

"It doesn't sound like Claire's idea of a good time. Night clubs seem to have been more in her line."

"Perhaps she wanted another look at her old haunts. Even Claire could have had a streak of sentiment in her make-up. If so, the visit couldn't have been more than a few days before her death. She wouldn't have kept the compact long. She'd have thrown it away the next time she turned out her handbag."

"A good many of the stall-holders must have known her when she worked there," said Althea. "If she visited the place recently, some of them are sure to have seen her. They'd remember if she was accompanied by a man."

"I think we have something here well worth following up," responded Julian. "Supposing I run down to Coney Island tomorrow afternoon and see what I can find out? Have we a picture of Claire I could show, in case she isn't remembered by name?"

"They'll remember her, alright," mumbled Barney. "She was bumped off, wasn't she? Folks always remember anyone they knew who came to a sticky finish. Better let me take care of this, Mr. Deering. I know Coney like I know my old mother. I wish I had a dime for all the kewpie dolls I've won in my time."

"Perhaps you could handle it better than I," agreed Julian. "My education was neglected, as far as Coney Island is concerned. Under the spell of the merry-go-rounds and Ferris wheels I might forget what I was there for."

"While Barney covers the Coney Island angle," said Kay, "I'm going to make the acquaintance of Mr. Morrie Stern, whose clandestine meetings in Central Park with Claire intrigue me greatly."

"I'll go with you," said Althea quickly. "From what you've told me about him, he's too dangerous a man for you to tackle on your own."

"Let's make it a party," proposed Julian. "It's an age since I've been to the Hoot Owl."

"Include me out," said Barney hastily. "My tux smells too strong of mothballs. I ain't worn it since the last Fourteenth Precinct Social."

"We'll make it a threesome, then. I'll be the envy of the wolves when I walk into the Hoot Owl with a lovely lady on each arm. Shall we make it this evening? I think I left a dinner jacket at my club last time I spent a night in town."

Chapter 15

He looked like a film gangster, the man who swaggered out of the Hoot Owl at a few minutes to ten that evening, when Julian, Kay and Althea were going in. Baleful, insolent eyes, shadowed by a snap-brim hat. Dinner jacket fitting too tightly at the waist, the padded shoulders standing, up like epaulettes. The chest of a gorilla; bulging muscles of an all-in wrestler. His face was broad, heavy, pugnacious, a broken nose spreading over it like some fungoid growth. Touching his peaked cap, the doorman said, "Evening, Mr. Mascagni"; and was rewarded with a grunt.

"Boris Karloff in a new makeup, no doubt," commented Julian with a smile and his companions laughed.

Above the plate glass doors which the custodian opened with a flourish, a large painted owl, whose neon eyes winked on and off, looked down at them with an expression more suggestive than wise. The music of a dance band in which each instrument retained its identity wafted out to them as they shed their wraps into the hands of a bowing male receptionist and a pert, smiling hatcheck girl. At the head of a short flight of steps leading to a long, many-mirrored room, the receptionist bowed them into the hands of a head waiter with body arched like a question mark, who saw them to a table bordering the dance floor. Another waiter offered a menu which Julian waved aside and a third produced a wine-card over which Julian ran a doubtful eye before ordering a bottle of Heidsieck, 1928.

On the black glass floor a score of girls in costumes too brief to have passed a beach inspector were going through the gymnastics of a dance routine. The routine was old but their powdered bodies were young. All of them were pretty; a few, beautiful;

their arms and legs uniformly slim, smooth and shapely. Artificial rosebuds adorned each cupped breast and, from dimpled stomachs to swelling thighs, abbreviated garments of black net and silken rose petals veiled scantily the rounded flesh.

Blaring cackle of a trumpet. Delirious moan of a saxophone on a three-day jag. Frenzied wail of a violin, like mad music tormented from the intestines of a living cat. Demented snarl of a muted cornet. Staccato stutter of a distraught banjo. Deep bass mutter of a hag-ridden sousaphone. Maniacal clash and clang of cymbals. A moonstruck clarinet shrilling high above the rest.

"Isn't the music ghastly?" murmured Althea.

Kay smiled. "I was about to say, isn't it swell."

"Really? To me, it is only an incoherent din."

"Listen to that clarinet. I doubt if even Benny Goodman could coax more out of it."

"I'd be satisfied with a good deal less."

"'Beat me, Daddy,'" said Julian. "'Bounce me, Brother.' 'Scrub me, Mama,' 'Sock it to me, Sister.' If you were a jitterbug, Althea, you'd find spiritual significance in every note.

"Give me Mozart," replied Althea, almost stiffly. "Give me Brahms."

"That's what they're giving you," said Julian. "Only, Basin Street and Tin Pan Alley have played tricks with the original themes."

"Isn't that Ben Firman over there?" asked Kay, craning her neck. "You know, the Broadway columnist."

"You mean the little man with the dead white face?" responded Julian, his eyes following her gaze. "I'm afraid I wouldn't know. I'm practically a stranger here myself."

"I'm sure it is Mr. Firman," said Kay. "I used to be a switchboard girl on his paper and I've seen him a good many times. I'd like to talk to him. He knows everyone on Broadway. He probably knew Claire."

"Shall I go with you?" suggested Julian, standing up.

"Thanks—but I'll probably get farther with him on my own. You'll excuse me? I shan't be long."

Skirting the dance floor, weaving between tables set too closely together, Kay made her way to the other side of the room. In a corner commanding the place, a thin little man, dapper in pearl grey, was sitting alone. His face was the unwholesome white of the underside of a fish. At his elbow stood a glass of amber liquid that might have been a highball but actually was ginger ale. He looked up at Kay with blank, inscrutable eyes.

"You won't remember me, Mr. Firman. I used to work at the switchboard in your office."

"Yeah?" was all the Broadway reporter answered. His expression did not change. He did not rise, nor did he ask Kay to join him.

Drawing out a chair, Kay sat down.

"Make yourself to home," said Firman.

"Thanks," she replied, ignoring the sarcasm. "If you'll spare me a few minutes of your time—"

"I'm not going any place."

"I'd like to ask you a question or two, if you don't mind."

"I don't hand out information, sister, I gather it in. That's Julian Deering, the photographer, at the table you just left, isn't it? Who's the tall woman with the air of a reigning queen?"

"Supposing we trade," proposed Kay. "I'll tell you about her, if you'll tell me what I want to know."

"Start telling, sister."

"That's Althea Archer. She's a woman attorney, with an office in Madison Avenue."

"And more dough than she knows what to do with," added Firman, in a bored drawl. "I didn't know she ever did the night spots."

"She doesn't, usually. This is a special occasion. In case

you're interested, my name is Kay Bannerman. I used to be Nick Abbott's secretary."

"The guy the police want for murder?"

"Yes. He didn't do it.".,

"That's what you say, sister. From what I hear, the evidence against him is good and strong."

"It isn't the first time an innocent man's looked guilty."

"Maybe not," conceded the columnist. "It wouldn't be the first time an innocent man sat on that old rocking chair up at Sing Sing, either."

"I expect you knew Claire Abbott?"

"Yeah, I knew Claire. She was strictly poison. I guess she got what was coming to her, when she was popped off."

"Nick wasn't the only person who might have wished her dead. There were several men whom Claire was blackmailing."

"I knew that, too, sister," replied Firman indifferently.

"How did you know?"

"Maybe I'm psychic. I get feelings about things. She used to pretend she knew me a lot better than she did. She'd walk up to me with some man at her elbow and call me, 'Ben, darling,' as if we were buddies. I figured maybe she was using me as a threat. You know—'Be a good boy, Or I'll tell Ben Firman what I know about you.'"

"More than likely. Do you remember who the men were?"

"Morrie Stern, for one. Morrie always smiled when she looked at him but when her back was turned, you could see he hated her insides. Arno Jannings, for another."

"Arno Jannings?" Kay frowned. "Who is he?"

"Don't scowl like that, sister, you'll get wrinkles. Arno calls himself an actor. He plays the lead in that farce at the Astoria Theatre. He got a Hollywood offer recently—but he turned it down."

"An actor and he wouldn't go to Hollywood?"

"Yeah, make sense of that, if you can. Most of them would give their store teeth and toupees for the chance."

"What does he look like? About thirty-two years old? Dark hair? Dark eyes? And around five feet, eight inches in height?"

"You sound like you were quoting from a police blotter. The description fits, such as it is, except for the height. Arno's half a head taller than me and I'm five feet, six. That makes him about five, ten."

"I see." For a moment, Kay looked disappointed.

"So far," said Firman, "you've had all the best of this deal. You wouldn't want to tell me why you're interested in Claire Abbott and her boy friends?"

"I'll tell you one day and there'll be a good story in it for you. I'll tell you this much, now: the man who shot Claire used to conceal his identity by using the name of a colour."

"What are you giving me? You mean, he called himself the Green Mask or something screwy like that?"

"Nothing so melodramatic. Plain Mr. Green—or White—or Black."

"I get it. Maybe I can use that in my column."

"If you do, please make the reference vague. Oh, and could you print something about Arno Jannings in the same column? Something, perhaps, suggesting that Jannings isn't his real name?"

"I could—but why should I?"

"I'll have to tell you that, too, another time. I promise there'll be a whale of a story in all this for you, one day."

"Maybe I'll string along with you, at that, sister. You talk like you knew your vegetables. I'll tell you a little something more about Claire Abbott. One night she spent half an hour in here at a rear table, talking a blue streak to a kid who used to kick her legs in the floor show. A kid called Janice Logan.

It interested me at the time, for Claire wasn't the sort to waste time on a little showgirl unless there was something in it for her. From the look on his face, Morrie Stern didn't like it—but he seemed reluctant to do anything about it."

"You say this Janice Logan used to dance in the floor show?"

"Sure, she wiggled her fanny with the other kids. She left about a week ago. I don't know whether she quit or was fired."

"How can I find her?"

"Some of the agents would have her address. You could ask Morrie Stern—but I don't advise it."

"Did I hear my name?" asked a cold voice.

Looking up they saw, standing between them, a man in evening clothes whose eyes were reptilian, whose pale skin looked oddly like curdled milk.

"Hi, Morrie," said the columnist offhandedly.

"Hi, Ben." The night club owner turned his beady eyes on Kay. "Who's your lady friend?"

"Miss Bannerman, may I present Mr. Morrie Stern? If you're looking for an expert secretary, Morrie, Miss Bannerman used to be Nick Abbott's Girl Friday."

"That's interesting," replied Stern. "I suppose you lost your job when your boss took it on the lam, Miss Bannerman?"

Finishing his ginger ale at a gulp, Ben Firman rose. "Be seein' you," he drawled. 'I've got a couple of items I want to phone in before my deadline."

"Don't put any slugs in my phone box," said Morrie Stern.

He looked bleakly at Kay, who returned his gaze steadily. She had risen to return to her own table.

"We're blocking traffic," said Stern. "Let's dance."

Without waiting for an answer, he led her out to the black glass floor, crowded with swaying couples now that the first show was over. Sinuous as a cat, he danced with an indolent grace.

"You used to work for Nick Abbott, huh?"

"Yes. Do you know him?"

"I ran into him a couple of times at Poli's bar."

"You knew his wife, Claire, rather better, I expect?"

The night club owner's expression was unfathomable. "She used to come here quite a lot," he replied. "I've been watching you," he added casually. "You and Firman had a lot to say to each other. What did you find to talk about?"

"Oh, one thing and another," said Kay airily. "People, mostly."

"Me, for instance?"

The girl was silent.

"I don't like people talking about me," said Morrie Stern, in the same detached tone. "It makes my ears burn."

They had reached the side of the room at which Althea and Julian were sitting. The night club owner dropped his arms and stood back slightly. "You'll excuse me. I've got things to do."

He turned away and Kay edged back to the table. "That was Morrie Stern," she said calmly.

"His face frightened me a little," said Althea, with a shiver.

"I believe he used to be on the list of public enemies," replied Julian, rising to hold Kay's chair, "although he's never been convicted of anything."

"Have either of you ever heard of an, actor named Arno Jannings?" asked Kay.

With a frown, Althea shook her head. Julian said, "Isn't he in that show at the Astoria?"

"Yes. And he's been seen here in Claire's company."

"I daresay a lot of men have," murmured Julian.

"Doesn't anything strike you about his name? Arno Jannings...Arthur Jansen...Arnold James. The same set of initials. And Arnold James was an actor in farce."

"Of course," said Althea. "I wonder how he compares with

the description of Arthur Jansen which Lieutenant Hull gave us?"

"It fits—except that he's two inches taller."

"An important difference," said Julian regretfully. "You know what the Bible says about the impossibility of adding even a cubic inch to one's stature."

"It can be done with lifts," replied Kay and, when the others looked bewildered, she added, "I mean, built-up shoes. It's a trick undersized actors use to make them look taller. If we only could find a way to inspect his shoes—"

"Nothing could be simpler," answered Julian, sipping champagne. "Don't I photograph celebrities? And isn't Jannings a celebrity, in a mild way? I'll drop in on him at the theatre with a proposal to make a camera study of him. There's sure to be more than one pair of shoes in his dressing-room. I'd be a poor detective if I couldn't find a way to examine one of them."

"Jannings had an offer from Hollywood but he wouldn't go. Isn't it possible he was afraid that, if his face appeared on movie screens all over the country, someone would recognise him as the Arthur Jansen wanted by the police of Kansas City?"

"Of course, it is," agreed Julian. "Perfectly possible. And, another thing, wouldn't an actor be the most likely person to think of wearing makeup to avoid being recognised, as the mysterious Mr. Black did?"

Sometime later, when they rose to go, Kay had the uncomfortable impression that someone was staring at her back. Looking round, her eyes met the cold gaze of Morrie Stern.

Chapter 16

Breakfasting early the following morning, Kay sipped strong black coffee and read Ben Firman's newspaper column. The Broadway reporter had gleaned four items from his chat with her: "...At a ringside table at the Hoot Owl, last P. M., your scribe spotted the social-register beauty, Althea Archer, who only steps out once in a moon blue to match her blood. The lady, whose papa left her enough folding money to stuff a mattress, was head-to-head and cheek-to-cheek with socialite Julian Deering, whose papa died in the depression, leaving him a juicy red apple... Also at Morrie Stern's torrid spot was Kay Bannerman, who didn't let her evening be spoiled by the knowledge that her ex-boss, Nick Abbott, is still badly wanted for murder... A little bird—could be a stool-pigeon—tells me that the murder rap against Abbott is one lovely frame. The rumour goes that Claire Abbott was popped off by a gent using as his alias the name of a colour... Set for a marathon run is the back-bedroom comedy in which one Arno Jannings made his first New York appearance. The face is familiar, Mr. Jannings—but I can't quite place the name."

That morning, Kay made a round of the theatrical agents, in quest of Janice Logan's address. After a series of fruitless calls her feet began to ache but she forced herself to carry on. She plodded up four flights of steep stairs in a down-at-heel building without an elevator and, panting a little, entered an office little larger than a sentry-box, in which a plump bald man was having hysterics into a telephone. Hanging up, the agent waved a podgy hand at her.

"Nothing today, sweetheart," he said, out of a corner of a mouth occupied by a frayed cigar.

"I'm looking for a girl named Janice Logan."

"That two-timing little chippy? I book her into Morrie Stern's club at good dough and what does she do? She runs out on the job without a word. What does she think? jobs grow on trees, maybe?"

"I wouldn't know what she thinks. I'd like her address, if you have it."

"Help yourself, sugar," replied the agent, indicating a shoebox full of grubby file-cards. "And, when you find her card, tear it up. By me, that goil is all washed up."

Kay quickly leafed over the cards until she came to one on which Janice Logan's name, address, telephone number and description was scrawled in pencil. She put it in her handbag and turned to go.

"You got a cute shape, baby," grunted the agent, shifting the cigar with a twist of thick lips. "Maybe I could find a spot for you, at that."

"Thanks," said Kay, "but I'm working."

"Okay—but if your job flops on you, look me up again."

At a rooming-house in the West Forties, a landlady whose face expressed an eternal distrust of the human species, shook her head sourly when Kay asked for Janice Logan.

"She don't live here no more."

"When did she leave?"

"Oh, about a week ago."

"It wasn't on the seventeenth, I suppose?" The seventeenth of the month was the day on which Claire Abbott had been murdered.

"Maybe it was." The landlady's voice was a bored drone. She scratched her head languidly, eyeing her caller from neat head to trim ankle. Her expression hinted that she cared even less for pretty girls than for the rest of the human race. "Lemme see, now. Yeah, I guess it was the seventeenth. She came home in an awful hurry in the late afternoon, paid me for the week and checked out."

"Did she leave a forwarding address?"

"No, she didn't. She just called a cab and away she went. I didn't ask no questions. I got no time to worry about roomers after they leave me. It's all I can do to bother with 'em when they're in my house."

"May I use your phone?"

"If you've got a nickel," replied the drab, pointing to the rear of a dark and dusty hall.

Someone had scrawled the word 'taxi' and a telephone number on the dingy wallpaper. Kay dialled the number and asked the garage employee who answered to send her a cab. It appeared in a few minutes and she met it on the sidewalk in front of the house.

"Did you pick up a girl with a suitcase at this house on the seventeenth?" she asked the driver.

He gave her a sullen stare. "No, I didn't. You bring me over here just to ask me that?"

"The cab she took almost certainly came from your garage. I'll give you five dollars if you help me find the driver."

"Get in," he said, opening the door.

He drove her two blocks west and one block north, stopping with a jerk outside a cafe in front of which a line of taxicabs was parked. "Wait here a moment," he said, "while I ask around." Climbing out from behind the steering-wheel, he walked to a group of men in peaked caps who were lounging on the sidewalk. In a few minutes he returned with one of them in tow. "This is the guy, lady. I guess that's the easiest five bucks I ever earned."

After making sure that he had produced the right driver, Kay parted with the reward she had promised.

"Do you remember what address the girl gave you?" she asked the second driver.

"It wasn't exactly an address, miss. I didn't take her to a house or anything like that. She told me to drop her at the corner of Seventy-Ninth and Broadway."

"Did you notice where she went when she got out?"

"Well, I asked if she'd like me to carry her suitcase—it looked kinda heavy—but she said no, she could handle it herself. She lugged it round the corner and I cruised back to the hack-stand. It wasn't any of my business where she went."

"Which is your cab? I'd like you to drop me where you dropped the girl that day."

"Sure, miss."

The driver led her to a yellow vehicle and opened the door. He swung the cab out from the pavement and turned it to head north. After driving for about ten blocks, he put his head slightly to one side and said, "I think there's a car following us. It sticks pretty close on my tail."

Looking back through the rear window, Kay saw the car he meant; a long black sedan. She could not distinguish the features of the driver, or whether there was more than one occupant. It occurred to her that it was probably a police car, that she was still being followed, in the hope that she would lead the way to Nick Abbott. "Try to shake it off," she said.

At the next corner the driver cut through a changing light and turned left, accelerating rapidly. On a parallel street to the one they had been travelling he drove five blocks in the direction from which they had come before changing course again and heading north once more.

"I think we lost our shadow," he said, after a while.

Where Seventy-Ninth Street meets Broadway, Kay alighted and paid the driver, tipping him well.

"The goil went that way," he told her, pointing a finger.

Kay thanked him and went the way he had indicated, walking between two rows of brownstone fronts. I'm looking for a room, she said to herself; and I have a suitcase in my hand. It is heavy and I don't want to carry it far... Crossing an intersecting street, she spotted a card in the window of a house at the middle of the next block. Going up a flight of stone steps, she rang a bell. In a little while, an aproned woman with straggling grey hair opened the door.

"I'm looking for a friend," said Kay. "She's a brunette, about twenty-three years old. I think she moved here about a week ago."

"You mean Miss Smith," answered the woman readily, opening the door wider. "She's in number 12, on the third floor. Can you find your own way up? These stairs is killing me."

Kay went up three uncarpeted flights and tapped softly on a door which had '12' in white paint on one of its panels She heard a bedspring creaking and an anxious voice called, "Who is it?"

"It's only me, dearie," replied Kay, assuming a cleaning-woman's tired whine.

After more sounds of movement and shuffling of feet, the door opened slightly and an eye and part of a cheek appeared in the aperture.

"I thought it was Mrs.— You must have the wrong room."

Surreptitiously putting her foot into the opening to prevent the door being closed, Kay replied softly, "No, it's you I want to see."

"I don't know you."

The girl tried to shut the door, giving Kay's toes a painful squeeze. The necessity of rescuing her foot made Kay exert every ounce of her strength. Bracing a shoulder against a panel, she thrust her way bodily into the room.

"You've got your nerve, busting in here like that. Yoli get right out this minute, or I'll call the landlady."

"I want to talk to you, Janice."

For a moment, the girl seemed about to faint. Wearing something flimsy that displayed her young body to advantage, she was pretty in the doll-like, big-eyed fashion of youngsters who prance in night club floor shows. Her looks were slightly marred by the knowing air such girls acquire after a time.

The outline of her figure was still imprinted on the unmade bed.

"That's not my name," she declared, her lips quivering a little.

"I know you're Janice Logan. Why bother to deny it?"

"Listen," said Janice, showing two rows of small pearly teeth, "I don't know who you are or how you found me but I haven't a thing to say to you. Not a thing. Now, get out of here. Go on—get out."

"I'm not going until I've had a talk with you."

"About what?"

"About Claire Abbott."

Janice Logan sat down abruptly and hard on the bed, looking sick and white and frightened.

"I never even heard of the woman."

"You had a long talk with her one night at the Hoot Owl."

"If I did—and I'm not saying I did—is it any of your business?"

"When you read in the papers that she'd been murdered, you went straight home and packed your things and moved out."

"I can change my room when I feel like it, can't I?"

"You took care not to let anyone know where you were going."

"But you found me," whispered Janice and her voice shook with fear. "You found me."

"What are you scared of, Janice? From whom are you hiding?"

"I'm not scared," the showgirl retorted, with a weak attempt at bravado. "Why should I be scared? What makes you think I'm hiding? Say, you must be nuts."

"From the look of this room—and your pale face—you haven't stirred out since you moved in."

Dropping her head on her trembling hands, Janice began to sob. Kay sat on the bed and put her arm about the slim, shuddering shoulders.

"I haven't had a breath of fresh air in a week," wept Janice. "I haven't even had a decent meal. Doughnuts and milk, that's all I've had. Doughnuts and milk, three times a day until I'm sick of them. And why? What have I done to be hiding out?"

"Tell me about it," urged Kay. "If I can, I'll help you. I promise that."

"You can't help me. No one can help me. I thought I was safe here as long as I lay low—but, if you found me, someone else can."

"If you'll tell me everything, I'll find a way to protect you."

"If I tell you everything," said Janice, with a hysterical laugh. "That's what she wanted me to do. But she couldn't protect herself, could she?"

"You mean Claire Abbott?"

"I don't mean Baby Snooks," replied Janice, wiping her red eyes with a wisp of handkerchief. "She was after me to tell her what I knew about Morrie Stern. She promised me a thousand dollars if I'd sign a statement about him. She swore nothing would happen to me, if I did."

"And did you?"

"Do you think I'm crazy? I wouldn't have signed that statement for a million. I was too scared. I dunno. Maybe I should have signed it. With a thousand dollars I could be a thousand miles away. Two of the other girls who talked to Claire Abbott are out on the Coast trying their luck in the movies."

"What could they know about Morrie Stern that would be worth so much to her?"

"I should give you a thousand dollars' worth of information just for the asking."

"If it's worth a thousand dollars," said Kay simply, "I'll see that you get it."

Janice clutched at her fiercely. Janice was shaking like a twig in a gale. "Will you get me out of here safely? Will you buy me a ticket for Chicago and put me on the train? I've got a boyfriend there. I'd be safe with him."

"I'll put you on a plane for Chicago," said Kay. "What do you know about Morrie Stern?"

"Maybe I'd be a sap to trust you."

"What else can you do? Go on hiding out until the thing you're scared of catches up with you?"

"Oh, God, no. But he shot Claire Abbott—how do I know I won't be paid off the same way?"

Kay's spine tingled as if at the touch of icy fingers. "Morrie Stern shot Claire Abbott?"

"Either Morrie or his strong-arm man, Pretty Boy Macagni.

"How do you know?"

"I just know, that's all. I knew it the moment I read about the killing in the paper. He had plenty of reason to shoot her, If Claire Abbott had ever used the papers, she got those two girls to sign, Morrie would have landed in a cell."

"You mean Stern is mixed up in the vice racket?"

"He used to be. He quit with cold feet when the cops moved in on some of the other operators. The club was only a front. Morrie had call apartments all over town. He used the club as a show-window, to display the best-looking girls. You don't think he'd let Claire live when she had the goods on him, do you? When I read about the murder, I was scared he'd kill me, too. He'd seen me talking to her. How would he know I hadn't ratted on him? That's why I took a run-out powder."

Kay stood up. "I'm going to take you to a friend of mine, a woman lawyer."

With an emphatic shake of her head, Janice replied quickly, "You don't get me walking out of here in broad daylight without an armed guard."

"If I phone her and ask her to come, will you talk to her?"

"Do I get that plane ride to Chicago and some cash to tide me over until I land a job?"

"I can promise you that."

"Alright," said Janice, stiffening her lip. "Call your friend. There's a phone in the hall."

A man in trousers and woolly undershirt, with suspenders dangling down his back and his hair standing on end, was talking on the telephone when Kay went downstairs. He kept saying, "Yeah" and "Sure" and "I get you"; and shifting from one foot to the other. Avoiding Kay's eye; he hooked his ankle under the rungs of a chair, pulled it closer and sat down. It looked as if it would be a long time before he was ready to relinquish the telephone. Kay decided to run out and make her call from a drugstore.

Coming out of the house, she noticed a man on the other side of the street whose face was vaguely familiar. He turned his back on her. He was dressed in blue serge and his shoulders were broad. She came to the conclusion that he must be a detective from the Homicide Bureau, still sticking doggedly to her trail.

The nearest drugstore was two blocks away. While she was in the telephone booth, talking to Althea, she suddenly remembered where she had seen the man before and uttered a startled gasp. He was the big man with padded shoulders and mashed features who had swaggered out of the Hoot Owl the previous evening when her party was going in. 'Mr. Mascagni,' the doorman had called him.

In frantic haste she told Althea how to find Janice Logan's room and said, "Come right over as fast as you can." Hanging up the receiver, she ran out of the store and went back to the rooming-house as fast as her legs would carry her. The three long flights of stairs she took two at a time, arriving out of breath at Janice's door. She walked in without knocking.

A curious bubbling sound was coming from the bed, across which lay Janice Logan, face down. When Kay gently turned the girl over, the bubbling sound turned out to be the showgirl's breath, coming through the bloody pulp of a fractured nose. Janice had been horribly beaten and was mercifully unconscious. With a cry, Kay covered her eyes. She could not bear to look.

Running downstairs, she snatched the telephone from the man in undershirt and trousers, who was still talking into it. Ignoring his angry protests, she cut the connection and dialled the emergency operator.

"I want an ambulance in a hurry. Someone's been hurt." She gave the operator the address of the rooming-house, repeated the injunction to hurry, and hung up.

"You ought to ask first before you snatch a phone out of a guy's hand," grumbled the irate man. "That was an important call I was making."

"Did a man come in and go upstairs during the past ten minutes?" asked Kay.

"I should keep track of who goes in and out, I suppose? What am I, a doorman? People come in and go out alla time. I don't pay them no heed. Gimme that phone."

Kay went slowly upstairs to wait for the ambulance. Before it came, Althea arrived. In a few terse sentences, Kay told the woman attorney the gist of what had happened.

"Her face," said Althea weakly, turning away from the bed. "Her poor, poor face."

"She was a pretty kid," said Kay, in a burst of anger. "Such a pretty little kid."

"I'll get the best plastic surgeon in the country. I'll do everything possible for her. A private room in the hospital; every conceivable care and attention."

Kay said bitterly, "Will your surgeon iron out the scars inside that are left by a beating like that?"

"I shan't rest until the brute who attacked her is in prison."

"She'll never tell who did it. She'll be more frightened than ever."

"But you saw the man."

"Yes, I saw him—on the other side of the street. You ought to know that proves nothing."

The girl on the bed moaned and Kay swiftly turned and bent over her. Janice's eyes were open. They stared up wildly as if a nightmare still held her in its grasp.

"Who did it?" asked Kay pleadingly. "It was Morrie Stern's bodyguard, wasn't it? Mascagni?"

The bruised mouth moved convulsively for what seemed a long time before any words came out.

"I—I—"

"Who did it, Janice?"

Unable to speak, Janice Logan made a painful effort to shake her head. She was not going to name her assailant.

"Where the hell's that ambulance?" cried Kay, bursting into tears.

Chapter 17

"Now I know why men drink to forget," said Kay, in a half-dazed voice, looking chilled to the marrow although it was a sunny afternoon. "I can't get her poor broken face out of my mind. I simply can't forget it, no matter how hard I try."

Kay sat huddled in a booth at Muldoon's, an ashtray overflowing with half-smoked cigarettes in front of her. She was staring in horror at the varnished partition, as if some ghastly picture was projected on its surface. Barney sat opposite her, in shirt sleeves, soiled apron and striped trousers, his long face expressing sympathy from wart on scalp to wart on nose.

"Listen, kid, you're in a fair way to go screwy. It's no good torturin' yourself. That won't help the goil."

"If I'd left her alone it might not have happened. Pour me a stiff drink, Barney. I'll see what that can do for me."

"You don't want no drink. You'd only get a cryin' jag on. A hot cup of strong tea is what you want. My old lady always says nothin' brings her out of the doldrums quicker." Turning his head, Barney shouted, "Hey, Joe!"

A dark face appeared in the kitchen hatch. "Wharra you want?"

"Make a pot of tea. Be sure the water's boilin' before you pour it in. And remember to warm the teapot."

"Nice fuss for a cups-a tea," said Joe caustically. "What am I—a lady's maid, or sump'n?"

"I'll tell you what you are when there ain't a lady around. Put three heaping spoonfuls in the pot. It better be good, or I'll have your blood."

In the kitchen, Joe made clatter with pots and pans, keeping up an indignant grumbling below his breath. "He can't talk-a to me like-a that. What does he think he is, the poltroni, the birbante, the no-good bom? I'm-a the union man. I pay-a my dues. I gotta my rights. I don't got to take nuttin' from nobody."

"You better lay off Morrie Stern, Kay," said Barney soberly. "You seen what happened to the Logan goil."

"That's one good reason I can't lay off, Barney. And if he killed Claire Abbott, I've got to prove it for Nick's sake."

"You'll get your throat cut. Let me take over this part of the job. I'd like to tangle wit' that ape, Mascagni."

"I can handle this better than you, Barney. I'm close to Stern already."

"Too close, 'maybe."

"We set out to prove Nick's innocence. I'm going through with that."

"Nick wouldn't want you to stick your pretty neck out for him."

"I know it—but that isn't the point."

"Look, Kay. Muldoon is still in hospital wit' stomach ulcers but I can get my brother to look after things here for a few days. Supposin' I tag along wit' you and make sure you don't get hoit?"

"Thanks, Barney, but that won't do. We'd get nowhere."

"Might save a lot of grief."

"Perhaps—but this is something I can do best on my own."

"If you get in a jam, try to tip me off. I'll come a-runnin'. You know me—a whole squad of marines, when I go into action."

"I'll bear it in mind."

The scowling olive face of Joe appeared again in the kitchen hatch. "One pots-a tea." He said something else as well but Barney did not quite catch the last word. Barney hoped it wasn't what he thought it was, for Joe did not smile when he said it.

Sipping the steaming brew, Kay felt her overwrought nerves relaxing. She reached for another cigarette but Barney shook his head and poked the pack deeper into her handbag.

"What you wanna do? Tan your lungs like leather?"

"Old Mother Barney," smiled Kay. "Whistler ought to have painted you, bald head and all."

"If you don't think I been runnin' a kindergarten for years," responded Barney' grimly, "try handlin' my customers for a coupla days. It'd open your eyes."

In Kay's second cup of tea, he allowed her a spoonful of rum. She felt much better when, at last, she rose to go.

She spent the late afternoon and early evening at her apartment, writing down everything Janice Logan had told her and a detailed account of what had happened to the showgirl. She added to it the fact that she had seen Pretty Boy Mascagni lurking across the way from the rooming-house; and that it was Mascagni and his employer from whom Janice had been hiding. When her story of the beating was as complete as she could make it, she signed and enclosed it in an envelope addressed to Police Lieutenant Hull. The police might find some way to prove Mascagni's guilt of the brutal attack on the showgirl. It was worth-while, at least, to make them work on it. Going out, she bought a stamp at a corner drugstore and mailed the letter.

Returning to her flat, she tried to concentrate on a plan for coming closer to Morrie Stern. She had no illusion about the risks involved in such an undertaking but even if she had known positively that the venture would end in disaster to herself, she still would have carried on with it. That was a duty she owed to Nick and to a heartbroken girl in a hospital bed.

After dark, the telephone bell rang and, when she answered, a woman's voice came to her from the other end of the wire. It sounded strained and uneasy, as if the woman was mortally afraid.

"Is this Miss Bannerman?"

"Yes. What can I do for you?"

"I'm a friend of Janice Logan, the poor kid that got beaten up. I've got something to tell you, if you want to hear it."

"Certainly, I want to hear it."

"This is something I can't say over a phone."

"Then come up to my apartment."

"I'd be scared to. Someone might be watching the building. I've been riding around in a taxi for over an hour, getting up nerve enough to make this call. The cab's parked across the street from your apartment right now. If you'll join me, we can keep going while we talk."

"How did you get my name?"

"I heard a couple of girls talking."

"Who are you?"

"I'll tell you my name when I see you. Like I said, I'm a friend of Janice Logan. A lot of the girls are burned up about what happened to her but they're all too scared to do anything about it. I've got the jitters myself but I thought maybe you— If you're coming down, you'd better make it snappy. I don't want to hang around."

"I'll be right down," promised Kay.

As soon as the woman hung up, Kay dialled the number of Muldoon's Tavern but the line was busy. This was the hour at which impatient wives were tracking down erring husbands. She went to the window, parted the curtains, looked down through the darkness at the lighted street. The taxicab was there, parked beside a tree but the woman had made it plain that it would not wait there long. Again, Kay tried to telephone Barney and again she heard the droning burr that meant 'busy. Snatching up her hat, gloves and handbag, she hurried out of the apartment and pressed the button to summon the elevator.

The taxicab was still waiting across the way when she came out of the building into the quiet street. There was no traffic in sight, so she cut across the roadway in an oblique line to the vehicle, the door of which opened at her approach. Kay paused with one foot on the running-board,

peering into the darkened interior, looking for the woman who should be there. But the sole occupant of the taxi was a man. She looked into the smirking face of Pretty Boy Mascagni. He gripped her by both arms and dragged her in.

"I figured that phony call would bring you out," he gloated.

He hit her once on the jaw and her struggles ceased. Kay fell back limply against the cushions, her eyes shut.

Pretty Boy Mascagni slammed the door shut and snapped, "Get going," to the driver.

* * * * *

There were voices talking. They seemed to come from a long way off.

"I think she's coming round, boss."

"What did you have to hit her so hard for?"

"Aw, I didn't break no bones. Should I twist her ear, boss? That'll snap her out of it in a hurry."

"Nothing you enjoy so much as getting your hands on a dame, Pretty Boy."

"It's me playful nature, boss."

"I told you to bring her here, not knock her cold."

Kay opened her eyes, a dizzy awareness coming slowly back to her stunned senses. She was sitting on a wooden chair with curved arms and her hands were tied behind her back. The room was a sort of small office, walled with matchboard and glass and floored with concrete. It held a rolltop desk littered with papers, a few bentwood chairs, an antiquated safe and a filing-cabinet. A huge calendar on a wall advertised lubricating oil. The air smelled of gasoline, rubber and grease, suggesting that the office was in a garage, and the place was very quiet, except for the subdued hum of traffic from a street the building's length away.

In a swivel chair at the desk sat Morrie Stern, his snakelike eyes watching her coldly, his gloved hands toying with a long paper knife. He wore a lightweight black coat over a dinner jacket, a soft black hat drawn low on his narrow forehead, a red carnation in his button-hole. His sharp pallid face, mottled with lumps like cream cheese, was void of expression.

Behind Stern, leaning against a wall, Kay saw the bulky figure and misshapen face of Mascagni. The big man grinned at her.

"If you feel like making a noise, go ahead," said Morrie Stern, in a voice all the more frightening because it was so very quiet. "It won't do you any good—there-isn't another soul in the building and there's a vacant lot next door—except that it might relieve your feelings."

"I'll make a noise at the right time," retorted Kay defiantly. "You know there's a Federal law against kidnapping?"

"They make all kinds of laws. A fellow can't keep track of 'em. They ought to make a law against people who can't mind their own business. I hinted last night I don't like nosy dames poking into my affairs?

"That's why you killed Claire Abbott."

"Any more cracks like that," declared Pretty Boy Mascagni hoarsely, "and I'll slap you down."

"The way you slapped down Janice Logan."

The big man stepped forward menacingly, but Morrie Stern motioned him back with a languid wave of his hand.

"Let her talk. She likes to talk, don't you, baby?"

"She's got too much lip," snarled Mascagni. "Leave me take a sock at her, boss."

"You're too impatient, Pretty Boy. Always in a hurry." The

night club owner's dark glittering little eyes studied Kay's face with a detached interest, as they might have studied a laboratory specimen. "Maybe you'll have the privilege of working on Miss Bannerman later. Right now, I've got things to talk to her about. Things like this, for instance."

Producing a clipping from his wallet, he held it out to Kay, who took it in fingers whose tremor she could not control. It was a sentence from the Broadway gossip column which Kay had read that morning. "…The rumour goes that Claire Abbott was popped-off by a gent using as his alias the name of a colour…"

"You had a lot to say to Ben Firman last night," said Morrie Stern very quietly, very coldly. "He didn't think that item up himself—you gave it to him. What are you trying to do, Miss Bannerman? Frame me?"

"That's funny," replied Kay. "Very, very funny. You'd make a lovely picture."

"Go ahead, laugh. Have a good time. Maybe things won't seem so funny after a time. Maybe you'll find out that I have a sense of humour, too. A different sense of humour from most people, perhaps."

"Are you trying to frighten me, Mr.—" Kay paused. "I'm afraid my memory for colours isn't good."

"I don't have to frighten you, sister. You're scared to death already. It's only your nerve that's keeping you sitting on your fanny, instead of falling on your face. How did you find out about the 'Mr. White' gag?"

"Perhaps I know a lot more than you think—Mr. White."

"Perhaps you do, sister, but you're going to tell me all of it. It may take time—but you'll tell me. The Pretty Boy, here, has an awful persuasive way with little girls."

"I'd like to see him stand up to a man," said Kay contemptuously.

Mascagni lunged forward like a snarling animal but once more his employer waved him back.

"Take it easy, dimwit. You don't start to work until her tongue stops wagging. What did you do with the papers, Miss Bannerman?"

"The papers?"

"Quit stalling. You know the ones I mean."

"Oh, those," said Kay, trying desperately hard to speak calmly. "The papers Claire Abbott held over you like a club? The signed statements that implicate you in the vice racket?"

A muffled grunt came from Pretty Boy Mascagni but his master only looked bleak.

"You're a pretty smart number, Miss Bannerman."

"Claire Abbott must have wanted a heavy price for her silence, Mr. White."

"I paid her plenty. She collected—but good—every week. That's over now and I'm not going to let it start again. I want those papers."

"What makes you think I have them? After all, you killed Claire Abbott to get them."

"I'm telling ya," rasped Pretty Boy Mascagni, "just one more crack and I slap you down."

"And I'll sit here and watch him do it," said Morrie Stern. "He does a thorough job when he starts, sister. You ought to know that."

In spite of herself, Kay swallowed convulsively and her face, already pale, became deathly white.

"And, sister," said Morrie Stern, quite wearily, "don't imagine you're going to live to squawk about what happened to you. When Pretty Boy gets through, you'll need the death wagon, not an ambulance. Better tell me where those papers are."

"I haven't got them."

"Too bad," sighed the night club owner. "They might have saved your life."

With a shudder, Kay closed her eyes. This is what Barney was afraid of, she thought; this is what he wanted to protect me from. If I'd listened to him… But, if it was all to do, over again, she would still refuse to listen, she knew that.

"Wait a minute," she said, opening her eyes again. "I'll talk. I left the papers with a friend."

"Now we're getting somewhere. What's your friend's name?"

"His name is—is Dorian."

The night club owner stared. "That's a crummy name for a man. Where does he live?"

"He wouldn't be home now. I can reach him by phone."

"You wouldn't be trying to pull a fast one?"

"Is it likely?"

"I wouldn't know. You're a new kind of dame to me. I never met anyone just like you before. How would I know how to figure you?"

"My friend has the papers on him. I could tell him to bring them here."

"There's the phone," said Morrie Stern, "but don't tell him a word more than I tell you to say."

"You're forgetting my hands," said Kay, twisting her body to show that her arms were still tied.

"Cut her loose," said Morrie Stern, to Mascagni.

When the ropes fell from her wrists, Kay massaged the chafed members. She picked up the telephone.

"Don't say anything to warn this guy."

"How could I, with you listening?"

"You might take a chance. Don't. It wouldn't be healthy."

Kay dialled the number of Muldoon's Tavern. When Barney answered, she said, "Is that you—Dorian?"

"I told you I come out fightin' when anyone calls me that," he retorted angrily.

"That's fine," said Kay steadily.

There was a pregnant silence at the other end of the wire and then Barney said, "I get it. You're in a jam."

"Tell him you want the papers," prompted Morrie Stern, leaning forward in his chair.

"You remember those papers I gave you to keep for me?" said Kay, into the mouthpiece. "Well, I need them at once."

"Everything is okay,' whispered Stern. "You're with friends. You just need the papers, that's all."

"Everything is okay," repeated Kay, "I'm with friends. I just happen to need the papers."

The night club owner covered the mouthpiece with his hand. "Could this Dorian guy make it to the corner of Fortieth and Broadway from where he is in thirty minutes?"

"Easily," replied Kay.

"Then, tell him a black sedan will pick him up there in half an hour," said the night club owner. "Then tell him 'au revoir.'"

Kay repeated the message into the telephone. "Don't give the papers to anyone but me," she added, the moment before she hung up.

"What was the idea of that last crack?" demanded Morrie Stern. "I didn't tell you to say that."

"It was a little idea of my own."

"I told you not to get ideas."

"There isn't any harm in it. After all, you're trading my life for the papers, aren't you? I only wanted to make sure my friend wouldn't part with them until I gave the word."

"Okay," said Morrie Stern softly. "In fifteen minutes, Pretty Boy, you can drive over and bring that guy back here. You've got a gun, in case he starts anything?"

Mascagni patted his left armpit and nodded.

"My friend won't start anything," said Kay lightly. "You didn't hear me say anything to warn him, did you?"

"Frisk the guy when he gets into the car. Make sure he isn't armed before you bring him here."

"I'll see he ain't got as much as a toothpick on him, boss."

To Kay, it seemed a long time before Mascagni left to fetch Barney and a still longer time while she and Morrie Stern sat in the little office awaiting their arrival. The night club owner took an automatic pistol from his pocket and laid it on the desk close to his drumming fingers. "Just to make sure," he remarked, with a baleful, glance at Kay, "that this little party is run my way."

When the bodyguard ushered Barney in he was holding a gun against the barman's ribs. Kay's eyes went at once to Barney's hands. It was the first time she had seen him wearing gloves. They were at least a size too big and made his hands look even larger than usual.

"I frisked the guy from head to heels, boss," said Pretty Boy. "He ain't got a thing on him but a long envelope."

"I'll take that," said Stern quickly, holding out his hand.

Barney glanced questioningly at Kay. She did not know the right answer but she nodded her head numbly. The barman reached for an inside pocket.

"Keep your hands down," ordered the night club owner, his fingers closing on his automatic. "Mascagni will find the envelope."

Shifting to the barman's front, Mascagni put a hand inside Barney's coat and brought it out holding a long envelope. He handed it to his master, who tore it open, revealing some folded sheets of newspaper. At that moment, Kay learned why Barney was wearing gloves. Barney hit Pretty Boy full in the face and his glove split up the back, uncovering the brass knuckles they had been worn to hide.

The punch, given authority by several ounces of brass, rendered Mascagni unconscious on his feet. He toppled forward, his large body unnaturally stiff, and the gun fell from his nerveless fingers and clattered across the floor.

Morrie Stern brought up his own gun and Kay kicked it out of his hand. She had been planning the kick ever since the night club owner produced the weapon and it was as successful as if she had rehearsed it many times. Barney pulled Stern up by the lapels with one hand and knocked him back into the chair with the other. There was no need for a second punch.

Kay tried to pick up the telephone but sank back, shaken and helpless, into a chair. "Barney, I can't. Oh, Barney, I think I'm going to have hysterics."

"If you do," said Barney grimly; "I'll slap you, too. What number d'you want?"

"T-the p-police."

Barney put the call through. It was due to sheer absentmindedness—and the crowded state of the tiny office—that he stood on Pretty Boy Mascagni's face while he did so.

Chapter 18

When the curtain fell at the end of the first act, Julian turned his face to his companion. "Shall we go out for a smoke?" His smooth yellow hair and long aristocratic nose reminded Althea for a moment of the neat, yellow-feathered head of a canary. "I shan't smoke," she replied, rising, "but I'll come for a stroll while you do. The air in here is rather stuffy." Julian placed her light evening wrap, almost reverently, around her lovely shoulders and they inched their way over feet and ankles to the aisle. The doors at the rear of the auditorium stood wide open. Little groups of playgoers were flocking out to the sidewalk, fanning themselves with programs, fumbling in pockets for cigarettes.

"Hello, Althea. Hello, Julian," said a tall man in tails. He was a successful publisher whom they both knew. "I say, Julian, what about that book you promised me? It's long overdue, you know."

"I'm sorry, Dick," replied Julian, looking annoyed. "I'm afraid the whole idea has turned out to be a bore. I'll drop in on you in a day or two and we'll talk about something else I have in mind."

Reaching the sidewalk, Julian drew Althea a little apart from the knots of men in starched shirts and women with bared bosoms.

"I've seen this thing before. Jannings hardly appears in the second act, until just at the end. I thought, with your approval, it might be an idea to tackle him now."

"I'd like to," replied Althea without. hesitation. "I don't really care about seeing the rest of the play. I've seen it so many times before—under different titles."

"That's the nostalgic quality about farce. Always the same

time-hallowed situations. I think we'll find the stage door round that corner. Will you back Mr. Jannings against the wall of his dressing-room and force him to tell all, or shall I?"

"We'd better feel our way, at first. After all, we can't ask the man point-blank if he's a criminal masquerading under an alias."

"It would be rather fun but I suppose we'd better not. You have the clipping, haven't you?"

"Yes, it's in my handbag. I thought we'd try him with that first."

"Clever of Kay to think of it," said Julian, pushing open the stage door.

"Kay is clever. And a dear person. I hope she doesn't get in deep water with that Morrie Stern. I haven't seen her since we parted company outside the hospital."

A fat man, with a discouraging eye, sat just inside the stage door, in a chair tilted at an alarming angle. In a blackened pipe, he was smoking what smelt like scraps of old sock.

"We'd like to see Mr. Jannings," said Julian.

"Ar," said the doorkeeper grudgingly.

"Will you see that he gets my card?"

Holding the calling card daintily between thumb and forefinger, as if suspecting germs, the doorkeeper let his chair down, rose with a grunt and a sigh, and waddled into the bowels of the building. In a few minutes he waddled out again, lowered himself wheezily into the chair, balanced it on its back legs; and jerked a nicotine-stained thumb at a corridor.

"End of the passage. First left. Third door on the right."

"Thank you," said Julian politely.

"Ar," said the doorkeeper.

They followed instructions to the letter and found the dressing-room occupied by Arno Jannings, who received them in a red silk robe.

"Mr. Deering?"

Julian nodded his head and introduced the actor to Althea. Arno Jannings said it was a pleasure, he was sure.

"We liked your performance in the first act," said Julian. "It had a subtlety all too rare these days."

"Do you really think so?" cried Jannings delightedly.

"My dear chap, I thought the delicate shades of meaning, you insinuated into your scene with Miss What's-her-name a superb piece of stagecraft. I'd like you to come to my studio for a sitting one day soon, if you will. The illustrated papers are always after me for photographs of important stage personalities."

Althea looked as if she thought Julian was laying it on much too thick but the actor was unaffectedly pleased. He said, however, that he rarely cared to have his photograph taken; the camera so seldom did him justice.

"I can see what you mean," replied Julian, studying the actor's face from a number of angles (and having difficulty in keeping his own face straight). "I'm quite sure, though, that with care—I could do justice to that chin and the Grecian quality of the nose."

"Supposing I think it over and give you a ring? By the way, won't you sit down? Stupid of me, I should have suggested it before."

The actor brought a chair for Althea and Julian seated himself in a corner, conveniently near a row of highly polished shoes. While Jannings gave Althea a cigarette and a light, Julian ran an exploring hand over one of the shoes, inside and out.

"No, thanks," he said, when Jannings turned to him, holding out a gold case, "I prefer the longer ones. Do you know, I used to smoke some that were quite two inches longer than the ordinary size."

"I don't think I've ever seen any as long as that," commented Jannings, lighting a cigarette himself.

"Oh, yes, I assure you," replied Julian, catching Althea's eye. "Quite two inches."

Althea made a barely perceptible nod to show him that she understood. Opening her handbag, she produced a newspaper clipping.

"We were rather interested in this item about you in Ben Firman's column," she said casually, offering it to the actor. "Have you read it?"

Running his eyes over the clipping, Jannings read the first line or so and his face blanched. "...The rumour goes that Claire Abbott was popped-off by a gent using as his alias the name of a color..." The actor gaped at Althea, his, mouth open, his eyes goggling.

"Wh-what makes you think this is about me?"

"It gives your name, doesn't it? Oh, I see. You thought I meant the first part."

Looking over the clipping again, Jannings realized that there was more to it than he had read at first. "...Set for a marathon run is the back-bedroom comedy in which one Arno Jannings made his first New York appearance. The face is familiar, Mr. Jannings—but I can't quite place the name..."

"Foolish of me. For a moment, I thought—"

"That I meant the part about the man who killed Claire Abbott."

"Absurd, isn't it? Why, I didn't know the woman."

"Not even under the name of Claire Jansen?" asked Julian.

Sitting down rather heavily, Jannings put out a hand that trembled and laid the clipping on his dressing-table. His upper lip and brow were moist with perspiration.

"D-did she go by that n-name once? No, I never met her. I read about the murder in the p-papers, of course. I suppose most p-people did, didn't they?"

Neither of the others spoke. The actor picked up a comb and twiddled it in his fingers. He dropped it. Picked it up. Dropped it. Let it lie. He opened his cigarette case and snapped it shut.

"Would either of you care for a drink or—or anything?" he said, unable to bear the silence.

With an air of idle curiosity, Althea looked into the actor's make-up box, open on the table. Watching Jannings's face in the mirror, she took out a stick of white greasepaint. He looked at the white stick but his expression did not vary. She selected a brown one; but that colour, too, seemed to have no particular significance for him. Even a stick of black produced no reaction in the actor.

"There's no green here," she remarked, as if musing aloud. "I suppose green isn't a colour for which you'd have much use."

"They used green a lot in the old-time melodramas," said Julian, following Althea's cue. "The villain's face was always bathed in green light. I imagine there is something sinister about green. Do you feel the significance of colour, Mr. James? What, for instance, is suggested to you by green?"

"I don't know why you keep harping on the word," said Jannings shakily, irritably. "And my name isn't Mr. James."

"Absentminded of me, Mr. Jansen. Do forgive me, Mr. Jansen."

"It isn't Jansen, either. What are you trying to do? I don't understand all this."

"Don't you really—Mr. Green?" murmured Althea softly.

The actor's face turned a ghastly shade remarkably like the colour they kept repeating.

"I think you do, Mr. Green," said Julian pleasantly.

"You'll have to excuse me now. I'm due back on the stage."

"You aren't due on the stage for"—Julian consulted his watch—"fully twenty minutes, Mr. Green. That will give us time for quite a long chat. Even if the audience has to wait for you, Mr. Jansen, it won't have to wait nearly as long as the Kansas City police. They've waited almost four years for you, Mr. Jansen."

In a panic, the actor jumped up and backed to the door, glaring about him distractedly like a rat cornered by two determined terriers.

"I shouldn't advise you to make a run for it," remarked Althea. "That would only make things look even blacker for you, Mr. James."

"Or Mr. Jansen or Mr. Jannings," added Julian. "We really must make up our minds what name we're going to use. We can't go on peopling this little room with conflicting personalities. Personally, I agree with the late Claire Day-Jansen-Abbott in preferring 'Mr. Green.' Such a nice simple name for use on the telephone. I advise you to shut that door again, Mr. Green. There are two policemen waiting in the passage."

The actor quickly slammed the door and went backwards across the room until halted by the dressing-table.

"You might have given me a chance, instead of bringing the police with you. After all, it happened a long time ago and I've paid plenty for it— I've gone through hell. I don't know how you found out all about me—"

"Oh, we don't know quite all about you," replied Julian offhandedly. "There are one or two details you might fill in for us. We may be able to make this easier for you, if you do. Sit down and smoke a cigarette and tell us the whole story."

The actor sat down but did not smoke the cigarette he took from his gold case. His twitching fingers plucked at it until they had reduced it to shreds. "I was only a kid," he said, "at the time of the holdup."

"Oh, yes, the holdup," said Julian, blinking a little. Althea, too, looked surprised. "By all means, let's start with the holdup."

"I was broke and friendless in a strange city and hadn't had a bite to eat for two days. The show I was in had folded, leaving me high and dry. It happened that one of the props I'd used in my part was a gun—not a real gun, just a dummy that fired blanks. I—I—well, I was desperate and starving and couldn't think straight. All I knew was that I had to have money, so I walked into a store and threatened the man behind the counter with the gun. He handed over all there was in the till—about forty dollars—but when I made for the door he crouched down behind the counter and started to yell. Scared stiff, I dropped the gun and took to my heels. I don't know to this day how I got away. I simply kept on running and never looked back until I stumbled across the tracks of a freight yard. A train was pulling out. I swung aboard it; and was two hundred miles away by morning. I was still scared, though, for I knew my fingerprints were smeared all over the dummy gun I left behind."

"You can be sure those fingerprints have been very carefully preserved," said Julian.

"Do you think they haven't haunted me? Well, my luck changed a little. Nothing to write home about but I got one part after another in third-rate touring shows—it was a living. And then, I met Claire."

"She was Claire Day then," remarked Althea. "You appeared together in a farce called 'You Can't Fool Margie.'"

"That's right. You've got it all down pat, haven't you? It's a wonder you bother to listen to me. Well, I fell in love with Claire—there was something about her that got me—and in a weak moment told her about the holdup."

"There's one thing I'd like to get straight," said Althea. "Were you married to Claire?"

The actor shook his head. "She wouldn't marry me. I hadn't enough to offer her. We—we just roomed together on tour."

Althea looked disappointed.

"After the show we were in folded in St. Louis, Claire and I were on the rocks for a time. Being broke bothered Claire more than it bothered me. I was satisfied if we could eat. She wanted a lot more. So, she suggested a plan to make money. She'd pick up some rich sucker and take him to her room. After a while I was to rush in, posing as her husband—and we'd shake down the sucker."

"The badger game," said Althea.

"Sure, the badger game. I didn't want any part of it, but Claire threatened to turn me in for that holdup unless I agreed to her scheme, so I strung along with her—for a while. The first chance I got; I ran out on her. It was only a coincidence that the cops walked in almost as I ran out, but I guess Claire thought I had ratted on her.

"Well, I changed my name again and lay low for several years, working at a soda fountain, clerking in a store, doing the best I could, always avoiding the stage, for that's where she'd look for me. All that time I hadn't the slightest idea where Claire was. I thought she'd still be out West, where I met her, so I worked my way East. And then I got a chance to join the company of a summer theatre in Maine and I just couldn't refuse it. I was itching to walk onto a stage, again. Abe Meyer saw me up there and offered me the part I'm playing now. I knew it meant taking a chance, appearing on Broadway, perhaps having my picture in the papers, but the offer was so good I couldn't turn it down.

"My first visitor, a few nights after we opened, was Claire. She came straight to the point. I was still wanted for that holdup. I could go to jail—or pay her to keep her mouth shut. What could I do? Every Week, after that, she collected two thirds of my salary."

"You used the name of Mr. Green when you phoned her? When you paid her, you did it in a taxi in Central Park?"

"Yes, those were her ideas."

"And at last," said. Julian, very softly, "you became so tired of parting with the lion's share of your income, that you went to her apartment and put a bullet through her?"

The actor almost fell off his, chair. He stared from Julian to Althea, his face working pitiably.

"My God, no. It wasn't I who killed her. You've got to believe me. I swear I didn't do it. I was never even in her apartment. God, you wouldn't try to frame me, would you? I couldn't kill another human being—not even a harpy like Claire."

"We wouldn't frame you," said Althea coldly, standing up. "Nor are we prepared to accept your unsupported word in the matter. You're very convincing but then, you're an actor, aren't you? We'll want to see you again. If it turns out that you didn't kill Claire Abbott, we might be prepared to suppress what we've learned about the holdup—but I warn you not to try to run away in the meantime."

"What about the policemen waiting in the corridor?"

"They don't exist."

Julian took something small from his pocket and held it upon a level with his eyes. There was a little click. "Look over there, please," he said casually, pointing a finger at a wall.

Too dulled in mind to comprehend what was happening, the actor numbly obeyed. There was another click and Julian replaced the small object in his pocket.

"I've just taken two candid camera shots of you, Mr. Green. They'll be invaluable to the police, if you try to make a getaway."

* * * * *

Althea kept an apartment on Park Avenue for the rare occasions on which she spent the night in town. She and Julian went there from the theatre and dialled Kay's telephone number. There was no answer. They chatted, for half an hour and tried again to put the call through, with the same result. Julian telephoned Muldoon's Tavern and was told that Barney had gone out, leaving his brother in charge. It was late—and Althea was anxious—before they succeeded in talking on the telephone to Kay.

Coming to Althea over the wire, Kay's voice shook with elation and excitement. "The police have arrested Morrie Stern and Mascagni. Stern was Mr. White in Claire's colourful list of acquaintances."

"Mr. Deering and I have discovered Mr. Green. He is Arno Jannings, alias Arthur Jansen, alias Arnold James. He had quite a story to tell."

"That's swell. Morrie Stern and his henchman both have alibis for the time of the murder—but, of course, men like that would arrange their alibis in advance. The police are holding them for the attack on Janice Logan, for violations of the Sullivan Law—and for kidnapping me."

"For kidnapping you?" gasped Althea faintly.

"Yes. I'll tell you all about it in the morning. The police are questioning them separately, in the hope that one of them will break down and rat on the other. For once, I don't feel the least bit indignant about Third Degree methods!"

Chapter 19

The bed was soft and warm and had a piney fragrance. It held him in loving embrace, yielding to the contours of his body. It seemed to know that his body was weak. He felt he wanted to stay in it for ever. Age had softened the blanket and through its fluffy weave he could see daylight. He put one eye out, glimpsing an uneven plaster wall, yellow-washed, and a corner of a low ceiling, freshly white. The bit of a room he could see was bathed in bright sunlight and sweet with the smell of flowers and other growing things.

He could not remember what had happened to him after he dived from the rail of the rusty tramp but this part of it was good. He had a reluctance to know more: nothing could be as good as this bed. The way he felt, puny and new-born, one could quite easily fall in love with a bed like this.

"Appears you're beginnin' to take notice," said a dry old voice.

Nick had not known that anyone was nearby. For a time, he lay quite still, hoping that whoever was there would go away. He heard a chair creaking and knew that this person had been sitting in the room when he opened his eyes and was settling comfortably, unlikely to budge. With turtle-like caution, he put his head out, stretching his neck to look across the room.

By the huge black mouth of a fireplace a very clean old man was sitting in a wheel-backed chair, with a blackthorn stick across his knees. His skin was pink; his hair and moustache white; his eyes, by far the liveliest part of him, blue as a summer sky. He wore faded overalls and a white shirt open at the neck. He was a kindly old man and a shrewd old man— Nick saw that at a glance—and his wrinkled brown hands told that he had worked hard all his life. Stretched at his slippered feet lay a full-grown red setter.

"Right nice day for a man to open his eyes to," said the old man, with a smile. "I was born on a day like this and I know."

"I feel as if I'd just been born myself," said Nick feebly.

"A man is born more times than one and that's a fact. There's nothing you'd want that couldn't wait a spell, I s'pose? My old bones make slow work of risin' once they're set in a chair and my boy Seth won't be home for a good hour."

"No, there's nothing I want." Nick lay back on the pillow and closed his eyes. "How long have I been here?"

"This is the fourth mornin' since Seth fished you out'n the sea. I guess you're mighty nigh the bigges' fish he ever did catch. He was alone in his motorboat and it was all he could do to haul you in. You were a good seven miles out, so Seth reckoned you must have fallen overboard from some ship."

"Yes, I remember. I fell overboard. Seven miles out, you said? I made a good try at swimming—the wrong way." There was a pause before Nick spoke again. "Who knows I'm here?"

"We couldn't let your folks know," replied the old man evenly. "Wasn't a thing on you to tell who you were. We had the doctor up from the village to look at you. He said he reckoned you'd live, so we saw no call to have him more'n just the once."

"Who lives here?"

"Why, I do," said the old man reasonably.

"I mean, apart from you."

"My boy Seth; Old Jed, here"—the dog looked up, wagging his tail at the sound of his name—"and a passel of chickens. There ain't another livin' soul within three-four miles—less'n you count a whole ocean full of fishes."

"And I've been unconscious for four days?"

"Close on four. You had one lucid spell when you told me you were workin' your way through college—but I guess you weren't rightly clear in the head, at that, for if a man ain't had his share of schoolin', time he's your age, I don't know when he'd expect to get it."

Nick must have fallen asleep again, for he knew no more until he opened his eyes in the scented dusk and lay listening to the beat of waves on a beach. Curious to find out whether he could stand, he sat up and slid shaking legs out from under the blankets, onto the floor. He was wearing a long flannel nightshirt. He almost fell the first time he trusted himself to his feet. At a second try, he tottered to the window and looked out at a garden hushed in moonlight, enclosed by a white picket fence, beyond which foam-crested breakers lapped and swished on the sentinel rocks of a pebbled beach.

Hearing a sound behind him, he turned unsteadily and saw a man peering into the room with a lantern in his hand. So tall he had to keep his head bent to avoid bumping it on the ceiling, the man was as thin as a scarecrow limbed with broomsticks. He came further in, placing the lantern on a table. He was dressed like the old man, in overalls, his shirtsleeves rolled above knobbly elbows. Approaching forty; thin of face; mild of eye. The short hair that bristled all over his head made him look as if he had fallen under a lawnmower.

"Heard you stirrin', figured maybe there was somethin' I could do for you. I'm Seth Jameson. My dad said you come alive this mornin'. It's a mite soon for you to be walkin', seems like."

"I'm afraid you're right," agreed Nick.

His legs would not stop trembling. Putting an arm about his shoulders, Seth helped him back to bed and covered him as gently as a woman might.

"You must be plumb hollow inside. Ain't had a bite to eat since I fished you out'n the sea, less'n you count a spoonful of gruel you like to choked on when I tried to feed you. I'll fix you somethin'. Could you stomach an egg?"

She Got What She Asked For 203

"I could stomach an ostrich egg," said Nick, who was famished.

"We don't keep ostriches," replied Seth soberly, "but we keep hens."

He went out. Before long he returned bearing a laden tray spread with a checked cloth. The food was good and Nick did justice to it. While he ate, Seth sat on the edge of the bed, his eyes politely averted.

"Old Doc said he couldn't do nothin' about your nose. Needed a surgeon, he said—he didn't care to risk tackling the job himself."

"My nose?" Nick put up a hand and felt his face. It was oddly unfamiliar to the touch.

"You must have hit your nose when you fell off'n the ship. It's pretty badly out of shape. Old Doc said, though, a good surgeon could fix it up like it was before."

The lanky fisherman took a roll of crinkled and discoloured bills from his pocket and laid it by Nick's knee.

"Found this money on you when I took off your pants. More'n two hundred dollars. It was pretty much of a mess, all squelched up together, so I dried it in the sun. Don't look like money ought to look but you can still make out the numbers on the bills, so I reckon a bank will change 'em. 'Fraid your pants won't be no more good to you. The salt water shrunk 'em plumb up to your shins. Don't reckon, my things, or my dad's, would fit you, so when you feel well enough to be up and about, I'll fetch you something to wear from the village store. Old Man Farley don't carry much of a stock but you're a handy size, so I guess he'll be able to fix you up one way or another.'

"Could you get me the things tomorrow? A suit and a shirt and underwear and socks and a tie and shoes?"

"Reckon I could. Don't figure to be needin' 'em that soon, though, do you?"

"I'm feeling fine," said Nick, pushing aside the tray. "Just fine. I'll be walking tomorrow. I can't impose on your, hospitality much longer,"

"We don't look at it that way. Stay as long as you like. My dad and me, we're mighty glad to have you."

Alone again, Nick lay on his back in the darkened room, looking up at the silvering of moonlight on the ceiling and listening to the murmur of the sea. When you run away from something, he thought, no matter what it is, you're running away from yourself. A man's a fool to try, for he keeps catching up with himself. His inner self, the self that knows him utterly and minutely. The self that wakens him in the still, small hours and forces him to look while it parades before his eyes his follies and misdeeds; that forces him to listen while it whispers his shabby story in his ears. The self with which a man cannot win an argument, for it knows all the answers.

He had tried to run from himself, dulling his senses with drink, drugging his wits with apathy, in the months before Claire's death, after she told him to go. He had let himself become a drifter and a wastrel, squandering his youth and denying his intelligence, because in his love for her he had thrown at Claire's feet all that he had, all that he was; and because his manhood had not been strong enough to rise above humiliation and rejection. He had crawled on his belly like the lowliest thing that lives, and his flesh crawled now at the thought of it.

In running from the law, what had he done but run from himself, tacitly admitting his guilt in the eyes of men? Avoiding a question does not answer it; evading an issue does not solve it; skirting a difficulty does not surmount it.

He had run away from New York in the same weak spirit as he had run away from himself four months before. He had not tried to prove his innocence; he had not thought of trying; he had left that to others. If there was risk to the undertaking, he had left the risk to others also. The truth about Claire's death was hidden in New York but he had not sought it there. He had turned his back on the truth and on the self-reliance that makes a man a man. To have remained in New York might have cost him his life but running away was costing him everything that makes life precious. A man is not born to hide himself in a hole like a hunted animal. A man cannot live under a stone. A man must live among men and be able to look them in the face. A fugitive is only an uncoffined corpse, denied the rights, the friendships, the familiar hearth and precious home of the living.

Nick turned and tossed and said, aloud, "For God's sake, shut up"; but his inner self would not be stilled.

Against his will, his thoughts went back to the night on which he saw Claire for the first time. Until that night he had had little time to spare for anything but work; he knew little about women; less about gaiety. A friend had persuaded him to go to a party at somebody's penthouse and Nick had been very bored with it all until a blond woman came in, moving as if to the music of an unseen orchestra. Nick thought her the loveliest thing he had ever seen. Her escort was drunk and became obnoxious, and Nick rescued her from an awkward situation. Soon after, they left the party and went to a little café Claire knew. Nick talked a lot—words intoxicated him that night—and Claire listened, seeming to understand him as no other person ever had. It was late when he took her home and, in the morning, he telephoned her and they had luncheon together. For three breathless weeks they had been together almost constantly and then one evening they drove over to New Jersey and were married by a sleepy Justice of the Peace in a nine o'clock town. Nick did not realize then that he did not know a thing about Claire, except that outwardly she was lovely. She had never said a word which would give him a clue to her real self; everything she said as guarded and considered, although having the air of spontaneity. He found out about her, about her shallowness and selfishness, about her greed and cunning, all too soon. One day he realised that the unseen orchestra to whose music she seemed to move was playing something like 'Frankie and Johnny.'

Long into the night, Nick's brain was restlessly filled with things he would far sooner have forgotten.

In the morning, he told the old man that he must leave as soon as he could walk with confidence.

"Couple of days of sun and good food'll put the strength back in your muscles," said the old man, eyeing him calmly. "But what's your hurry? Time goes slowly here."

"I have to get back to New York. I have business to attend to."

After a pause, the old man said, in a kindly tone, "I kind of hoped you'd tell me that. When you're in trouble, son, it's best to face it—even when it's trouble with the law."

"Then you know?"

"You were delirious, the first day you were here. You raved a good deal."

"You didn't think of calling the police? For all you know, there might be a reward for me."

"I wouldn't want money with another man's misery in it. You haven't the eyes of a bad man, son. I figured I'd leave you to work out your own salvation."

Nick found it easier to rise than he had done on the previous evening. His legs still shook but they carried him, without stumbling, across the room. On his slow and careful journey to the window he glimpsed himself in a mirror and uttered an exclamation of surprise. Going closer to the mirror, he stared into it at a face that must be his own —and that was the face of a stranger.

Chapter 20

The scenic railway, an octopus hunched against the sky line, with beetles crawling and darting over it; the gay-striped tents, dotting the area like colourful fungi; the Ferris-wheel, whirling its cargo of shrieking girls in the arms of boys; a score of asthmatic calliopes, murdering last year's melodies; a giggle of children, eyes big, mouths never closing, going round and round on sedate painted horses with solemn painted faces; a deadpan spider droning, 'Fanny the Fat Goil, ladeez and gen'l'men. Two quivering tons of femeenine allure'; a little man with bone-ridged face, a moustache like a misplaced eyebrow and an open suitcase on metal legs in front of him, saying persuasively, 'Step a little closer, folks, if you please'; the bang and ping of the shooting gallery; the metallic laughter of the machinegun range; a stentorian voice shouting, 'Everyone a winnah, folks, everyone a winnah.'

"Get 'em while they're hot, folks."

"Get 'em while they're cold."

"Get 'em while they last."

With the uncomfortable feeling of eyes boring into his spine, Barney ducked into an opening between two stalls and scrutinised the scantily clad amusement-seekers who meandered by, but spotted no one of whom he could be suspicious. Cutting across untidy lots behind wooden structures, he covered two hundred yards in the direction from which he had come. Reaching the boardwalk again through another gap, he tried to detect a possible shadower, but decided, at last, that he must have been mistaken.

Pausing at a hotdog stand, he selected the plumpest and juiciest of a row of frankfurters sizzling on a grill.

"That one," he said, pointing.

"Kinda choosey, ain't ya?" grinned the white-capped counterman.

"I know what I like. Dab on plenty of relish."

The counterman smothered the hot dog in moist green fragments.

"And a good big pickle," said Barney.

"We got two kinds. Which d'ya want?"

"Both."

"It's your mouth, mister—but you're gonna hafta stretch it."

"Now a scoop of mustard."

"Here you are, mister," said the counterman, presenting the bulging bun with a flourish. "An', if that ain't the biggest value on the boardwalk, bring it back an' I'll stuff it with cheese and chili."

"I don't care for chili—but a little cheese would go good."

The counterman sighed. "Sarcasms wasted on some folks," he remarked, cutting a strip of cheese and topping the hot dog with it.

As Barney walked on, a hand plucked at his arm.

"Here you are, buddy, get your picture taken. A beautiful portrait for the piano and only a quarter."

A perspiring man in startling checks and a vivid orange necktie tried to drag him into a curtained booth flanked by photographed faces, toothily smiling. "You took my picture two-three years ago. At least, I guess it was you. The guy who took it had been woikin' a pitch here for a long time."

"That's me, buddy. Twenty years on the boardwalk. Step right inside, buddy."

"If you been here so long you probably knew that jane that was murdered, Claire Abbott."

"Did I know her? He's askin' me, did I know her? Miss B.U., I used to call her."

"Huh?"

"Miss Biological Urge, buddy. She bared a lovely torso ten times a day, right over there where the bearded lady is now."

"I guess she got too high hat for Coney, after she fixed herself with an apartment on Park Avenue."

"That's where you're wrong, buddy. She was here only a couple of days before she was bumped off."

"There wasn't a man with her, I suppose?"

"You don't think she was leadin' a trained seal? Sure, she had a man with her. With a shape like she had, there'd always be a man with her."

"Remember what he looked like?"

"Well, I'll tell you, buddy. He had two legs, two arms and a face. More'n that, I wouldn't care to say. When a goil walks by with a fanny like Claire's, giving it that old swing, I don't waste no time lookin' at no man. Step inside, buddy, a lifelike camera portrait for only two bits."

"I guess not," said Barney. He had no illusions about his own excessive homeliness. The twin warts embellishing his face had a sad habit of dominating such rare pictures as were taken of him.

"Only two bits, buddy, the fourth part of a dollar, for a portrait to grace your parlour piano."

"We ain't got a piano. And we ain't got a parlour."

"Don't tell me you ain't got a quarter. Tell you what I'll do—business is slack—I'll make you a special price of a dime. One thin dime, buddy."

Barney turned away, licking relish off his chin.

"I don't blame you, buddy," the photographer shouted after him. "With a face like yours."

Wheel of fortune. Wall of death. Wave of the future. 'Here you are, folks, it's ice cold. Get your ice cold pop here.' 'Fresh roasted peanuts, a nickel a bag.'

Barney stopped at a shooting gallery and picked up a rifle.

The attendant made haste to load it. A blasé look on his long face, Barney downed ten toy parachute troopers in ten shots.

"Fancy shootin', mister. Try another load?"

"What for? It don't hurt Hitler none."

"Maybe not—but it's good practice in case the bastard ever shows his face over here."

"You're a bright kid," said Barney, accepting the reloaded gun the youngster thrust into his hands. "I'll bet you keep, your eyes open."

"Leading up to what?" asked the lad suspiciously.

Repeating his previous performance with the rifle, Barney looked bored. "Maybe you knew Claire Abbott?"

"The dame that was killed? Sure, I knew her. She stopped at this stall a day or two before she was shot. So what?"

"So maybe you noticed the guy that was wit' her ?"

"Sure, I noticed him. He was a swell shot."

"That ain't what I mean. What did he look like?"

"He looked like he could handle a rifle. 'At's all 'at interested me. I'll load her again, mister."

"What's the good?" grunted Barney, flipping a coin to the boy. "I'm shootin' at the wrong target."

He went on down the boardwalk, stopping briefly here and there to spend a nickel or dime judiciously and fish for information. He had little luck. Most of the concessionaires had known Claire Abbott and noticed her on the visit to Coney Island shortly before her death, but they shook their heads and shrugged their shoulders when he asked about her male companion.

At a hoopla stall, he ringed a cheap compact, a 'solid gold' bracelet which would turn the wearer's wrist green, and a pair of binoculars. Handing the latter article to Barney, the attendant looked glum. Those binoculars were only intended as a lure. It was supposed to be impossible to ring them.

"Keep 'em," said Barney, pocketing the compact.

"Gee, t'anks. The boss gits sore when someone walks off wit' binoculars. They cost him ten bucks a dozen. That ain't hay."

"Yeah, I know. They tell me Claire Abbott was out here a coupla days before she was bumped off."

"That's right, mister. Saw her myself. Boy, she had everything."

"You notice the guy wit' her?"

"Well, you know how it is—"

"Yeah," said Barney disgustedly, "I know how it is."

"She had a lot on the ball, that Claire Abbott. I coulda gone for her in a big way. I made a play for her when she did her striptease here at Coney but she never give me a tumble. Boy, she was certainly hard to get. I was boined up plenty when she ups and marries Steve Grady."

"Who did you say she married?" asked Barney, his eyes goggling.

"Steve Grady. He run a sandwich and soft-drink stand."

"Yeah? No one else seems to know about this."

"Well, maybe they didn't get married. What's the diff? Steve drew all his dough out of the savings bank and they went off together. He bought her a ring—he showed it to me—so I figured they were fixin' to get married."

"Where would I find this Steve Grady?"

"Jeez," muttered the attendant, scratching his head, "I wouldn't know. What are you, anyway, a dick?"

"Hell, no."

"Well, you could ask around. Someone might know where Steve is. Me, I ain't seen him in a good three years."

To his later questions about Claire and the man she had brought to Coney Island, Barney added an enquiry about Steve Grady. Most of the concessionaires had not seen or heard of Grady for a long time; but a girl running a wheel of fortune thought he was working at the sandwich counter of a drugstore in New York.

"New York's a big place," objected Barney. "Can't you narrow it down a little?"

"No, I can't. I run into him one night in Brooklyn and that's what he told me. I didn't pay no heed to where he was woikin'. Why should I? Steve Grady was nothing in my young life."

"What does he look like?"

"Oh, kinda tall and skinny and when he looks at you his eyes sorta blaze as if he's boinin' up inside. What's he done? Robbed a bank?"

"No, I'm his aunt's sister's mout'piece, lookin' for him to hand him a legacy of a million bucks."

Her jaw dropped. "You don't say!" And then, realising that she was being kidded, she snapped "Wiseguy!" and turned away. Barney drifted on.

"Here you are, mister," said a gin-husky voice. "Your picture, drawn by hand, in ten minutes."

Barney looked down at a grey-haired man with strawberry nose and moist mouth, sitting in a canvas chair at an easel, surrounded by black-and-white drawings.

"Fifty cents, mister, for an artistic sketch your grandchildren will prize in afteryears. What d'you say? I'll leave out the warts."

"Observant sort of guy, ain't you?"

"An eye like a hawk, mister. And a memory like an elephant. One look at a face is all I need to put it down faithfully on paper."

"I'll test your memory. You happen to see Claire Abbott when she did Coney a coupla days before she was murdered?"

"I'll say I did. Say, there was a shape worth noticing. I must have done a hundred sketches of her when she worked here—did 'em for nothing, just for love of my art. Say"—the alcoholic mutter dropped to a furtive whisper—"I got one hidden away here that I did of her at the climax of her striptease act. Hot? Say, mister, on a cold day one look at that picture would raise your temperature fifty degrees. Tell you what I'll do, I'll let you have it for a five-spot. You could get your dough back in no time, charging your friends a quarter a look."

"I guess you remember Claire, all right," admitted Barney. "But what about the guy that was wit' her that day? I'll bet you couldn't describe him."

"That's where you're wrong, mister. I sized the guy up; I figured a snappy dresser like him might be good for a two-buck sketch in colour."

"What did he look like?"

"What's it to you?"

"A lot," said Barney. "Come on, gimme the dope on him."

"I could draw you a picture of him," replied the artist, watching Barney's face closely, "if there was enough in it for me."

"On the level? You wouldn't draw just any old face and claim it was him?"

"I'll play square with you, mister. I'll do you a sketch that'll walk off the paper and talk to you. What's it worth?"

"Five bucks."

"Now you're kidding," said the artist, with a crafty smile. "This means a lot more to you. than a lousy fin. What's your racket, anyway—you ain't a dick?"

"I'll make it ten. That's all I got on me."

"But you could get more. I got a hunch you'll pay fifty bucks for that picture."

"Listen, chiseller—"

"So, I'm a chiseller. Names, he calls me. That crack will just double the price, mister. You'll lay a hundred smackers on the line for the picture—or no dice."

"You should live so long," said Barney scornfully. "I'll make it twenty bucks. That's a lot of dough for a fifty-cent picture. Be smart and call it a deal before I change my mind."

"I wouldn't want to cheat myself," replied the artist, shaking his head cannily. "A picture is worth what you can get for it. I still think a hundred is the right price."

"It's been nice knowin' ya," said Barney, turning away. He had walked a hundred yards without looking back when he felt a tug at his arm.

"Let's not be hasty," said the artist, walking at Barney's side.

"Go away," retorted Barney, "you bother me." "Supposing we say fifty bucks?"

Barney said, "Nerts."

The artist sighed. "Twenty-five."

"Twenty," said Barney flatly.

"Okay. Twenty."

"It might take me a couple of hours to raise it."

"There's no hurry."

"Maybe for you there isn't. But I want that picture today."

"You raise the twenty bucks today and you'll get it."

"It's five o'clock," said Barney, consulting his watch. "I could get the dough and be back between seven and eight."

"How far you got to go?"

"Muldoon's Tavern on Twenty-Eighth Street. I woik there."

"Maybe I can save you a trip. I like taverns"—the colour of the artist's nose testified to that. "I'll drop in on you there about ten this evening. You'll have the dough then?"

"Yeah, I'll have it."

* * * * *

On his return to Muldoon's, Barney found the brother he had left in charge standing a round of drinks to a bar full of customers.

"Always the same," grumbled Barney, taking the soiled apron from his brother's waist and tying it round his own. "Leave you in charge for a couple of hours and you get tanked and wanna give the joint away."

"If that's the way you talk when a guy does you a favour," replied the brother, with an austere dignity marred only by a hiccup, "you needn't ask me again."

"Don't worry, I won't. Go on—get. When I tell Mom you been drinkin' again, she'll give you hell in Technicolor."

Barney had no patience with barmen who drank at work. Never so tactless as to refuse a customer who wanted to treat him, he kept cold tea in a whisky bottle under the bar and filled his own glass with that. The price of the drink went into his pocket.

Only for the briefest of moments did he consider expending his own money on the sketch of the man who accompanied Claire to Coney Island. He cared enough for Nick to have used his own, if necessary, but told himself that Miss Archer and Mr. Deering had plenty; it would be ungracious to deny them the privilege of parting with some in a good cause: When the crowd at the bar thinned out, he telephoned to the apartment Althea maintained for occasional nights in town and explained to her the results of his trip to Coney Island. Althea promised to bring the money to Muldoon's right away.

It was actually Julian Deering who brought the twenty dollars into the bar. He gave it to Barney and told him Miss Archer was outside in a taxi and wanted to speak to him. "While you're talking to her, I'll have a Tom Collins."

Mixing the drink, Barney placed it in front of Julian, whose grey suit emphasized the sunburn on his nose and brow.

"Looks good," said Julian, smiling at the tall glass. "It's been a stifling hot day."

Removing his apron, putting on his coat, Barney hurried

out to the sidewalk, straightening his necktie. Althea pushed open the door of the taxi and motioned to him to sit beside her.

"I want you to do something for me. I hear your police connections are impressive."

"Well, ma'am, I know a good many of the boys."

"Do you happen to know a ballistics expert?"

"A guy that monkeys wit' bullets and gives you their pedigree? I guess Joey O'Leary would be the one to see about that."

Handing him two discharged bullets, Althea gave him some detailed instructions. "Do you think you can manage all that?" she asked.

"Sure. It may take a little time. You got me wonderin', ma'am, what this is all about."

"That's something I'd rather keep to myself for the present."

"By the way," said Barney, pulling his long nose, "I got a lead at Coney on a guy named Steve Grady who may have been married to Claire."

"Do you know where to find him?" asked Althea, leaning forward with prompt interest.

"He's supposed to be a sandwich-cutter in a drugstore. Don't ask me which drugstore. There's only about ten thousand of 'em in New York—you can take your pick. He's tall and sort of skinny and his eyes blaze up when he looks at a goil—at least, that's how I heard it."

Writing down name and description in a little book she had taken from her handbag, Althea said that she would start the detective agency looking for Grady without delay. Julian came out of the tavern and took the seat which Barney vacated; and the taxi moved off.

At fifteen minutes to ten that evening, the black-and-white artist appeared with a roll of drawing-paper and a thirst which had to be assuaged with four gin rickeys before he would start to work. After much persuasion and by rustling the bills to be paid for the portrait, Barney coaxed the man into a booth with a fifth drink and his drawing materials. For ten minutes Barney was kept busy refilling the glasses of his customers and then he went back to see how the sketch was progressing.

The artist was sitting up stiffly against the wooden partition, paper and pen and ink arrayed before him. He had finished the fifth gin rickey but he had not started the drawing.

"What's the idea? You going to take all night?"

The artist did not answer. Nor did he stir. He simply sat there, bolt upright, his eyes staring straight in front of him. It was then Barney noticed the handle of a knife protruding from the wooden back of the booth and the short hairs rose at the nape of his neck. His hand shaking slightly, he pulled out the knife, whose long blade dripped blood. It had pinned the artist to the partition like a butterfly to a board and, when it was withdrawn, he fell forward, sprawling face-down on the table. Without touching the body, Barney knew there was no life in it.

The side door, rarely used, leading through the adjoining building to the street, was ajar. Barney went through, down a dim corridor, out to the sidewalk. He peered up and down but there was no one in sight. Returning the way he had come, he shut the door behind him.

Picking up the empty glass, he carried it back to the bar, holding the long knife in his other hand in such a way as to conceal it from his customers. Under cover of the bar, he dropped the knife into the sink in which he rinsed soiled tumblers. He mixed another gin rickey.

"That guy in the back certainly has a thirst," he remarked, with a laugh. "He's drunk now—but he won't quit until it runs out of his ears."

Carrying the replenished glass to the booth, he placed it at the elbow of the corpse. Making sure those at the bar were not watching, he shifted the dead artist slightly so that the blood on his back would not show if someone glanced, in passing, into the booth. Walking back to the bar, he poured himself a drink, downing it at one swallow. This time, it did not come out of the bottle containing cold tea.

Someone put a nickel in the jukebox and a band, dominated by a strident trumpet, started to play.

A glassy-eyed drunk, perched on a stool, kept time with a wavering hand and sang the words in a maudlin tenor:

'Oh, Daddy, I wanna brand-new car…champagne…caviar…'

There ought to be at least one hymn in that jukebox, thought Barney. You got to consider all your customers. How do you know a corpse is going to like boogie-woogie?

Chapter 21

Barney raised his eyes from the thing lying like a bundle of old clothing against a wall in the alley.

"Well?" said the police sergeant sharply, at his elbow. Other police officers, at both ends of the alley, were holding back the morbidly curious crowds. Barney shook his head.

"Don't know the guy. Never seen him before."

"A policeman found him lying here early this morning. He wasn't here at midnight, so someone must have dumped him against the wall after that. There's a knife stab in his back. He stinks of liquor."

"Muldoon's ain't the only joint in the neighbourhood."

"It's the only one in the block." The police sergeant gave the barman a shrewd up-and-down stare. "It ain't the first time we found a corpse behind Muldoon's, Barney."

"Always castin' up the old days," said Barney sourly. "That was durin' Prohibition, Sweeney. Things was different then. Why, we ain't even had a fight in the joint in months. My hunch is he wasn't even croaked in the neighbourhood. He could have been brought here by car."

"Maybe he could. Whoever brought him did a fancy job of trimming the labels out of his clothes and emptying his pockets. There ain't a thing on him to help identification. Well, I guess we can trundle him off to the morgue. The coroner's seen all he wants to see for now."

"I've seen more'n I want to see," growled Barney. "Next time you boys find yourself a corpse, don't go draggin' me out of bed first thing in the mornin' to look at it. I got a sensitive stomach. Besides, I woik late— I got a right to sleep late."

"You know how it is, Barney. I had to have you look at it, as a matter of form. See you later. I'll be in for a drink after they cart the stiff away."

For an hour of more Barney was occupied ministering to the thirsts of half-clad people from nearby tenements, avidly discussing the body in the alley. He worked with his usual deftness but his heart was not in it. Although he had relieved the corpse of everything that might identify it—short of removing the strawberry nose, which would have required a surgical operation—he had little doubt that the police would eventually trace the dead man to Coney Island and hear something about an individual with two conspicuous warts who had spent an afternoon there asking questions. Those twin warts would put Barney on the spot, unless the real murderer were promptly unmasked. The slaying of the artist proved two things beyond all doubt; that Barney had come close to the man who killed Claire; that the murderer was almost certainly her male companion at Coney Island. Barney remembered his impression of being followed on his tour of the boardwalk.

It was one of the longest days of his life and, when he went home still a free man, Barney had nothing to anticipate on the morrow but another agonising period of suspense. Soon after he opened the tavern the next day, he had a phone call from Althea, who told him that the detective agency she had employed had found Steve Grady.

"It wasn't difficult, as he works for one of the big chains of drugstores."

She gave Barney the address of the store and of the rooming-house in which Grady lived.

"Before we make a move to find out what Grady knows," she added, I want Mr. Deering to take a good photograph of him. He can do that without Grady's being aware of it. I have an excellent likeness of Arno Jannings which Mr. Deering took and one of Morrie Stern which I obtained from the picture editor of a morning newspaper. I mean to try an experiment with them."

Althea did not explain the experiment and Barney did not question her about it. He said he expected to have information that day or the following morning about the bullets she had given him.

"Good. Do you know, Barney, I think we're coming closer to the killer every hour."

"I hope to God you're right," declared Barney fervently.

At about noon, when there was only a sprinkling of drinkers at the bar, a man walked in and made a beeline for one of the booths. His appearance was unfamiliar to Barney, which made the barman uneasy, for at the moment he was allergic to strangers. Setting down the glass he was polishing, Barney wiped his hands on his apron and came from behind the bar to take the stranger's order.

The man was clad in a misfitting blue suit and gaudy yellow shoes no city store would dream of having on its shelves. He was a good ten pounds underweight and his skin had an unhealthy pallor. Beneath a nose with a twisted bridge, which looked as if it had been tweaked before it set, sprouted the short hairs of a moustache covering the upper lip from cheek to cheek. He looked at Barney with inscrutable eyes and the barman felt an odd tingling along his spine. Barney had a hunch he ought to know this man, although he would have sworn he had never seen him before.

"What'll it be ?"

The man pushed a nickel across the table. "Put that in the jukebox while I make up my mind."

"Sure." Barney spun the coin. "Any particular record you'd like to hear?"

"Make it number ten."

The barman blinked at that. Only a regular visitor to the

place would know the records by their numbers and he could think of only one regular who would ask for that particular record. He put the coin in the slot and pressed a button. His large hand trembled a little as he did so.

The jukebox started to play 'Melancholy Baby.'

"A shot of rye, huh?" asked Barney, staring at the man in the booth.

"No. Make it plain ginger ale."

"I could have sworn it would be rye."

"It used to be rye. Not anymore."

Going back to the bar, Barney filled a tumbler with ginger ale.

"When did you come back?" he asked in a whisper, bending over the man in the booth and placing the tumbler at his elbow.

"This morning," answered Nick Abbott.

"Could you prove that?"

"Certainly."

"Boy, is that a load off my mind."

"Why?"

"A guy was bumped off in here night before last. The cops don't know it happened here but they're liable to find out any time. In a roundabout way, the killing could be pinned on you if you was in New York at the time."

"I was hundreds of miles away."

"What you want to come back for?"

"I couldn't stay away, Barney. My place is here, proving my innocence."

"Well, things have certainly happened while you was gone. Me and Kay, Miss Archer and Mr. Deering, we've all gone to bat for you. I got a lot to tell y—"

The barman stopped talking very suddenly, for a policeman in uniform had come into the tavern. With as casual an air as he could contrive, Barney returned to the bar.

"Small beer, Barney," said the policeman, mopping his brow with a handkerchief as large as a tray-cloth. "Jeez, it's another scorcher."

The policeman's eyes roved over the place while he drained the frothing glass, coming to rest briefly on Nick. He made a face at, the jukebox, still playing 'Melancholy Baby.'

"That record stinks. Why can't you play something snappy for a change?"

"I like it," said Barney, wiping the mahogany.

"You would. Well, see you in church."

"See you in the funny papers," replied Barney.

He poured himself a drink, realized too late that it was from the cold tea bottle, and spat it out.

"Everythin' happens to me," he complained, walking back to Nick.

"That cop didn't give me a tumble."

"Who would, in that getup? How did you fix your nose?"

"I didn't do it on purpose. A certain Mr. Hennessey's fist fixed it."

"It certainly changes the looks of your map. You lost a lot of weight. Been sick?"

"I stayed too long in a saltwater bath."

"The way you look, your best friend wouldn't know you."

"You said you had a lot to tell me?"

"There's too many people around now," responded Barney cautiously. Two more customers had come in. "Come back in about an hour."

With a desire to ascertain whether Barney was right in thinking him safe from recognition, Nick went uptown to the grill-room where Julian lunched when in New York. The photographer was sitting at a table, sipping a dry martini and studying a menu and, in passing, Nick jolted his friend's arm.

With a frown of irritation, Julian glanced up and Nick made a gesture of apology before moving on. Although they had stared at each other, Nick felt sure that Julian—his best friend—had not the slightest idea who he was. He ate a chop at a table not far from Julian's. When the photographer rose to go he glanced directly at Nick again but without the faintest glimmer of recognition in his eyes.

Later in the afternoon Nick returned to Muldoon's, this time finding Barney alone. They had a long talk at the bar and Barney told all that had happened in Nick's absence, concluding with the murder in the tavern.

"We've got to work fast," said Nick thoughtfully, "before the police link the dead man with Coney Island—and with you."

"I get the jitters just thinking about it."

"You have this Steve Grady's address?"

"Yeah, he lives in a rooming-house on Tent' Avenue. I'll write the number down for you. What you going to do?"

"If I can think of a way to do it, I'm going to look over his room. I might find a clue."

"You'll be stickin' your neck out."

"That's what you and Kay and Miss Archer and Mr. Deering have been doing, isn't it?"

"Okay—but be careful."

"I'll be careful," promised Nick.

He bought a cheap suitcase in a store on Eighth Avenue and filled it with rubbish he found in an alley. Weighed down on one side by it, he panted up the steps of the brownstone front on Tenth Avenue in which Steve Grady lived.

"Steve isn't in, is he?" he asked the plump woman who opened the door.

"You mean, Mr. Grady? He won't be in from work until eight."

"He asked me to leave this in his room," said Nick, indicating his burden.

The woman eyed it curiously.

"Did he give you his key?"

"No, he didn't say anything about his door being locked."

"That's funny. He's always very, careful to lock his room when he isn't in it, even when he's only down the hall taking a bath. Maybe you better leave the case outside his door."

"He said to put it in his room," answered Nick doubtfully. "I guess there's something pretty valuable in it."

The landlady sniffed. "I don't know what he'd have that would be worth much. How did he expect you to get into his room without the key?"

"Maybe he thought you'd have a spare key."

After a moment's hesitation, the woman said unwillingly, "Well, so I have—but I don't know as I'd care to use it."

"This thing is heavy. I wouldn't want to lug it all the way back again."

"Well, I'll lend you my key," said the landlady grudgingly, fumbling under her apron, "but be sure to tell him you asked me for it."

"I will," replied Nick quickly, taking the key before she could change her mind. "Don't bother to come up. Those stairs look steep. I'll find the room myself."

"Second on the left on the first landing," she told him; and he carried the suitcase up the winding staircase. Closing the door of Steve Grady's room behind him, Nick set down the suitcase and went swiftly to a chest of drawers on which lay a near-bald brush and a hair-wreathed comb. He pulled out the drawers, one by one, rummaging through them with more haste than tidiness. All he found to interest him was a snapshot of two people in bathing-suits. One was Claire and the other, a lanky man with prominent adam's-apple, must be Grady. The photograph had been torn in half and stuck together with gummed paper.

Nick went through the pockets of the one threadbare suit hanging in the closet; inserted his fingers into the toes of a pair of shoes; examined an empty suitcase for a possible hidden compartment; ripped the covers from the bed and felt every inch of the mattress, turning it over to make sure nothing was hidden beneath it. He picked up a worn strip of carpet, shaking it before he replaced it; opened the window and ran his eye along the crumbling stone ledge; turned over the single chair, causing the upholstered seat to fall out.

He pressed the padding of the seat with his fingers and heard a faint rustling. With a penknife, he gouged out the thumbtacks holding the shabby leatherette covering. Between cover and padding, he found five clean new one-hundred-dollar bills. After taking the numbers, he replaced them and drove in the thumbtacks with the handle of his knife. He went over the room hurriedly, tidying up. Locking the door behind him, he went downstairs and returned the key to the landlady.

From a nearby telephone booth, he called Barney and told him about the money.

"You can bet your life he didn't come by it honest," declared Barney virtuously. "It would take a sandwich-cutter about five years to save five hundred bucks and you can bet he didn't have a dime when Claire was through wit' him."

"That's what I thought. If he was really married to Claire and if she never got a divorce, he'd have a hold over her. Maybe he played her game in reverse—blackmailed her out of some of the money she got from other men."

"Could be. How do we go about provin' it?"

"I thought the two of us might try to throw a scare into him."

"I'll be right over," said Barney promptly. "There's a guy

at the bar who's helped me out a couple of times. He'll keep an eye on the place while I'm gone." Before hanging up, the barman said grimly: "Muldoon will have woise than stomach ulcers when he comes out of hospital and loins how I've been neglectin' the joint."

Nick met Barney on a corner and they went into a drugstore to confer. The barman produced two metal badges which appeared, at a glance, to be police shields. "I thought these might come in handy," he remarked, giving one to Nick and pinning the other to his suspenders.

"Grady won't be home from work until eight."

"I got a hunch I could make him come home right away," replied Barney. "There's a phone in the corner. You got a nickel?"

"Yes. Here."

Barney looked up the telephone number of Steve Grady's place of employment. He dialled that number and, when the call was answered, asked for Grady. In a few moments a nasal voice came to him over the wire:

"Is this Mr. Brown?" asked Barney.

There was dead silence for a moment and then, in a hesitant stammer, the nasal voice said, "T-this is Walman's Forty-Second Street branch. May I take your order, please?"

"Listen, Mr. Brown," rasped Barney, "I wanna talk to you. I'll be at the store in about ten minutes. If you know what's good for you, you'll be there."

Without waiting for an answer, he hung up. "I've a hunch Grady will go straight to his boss and ask for the rest of the day off, on account of he's sick," he remarked. "And, boy, that will be no lie. He certainly sounded sick."

"What's this 'Mr. Brown' gag?" asked Nick.

"I forgot to tell you about that. The guys that did business wit' Claire always used the name of a colour when ringin' her up. We found Mr. White and Mr. Green—I guess Grady is Mr. Brown."

On a corner near the Tenth Avenue rooming-house, they waited for Steve Grady to appear. They had not long to wait. Within fifteen minutes a taxi drove up and a tall, spindling man alighted and paid the driver. He started up the steps with a jerky, blundering gait as if too agitated to see straight or move in a coordinated manner. When Nick and Barney fell in on either side of him, he stared at them with popping eyes and almost slipped down the steps. Barney briefly exposed the badge on his suspenders and Nick held out a cupped hand with his badge in it.

"Walk into the house like nothing was wrong," ordered Barney. "We want to talk to you."

"I—I— There must be some mistake. Y-you've got nothing on me."

"You heard what the sergeant said," grunted Nick, prodding the man in the ribs. "Get going."

With a frightened look on his bony face, Grady obeyed. He unlocked the front door and they went in a body up the stairs. While groping for the key to his room, Grady blinked nervously from one grim face to the other.

"You guys are making a mistake," he whined, preceding them into the room. "I've done nothing to be in trouble with the cops."

Barney pushed him down on the bed roughly.

"What d'you call blackmail? Is that nothing?"

His adam's-apple bobbing, Grady faltered, "I—I don't know what you mean."

"Where did you get the five hundred bucks hidden in that chair?"

"I—I—"

"Don't stall."

"Should I call the patrol-wagon, sergeant?" asked Nick.

"You might as well," growled Barney. "We can give this guy a good going-over at headquarters."

"Wait a minute," quavered Barney. "Give me a chance. I can explain. I—I got that money from my wife."

"From Claire Abbott," said Nick.

"Yeah, that's what she called herself—but she was my wife. We were never divorced."

"When did you get it?" demanded Barney. "Before you shot her—or after?"

Steve Grady looked sick. "Oh, Jeez. Oh, God. You don't think I shot her? Why, I hadn't even seen her for a week when I read about the murder in the papers. Would I be likely to kill her, just when I was getting back a little of the dough she gypped me out of?"

"Talk-fast. When did she give you this dough?"

"A hundred bucks at a time, with ten days between each payment. The last was a week before she was shot. You got to believe me; I'm telling the truth. I tried to make her pay up faster but she swore she didn't have the dough. I knew she was lying—but what could I do?"

"To make her pay, you threatened to squawk that she was your wife?"

"I had to threaten her. If you knew Claire, you'd understand that getting money out of her was like squeezing it out of a turnip. She married me because that was the only way to get her hands on my savings—almost four thousand bucks—every cent I'd scraped together in a lifetime of hard work."

"Go on."

"She said she knew how we could double it and, like a sap, I let her take it. As soon as I parted with it, she ran out on me." A look of pain crept into his eyes and a wistful note into his voice as he added, "We didn't even spend the wedding night together.

I didn't catch up with her until a few months ago and then I knew she had dough, because she was living on Park Avenue. I put on the pressure but she stalled and stalled. That five hundred bucks is all I was able to squeeze out of her."

"So, you got sore and shot her?"

"I didn't!" Grady's voice rose to a shriek. "I didn't kill her."

"Listen," said Nick, with assumed ferocity, "you came home this afternoon to pack your things and make your getaway."

"I—I was scared. That don't mean I killed her. Even an innocent man can be scared."

"Yes," said Nick, "I guess he can. But forget about running away. We won't arrest you for the present but we'll have a man watching every move you make. If you try to run out on us, you'll find yourself behind bars."

"I'll stay. You can trust me."

"You'll stay," said Barney darkly, "or else."

In a taxi, Barney and Nick went back to Muldoon's. Nick said, "Poor devil," in a pitying tone. The tavern was unusually crowded and, as they went in, half a dozen burly men in dark clothes came out of neighbouring doorways and walked in at their heels. In each man's hand was a service revolver and two of the men in the bar had submachineguns. One of them said grimly, "We want you, Abbott," and Nick quietly raised his hands above his head.

While the detectives crowded round Nick, Barney walked straight through to the kitchen, expecting every moment to feel a hand on his shoulder. He went out by the back door and saw a couple of police cars parked in the alley. Walking at a disarmingly slow pace, he reached the other end of the alley, rounded the corner and took to his heels.

From a cigar-store several blocks away, he telephoned to Althea. "They just arrested Nick," he said.

A gasp came over the wire. "I thought Nick was on his way to South America?"

"He came back."

"I'll find out where they've taken him," said Althea, "and go right over. As his attorney, they're bound to let me see him."

"About those bullets. You can get the dope by phoning O'Leary at Central Headquarters."

"I'll do that. Where can I reach you?"

"You can't reach me. Nobody can, for a couple of days—I hope, I hope."

After a long talk with Nick at Police Headquarters, Althea went to the apartment building in which Claire had been shot. She spread some photographs on the desk in front of the reception clerk, who bent over them. They had been altered by an artist, who had added to each a scrubby moustache, a pair of tinted eyeglasses, a hat, with the brim turned down and a muffling greatcoat with the collar turned up.

"That's him," cried the clerk in his shrill falsetto, pointing to one of the pictures. "That's Mr. Black!"

Chapter 22

They had turned off the Parkway and were driving along a winding back road, overhung by spreading trees, when a little dog ran into the glare of the headlights. Julian was at the steering-wheel of Althea's smart coupe. He trod the brake to the floorboards but did not attempt to swerve. There was a bump; a shrill yelp; a silence. Althea's teeth sank into her lower lip until they drew blood. The car crawled to a halt at the grassy verge of the road and Julian stepped out and walked back to bend over the limp white body of a Sealyham. After a while he lifted it by the hindlegs, carried it into the long grass, and came back to the car.

"I'm sorry," he said, settling himself behind the wheel. "The poor little beggar's dead. No good trying to find his owner at this hour. In any case, he'd want us to pay through the nose for the dog, although it was his own stupid fault, letting the poor little beast run wild in the middle of the night."

"You didn't even try to avoid hitting it," said Althea huskily, her face very white, her nostrils pinched.

"What could I do? The little beggar ran slap in front of me."

"You could have swerved."

"And risked hitting a tree?"

"Most people would have taken the risk to save a dog's life."

"And broken their own fool necks. Be reasonable, Althea. I'm as sorry about this as you are—but it was the dog's life or ours."

"You'd always be sure to save your own life, wouldn't you, Julian, no matter who was sacrificed?"

There was a pause that seemed unending, while Julian lit a cigarette. "I don't know just what you're getting at," he murmured, letting smoke trickle through his thin nose. "Sounds as if you were going out of your way to be unpleasant. I'll drive on, shall I?"

His companion made no reply; they were both silent as the car purred round the bends and twists of the rutted road. When the colonial farmhouse in which he lived came in sight, Julian braked gently, stopping the coupe outside the wide entrance to his garden.

"Shall I drive you home or would you prefer to take over?"

"I'd like to come in for a minute, if you don't mind."

"Please do." Julian ran the car in through the gap in the wall and up the curving driveway to the old white house. A light over the front door came on at their approach. Climbing out, Julian walked round the car and held the nearside door open for Althea. They mounted the front steps and were bowed in by an elderly man in black suit and black bow tie.

"Good evening, Miss Archer. Good evening, Mr. Julian."

"You might stay up a little longer, Hodges," remarked Julian, stepping aside to let Althea precede him into the living-room. "We may want coffee. I'll ring if we do."

"Very good, sir."

Following Althea into the long-panelled room, Julian took her wrap and laid it on a chair. While lifting the wrap from her shoulders, he tried to kiss her but she moved her face and his lips barely brushed her cheek. With a shrug, he knelt and put a match to some crumpled paper beneath apple logs in the huge fireplace and a crackling tongue of flame began to lick the bark. His hand on the round-knobbed stopper of a decanter, he shot an enquiring glance at Althea. "Care for a drink?"

"No, thanks."

"Mind if I do?"

"Of course not."

The cool clinking of glass on glass; pleasant gurgle of liquid; swish of soda. Julian turned, with a tumbler of amber fluid in his long fingers. "Perhaps you'd like coffee?"

"No, thanks."

"A cigarette, then?" He offered a platinum case.

"Thank you, I won't have anything. I want to talk to you, Julian, on a horribly unpleasant subject."

Julian said lightly, "Is that why you're armed?"

Althea looked at him without speaking, her eyes deeply troubled.

"I felt the gun in your handbag," he explained, in the same casual tone, "when I helped you out of the car. You don't expect to use it? You, look serious enough even for that."

"I'll use it if I must. If you force me to use it."

"My dear Althea, you're talking over my head. You aren't afraid I'll make violent love to you? I'm hardly the type."

"No, your emotions are remarkably under control. I'm not afraid you'll force unwelcome attentions on me. But I'm quite sure you wouldn't hesitate to kill me to save yourself, the way you killed that little dog, the way you killed Claire and the Coney Island artist—the way you plan to let Nick die in your place."

The glass poised in his hand, his eyebrows raised, his thin lips parted, Julian stared at her in surprise. "Good Lord, Althea, are you out of your mind?"

"I don't think so."

Julian took a hasty gulp at his drink. "You'd hardly joke about anything so serious."

"No, I'm not joking."

"Then what on earth's got into you? It isn't— Oh, good Lord, Althea, I knew you were beginning to care quite deeply for Nick but surely you wouldn't go quite so far in your efforts to free him as to implicate me. It's too absurd. I never even saw Claire Abbott."

"Didn't you? I asked Nick Abbott about that. He said you were to go to dinner with them one evening but he was detained at the office."

"I phoned my apologies to his wife. Something came up —I forget what—and I was unable to keep the engagement."

"That's what Claire told Nick when he went home. But—I've been wondering—did you turn up that evening, after all? Did you and Claire dine alone and decide to pretend you hadn't? Did you, perhaps, fall in love with her?"

"A woman like that?"

"How do you know what she was like, if you never met her?"

"I should think we have found out enough about her."

"She was attractive."

"I can't argue with you, my dear. I can only repeat that I didn't go to dinner that night. I never met Claire."

"It was soon after that particular evening that she got rid of Nick."

"Life is full of coincidence."

"Was it only coincidence? Or did she get rid of him so that you could step into his shoes, in the guise of the mysterious Mr. Black?"

Throwing up a hand in a despairing gesture, Julian said, "If your mind is set on this absurd theory, what can I say to change it?"

"I'm afraid it isn't absurd. You remember the night at the theatre when Dick Stanley, the publisher, reproached you for failing to do a book you had promised him? I telephoned Dick today and he said it was to have been a book of camera studies of Coney Island."

"The idea bored me and I dropped it. I didn't even go to Coney Island to line up camera angles."

"I think you did. I think you went with Claire. She'd be able to show you round. This evening I made Nick try to remember everything that happened on the night of his escape. He recalled looking at a strip of negative in your darkroom. One of the pictures was of a very fat woman."

"My dear Althea, you needn't go to Coney Island to find fat women. You should see some of my clients out of the Social Register."

"You made haste to burn that strip of film when you saw Nick examining it."

"It hadn't come out well, I suppose. There's nothing to that."

"Perhaps you can tell me how it was that the police arrived at this house to look for Nick so soon after he came to you for help?"

"It's no secret that Nick and I are friends. They'd naturally look for him here."

"I talked to the two state policemen who came here that night, Julian. A man told them on the phone they'd find Nick here. You phoned them, Julian, while you were supposed to be making sure that the Hodges were asleep."

"All this is a great strain on my patience. I don't like to be accused without proof of betraying a friend."

"I happen to have proof. Some days ago, I stopped to talk to those two policemen and they were arguing which was the better shot. Each claimed to have fired the bullet that wounded Nick. To decide the question of superiority, I had them fire at targets in my grounds. They both did fairly well but that isn't the point. They used the guns they carried that night. I gave two of the spent bullets—one from each gun—to Barney, asking him to have them compared with the one taken from Nick's shoulder. Neither of them matched. Neither of the policemen shot Nick."

"And you think I shot my friend while he was running away, to make sure he'd be captured?"

"That's precisely what I think. You have a revolver. You are an excellent shot."

"You forget I'm fond of Nick."

"I remember you're fonder of yourself. If you could pin the murder of Claire on Nick it would ensure your own safety."

Heaving a long-drawn sigh, Julian said, "We return to the question of why I should kill Claire Abbott, who meant nothing to me."

"To prevent her persuading Nick to divorce her, naming you

as co-respondent. You've asked me to marry you a good many times, Julian, and I've never given you a flat refusal. I always knew you were more interested in my money than in me, but I probably would have overlooked that, for I rather liked you in spite of it. But you knew perfectly well you'd never get me or my money if you were involved in a scandal."

"If what you suppose is correct, I could have bought her off. There would have been no need to kill her."

"I imagine she wanted a lot of money. You care too much for money ever to part with a large sum."

"So, I killed her and framed my friend? You make me sound like a charming character, Althea."

"You keep talking of Nick as your friend. But didn't you tell me a shocking lie about him, in the hope it would prevent me from helping him? You said that at college he almost killed a man in a fight over a girl. I asked Nick about that and he says there isn't a word of truth in it."

"What did you expect him to say? He'd hardly admit it."

"You lied about him, to turn me against him. There's something else; how did the police know to look for Nick today at Muldoon's Tavern? How did they recognize him?"

"Don't ask me," said Julian, shrugging his lean shoulders. "I didn't know he was in New York."

"He lunched two tables from you today. You didn't let him see that you recognised him—but your trained eye would pierce any disguise. How did you get a sunburnt nose? At Coney Island, when you followed Barney?"

Julian rolled his eyes, spread his hands, but said nothing.

"Only three people knew that Nick had escaped from New York by boat—until I was foolish enough to tell you. No sooner had I told you than the police were radioing ships at sea, bound for South America, to the effect that Nick was aboard one of them."

"Determined to believe the worst of me, aren't you?"

"There's one other thing I haven't told you. This afternoon I had photographs of Morrie Stern, Arno Jannings and Steve Grady touched up by an artist, who painted in the various props used by Mr. Black. I showed them to the receptionist at the building in which Claire lived but he didn't recognize any of those as the mysterious Mr. Black. Without hesitation, he picked a fourth retouched photograph—your photograph, Julian."

"I'm expected to shrink with horror and confess my guilt?" murmured Julian, rising and. sauntering toward her.

With a swift movement, Althea took a small plated revolver from her handbag and pointed it at him.

"Don't come any nearer, Julian."

Julian halted and laughed out loud. "My dear girl, I wasn't going to lay a finger on you. I was merely going to ring for Hodges and make an end of this absurd nonsense."

"Please keep your distance. I'll ring for Hodges."

While they waited for the manservant to appear, Julian helped himself to more scotch and soda. "The poor old chap will throw a fit at sight of that gun," he remarked calmly.

Althea dropped her handkerchief over the weapon, concealing it but making it no less ready for use.

Julian's manservant came in. "You rang, sir?"

"You remember the night the police came here looking for Mr. Abbott? The night there was all that shooting and commotion in the garden."

The old man said gravely that he did not expect ever to forget that particular night.

"Please tell Miss Archer everything I did that day."

"Everything, Mr. Julian?"

"Everything, Hodges."

The manservant turned to Althea, drawing a deep breath. "Mr. Julian rose at eight sharp, Miss Archer, took a lukewarm bath and had his breakfast. Let me see now, I think his breakfast that morning was—"

"You may omit the menu for the day, Hodges."

"Very good, sir. After breakfast, I accompanied Mr. Julian on a tour of inspection of the grounds and he gave me some instructions for the gardener, who comes in thrice weekly. At about ten, Mr. Julian went into his darkroom to work for a couple of hours. He rang for me several times to help him. After luncheon, he put on bathing trunks and lay in the sun all afternoon. He dined quite simply at seven and spent the evening working in the darkroom."

"That's odd," said Althea, frowning. "I could have sworn Mr. Deering was in New York that afternoon."

"Oh, no, Miss. He did not leave the grounds all day."

"Isn't it possible you're mistaken, Hodges?"

"Mr. Julian was at home, Miss. I am perfectly certain of that."

"Does that satisfy you, Althea?" asked Julian quietly, "or would you like Hodges to waken his wife and bring her down?"

"That won't be necessary," replied Althea. "Thank you, Hodges."

The manservant looked at his master. "Will that be all, Mr. Julian?"

"That's all, Hodges. You may go to bed."

When they were alone together, Julian made a move toward Althea but changed his mind, seating himself, instead, on the arm of a chair facing her.

"You see, my dear," he said sadly, lighting a cigarette, "the elaborate case you built up against me has collapsed like a house of cards. When you think it over, you'll realise how needlessly you've hurt me."

"The Hodges have been with you and your family all your life. They'd do anything for you."

"Oh, for heaven's sake, Althea," cried Julian, throwing the cigarette into the fire, "won't anything silence your absurd suspicions?"

"Hodges was lying," replied Althea flatly. "You were in New York that day. You killed Claire Abbott."

"That's something you'll never be able to prove," retorted Julian angrily.

Althea had the despairing feeling that he was right.

* * * * *

In the morning, after making sure by telephone that Julian had left for New York, Althea drove over and interviewed the manservant again. This time she saw his wife as well but nothing she could say budged the elderly couple from the flat assertion that Julian had been at his Connecticut home on the day of Claire's murder in New York. Althea was convinced they were lying but they stuck doggedly to their story. She knew the police would be no more successful with them. In face of bullying and cajoling, they would simply go on repeating that their young master had been at home on the day of the murder.

"You realise, don't you," said Althea in exasperation, "that you are placing your lives in Julian Deering's hands? He's already killed one man who might have identified him as the murderer of Claire Abbott. How long do you think he'll trust you to keep his secret, knowing that you two can tell the truth which can send him to the electric chair?

"Oh, I know you think of him as the boy you helped to rear—but he's grown into a monster who could kill a woman in cold blood. You think he'd never harm you—but how can you know he'll always trust his life in your hands? At this moment he may be wondering whether he can depend on you to go on telling the same false story. It would be simple, so very simple, to dispose of both of you and make it look like an accident."

Although ashen to the lips, the old man raised his head and looked Althea in the eyes. "I can only tell the truth, Miss Archer. Mr. Julian wasn't out of my sight all that day for more than a few minutes at a time."

"If you've turned against him, Miss," added Mrs. Hodges, pursing her bloodless mouth, "we haven't. And never will."

"A man may die for the crime your master committed. Does that mean nothing to you?"

"You're asking us to trade Mr. Julian's life for that of this other man," replied Hodges, his hands shaking.

"Mr. Julian wasn't in New York that whole day," said Mrs. Hodges firmly. "He was at home every minute."

"Yes, indeed, Miss—every single minute."

In a mood of frustration and despair, Althea drove in to New York and found Kay waiting for her at the Madison Avenue office. Kay's eyes grew large while Althea repeated, one by one, the damning facts and well-founded suspicions she had accumulated against Julian Deering. Marshalled in order, they left little doubt of Julian's guilt.

"But that won't prevent Nick's execution for the murder," Althea added bitterly, "if we can't prove the crime against Julian up to the hilt—and as long as the Hodges tell the same story, we never can prove it."

"We've got to find a way to make them tell the truth."

"It's the only way to save Nick—but how?"

"I don't know. Let me think."

"I've thought and thought," said Althea hopelessly. "It's no good, Kay—we're licked."

Chapter 23

Pouring a liqueur for his master, Hodges's wrinkled hand shook and a splash of green stained the white cloth. "I'm sorry, Mr. Julian," he said, spreading a fresh napkin over the place.

"Nerves," commented Julian, lighting an Egyptian cigarette, the variety he preferred as an after-dinner smoke.

"I—er—haven't been myself all day, sir. After you left, we had a visit from Miss Archer and it upset both Mrs. Hodges and me."

"You told her exactly the same as you told her last night?"

"Exactly the same, Mr. Julian."

"And still she wasn't satisfied?"

"No, Mr. Julian, she wasn't satisfied."

Blowing two smoke rings, Julian put a pillar of smoke through them. "Women get strange notions, Hodges—and are apt to twist the truth to fit their notions."

"Yes, Mr. Julian. More coffee, sir?"

"No more coffee. There's something on your mind. What is it?"

The old eyes were downcast. "Well, sir, I wonder if— You see, we're not feeling at all well, Mrs. Hodges and me. If you could possibly spare us, we thought a short vacation—I have a sister in Vermont, Mr. Julian, who would be happy to have us for a week or so."

"A little later I shall be delighted to let you take a vacation, Hodges, but for the present I'd rather you stayed here. You and Mrs. Hodges may have to tell your story again. Don't let that upset you. Simply repeat what you said last night and everything will be alright."

"Yes, Mr. Julian."

Liqueur in one hand, cigarette in the other, Julian strolled across the room to the fireplace. In a mirror above it, he saw the elderly manservant staring oddly at his back. "What is it, Hodges?" he asked sharply. "Are you, too, wondering if I'm a murderer?"

His gnarled hands gathering in finger-bowl and coffee-cup and clattering them together in his agitation, Hodges replied in a tortured voice, "That's something I'd rather not think about, Mr. Julian."

"But you can't help thinking about it?"

"We knew you as a child, Mr. Julian. Need I say more, sir?"

"I don't think of you as servants, Hodges. I think of you as friends."

"I am happy to hear you say that, Mr. Julian. You—er—may rely on us always to be your friends."

After the old man had cleared the table and withdrawn, Julian threw the stump of his cigarette into the fireplace and stood for a long time staring at the hissing, flame-lapped logs.

It was not much after dawn the following morning when Hodges came downstairs and started to make an early cup of coffee for his wife and himself. He took cream from the refrigerator, placing it on the kitchen table, and set out two cups and saucers and spoons. The kitchen was filled with a pleasant warm aroma when his wife joined him in a faded wrapper, her hair in curlers. They sat on opposite sides of the table, sipping the strong sweet coffee in silence. On most mornings they had a lot to say to each other but today they felt a strange reluctance to speak.

It was Mrs. Hodges who first complained of cramp. She put a hand to her side and said it hurt her there, when she breathed.

"You've been doing too much, my dear. Better go back to bed."

Raising her cup, Mrs. Hodges took a defiant swallow. "I've never been one to lie in bed, whatever ailed me, and I don't intend to start. The pain'll go away. I'll work it off. Whatever did you put in the coffee?" She tasted her lips dubiously.

"I made it the usual way. You're imagining things, my dear."

Hodges put a hand to his abdomen. "Darned if I don't feel

a touch of those cramps you were talking about. Funny. Never had a sick day in my life."

After an attempt to rise; his wife sank back with a groan. She was trembling and her face had a sickly pallor. "It's getting worse, Alfred. Catches me right here."

"You look awful, my dear. Like death warmed up."

"Alfred!" she cried, in a hoarse, shocked voice.

"Just a manner of speaking, my dear. It can't be anything much if it takes us both the same way. A touch of the sun."

"We were alright until we drank that coffee."

The manservant sniffed the cream jug. "The cream's turned, my dear. That's what's done it."

"It was fresh yesterday. It wouldn't spoil in the icebox."

Dipping a finger into the jug, Hodges brought it out covered with a white film. He licked it. "Yes, it's the cream. Tastes quite funny."

His wife did not answer. She was lying back limply, breathing stertorously, her head lolling on one side, her neck starting to swell. Hodges bent over her, administering ineffectual pats to her flabby hands, saying reassuring things with a confidence he did not feel. His own stomach felt as if tied in knots. Doubled with pain, he hobbled to the kitchen telephone and summoned a doctor.

When the doctor arrived, entering by the back door as he had been requested, he found the elderly couple writhing with agony. They were sitting miserably in hard kitchen chairs, unable to make the effort to reach their beds; and they had locked the door between the kitchen and the rest of the house. Hodges was able to explain how these sudden pains had gripped them but his wife could do nothing but moan and clasp her stomach; as if holding herself together.

"You think there's something wrong with the cream?" The doctor tasted it and quickly spat into the sink. "I'll say there's something wrong with it. The taste of strychnine is unmistakable. You've been poisoned."

The old man and his wife exchanged looks of horror but not of surprise, as if this was the confirmation of a dread. "She was right, then. He couldn't trust us."

"How could he think we would give him away?"

"She said he'd find a way to get rid of us."

"What on earth are you talking about?" demanded the doctor. "And how did strychnine get into the cream? It couldn't have been an accident."

"No," whispered Hodges brokenly, "it wasn't an accident." A tear squeezed through his half-shut eyelids and trickled down his withered cheek. "Are we going to die?"

"Not if I can get the right appliances here at once. I'll phone for them."

Hodges and his wife looked at each other again. "Before you phone the hospital, Doctor," said Hodges huskily, "please call Miss Althea Archer and ask her to come quickly. We have something to tell her."

The doctor telephoned to Althea and gave her the message. He put through another call, reeling off a long list of medical equipment and supplies. It appalled the Hodges to listen to the great amount of stuff he would need with which to save them. They hoped their master would not waken and come down before Miss Archer arrived; they would not feel safe until she was with them.

The doctor gave them something to drink, easing the pain but not lessening their horror. In fright and misery, they kept listening for the step on the stairs which would mean that Julian Deering was coming down. The step did not come but fear made them hear it a score of times before a car turned into the drive.

Althea came in through the back door, followed breathlessly by Kay.

"He tried to do it," whispered Mrs. Hodges. "He tried to kill us."

"Don't be afraid," said the doctor soothingly, "I shan't let you die."

"It was all lies, what we told you before," groaned Hodges. "He made us say it. He rehearsed us in every word. Not a bit of it was true—he was in New York that day from early morning until the evening."

It was then that the Hodges heard the step on the stairs they had been dreading and, a moment later, a hand rattled the doorknob. A voice demanded to know what was going on.

"Don't let him in," quaked the old manservant. "He tried to kill us. We'd never have given him away—but he wouldn't trust us."

Althea wrote a few lines on a piece of paper, the Hodges signed it, and the doctor and Kay witnessed the signatures. And then, Althea opened the door and confronted Julian, who was hammering on it, clad in pyjamas and silk robe. He glared at her and, over her shoulder, at the cringing elderly couple, who avoided his eyes.

"What are all you people doing in my kitchen?"

"I'm about to telephone the police," replied Althea. "The Hodges have signed a statement which destroys your alibi. I think you know what that means."

After a moment, Julian said, quite calmly, "Yes, I think I do. One would say that I'm all washed up, wouldn't one? I don't know how you inveigled them into giving me away. I'd have sworn I was safe in their hands."

"I can understand why you killed Claire," said Althea, "I can even feel sorry for you, as far as that goes. What I can't understand or forgive is that you tried to put the blame on your best friend."

"Oh, Nick," responded Julian casually. "I've hated his guts as long as I've known him. Don't ask me why. One of those delightful hatreds that need have no particular basis and are so satisfying to the soul. Good morning, Doctor. I don't know why Miss Archer brought you into this, unless it was to witness my confession that I shot Claire Abbott. She had it coming, by the way. I don't know of anyone who asked to be murdered as persistently as she did. Oh, and I stabbed a grubby drunk the other night at a tavern on Twenty-Eighth Street. Don't ask me to be sorry about that, Althea. He was another most murderable type."

Taking Althea's hand, Julian held it to his breast for a moment before releasing it. "I shan't wait to meet the police. They'd make a fuss and I abhor fusses."

He turned and went through the house, pausing briefly in the living-room to take something from a drawer before going out to the garden by the front door, which he closed gently behind him. He walked across the springy turf, skirting the flowerbeds and the sunken garden, with its slabs of mossy rock. It was a smiling day; the garden looked its best; he halted to pluck a rose for his buttonhole before sauntering on to where a brook danced over pebbles to swell the placid waters of a pool.

In the kitchen, they heard the single shot which Julian fired into his brain.

Althea put a hand on her heart. "I don't know if you can ever forgive me," she said, gently and very sadly, to the Hodges. "We tricked you rather shabbily. I came here last night, found my way in through an open window, and tampered with the cream. I had to do it; you see—it meant the life of a friend."

The Hodges looked wonderingly from Althea to the doctor, who also was embarrassed. "It wasn't strychnine in the cream," he explained. "I gave Miss Archer a harmless drug to make you sick. Imagination did the rest."

"We had to make you tell the truth," said Kay humbly. "You do see that, don't you? We're terribly sorry."

The Hodges wept in voiceless misery. They were sorry, too.

Chapter 24

There was a curious mixture of bravado and dismay in Kay's expression as she perched herself on a stool at the bar. Her once jaunty hat with its gay cock-feather had a crushed look, as if rammed on her head without benefit of mirror. Her lips were blurred, as lips are likely to be if makeup is applied as a gesture, a face-saving device in a moment of discomposure.

"Rye highball, Barney," she said, in the dismal tone that goes with funerals. "Two highballs—a lot of highballs. This time, I don't care what you say, I'm going to get good and plastered. If you offer me a nice cup of tea, I'll—I'll hit you with a bottle."

Scratching his head, Barney said, "I don't get this. Nick's in the clear, ain't he?"

"Yes, they let him out an hour ago. They found all the stuff from Claire's safe-deposit box hidden behind a stone in the fireplace at Deering's place. A lot of bonds and papers and cash and jewellery—he'd have been wiser to destroy it all but he loved money too much; and it represented a sizable fortune. Rather a joke, by the way; all Claire's ill-gotten gains will go to the husband she never bothered to divorce—Steve Grady. There was also enough evidence among the stuff to send Morrie Stern and Mascagni to prison for fifteen or twenty years. Are you going to keep me waiting all day for that highball?"

"You were so crazy keen to clear Nick. I'd have thought you'd be dancin' a jig, instead of looking like Gloomy Sunday. What's eatin' ya? Where's Nick?"

"I left him with Miss Althea Archer," replied Kay viciously. "Dear Miss Althea Archer, of the Social Register —and Godey's Lady's Book. She's got everything, Barney, looks, blue blood, money, brains. She'll make him a lovely, lovely wife—even if all their children do grow up to be Republicans. Coming from the jail, they were wrapped up in each other—a sickening sight to see. I know when I'm not wanted, so I said, 'Bless you, my children'— I nearly choked on that one—and bowed myself out. Where's that drink? I want to weep into it."

"What a sissy you turned out to be. Didn't you tell me if the guy was ever free to marry again, you'd drag him to the altar if you had to fight off dames every step of the way?"

"I couldn't do it, Barney. Call it foolish pride, call it anything you like. All I could do was walk out and leave them to it."

"I guess, maybe, you do need that highball," conceded Barney, polishing a glass.

Someone entered the tavern in a hurry and jerked Kay's stool round, so that she looked into a pair of angry eyes. Nick's eyes. "What do you mean by handing me over to another woman, like a frock for which you have no further use?"

"Why, I—"

"Don't deny it. That's exactly what you did. Althea's a swell person; it's a good thing she didn't take you seriously."

"Well, but—"

"And now, you're making excuses. I ought to sock you right on the chin."

"But—Nick—"

"Don't give me that. You deliberately turned me over to Althea, with your blessing. It's a wonder you have the nerve to look me in the eyes. What am I—a bond-slave or some-thing?"

"You're a dope," said Barney caustically. "Why don't you kiss the goil, insteada wasting, time?"

"How right you are," said Nick, taking Kay in his arms.

It was a kiss from which Kay came up gasping for air. Blinking her eyes, she took a quick swallow from a glass filled with amber fluid, which Barney had placed on the bar. "Why, Barney," she said, accusingly, "this is plain ginger ale."

"It ain't champagne," said Barney. "I'm savin' that for the weddin'."

THE END

THE LONELY MAN

Chapter 1

On a wild night, pitch dark, a night of howling wind and lashing rain, Deborah Vail drove a dilapidated car over an unfamiliar road. The road twisted and wound, rose and fell, narrowing to little more than a rutted lane. On either side, gnarled old trees reached out branches as deformed as arthritic fingers.

The little car kept threatening to give up. It laboured, panted, faltered. The windshield wipers moved jerkily, in spasms. The leaky roof sent a steady drip down on the girl's neck. She had planned the journey from London in one day, with an early start, but had fretted away two nights in drab hotels in soot-blackened industrial towns while mechanics worked at overtime rates on the asthmatic engine. Everything was wrong with it that could be wrong. The wonder was that the wretched thing ran at all.

More than an hour before, Deborah had crossed the border from England into Scotland.

She should now be nearing the market town of Garnock that was her goal; but between the rain, the dark, and her ineptitude with road maps, she had lost the main road and blundered on to some track across the moor. The only signs of civilization were the tall poles at intervals along the roadside and the wires, humming in the storm, strung from the crosspieces.

Soon after passing the last crossroads, she had suspected herself of taking the wrong fork but was too stubborn to turn and go back. It would do no harm, she had reasoned, to go on a little farther and see. But she had gone on and on and on without getting anywhere. Not a soul to help her. No wayside cottage with a friendly light. Not even a signpost or a milestone. Only dark, rain, wind, and desolation.

She told herself sharply not to be a fool, not to panic. She had lost her way. She would find it again. It was as simple as that. But her scalp prickled as she gripped the steering wheel and peered through streaming glass at the boisterous night.

A sudden flash of lightning. A thunderclap. Startled, she lost control and the little car swerved. Before she could master it, she heard a loud bang and, a moment later, the thumping of a blown-out tyre. Halting the car, she sat for a while, fuming with exasperation, before stepping out into the downpour to examine the damage.

The tyre was at flat and flabby as she had known it would be. There was nothing she could do about it. The jack only worked, in apparent self-justification, when she complained of it to a mechanic.

She looked up and down the road. Not a glimmer of light to be seen; and the last house she remembered passing was miles behind. In all those miles she had not seen a single wayfarer or a vehicle. But there might be a village round the next bend. The important thing was to keep calm, to keep her head.

By the luminous dial of her watch, it was ten-thirty. Past bedtime in a country district but not too late to arouse someone if she could find a house. It meant plodding along a muddy road through the murk with no other guide than her faulty sense of direction and becoming wetter and wetter with every step.

On the other hand, she could sit in the car until help came or the storm passed: but that might mean sitting there all night, a chilly prospect, and she was already drenched to the skin. Apart from her own plight, she ought to make an effort to find a telephone for the sake of her cousin who would be expecting her and would worry.

With a wry smile, she remembered the phone call to her cousin the previous evening, and the one the evening before that. "I'm quite all right, only the cars broken down. They're mending it now; you can expect me tomorrow." The same story, two nights in a row. And now the wretched thing had broken down again. But this time there was no handy garage, no convenient telephone booth, no near-by hotel to shelter her.

A more phlegmatic person might shrug her shoulders and go complacently to bed when Deborah, for the third time, failed to turn up; but this cousin was not like that. Probably she had begun to worry already and by midnight, if there was still no word, she would be thoroughly alarmed.

Reaching into the car, Deborah switched off the engine and lights. Turning up her sodden coat collar, digging her hands deep into the pockets, she started trudging along the road in the direction she had been taking. There was no point in turning back, no help to be looked for in that forlorn stretch.

The wind was slackening but the rain beat pitilessly on her shoulders. It quickly made a soggy mess of her pert hat. The rough muddy surface of the road was ruinous to her smart shoes. She had brought the flashlight from the glove compartment, but the battery was low and she dared not use it longer than seconds at a time.

She plodded on, stumbling now and then, watching avidly for some sign of human habitation, beginning to despair of ever finding any. After a while of this she was too cold and miserable to go farther. She stopped, drew a deep breath to hold back tears, and half-turned to go back to the car. And then she saw a light. Not far off. Half-hidden among the trees. Incredulous but delighted she started to run.

Drawing closer, she saw the uneven shape of a house, a dark and gloomy outline except for one lighted window. Her eyes fixed on the hopeful glimmer, she bumped into a gate whose rusty hinges creaked when she opened it. The pale-yellow glimmer of her flashlight found a flagstone path, sprouting tufts of weeds, which she followed to rough stone steps leading to a front door.

While rapping sharply with the heavy brass knocker, she mentally framed some polite explanatory phrases. She listened, expecting to hear the footsteps of someone coming to answer. But there was no sound. As she lifted her hand to grasp the knocker again the one light that showed abruptly went out. It was as disconcerting as a rude answer to a polite inquiry. For a moment she was completely taken aback. But she was not going to let herself be rebuffed and shut out, not it her predicament, not in a storm like this.

Gripping the knocker firmly she set up a pounding that echoed through the house. For extra measure she pressed a button beside the door and heard the shrilling of a bell. For what seemed a long time she knocked and rang, knocked and rang, pausing at intervals to listen, hearing nothing but the pattering of rain.

She noticed a faint stirring at a curtained window on her left. Someone was standing there. watching her through a slit between the curtains. Furious, she reached out and rapped on the window.

The narrow parting between the curtains closed as the person who had stood there moved away. Afterwards, Deborah was to wonder why she had not been terrified. At the time she was not frightened, only very angry.

Her anger went into another prolonged knocking.

Suddenly a light went on in the passage beyond the door and she heard footsteps. The door was flung open by a large man who regarded her with a cold, inhospitable stare. There was enough light for her to see that he was in the early thirties, that he needed a shave, that he wore a torn flannel shirt, stained trousers and worn sandals. She had the fleeting thought that he might be attractive if his expression were less boorish and hostile.

"Can't you go away and leave me in peace!" the man said savagely. "You're all the same— What do you think I am—a bloody peep show? By God—I ought to welcome you with a gun!"

Chapter 2

The man was about to shut the door in Deborah's face.

She said weakly, "I only came because I—"

Deborah felt like crying but she was determined not to cry. She would not give this bewildering brute the satisfaction of seeing her in tears.

"Well, go on. Explain yourself, if you can," he said impatiently.

"I don't know what this is about," she said. "I'm a stranger. I've lost my way. My car is stuck down the road with a flat tyre."

In the slanting oblong of light from the open doorway he studied her mistrustfully from bedraggled hat to scraped toecaps. Gradually, his expression changed. It was infuriating. She did not want his pity. It was sufficiently mortifying to know that she looked like a drenched scarecrow. It would have given her satisfaction to slap his face.

It took no clairvoyance to read his mind. He did not want to let her in. He only wanted to be rid of her. But in the circumstances, he did not see how he could turn her away. He made the invitation gracelessly, without words. He stood back, with a jerk of his head, to let her pass.

"If there's another house within miles," said Deborah, making feeble stand on her dignity, "I prefer to take my chance there."

"There's another house at the next bend—but the old lady who lives there is as deaf as a post."

Deborah started to say that she would rather crawl on hands and knees through mud than be beholden to him. In the middle of this haughty speech the floor teemed to rise up and hit her in the face.

The next she knew she was lying limply on a couch beside a fire and the man was kneeling beside her, chafing her small hands between his large capable ones.

"Don't move," he said, when her eyelids flickered open. "Don't try to speak."

"I—I fainted," she said, in dizzy wonder.

"You'll be alright in a minute."

"But—I never faint."

"You did this time. Don't move while I get you some brandy."

The moment he left the room she forced her trembling body to rise, supporting herself by a slender arm braced against an arm of the couch. The hat, bought with pride and pleasure a few days before but now a sodden, hateful thing, still clung like a leech to her head. Snatching off the ridiculous headgear, she threw it in a corner. Slipping out of the dripping coat, she let it fall to the floor.

In a huge stone fireplace with a basket grate an aromatic armful of apple logs blazed and sizzled. It drew her irresistibly. She went over, with a little cry, and stretched out slim, pretty hands. In a graceful movement she flung back her head to loosen her silken curly hair.

The man came in, carrying a bottle and a glass. Although he shook his head sternly when he saw her standing up, his eyes were appreciative. Until now he had not realized how lovely she was. Her figure was enchanting.

He set the bottle and glass on the mantelpiece. He pushed an easy chair nearer the fire and made her sit down. He poured a generous measure of brandy and put it in her hand.

"Would you like something to eat? I'm not much of a cook but I could scramble some eggs."

"No, thanks, I'm not hungry."

She sipped the strong liqueur. It had a pungent flavor and warmed her like liquid fire.

"I'm sorry I made such a fool of myself. You see, I seem to have been driving forever, I've been three days on the way from

London. The car's been acting up all the time. It's discouraging, the way mechanics shake their heads when they peer at its innards as if they couldn't make out how it ever runs at all."

"Where are you heading for?"

"Garnock."

The man looked surprised. "You certainly came the long way round. You must have left the main road about fifteen miles back."

"I took the wrong fork. I have never known left from right, was so pleased when I crossed the border from England into Scotland. I thought, well, you haven't far to go now.

When I realised I was wrong, I was too stubborn to go back. But all those miles of moorland…and the storm. I kept expecting a tree or a telephone pole to topple over and smash into the car."

"Where did you leave the car?"

"About a mile down the road, to the right."

"Have you got a spare tyre?"

"Yes…at least, the garage man at Doncaster called it an apology for a spare tyre. But he said it might last a few miles, at a pinch."

"A few miles will get you to Garnock," she half-expected him to add, "and then you'll be someone else's headache." Instead, he said, "I suppose you have a jack?"

"Yes…but it won't work for me."

His stern expression suggested that it had better work for him.

A question trembled on her lips. You're alone here? But she did not ask it. She knew what the answer would be. She could feel for herself the unpeopled atmosphere of the place. Yes, I'm alone. But he would mean more than that. He would mean aloneness so utter that it was a physical hurt. The aloneness of a solitary man crouched by a dying fire in a waste of snow and ice with ravenous wolves in a circle about him where the shadows were thick.

She shivered slightly. The man looked at her inquiringly and, to cover her confusion, she asked for a cigarette. He brought out a half-filled pack, gave her one, and lit it for her with a silver lighter. He left the lighter and the cigarettes on a table at her elbow.

The thought struck her that she ought to get in touch with her cousin.

"May I use your telephone?"

"I haven't got one," he answered, without hesitation.

He knelt on the hearthrug to tend the fire. While his attention was engaged Deborah studied his lean jaw, the sunken, haggard eyes; the tight-lipped mouth. All his features were good but the face was that of a man starved, friendless; forsaken. Never in her life had she seen a face in repose that looked so unhappy. Something inside him was eating him alive. Some inner despair. He glanced round suddenly, as if her intent gaze scorched him, and Deborah flushed and looked away, her heart pounding. She felt a premonition.

Chapter 3

Except for dirt, untidiness, neglect, the room Deborah was in would have had considerable charm. It was large and well-proportioned. The walls were panelled in rosewood to the height of a tall man and painted dove grey above that. Someone of taste had taken pains to furnish and decorate it attractively. The few pictures and ornaments had been chosen with discrimination. There was no attempt at uniformity but the result was harmonious.

But everywhere she looked she saw dust and disorder. On tables and chairs lay the debris, the soiled plates and cutlery, of several snatched meals. Even a greasy frying pan; an encrusted coffee pot.

A camp bed with tousled blankets stood against a wall. With a large house at his disposal, the man was camping one in one room.

Apparently, he also used it as a studio, for an easel stood in the middle of the floor and on a table beside it lay a palette, and a litter of brushes and tubes of paint. The easel supported an unfinished portrait of a very beautiful woman. Seeing Deborah looking at it, the man went forward quickly and threw a cloth over the picture. The action was like an abrupt admonition to mind her own business.

"I'll see what can be done about your car," he said.

He left the room and came back in a few minutes, clumping on thick-soled boots and wearing a shapeless felt hat and an old raincoat, he asked about the car keys and Deborah said she had left them in the ignition. She always did; it was not a car that any self-respecting thief would steal.

"Shall I come with you?" she asked, doing her best not to sound as unwilling as she felt.

"No, you stay here and get warm." Pausing in the doorway, he looked back with a frown. "You'll be alright? You're not afraid to be left alone?"

"No, I'm not afraid."

"Good."

With that, he was gone. She was alone in the one lighted room of a dark house; a house that conveyed an impression of morbid antagonism. She was afraid now. She had said lightly that she would not be afraid, but she could not repress a rising queasiness, a gripping foreboding. She was not in the least a timid person but the events of the night had set her nerves on edge.

A sudden sound made her jump. An imperative ringing, unquestionably the summons of a telephone bell. But he had said he had no telephone. The ringing went on and on. It came from the hall. Leaving the door of the living room open to light her way, she followed the sound to a nook under the stairs where the instrument stood on a small table.

An ordinary dial telephone. Why lie about something so commonplace? Deborah bit her lip. Should she answer it? No, she was an unwanted intruder. Her grudging host's affairs were no business of hers. Let it ring. In a little while it would stop. But the thing went on clamouring for attention.

The strain was too great. Deborah lifted the receiver.

The moment she raised it to her ear she heard a voice saying:

"Get out and stay out. You're not wanted here." The words were followed by a string of shocking obscenities that made her cringe. There was a click as the speaker hung up. Appalled, she stood holding the dead instrument for a while before shakily restoring it to its cradle. Numbly, she walked back to the lighted room.

Never before had light and a fire's warmth been so welcoming, so reassuring. "Get out and stay out." The snarled command echoed in her brain. But who could know she was here? And why should anyone care? And then she realized that the words, though grated in her ear, were not addressed to her. The voice with its gutter insults had spoken the instant the receiver was lifted. Obviously, the speaker had expected the lonely occupant of the house to answer. He was the one who was not wanted. But why? What had he done?

Uneasily, she moved about the room. Her feminine curiosity was piqued by the shrouded portrait on the easel. Why had the man been so quick to throw the cover over it?

Throwing back the cloth, she took a long look at the painting. Yes, the woman who was the subject was very beautiful. Not only beautiful, but striking. Her mouth a scarlet bow against a pallid oval face. Hair of Venetian red, exquisitely moulded nostrils, a slender throat proudly held, large grey-green eyes that were oddly expressive and compelling. It was a really lovely face, strangely intriguing, a face so unusual, so challenging to the imagination, that one could not conceive of ever tiring of it.

All that marred it was the evident discontent underlying the loveliness. Although she did not know the sitter, Deborah felt an irrational annoyance with the painter for betraying the inner discontent so unmistakably. He could have been a little less perceptive, a little more kind.

Touching a corner of the canvas, she found that the paint was still wet. It was evident that the artist had been working on the portrait that evening.

She reminded herself that she was prying. The artist had shown her most pointedly that his work was no concern of hers. Now that her curiosity was satisfied—and, at the same time, titillated—she felt a twinge of shame. Draping the cloth again over easel and canvas, she walked back to the fire and lit a cigarette from the lighter she found on a table.

As a fascinated child might do, she clicked the lighter several times, admiring the tiny flame that instantly and invariably responded.

It irked her to see the messy plates and saucepans that cluttered various parts of the room. It was only fair to make some payment for the trouble she was giving her host. It was stupid to be frightened of an empty house, to be ruled by her nerves. But she felt an inward quailing again as she went out again to the hall—prudently leaving the living room door open as wide as it would go—turned on the light there, and explored a connecting passage until she found the kitchen.

It was as repellently untidy as she had feared: a cockroach scuttled madly about the sink when the light went on: but she rolled up her sleeves and donned a soiled apron. She gathered the dirty dishes and the other things, washed them thoroughly, and put them away as neatly as possible.

While rinsing the sink she glanced up and saw a brutish male face staring in at her through the window. An ugly, stupid, bestial face with bulging eyes and a snoutish nose. It was like something monstrous from another world.

She screamed…and the face withdrew in a flash.

Chapter 4

Deborah's involuntary host returned and found her shaking with fright.

"A face at the window," she stammered.

"That's nothing new," he said bitterly. "Didn't I tell you? I'm a regular peep show."

And then his expression changed. The bitterness faded out of his eyes and he became simply a human being honestly concerned over another human being.

"You've really had a shock," he said, putting a hand gently on her shoulder. "I shouldn't have left you alone. Come to the fire and I'll get you another drop of brandy."

"No—I'll be all right I—I only…"

"You only want to get away," he said, with a wry smile that brought back all the bitterness to his gaunt face. "You sense that there's something terribly wrong with this house—and with me. Well, I can't blame you. Fortunately, your car's ready. It's at the door."

"I don't know how to thank you."

"I couldn't very well do less than I did. Keep on this road for a mile or so and you'll come to a crossroads. Bear to the left and Garnock is about three miles further on."

She went into the living room to find her overcoat. It was too sodden to wear, so she slung it over her arm.

"You're forgetting your hat," he said.

"Throw it out," she replied with a wan smile.

It pleased her to see the answering smile that fleetingly lit up his features. She was trying to find words to express what she wanted to say. She could not say goodbye. She was quite certain in her mind that they would meet again. You couldn't feel so deeply affected by a man unless he was to mean something in your life.

"My name is Deborah Vail," she said. "May I ask yours? My cousin will want to thank you."

"Will she?" He shook his head. "No, I really don't think she will."

"I don't know what you mean."

"My name is Andrew Garvin."

Obviously, he expected the name to mean something to her but it did not.

He was watching her face, "It doesn't register?"

"No, it doesn't. Ought it to?"

"It will," he said flatly.

As she walked down the garden path he left the door open to light her way, but when she neared the car he shut it firmly.

* * * * *

Near the statue of Robert Burns that stands in a square of sandstone buildings in Garnock, a policeman in a glistening oilskin cape told Deborah how to find her cousin's house. Although he gave the directions painstakingly, her first thought on reaching the house was that he had made a mistake. She expected a modest bungalow such as a schoolmaster might afford, not an imposing residence set in a large garden.

However, the moment she stopped the car, the door of the house was thrown open, spilling light into the darkness, and the small roly-poly figure of Joyce Monteith came running through the rain, followed by the stork-like form of her husband, carrying an umbrella, and the stridently barking hairy bundle on legs that was Paddy, their Sealyham terrier.

"Well, here you are at last. I'd begun to think—" Joyce burst out.

"If you knew what I've been through with Joyce! For hours her imagination had been working overtime...every dire fate—" her husband interjected.

"I wanted to phone the police—" Joyce cut in.

"And the fire department and the hospital and the lifeboat station—" her husband added.

"On a night like this," said Deborah, "it was certainly an idea to call the lifeboats."

"Ewan almost sat on my head to keep me from the telephone. He said if anything was wrong, we'd hear. Let me look at you. Oh, you poor drowned kitten. Whatever happened to you?"

"Everything went wrong that could go wrong," said Deborah, hugging her cousin, "but here I am at last, so it's all right."

Ewan thrust the umbrella into his wife's hand, telling her to get Deborah out of the wet and not to bother about the luggage, he would fetch it. She made no move until he gave her a gentle push that started her toward the house, arm-in-arm with Deborah. Lugging in three suitcases several minutes later, Ewan found his wife and Deborah still in the hall.

"I was sure this was the wrong house. Why, Joyce, it's a mansion!"

"Darling, we couldn't possibly afford it, only no one else would have it as a gift."

"Even so," said Ewan, "we've had to let out the top floor to help pay the rent."

"We spend our lives mending, painting and patching," said Joyce, "but we love it."

"I can't wait to see the baby," said Deborah. "If he's like his pictures, he must be a darling."

"He's a fat little dumpling like his mother," said Ewan, setting the suitcases at the foot of the stairs. "Now, will someone please make a move to go in by the fire?"

"He made a pot of coffee all by himself," said Joyce, "and he can't wait to hear us exclaiming over it. Oh…but I am awful, keeping you standing here. Come to the fire at once, you're soaked."

"An hour ago, I felt like giving up," said Deborah, following her cousin into a living room that was the very picture of comfort. "I was lost on the moors and a tyre blew out. I was being blown away by the wind and washed away by the rain. Heaven knows what would have become of me if I hadn't found a house and a man—"

"A man," repeated Joyce, giving Deborah a penetrating glance.

"A strange man," said Deborah thoughtfully. "I don't think I've ever known anyone who seemed quite so unhappy."

"A farmer, no doubt," said Ewan, pouring steaming coffee into huge cups. "Brooding over the state of the crops."

"No, not a farmer—an artist. He said his name is Andrew Garvin."

There was a silence so acute that it could almost be felt. Deborah stared in bewilderment at the startled faces of Joyce Monteith and her husband.

"What is it? What's wrong?"

"Andrew Garvin," repeated Ewan. "I didn't know he was back."

"How dare he show his face!" said Joyce.

"I don't understand. What has he done?"

Joyce drew a deep breath. Her normally cheerful face was set and severe.

"He murdered his wife," she said.

Chapter 5

"I can't believe that he murdered his wife," Deborah said angrily. She was as indignant as if they were speaking of an old and trusted friend. "I don't believe a word of it," she emphasized.

Ewan Monteith looked from one woman to the other. Joyce was bristling at Deborah, assuming an air of dignity. That was a prelude to throwing things. Afterwards she would hate herself and be humble for days, and he wanted to spare her that. To cause a diversion he walked between the two, mumbling an apology, and crossed to a window.

"I do believe it's stopped raining," he said, doing his best to infuse interest into the trite remark.

Joyce knew her husband fully as well as he knew her. She told him brusquely not to change the subject.

"You don't believe that Garvin murdered his wife," she said icily, to Deborah. "And what, may I ask, do you know about it?"

"I've met the man," said Deborah, equally chilly. "I've talked to him. I can't believe—"

"He changed a flat tyre for you. So that makes him a sterling character." Joyce clenched her plump fists. "Oh, you're so stubborn."

She turned to her husband. "She's always been stubborn. Ever since she was a child."

"If she's stubborn," said Ewan, with a sigh, "you're dogmatic."

Walking back to the fireplace, he started to fill a blackened briar pipe, spilling crumbs of tobacco down his front.

"Oh, of course! Trust you to put me in the wrong."

"My dear, if anyone is putting you in the wrong, it's yourself. We know that Erica Garvin was murdered—"

"Good of you to concede that much."

"What we don't know," said Ewan, striking a match, "is that Garvin did it."

"Ask anyone," snapped Joyce.

"Oh, by all means," said Ewan, puffing on his pipe. "They'll all tell you the same. That Garvin's guilty." Leaning on the mantelpiece, he exhaled a cloud of smoke. "But—is that proof?"

"Proof," repeated Joyce, as if the word were nasty. "Oh, you—you mathematician!"

"I teach mathematics for a living," said Ewan equably. "You can hardly expect me to agree with you that two and two makes six."

His tone was so amiable, his logic so exasperating, that Joyce looked about her for something to throw at him.

Joyce ran to her cousin and threw both arms round her,

"I'm a beast. Starting a fight before you're properly in the house. I ought to be given a shaking."

"You're a darling," said Deborah, hugging her, "but you haven't changed a bit."

The Sealyham had been standing, with ears cocked, at the living room door. Now he gave a sharp, commanding yelp and trotted forward to look up imperatively at his mistress. They heard a plaintive wailing from upstairs.

"The baby," said Joyce. "Paddy always hears him first. I believe he thinks it's his baby and he only lets us look after him."

Pressing her cheek against Deborah's for an instant, as a contrite and loving child might do, she hurried out of the room and ran upstairs with the little dog at her heels.

The three cups of coffee Ewan had poured were standing on a side table. Deborah handed one to him and took one for herself.

"Good," she said, after an appreciative sip. "But poor Joyce's will be cold."

"She likes it that way. Which is just as well, since it's the way she usually gets it."

Setting his cup on the mantelpiece, Ewan ruffled his thinning yellow hair. "You know, she's devoted to you, really."

"You don't have to explain Joyce to me. We've been rowing and making up since we were old enough to snatch each other's toys."

"You grew up together?" Ewan ran a masculine eye over her.

"I wish we had." A frown clouded Deborah's lovely face. "I was always so happy with Joyce and her parents. It was the only taste of family life I had. But that was only for a week or two, three or four times a year. For the most part I was a very lonely little girl, always being scolded, living with an elderly maiden aunt who was bound and determined to 'do her duty by me'."

"Sounds grim."

"It was. You see, my parents were killed in a car accident when I was three. Most of my relatives were only just making ends meet and this old aunt volunteered to take me. I suppose it was kind of her; but I grew up thinking that all sentences began with the word 'don't.' She had an attic, with trunks full of old clothes, where I played on rainy days. I used to dress up and pretend to be different people who'd come to call. Some of them were dull and I let them drop. The others came to call every single rainy afternoon until they were more real to me than real people."

"And that's why you became an actress?"

"It sounds so impressive…an actress," said Deborah, setting down her empty cup, "The truth is rather disillusioning. I spent three seasons in repertory, painting scenery, running errands, selling tickets, and occasionally walking on to the stage to say, 'Did you ring, Madam?' I've had two bits in pictures but you could have missed my deathless performance in either of them by stooping to tie your shoe lace."

"But surely, this London play you've been in—the one that just closed. Didn't it run for months?"

"Almost seven," agreed Deborah. "And it was like heaven to get a weekly pay check. But it was a thriller. And I played the corpse. I got strangled every evening before the curtain was up five minutes. The only line they gave me to speak was: 'You!'"

"Well, you're young. You've made a start."

"Young? Why, I'll be twenty-five next birthday."

"I apologize," said Ewan solemnly. "You're not young at all. You're a broken-down old lady with her future all behind her."

She smiled, but responded in a serious tone. "In the theatre, twenty-five can be old. It all depends on what you've accomplished."

She took a sip of coffee and went on. "When you're young, very young, you think you'll be someone by the time you're twenty-five. And then one day, you wake up to the fact that twenty-five is just around the corner and you're no one—no one at all."

"Perhaps round the next corner there's a producer with nice part for you."

"That dream belongs to eighteen," said Deborah, shaking her head. "And there's another thing. I've never admitted it to anyone before but perhaps I wasn't really meant to be an actress. Perhaps I've fooled myself…"

An impression Garvin had made upon her flashed across her mind.

Chapter 6

This is what I want, thought Deborah, appreciating the restful ease and domestic tranquillity of the room. A home of one's own.

But a home is nothing without someone to share it. And there was the snag. Deborah had enjoyed mild flirtations with a number of personable young men but none of them had touched her heart. Most of them were in the theatre, like herself, and a girl is a fool to marry an actor. She starts married life with a rival, for every actor is in love with himself.

"You ought to have a cat to sit before the fire," she remarked.

"Our dog, Paddy, won't have one," replied Ewan, choosing a fresh pipe from the rack at his elbow. "We got him a kitten as a present from the people two doors away but he carried it back in his mouth by the scruff of the neck and deposited it on their doorstep."

Paddy came downstairs slowly, looking back from almost every step at his mistress, his alert eyes cautioning her to be careful of the bundle in her arms.

With ill-concealed pride, Joyce put her baby son into Deborah's arms and the women exclaimed over him fondly while Ewan looked on.

Joyce kissed her cousin's cheek and said, "It's going to be grand having you. I'm going to make you stay a long time."

All the while Joyce talked; she was appraising Deborah without seeming to do so. She's pale, she thought, but it suits her. It goes with the medieval pageboy cap of dusky hair. If I were an artist, I'd go mad trying to capture on canvas the delicate texture of her skin.

An artist. The thought brought a certain artist to mind. Joyce's mouth, normally shaped for laughter, tightened determinedly.

Andrew Garvin was also in Deborah's mind.

"Darlings," she said, trying to speak casually, "let's not get all excited, but I do want to know—"

Joyce was silent and disapproving.

Ewan looked up and said, "I wondered when that was coming. It's no use, Joyce. You can talk about a dozen other topics but the same thought is in all our minds. Deborah wants to know about Andrew Garvin. I'd better tell her."

Leaning back thoughtfully, he said, "I've known Andrew since we were boys. We grew up in Garnock and went to school together. I always thought him an odd chap. Moody. A bit difficult to know. Andrew is a good artist. At least, I think he is. Don't know much about it but his work appeals to me. It was common knowledge that he didn't make much money as an artist. And then he won some big prize. Don't know the details but a thousand pounds went with it. He went off to London for the presentation and when he came back, a month or so later, he brought Erica."

"A lovely, lazy, social-climber with red hair, expensive clothes and questionable morals," declared Joyce.

"There you have the verdict of the good ladies of Garnock," said Ewan pleasantly. "The men were of somewhat different opinion."

"Whether it's Mayfair or Garnock," said Joyce, "it isn't the men who decide who's accepted and who isn't. It's their wives. And the women of the County set, the titled and wealthy lot, just wouldn't have her."

"However, that's not the point," said Ewan. "Life in Garnock was pretty dull for Erica with only people like us for company— and some of us a bit cool. Goodness knows why she married Andrew in the first place."

"Because she thought he'd win a thousand-pound prize every month," said Joyce.

"Well, that dream didn't last," said Ewan. "She found herself with barely enough to live on, snubbed by the people she wanted to impress. She made up for it by flirting with every presentable male and running up bills that Andrew couldn't pay."

"A flirtation is a flirtation," said Joyce. "Hers were affairs."

"In a small town like this," said Ewan, "everyone takes notice of what everyone else does, of course. It was all over the district that Erica entertained male callers when her husband was out. A few weeks ago, she was found; late one afternoon, dead in her bed, beaten on the head with a blunt instrument. The police estimated that Erin was killed about one in the afternoon, although the body was found in pyjamas."

"And made up to the nines," added Joyce.

"The police never found the weapon," said Ewan, "although they made tests of every possible object in the house and searched the surrounding fields for weeks. As far as the maid could remember, nothing that conceivably could have been used to kill Erica was missing from the house. The significance of that is that it the murderer brought the weapon in with him, the crime was almost certainly premeditated."

"The first person the police questioned was the husband," said Joyce, "and they've questioned him for hours several times since. Naturally, he hated her, for all she did to him."

Deborah had a fleeting thought: who can say what another being can forgive?

"He claims to have been painting all that day," Joyce continued. "On a hill near a farm. But the farmer's boy says he definitely wasn't there. He was seen on his way home shortly before the murder and even entering the house. I'm told they found blood on his jacket. The only mystery is why he isn't under lock and key, awaiting trial. He went off two weeks ago and everyone thought he'd got away for good. I don't see why the police let him walk about free."

Deborah's fingers trembled as she took out a cigarette and put it between her lips. From a pocket she brought a lighter. When she triggered it, she realized it was not hers.

"Mr. Garvin's lighter! I must have put it in my pocket by mistake."

"A psychologist," said Ewan teasingly, "would call that proof that you wanted an excuse for seeing him again."

"Well, she isn't going to see him again," said Joyce forcefully. "I'll wrap it up and post it back to him."

Paddy was whining to be let out. Deborah went to open the door for him. She looked up, startled to find a police inspector in uniform standing in the threshold.

"Joyce!" she called.

"I told you we'd let the top floor," said her cousin, as she came out to the hall. "This is our tenant, David Gray. Inspector, this is my cousin, Miss Vail."

The inspector was a tall, solid man of about thirty, with a serious expression. Nodding briefly, he walked past them and started up the stairs.

"I hear Andrew Garvin is back," said Joyce.

The inspector paused with a hand on the banister.

"We're keeping an eye on him," he replied.

This casual utterance irritated Deborah intensely.

Chapter 7

On the freshly washed morning following the night of rain, Andrew Garvin drove to Garnock in his Jaguar. He had shopping to do that could not be put off any longer. It might he more discreet to do his errands in Dumdires where he was less well known, but he was hanged if gossiping tongues were going to make him drive thirty miles out in his way.

He could not afford the car. He never had been able to afford it. Only...Erica had kept on at him until he bought it for her. Looking back, he saw their married life as an unending scramble for money, more money, and yet more money. He had been driven to abase his talent as an artist with hack work for advertising agencies. His overdraft at the bulk had long since reached its limit; his house was mortgaged to the eaves. Despising himself, he had borrowed from every approachable friend and acquaintance.

Now he must sell the car, sell the house, work like a fiend and scrimp like a miser to keep himself out of the bankruptcy court. He tried not to think of the infinitely more ominous court in which he shortly might find himself.

Driving through the rolling green countryside, he kept seeing Erica's beautiful petulant face. The very thought of her was pain and it was with him night and day. Erica. The subtle poison he had taken of his own free will. The poison that went on working it's mischief even though Erica was dead.

He was too absorbed in his thoughts to notice the sharp, avid stares of the pedestrians he passed on the outskirts of the town. In a quiet turning near the square, he parked the car. Walking along Market Street, he was conscious of hostile glances from passers-by, but steeled himself to ignore them. At the tobacconists the salesgirl gaped open-mouthed at him as she weighed his too ounces of cheap tobacco. Turning, he saw two or three faces peering in at the shop window.

By the time he came out half a dozen spectators were gathered to watch him. A commercial was being told in audible whispers the nature of the free attraction.

"That's Garvin…Did ye no' hen'…Aye, the murderer, the yin that bashed his wife."

Andrew walked on, with the pack at his heels, and entered a grocer. The aproned proprietor and his assistants were busy with customers but they froze abruptly as if stricken motionless: and for a while, their eyes wide with curiosity, were all that proved they were not statues. Then suddenly, as if a penny had been dropped into a slot, animating a peep show, the grocer and his assistants went about their business again, filling orders, enquiring about other necessities. But there was an artificial quality about this stir of activity, a falseness about the unctuous enquiries and the stilted replies. It was like a scene stage by amateur actors who were not up in their lines. None of them could keep their attention on the business at hand. Every pair of eyes kept wandering furtively to Andrew Garvin and their minds nibbled at him like mice on cheese.

When it was the artist's turn to be served, the grocer cleared his throat self-consciously and studiously avoided looking directly at him.

"Sir?"

Andrew ordered bread and beans, sugar and coffee. He added eggs and tinned milk, for the local dairy had stopped delivering to his house. The shop was bustling with newly arrived customers, most of them out of breath and uncertain of their wants, whose small purchases were transparent excuses for coming in. The grocer felt that he, himself, was on show. Out of the corner of his eye he could see the gaping crowd clustered round his shop front. His bearing became that of a man who plays an important role in a drama.

Outside the shop, the crowd bulged over the pavement. Rumours were being bandied from one to another, but a hush fell when Andrew appeared in the doorway. A hundred eyes stared at him with inquisitiveness and enmity. They formed a barrier between him and the street but until he tried to pass there was no telling whether they would fall back to make way or force him to shoulder a path for himself. Others were coming to swell the crowd, some with as much haste as dignity would permit, some frankly running.

Andrew moved forward with as matter-of-fact an air as if his path was clear.

A little girl who had jostled her way through from the rear worked herself between a pair of adult legs and popped up almost into the artist's belt buckle. Someone's arm struck her ear and she let out a plaintive howl. Andrew reached out a hand to steady her. She thrust herself back, yelling, "Dinna touch me!"

Someone on tiptoe at the fringe of the crowd shouted: "Whit's he daein' tae the bairn?"

"He grabbed at her."

"He hit her."

"On the poor wee thing."

The child, sensing the dramatic possibilities of the incident, began to cry.

That morning, Deborah was driving her cousin on a round of errands. When the car turned into Market Street they saw at once that something was wrong. At a safe distance from the disturbance, Deborah parked at the curb, and Joyce stepped out to see what was happening. Too small to peer over the jostling shoulders of the crowd, she button-holed the chemist who was standing in his doorway.

Joyce came back to the car. "It's Andrew Garvin," she told Deborah.

"What are they doing to him?"

"I don't know. Nothing very much, I don't suppose. Only staring and calling names. The man's asking for trouble, showing his face in the town."

She saw a look of determination forming on Deborah's chiselled features.

"Don't be an idiot," she said sharply, "There's nothing you can do. Leave it to the police."

"The police don't seem to be doing very much," said Deborah grimly, reaching for the gear lever.

"Deborah, please...you'll only get yourself talked about. After all, the man means nothing to you."

"He's in trouble. That ought to mean something to any human being."

With a final cry from Joyce ringing in her ears, Deborah shot the car forward. She was not at all sure what she was going to do. Perhaps the crowd would scatter and make way if she drove the car straight at it. Perhaps not...

Chapter 8

Deborah glimpsed an opening between buildings, a cobbled lane running through to the next street. It was close to the scene of activity but only a few stragglers were milling about at the mouth of the lane.

Disengaging the gear lever, she revved the car engine furiously and at the same time pressed the horn, setting up a racket that made those nearest her jump with alarm. She guided the nose of the car into the lane, jammed on the brakes, and left the engine running. Jumping out, she scrambled up on a fender, raising herself until she could see into the core of the mob.

Seeing Andrew hemmed in there, she waved frantically until she caught his eye. His expression, as recognition dawned, was one of almost ludicrous disbelief.

"Over here," she shouted.

He had been unable to clear a way for himself but now that Deborah was involved, he put a shoulder between the two nearest men and propelled himself through. The action was so sudden and violent that he reached the edge of the crowd before the people were aware that he was gone.

"You little fool," he exclaimed on reaching the car, "get away from here."

Jumping down from the fender, Deborah flung herself into the driver's seat and beckoned to him to follow. She saw the mingled emotions reflected on his face: a reluctance to run away; an unwillingness to involve her; a resentment of the mob that made him itch to lash out at the nearest gaping face. There wasn't time to stand there and argue with himself. Deborah shouted at him angrily and he crushed in beside her. Before he could close the door she drove ahead, into the lane. She raced the car over the cobbles to the other end. There she braked violently, almost throwing their heads up against the windshield, and looked right and left before turning into the next street. The pavements here were all but deserted. None of the few pedestrians troubled to glance their way. They drove a hundred yards in silence.

"I suppose I ought to thank you," said Andrew Garvin at last, "but I'm too angry with you for taking such a chance."

"I was afraid the crowd might get out of hand."

"My car's not far from here, if you don't mind dropping me at it."

"No, I don't mind," said Deborah quietly.

It was deflating, after her desperate effort, to hear him giving directions as casually as if she were a taxi driver. A few streets away, she brought her car to a stop behind his Jaguar. Someone had taken the trouble to daub the hood and windshield with mud. Andrew got out and turned to look at Deborah through a window.

"I'm a surly brute," he said. "Please forgive me. I—I'm not myself."

"If people did to me what they were doing to you, I wouldn't be myself."

"That's just the point. You ought to have kept out of it. People will talk."

"Do you think I care what they say?"

Andrew regarded her seriously. "I read once about an African native who took refuge in a tree from a wounded buffalo. He tied himself on so that the beast could not dislodge him when it butted the tree with its skull. He was just high enough to be beyond reach of its horns. But his feet were dangling. He could not bring them up, and the beast started licking them with its tongue. The tongue was like a rasp and in a few hours, it stripped the flesh and sinews from his feet and ankles, right down to the bare bones. By the time help came he had bled to death."

"What a horrible story."

"Human tongues are like that," said Andrew. "With their malice and lies they'll strip you to the bone...Well, I'll be on my way. It'll do you no good to be seen talking to me."

"I'd like to ask a question. About something that's none of my business."

Andrew studied her. "Fire away," he said.

"I suppose I'm giving you one more jab, asking about the—the crime. But I would like to know who found the—the—"

"The body? Well, that's an innocuous question, compared with some I've had to answer. My wife was found by her maid about five o'clock in the afternoon. I came home about twenty minutes later, to a house and garden swarming with police."

"But, if you had a maid how could the murder go undetected for hours? Surely, she heard something?"

"The maid was in Dumfries all day. My wife sent her on an errand by the early morning bus."

"Oh."

"I spent the day painting near Old Knowe Farm. At least"—he made a face—"that's my story. The first time the police questioned me they listened gravely and seemed to believe me. The second time, about twenty-four hours later, they had developed a certain scepticism."

He brought out a pipe. His strong restless fingers toyed with it while he talked.

"For a week they kept hauling me in at intervals. A few minor points needed clarifying, they said. And then they confronted me with the written statements of three witnesses. The dear old lady who lives at the bend of the road near my house, the attendant at the garage where I buy petrol, and the farmer's son from Old Knowe.

"The old lady had seen me arriving home about the time of the murder. The garage attendant had sold me petrol on my way home. The farmer's son, mending dikes all day near the spot where I claimed to be, was quite sure I was nowhere in sight. So, you see, I'm not only a murderer. I'm a liar."

"If they are to be believed," said Deborah. Her intent grey eyes searched his face. "Why did they lie?"

"You say it as if you were quite sure they did lie."

"Well, didn't they?"

"I don't know why they lied. If it was one person it could be an honest mistake. Three honest mistakes are a bit hard to swallow."

"What happened to the maid?" asked Deborah, remembering the dust and disorder of his house.

"Annie Manson? Her mother whisked her home that evening. To a small holding on the Edinburgh Road."

A baker's van was nearing. At sight of them, the driver slowed to a crawl. His mouth fell open as he craned his neck to stare. Andrew straightened up. His expression became rigid and impersonal. He spoke a curt word, made a stiff gesture, as if Deborah had stopped only to ask a direction. Turning, he walked quickly to his car and drove off.

Chapter 9

It stood close to the road. A low-roofed cottage of white-washed stone with outbuildings of rugged appearance. A sign on the gate, unevenly lettered by an amateur hand, proclaimed:

WM. MANSON

As Deborah pushed open the gate a buxom, middle-aged woman with flour on her muscular bare forearms and an apron round her middle came to the open door and looked out with an authoritative eye.

"Annie?" she repeated when Deborah inquired for the girl. "And whit wid ye be wantin' wi' her?"

"I understand she worked for the Garvins."

"Aye, that she did," said the woman, pursing her lips. "And got her heid filled wi' nonsense. Lipstick an' gaddin' about an' nae respeck for onybody."

"Oh, Mother," said a voice from within the cottage.

The fresh face of a girl in the late teens looked out over the woman's brawny shoulder.

"Dinna 'Oh Maher' me," said the woman. "I ken whit I'm talkin' aboot. It's bad enow, bringin' up lassies these days, withoot a redhaired hussy pittin' waur ideas in their heids."

Grudgingly, she edged her bulk to let her daughter pass. Mistrusting Deborah's elegance and self-possession, and her Englishy accent, she remained within earshot while her daughter conversed with the stranger.

"I shan't keep you; but there's something I'd like to ask."

"Yes, miss?"

"I'm afraid it's about the murder."

"Oh." The girl looked disappointed. She had hoped this attractive stranger would offer a position. "That's all anyone talks about."

"I expect it gets you down. Now, about the errand your mistress sent you on—the one that kept you away all day."

"Oh, that? That was only an excuse to get me out of the way," said Annie frankly. "Every so often she'd send me to Dumfries for something I could have got as well at Garnock.

When I came back it was easy to see that she'd had a visitor while I was gone. One she didn't want me to know about."

"A man?"

"Yes, miss."

"Always the same man?"

"I don't think so. I couldn't say for sure. On those occasions I never saw the caller. Except once, when I got a lift instead of coming by bus, and was back early. And then I only saw a gentleman driving off in his car."

"What did he look like?"

"I've no idea, miss. I was a good way off. I could just make out that it was a man. The car was one of those sports models, like the master's Jaguar."

"Was it usual for your mistress to be in pyjamas at one in the afternoon?"

"Not as a rule, miss. Usually, she was dressed by noon and off to Garnock or Dumfries for lunch."

"I want to get one point quite clear," said Deborah. "Annie, you're certain Mrs. Garvin was expecting a caller?"

"Oh, yes, miss. I'd come to know the drill, as the saying goes."

After thanking the girl and her mother, Deborah walked back to her car. It was long after lunchtime when she returned to Birch Drive.

There was an apology on the tip of her tongue but her cousin would not listen.

"Joyce," said Deborah gently.

An indignant sniff and a reproving glance was the only answer.

"I'm sorry," said Deborah.

"You're not sorry a bit," said Joyce. "I was never so humiliated. How could you make such an exhibition of yourself? In an hour it was all over Garnock that you drove slap into a crowd, knocking down half a dozen people, to rescue Andrew Garvin."

"I didn't knock down anyone."

"No, you didn't. More by good luck than judgment. Oh, Deborah, how could you?"

"I had to. I couldn't help it."

"Before you came, I boasted about you to all my friends. My cousin, the glamorous actress. Now what will they think?"

"Probably that I did it for publicity."

"Don't joke. It isn't funny. Everyone was dying to meet you. The Amateur Dramatic Society wanted you to direct their next play. I haven't had time to tell you of all the invitations to lunch and tea."

"And now I've blotted my copybook. Shall I pack my things and leave in disgrace?"

"Darling," said Joyce reproachfully, "you know I'm on your side. I'm all for you. Only...well, you do make it difficult. And then, there's the MacInches. They're bound to have heard."

"And who are the MacInches? You speak the name almost with awe. Ought I to make a low bow?"

"They're the only 'County' people we know. Hector is a Q.C. and very wealthy. Judith, his wife, is a dear. They live in Edinburgh but spend as much time as possible at their country house near Garnock. They're giving a dinner party for you tomorrow night. You'll get a fabulous meal—and a chance to wear your prettiest evening dress."

"Sounds inviting. I'll be on my best behaviour...Oh! I meant to tell you when I came in—I've talked to the girl who used to be the Garvin's maid."

"I don't want to hear about it," said Joyce, stiffening again.

"On the day she was killed, Erica Garvin expected a male caller. Doesn't that suggest a few possibilities? A lover, tired of her, perhaps, who couldn't be rid of her except by—"

"I tell you; I'm not interested."

"Oh, very well." Rising, Deborah said, "I think I'll put the car away. It's time I learned where it goes. Where did Ewan put it last night?"

"In the old coach house. You'll see it at the end of the garden. There's loads of room."

As she went out by the front door, Deborah heard a metallic clicking somewhere to the rear of the place. Steering her car slowly round the curving, moss-grown drive, she saw a man perched on a ladder, pruning a tall hedge with a pair of clippers. The wide doors of the disused coach house stood open and a ragged jacket dangled from a doorknob. The neck of a whisky bottle protruded from a torn pocket...

Chapter 10

There was space in the old coach house for half a dozen cars. After she had parked her own, in a convenient position for taking it out again, Deborah noticed the gleaming paint and chromium of a sports car by the far wall.

The man on the ladder turned his head to inspect her inquisitively as she walked back down the drive. He was unwashed, uncombed, unshaven, and the seat of his trousers ballooned out behind as if they had been made for a much larger man. He had an unhealthily yellow skin, a mouthful of decayed teeth, a shock of iron-grey hair. He might have been of any age between fifty and sixty.

The sight of his slack lips, protuberant eyes and porcine nostrils sent a shiver down Deborah's spine. Her pace faltered. It was a moment of shock. She was sure that his was the brutish face that peered in at her through the window of Andrew Garvin's kitchen on the previous night of blustering wind and rain.

When she returned to the comforting normality of the living room, Joyce noticed at once that Deborah was shaken.

"Darling, what is it? Seen a ghost?"

"There's a dreadful old man out there, on a ladder!"

"That's only Scobie," said Joyce, laughing at her. "He's a filthy old creature and he drinks like a fish—but he's the only odd-job man in the neighbourhood."

"He doesn't look human."

"He isn't...quite. But we're jolly glad to have him. He comes and goes as he pleases but at least he keeps the place from becoming an utter jungle. It's far too much garden for Ewan to cope with."

Seated beside the fire, with her baby son asleep in a huge

clothes basket beside her, Joyce told her cousin about Scobie. As long as anyone could remember, he had existed shiftlessly in a crudely converted shed on the outskirts of Garnock. He lived alone, except for a mongrel dog that looked most of all like a mastiff. Scobie was a scrounger, a poacher, a clothesline robber, every kind of petty rogue. But those who complained of him to the police generally lived to regret it, because of the vindictive annoyances he caused them.

He worked only when in need of ready cash. He knew all the tricks of living with the minimum of effort. The police had employed him for a week or two, to help in their search for the weapon that killed Erica Garvin.

Deborah looked thoughtful. "Joyce," she said suddenly. "Supposing it was Scobie who killed her. He'd know how to hide the weapon so that it never could be found."

"A while ago you said it was a male visitor who killed her. Do be consistent," Joyce responded tartly.

"You couldn't put anything past a man like that," Deborah pressed. "I have a hunch he's involved in some way. Perhaps he found the weapon and hid it again."

Joyce snorted. "Forfeiting the reward he'd have got from the police?"

"Perhaps he thought he'd get a bigger reward from the murderer."

"There must be something else to talk about," Joyce said fretfully.

"By the way, I saw a snappy sports car in the coach house. I didn't know you owned one."

"We don't. That's David Gray's M.G.A."

"A bit dashing for a police inspector."

"He likes to get out in the country when he's off duty. David lets Ewan use it any other time."

Deborah stretched and yawned in luxuriant drowsiness. "I ought to be writing letters but I'm too comfortable to go upstairs for my writing paper."

"No need for that," said Joyce. "You'll find note paper and pens in the top drawer of the desk over there."

The drawer opened an inch or so and then stuck. Taking out the photograph that had been the obstruction, Deborah straightened the crumpled corners.

"I know this face," she said.

"It's Erica," said Joyce, coming to look. "Wasn't she lovely?"

"Andrew is painting a portrait of her from memory. I saw it in his studio. The paint was still wet. Doesn't that mean he loved her very much…still loves her?"

"Or that she's become an obsession."

"You honestly do believe he did kill her, don't you?"

"I don't know anyone who has the slightest doubt of it."

"'To darling Joyce, with love'," said Deborah, reading an inscription scrawled flamboyantly across the lower right-hand corner of the photograph.

"She called everyone darling," said Joyce, reddening.

"Then you weren't a special friend?"

"Oh, perhaps I was," Joyce admitted reluctantly. "We saw quite a bit of Erica and Andrew when they were first married. They were different, somehow, from the ordinary run of people. More exciting to be with, I suppose."

The door opened and Ewan walked in, long, lean, ungainly, and glad to be home. He was demanding to be told what was for tea when the telephone rang. Joyce hastened to answer. After a brief conversation she looked surprised and said doubtfully, "Well…I'll see what he says."

"Who is it?" asked Ewan, dandling his son.

"Judith MacInch," said Joyce, covering the mouthpiece with

her hand. "She's a man short for dinner tomorrow evening. She wants to invite Inspector David Gray."

"I'll bet that was Hector's idea," said Ewan, frowning. "He has a perverted sense of humour."

"What do you mean?" asked Deborah.

"The Sinclairs will be at the party," said Ewan, "and Enid Sinclair is Andrew Garvin's sister. It's a bit thick, asking her to dine with the policeman who's doing his best to convict her brother. Not that Enid has a good word to say for Andrew."

"They fell out long ago," said Joyce. "If you ask me, it was because Bill Sinclair was too much attracted to Erica. Still, you'd think a sister would stand by her brother, not disown him in trouble as Enid has done."

Going to the foot of the stairs, she called: "David!"

Inspector Gray answered by running down to the first-floor landing and putting his head over the banister. When he heard Joyce's message, he gave a low whistle and came down into the living room.

"Pretty cool," he commented: "You'd better tell Mrs. MacInch that Mr. Gray admires her nerve but declines her invitation. No, wait a minute." His appraising glance had fallen on Deborah, who was regarding him with faint hostility. "On second thought, tell her Mr. Gray will be delighted to come to her party."

Chapter 11

"Stay and have a cup of tea?" Joyce cordially invited David Gray.

The police inspector hesitated for only a moment before replying, "Thanks, I believe I will," but in that instant a spark of antagonism seemed to leap between him and Deborah. She was aware that it amused him to know that she would not have seconded the invitation. Selecting the most comfortable chair he seated himself with aplomb.

Deborah thought him annoyingly sure of himself. She had no doubt he had ample self-conceit. At breakfast that morning, Joyce had insisted on giving her his history in brief, although Deborah had protested that no subject interested her less. He was the son of a local doctor. As a boy, David Gray had planned to be a doctor but when left almost penniless in his late teens he had joined the police force and for years had walked a beat. Although his career was interrupted by military service during the war, he had risen in the police force in record time.

He was fair-haired, fresh-skinned, clear-eyed and built like an athlete; but Deborah could not like him. There was a sardonic twist to his mouth, as if he was wary of the world and watchful for false moves.

"None the worse for your adventure this morning, Miss Vail?" he said in a mockingly solicitous tone.

"You heard about it?" asked Joyce, when Deborah failed to answer.

"A constable reported the incident. He gave a description of the lady who drove recklessly into the crowd and the registration number of her car. I told him to interest himself no further."

"I wonder you didn't have me investigated," said Deborah.

"Oh, I did," he replied, crossing his legs. "Just a routine phone call to London. The Scotland Yard people were commendably prompt. It seems you're reputed to be of very high character. No questionable associates. You were with a stock company in Bristol when Garvin was in London, so you didn't meet him there. You've never been in Garnock before, so he didn't meet you here. So, you needn't be afraid that the papers will liven up the case with hints about the artist's association with a beautiful—and mysterious—actress."

"Do you often get your face slapped, Mr. Gray?" asked Deborah furiously.

"Not often. I watch out for things like that."

* * * * *

The following morning, Deborah stopped for petrol at a wayside garage. About to drive off, she noticed that her receipt was wrongly dated. She called the attendant back. "This isn't Tuesday the ninth," she pointed out.

"Isn't it?" He scratched his chin. "No, neither it is. Wednesday all day, isn't it?" He grinned. "Ah, well, what's the difference? As long as we both know you've paid."

Deborah looked at the name of the garage. "Isn't this where Mr. Garvin gets his petrol?"

The attendant leaned confidingly on her car door, all set for a friendly gossip.

"He did—but he doesn't. I'm afraid I've offended the gentleman. Not that I lose any sleep over it. Aye, I could tell you a thing or two about that bold lad and the fancy lady he was married to. D'ye know, he bought petrol from me the very day of the murder, when he swore he was miles away? I don't think he liked me spoiling his alibi, but what's a man to do when the police come asking."

"When did the police question you? How long after the murder?"

"Oh, a few days. Maybe a week."

"How could you be sure of the exact day he bought petrol? It's easy to make a mistake."

"When they came asking, I looked up the sales slip. There it was, in black and white, no getting around it."

"And a week from now," said Deborah, "you'll look up the carbon of my sales slip—and be ready to swear I bought petrol on Tuesday the ninth."

* * * * *

Old Mrs. Craw lived alone but was never lonely. She had for company all the joys and sorrows of eighty years to live over again. And she had a window facing the road.

When not nodding before the fire, half napping, half remembering, she loved to sit by her window, watching placidly for an occasional passer-by. If someone stopped at her gate Old Mrs. Craw had the kettle on for tea and her hearing-aid in place before the caller was halfway up the path.

On this chill, cloudy morning she startled Deborah by opening the door to her while the girl's hand still reached for the knocker.

"Come away in, my dear. My, you're a bonny sight in that pretty dress."

Deborah hovered diffidently, half in the tiny hall and half out.

"Come ben to the parlour. Sit ye down by the fire. We'll have a nice cup of tea."

In a casual way Deborah remarked on the tall chimneys and grey walls of the house, far off down the road that was the only other dwelling in sight.

"That's where Mr. Garvin bides," replied Old Mrs. Craw. After a reflective pause she added, "Poor Mr. Garvin."

"Then you don't think he's guilty?"

"Ah, my dear. I don't let my mind dwell on it, one way or the other. Ye ken, it was I that saw him coming home that day. I've often wished I hadn't."

"Did he pass your cottage?"

"No, he came the other way. At the back of twelve, it was. And within the hour the poor lassie was dead."

"At that distance, how did you know it was him?"

"I've got eyes, haven't I?" said the old lady, with a touch of asperity. "He drove up in his motorcar. Dressed the way he usually is, in jacket and trousers that don't match."

"A sports jacket and slacks," said Deborah.

"Aye, it was him all right," said Mrs. Craw unhappily. "And I had to admit it to the police when they asked."

The old lady took her spectacles from her lap, wiped them on her apron, put them on, and blinked two or three times to focus her sight. She stared out of the window.

"It's an odd time for the postman," she said.

Deborah turned to look. A man on a bicycle was riding up the road but it was not a bicycle of official red, he was not in uniform, and his burden was a knapsack, not a postbag. Yes, the old lady had eyes; but they were unreliable at a distance.

Chapter 12

Joyce was making last-minute alterations to an evening dress when Deborah burst into the room. In mounting excitement, Deborah told her cousin of the wrongly dated sales slip the garage attendant had given her that morning and of her talk with Old Mrs. Craw.

Joyce refused to be impressed. Her manner was disapproving. "I don't see why you're so worked up. It doesn't seem that important to me."

"People who make mistakes in the date are likely to be in the habit of making such mistakes. After a lapse of a week, how could one have the slightest faith in the man's evidence? It may have been the day before the murder, or a couple of days before, that Andrew Garvin stopped for petrol."

"The police aren't stupid. They're bound to have taken that sort of factor into consideration."

"The police," said Deborah disgustedly.

"David's no fool, whate'er you may think of him."

"As far as Old Mrs. Craw is concerned—well, all she saw was a man in a sports jacket getting out of a sports car. It could have been anyone."

Joyce did not seem to relish that line of thought. She shook her head vehemently.

"All those little cars look much alike," Deborah went on, "and a sports jacket is normal wear for men in the country. It wasn't Andrew Garvin she saw, it was the visitor his wife was expecting when she sent the maid on a senseless errand."

"I wish you'd forget the whole business," said Joyce petulantly.

"How can I?"

They looked at each other. It struck Deborah that Joyce

seemed almost frightened by the suggestion that some man other than Andrew Garvin might have killed Erica.

* * * * *

The babysitter arrived at a quarter to seven, bringing a friend. She hoped Mrs. Monteith would not mind, but she was scared to be alone with a murderer at large. Joyce said that was all nonsense. She only wanted someone to gossip with.

"Clothes and boys. That's all you girls think of."

"What else is there?" asked the baby sitter's friend with a giggle.

Paddy, the Sealyham, was suspicious of the friend, he kept circling her warily, making low-throated noises. He was not sure this giggler could be trusted near the precious baby. With a firm tread on the stairs, David Gray came down, looking debonair in a double-breasted dinner jacket.

Ewan gave an admiring whistle. "That's what I should look like!"

In the driveway, Deborah's elderly coupé looked like a poor relation behind David's glossy M.G.A. David pointed out that there was not room for four in either car.

"I'll take Miss Vail in mine," he said. "You and Joyce can go in Miss Vail's car, Ewan."

"I don't think he could handle it," said Deborah stiffly. "No offence, Ewan, but the old thing's a bit erratic. You have to know her little ways."

"Then I'll go with you," said David promptly. It was no use snubbing the man; a snub went right over his head. "Ewan, you take the M.G.A. No fancy driving. Remember you're a sober old married man."

Ewan and his wife climbed into the sports car, which started at once and was quickly gone. To Deborah's annoyance, an attack of asthma seemed to be afflicting her car. The engine wheezed and spluttered but refused to catch. David sat beside her, cool and imperturbable, offering neither counsel nor help.

It was several minutes before she coaxed the engine into a laboured panting, let in the clutch and drove slowly, almost limpingly, out of the drive. She drove at a sedate speed through the town.

David offered a cigarette. She refused coldly. He said it was a nice evening. This she could not deny. She said "Very" as if the word choked her. After a time, he told her pleasantly to turn left and, a little later, to turn right. She was relieved when they turned in between high wrought-iron gates and crunched over gravel to the imposing doorway of the MacInches' large bright-lighted house. The moment they stopped David came around to her side swiftly and handed her out as urbanely as if they had come in a Rolls.

The door was opened by a butler who admitted them to a panelled hall and took David's hat and coat. A rosy-cheeked housemaid relieved Deborah of her wrap. The butler led them into a room humming with conversation. It was habit with Deborah, a part of her stage training, to make an entrance. Before joining a gathering, she always squared her shoulders, threw back her head and looked cordially expectant. David, at her elbow, was amused by this instinctive performance.

The room, of elegant proportions, was furnished with taste and charm. Warmed by a blazing log fire, lit by discreetly shaded lamps, it made a gracious background for the men in formal black and white and the women in colourful dresses. A tall, middle-aged man detached himself from the group by the fire and came to them with a welcoming smile, followed by a very thin woman with a wan, almost haggard face.

"I heard how lovely you were, Miss Vail," said Hector MacInch in his rich, fruity voice, "but I'm afraid they didn't do you justice." How like an actor, was her immediate reaction. Well, she supposed a brilliant criminal advocate must be an actor of sorts. He carried with him an aura of wig and gown and ceremonial. He enveloped one of her hands in a well-fleshed palm.

"It was good of you to come, my dear," said Judith MacInch, her smile giving Deborah a glimpse of vanished beauty. A kindly, gracious person, she made Deborah feel very much at home.

"Good to see you, Inspector," said Hector MacInch, with the merest hint of mockery in his twinkling eyes.

"Inspector on duty," replied David pleasantly. "Off-duty, 'David' to my friends and 'Mr. Gray' to my acquaintances."

"Then come and have a cocktail, David. You, too, Miss Vail. I suggest one of my special martinis. Five parts gin, one-part Noilly Prat and one drop of Pernod. Well shaken with plenty of ice." With a Latin flourish he kissed his bunched fingertips. "Perfection."

Chapter 13

While Hector MacInch busied himself with a cocktail shaker, his wife, Judith, presented Deborah to the other guests. First Enid and Bill Sinclair. Enid's manner was effusive but her gaze was sharply appraising. She had been pretty as a girl, but fretful lines were now etched under her eyes. Her husband wore the eager, guileless face of a schoolboy on the thickened body of a self-indulgent man in the thirties.

Deborah thought at once that nothing would ever touch him deeply. He would enjoy life heedlessly to the limit of his capacity, without ever understanding it. He held Deborah's hand a fraction too long. It was obvious his wife was aware of it but her tongue went on uttering blithe nothings without faltering.

The remaining guests, now talking to Joyce and Ewan Monteith, were a woman novelist and her son, a willowy youth with spectacles shaped like teardrops and hair as sleek as a seal's pelt.

In the regrouping that followed their arrival Inspector David Gray was taken captive and led to a window seat by the woman novelist. Deborah found herself, glass in hand, on a couch between Bill Sinclair and the willowy young man. Bill told her that the martinis were excellent. He knew. He'd had four already. He asked why he had never seen her on the stage during his trips to London. How could he have missed her?

"Probably by going to the wrong theatre," Deborah said blithely.

She turned to the novelist's son, who was talking about himself into her other ear. Something about a life of his own which he was not encouraged to lead.

The maid was handing round canapes. Tiny hot sausages on toothpicks. Fried shrimp with a sauce to dip them into. The young man helped himself with both hands.

Bill Sinclair had his glass replenished, then spoke confidentially in Deborah's ear. "Can't we meet somewhere one afternoon? I'd love to show you our local views. I could pick you up with my car. You've no idea how much I need someone to talk to."

"There's always your wife," said Deborah unfeelingly.

"I can't talk to her," said Bill peevishly. "She only listens with half an ear."

At the moment, Enid was giving them both eyes. Deborah turned back to the novelist's son. "You're an only child?"

"Well, you can't wonder at that. I took nine months and she can produce a book in six."

The compelling voice of his mother boomed across the room. She was not addressing a public gathering, only a single male, but the effect was the same.

"The young of today are spoiled, lazy, egotistical—"

"Mother judges everyone by me," said the youth indulgently.

The butler came to his master's elbow without the cocktail shaker. "Dinner is served," he intoned, like a judge pronouncing sentence.

While helping himself to enough for two at the dinner table, the novelist's son told Deborah of his uphill battle to make his mother buy him a car. Deborah grasped the opportunity to steer the conversation to cars in general.

Judith MacInch said that for sheer comfort give her their old Daimler, although the running expense was ruinous. Her husband retorted that the Daimler always made him feel he was being conveyed in a hearse. For driving pleasure there was nothing to beat his Aston Martin. Bill spoke boastfully of his Austin Healey.

"A ridiculous car for people in our position," said Enid. "It would be different if we could afford two cars."

The woman novelist listened judicially to something her host was saying. When her interest began to wane, she brusquely interrupted him.

"Naturally, I've heard all about it. In this part of the country, they seem to talk of nothing else. But the story is too hackneyed for my public. The only advantage to writing about a man killing his wife is that the motive is always so clearly understandable."

"Joke," said her son brightly and was stabbed by a maternal glare.

"In this case," Hector persisted, "you might find the victim an enthralling study. She had the beauty of an angel. I know that sounds trite, but it's true. On the other hand, she hadn't a scruple to her name. A curious mixture, wouldn't you say, Enid?"

"Andrew was a fool to marry her," said Enid angrily, "and he had no right to bring her here to live."

"My dear, how vehement you sound," said the novelist, regarding her with avid curiosity.

"Enid used to be Andrew Garvin's sister," explained Hector.

"Used to be?"

"She scrapped the relationship. Simply cut him out of her life. A pity there is no law enabling one to divorce a brother."

"What a perfect stinker you are, Hector MacInch," said Enid. "As if it were not enough, asking us to dine with a—a—"

"A policeman," said David Gray quietly.

"Really?" broke in the willowy youth, immensely intrigued. "A proper copper?"

"Who is doing his best to convict Andrew. I may have disowned my brother, but I must say it's a bit thick—" Enid went on.

"My dear Enid, surely the son of Old Doctor Gray is socially acceptable anywhere in the county." Hector paused before adding, with ironic emphasis, "I imagine even Erica found him... acceptable."

David was silent.

"As a matter of fact," said Hector suavely, "I invited Andrew himself to dine with us this evening."

"Hector, you didn't!" gasped his wife.

"It might have been amusing," said Hector, "but Andrew declined without thanks."

"You must be mad to do such a thing!" Enid blazed.

Deborah expected her to rise in righteous fury and walk out. But although Enid glowered at her host, she kept her seat. And Deborah remembered something Joyce had told her. The MacInches were principal shareholders in a hosiery mill managed by Bill Sinclair. Joyce had more than hinted that Bill was fortunate to have so well paid a job. Enid might fume but she would not dare to quarrel with her bread and butter.

"Sorry if I upset you, Enid," said Hector insincerely. "But, after all, I can remember a time when you and Bill and the Garvins were almost an inseparable foursome."

"When he brought her here, I did my best to like her, for Andrew's sake."

"Was that why Bill did his best to like her? Didn't find it difficult, did you, Bill?"

"Draw it mild, old chap," muttered Bill uncomfortably.

"This is all very interesting," exclaimed the woman novelist. "I do hope no one's feelings are being lacerated. After all, conversation should challenge and stimulate, should it not?"

"Not to the extent Hector would like," said Joyce, with fire in her eye. "It would suit Hector to see us all spitting at each other like cats across the table. You're an odd combination of joviality and malice, Hector. Like a jolly Santa Claus giving a live gun instead of a toy one to a small boy."

Chapter 14

The woman novelist glanced at her companions seated at the dinner table. "Apparently you all know this Mr. Garvin well," she said. "What is he like?"

"Andrew's a violent chap," said Hector MacInch, their host. "One evening when they were here he gave his wife quite a going over."

"Erica was not herself that night," said Judith MacInch, who would not have dreamed of suggesting that a guest was intoxicated. "She behaved foolishly and Andrew decided to take her home."

"Judith, he knocked her head against a wall."

"Perhaps she knocked it herself, Hector. People do, when—"

"When they're not themselves," said Hector. "However, the murder evidence against him, while black, is not as conclusive as it's made out to be. For instance, the dried blood on the sleeve of his jacket—"

"Blood?" Judith exclaimed. "On the sleeve?"

"It was of his wife's blood type."

"Well, then, surely—"

"Ah, but Andrew claimed to have cut himself and was able to show the wound. And, as it happens, his blood is of the same type as Erica's. An Rh. Plus, I believe. Of course, there are hundreds of sub-groupings but it is difficult in laboratory tests to make minute identifications of dried blood."

"I should like to know where you got that information," said Inspector David Gray.

"I have my sources," said Hector.

"But surely all that dirty linen was washed at the coroner's inquest?" asked the woman novelist.

"In Scotland," replied Hector, "we do not hold a coroner's inquest. In the case of a death by accident or any violent means except murder, the police themselves hold a public inquiry to establish the facts. When murder is suspected, a formal report is sent to the Crown Agent, in Edinburgh, for consideration by the law officers. If the case is pretty strong against a particular person, the law officers usually decide to prosecute, even if they have doubts of gaining a conviction. A prosecution has a way of clearing the air, if you see what I mean."

"Otherwise, gossip and surmise have full rein?"

"Precisely. That is why it is interesting that they haven't yet decided to prosecute Andrew. No one in the district seems to doubt his guilt."

"It's an absolute nightmare," said Enid Sinclair. "You don't know what the scandal is doing to Rill and me."

"Doesn't it matter what it's doing to your brother?" Deborah asked suddenly.

"It's Andrew's own fault he's in it. We were dragged in."

"Supposing he's entirely innocent?"

"What an awkward suggestion," said Hector MacInch with a smile. "If Andrew didn't kill her, young lady, one of us did." He paused to enjoy the concerted gasp of consternation before adding, "Unless it was a jealous wife."

Deborah noticed a quick glance pass between Enid and Bill Sinclair. It startled and disconcerted her to realize that with the exception of the novelist's son, who was a recent visitor to the neighbourhood, any of the men seated around the table could have been Erica's lover. Perhaps more than one of them was. Old Mrs. Craw had seen a man in a tweed jacket and slacks climbing out of a sports car shortly before Erica was murdered. The description might apply equally well to any of these men.

Though the thought was disloyal and she tried hard to reject it, the man might even have been Ewan Monteith. An old sports coat and baggy flannels were Ewan's normal wear. He had the frequent use of David Gray's sports car. But no. It simply was not possible to suspect Ewan.

"When one examines it closely," said Hector, "why should Andrew Garvin have killed his wife? Jealousy? Nonsense. He must have known all along what she was. Why should he suddenly resent it so savagely? If he wanted revenge, time would give it to him."

"We return to the question," boomed the woman novelist. "If Garvin did not kill his wife, who did?"

"If Garvin did not do it," said Hector, "every presentable bachelor and married man in the district is suspect. But I imagine the police have gone into such possibilities—eh, David?"

"A matter of routine," said David curtly.

"But perhaps it isn't routine for the police to investigate the police," Hector replied smoothly. "You're a presentable bachelor yourself, David. And you knew Erica."

"You sound as if I were under cross-examination," said David, his manner making it plain that he would not be inveigled into discussing his private life.

"Happy the man who has an alibi," said Hector. "Where were you at the time of the murder, Bill?"

"Where do you suppose?" answered Bill Sinclair sullenly. "At the office, of course."

"Since when do you lunch at the office?"

"I—I lunched with Enid."

"Naturally, your wife will back you up in that."

"For that matter," said Enid, biting off words, "where were you?"

"I?" Hector laughed easily. "Oh, I was at Drumbirlie, looking over a hunter I thought of buying."

"That was the day before," said his wife.

"Was it? Then I'm hanged if I know where I was. But I daresay the police do. What about you, Ewan? Didn't you find Erica the sort of woman who raises a man's blood pressure?"

Ewan Monteith only hesitated for a moment before drawling, "That's exactly how I'd describe her."

"You surprise me. I expected you to say you've never looked at another woman since you married Joyce."

"You may know all about the law, Hector," said Joyce, her Scots intonation unusually pronounced, "but you know gey little about women. A wife doesn't want her man never to look at another woman. That would be a bloodless sort of gowk. She wants him to look at them all and still prefer her."

"Well bowled, ma'am," said the woman novelist's son.

"When the truth is told," said Judith MacInch, "we shall all feel remarkably foolish, for I'm sure a tramp or a prowler did it. Someone like that dreadful man, Scobie."

"The biggest scoundrel in the neighbourhood," said her husband. "Or shall I say, the biggest scoundrel with the exception of myself? The man gets a lot more of my game than I ever see. I have no doubt he'd cut a throat for half a crown if he thought he could get away with it."

The butler appeared with a disconcerted look on his face. Failing to catch his master's eye, he gave a discreet cough.

"What is it, Gregson?" demanded Hector.

Before the man could frame a reply the reason for his discomfiture walked into the room. It was Andrew Garvin. There was a bitter twist to his lips. He stood in the doorway, swaying slightly, surveying the scene with sardonic contempt.

Chapter 15

Those facing the dining room door stared at the man who stood there. The others turned their heads and craned their necks.

"He's drunk," Enid Sinclair exclaimed in a tone of disgust.

But Deborah knew better. Andrew Garvin was not drunk. He was desperate. He uttered a curt, mirthless laugh in response to his sister's remark. "I was invited to the party," he said.

"Better late than never," said Hector MacInch, rising with a cordial smile. "Gregson, a chair for Mr. Garvin."

"No, thanks, I'm not staying. I saw your lights and decided to see for myself whether people still mingle on a social footing, as friends, as human beings, with their knives and claws sheathed. So, it's true. We haven't all gone back to the dark ages."

"If you've only come to wallow in self-pity," began Enid harshly.

"Not that," replied her brother. "Each of us makes his own prison. If yours is warm and bright, so much the better...I've been to Glasgow. I imagine I broke all the speed laws on the way there and back." He looked at David Gray and told the police inspector: "Your chap, the one on the motorbike, needs a valve-grinding job. I hadn't any trouble shaking him off."

"That's alright," said the police inspector in a matter-of-fact tone. "We got reports on you from points along the way. And one of the Glasgow men kept an eye on you."

"A burly chap in a bowler hat and a raincoat," said Andrew. "He didn't bother to disguise his calling."

"He wasn't supposed to," Gray responded curtly.

It had made Andrew seethe with resentment to be spied on in Glasgow by an obvious policeman in plainclothes. On the drive back to Garnock his anger mounted. He determined on arrival to go straight to the police station and have it out with Gray. He was going to demand either to be arrested or left alone. He could not stand this cat-and-mouse game any longer. It was a setback to be told that Inspector Gray was off-duty; if the matter was urgent, he could be reached at the MacInches, where he was dining. He had decided to go home and postpone his verbal battle with the police official until the following morning.

The bright lights of Hector MacInch's house had rekindled his ire. He knew perfectly well that Hector had only invited him to the dinner out of a warped sense of humour. It was even more insufferable that, on the heels of Andrew's refusal, he should invite the very man who was doing his best to convict Andrew of murder. The original list of guests which Hector had mentioned had not included Inspector Gray. The affront was too great to be borne.

Moved by wrathful indignation, he swung his car between the gates and halted it in front of the house. He marched up the steps and pounded on the knocker, impatient to tell the police inspector and his malicious would-be host, face to face, exactly what he thought of them.

Now, in the presence of this formally clad company, he knew that he had blundered. If he launched on recriminations, he would only delight Hector and play into his hands. As the anger ebbed out of him, it left him drained and weary. Now he only wanted to explain himself briefly and go.

"I went up in a hurry to see an art dealer who handles my work. Almost overnight, oils by Andrew Garvin are in demand. People are willing to pay two and three hundred pounds for paintings they could have had for twenty a couple of months ago."

"Well, that's a bit of luck, old boy," said Bill Sinclair, reaching awkwardly for his wine glass.

The crass stupidity of the remark irritated Deborah. Didn't

the idiot realize what the demand for Andrew's work amounted to? It was not a sincere tribute to an artist. It was because it might be the last work of a notorious murderer. If he was hanged or imprisoned for life there would be no more oils by Andrew Garvin; and the prices would go on rising.

"He had already sold two," said Andrew. "Naturally, I took the money. My creditors will want it. But I forbade him to sell any more. He's crating them and sending them back to me."

Deborah saw him reach out to grip the doorknob. He was all in.

"Shall we have coffee and liqueurs in the drawing room?" suggested Hector.

As they rose, Judith went to Andrew and laid a gentle hand on his arm.

"Andrew, you'll join us?"

"You're very sweet, Judith," he answered, looking down at her with a faint smile, "but...I think I'll be going. Forgive me for being a boor and spoiling your party."

While the rest of the party straggled uncomfortably to the drawing room. Andrew walked to the hall with Deborah at his heels. She came to his side when he was opening the front door.

The butler hovered in the background, doing his best to pretend that he was not there at all.

"I almost forgot." Deborah fumbled in her embroidered evening bag. "I have your lighter. When I stopped at your house that night, I carried it away by mistake."

She held it out. He squinted at it. "It's not mine. I smoke a pipe. I use matches."

"But you handed it to me yourself when I asked for a cigarette."

"Did I?" Frowning, he rubbed his chin. "Come to think of it, I believe I did pick it up somewhere about the house. Yes, I remember wondering where it came from."

Coming out of the drawing room, Bill Sinclair walked unsteadily over to them. He made some scoffing remark, annoying them both, and Andrew went out abruptly, slamming the door. He was gone before Deborah realized that she still held the lighter in her hand. She dropped it into her handbag and for the time being thought no more about it.

Holding her head high, she walked straight past Bill, who followed her closely.

They were met at the drawing-room door by Enid. "You make it so simple for me to find my husband," she said with mild sarcasm. "I only have to look where you are, Miss Vail."

* * * * *

Sleepless in the night, Deborah lay listening to footsteps pacing the floor of the room above her head. The footsteps of Inspector David Gray going to and fro in a restless rhythm.

For the time being the police inspector had gone as far as he could along the road he had set himself to travel. He had made strides in Garnock but there was no future for him here.

The next step must be an appointment to the C.I.D. in a large city like Glasgow or Edinburgh. One day—who could tell?—he might sit in the chair of the man in command in London itself. It all depended on his handling of his first really important case.

If he could convict Andrew Garvin, promotion was certain. And Deborah, lying sleepless in the dark, listening to his ceaseless pacing, hated him for his singleness of purpose. Suddenly she sat bolt upright in bed under the stimulus of a startling thought. Perhaps he had another reason for being so anxious to convict Andrew. Perhaps it was to protect himself.

Chapter 16

One morning Deborah and Joyce set out to go shopping in Deborah's car. They took the baby and his guardian Sealyham to be left for an hour or two with a friend and neighbour. A newish mother, she had offered the accommodation under the delusion that two babies would not be more trouble than one.

"She'll learn," said Joyce.

Backing out of the drive, Deborah noticed Scobie the handyman, cutting the grass. Although well aware of their passing, the man did not offer even a grudging "Good morning." He kept his surly face bent over the lawnmower.

Before they had gone far, Joyce exclaimed that she had forgotten a library book she had promised faithfully to exchange for Ewan. Since it would be a bother turning the car in the narrow street, Deborah parked it at the curb, hopped out quickly and walked back. On nearing the house, it struck her that Scobie's grass cutting had ceased.

The mower stood idle in the middle of the lawn. Scobie was nowhere in sight.

Entering the house quietly, Deborah saw at once that the living room door, left shut, now stood ajar. For once it would have been reassuring to have Inspector Gray within call; but he had risen early and gone about his official duties.

Mustering all her courage, she crept to the slightly open door and pushed it wider. She breathed easier when she saw that the room was untenanted. She wondered what she would have done if she had surprised Scobie in the act of rifling Ewan's desk. Screamed and run, probably, if her legs would carry her.

Listening intently, she heard a faint movement from the direction of the kitchen. Tiptoeing along the passage, she peered in but no one was there. Beginning to think she had alarmed herself over nothing, she noticed that the door to the basement was open. Stealing across the smooth linoleum, she halted breathlessly at the head of the basement stairs.

The basement was shadowed, but a patch of light from a window gave her a distinct view of Scobie. He was kneeling on the floor, scowling with the effort to concentrate, clipping small bits out of old newspapers which were scattered all round him. He had borrowed the shears and pastepot from Ewan's desk and was pasting printed words on to a sheet of foolscap.

Deborah drew back to an angle from which she could glimpse Scobie without herself being seen from below. What now? Should she challenge him? And perhaps feel his gnarled hands on her throat before she could make an outcry?

After some uneasy deliberation she put out a hand, soundlessly opened the refrigerator, and noisily banged it shut. At the sound, Scobie turned his head. In an instant he was on his feet, crouched like a predatory animal. For a dreadful moment Deborah expected him to start upstairs toward her.

Hastily, Scobie folded the foolscap sheet and stuffed it into a pocket of his ragged jacket. With a furtive backward glance, he slipped out through a creaking door leading to the garden. Soon after, Deborah again heard the plaintive whine of the lawnmower.

Shaking at the knees, she retraced her steps to the front hall. When opening the door, she remembered the book she had come for. Every nerve in her body urged her to go, to get away quickly, but she forced herself to delay long enough to find the book and snatch it up in trembling fingers.

On her return to the car, Joyce was blissfully cooing to her son. Otherwise, she could not have helped noticing how shaken Deborah was. And Deborah had decided not to tell her cousin about Scobie until later. It would only frighten and upset her for the rest of the day.

* * * * *

No matter how much shopping remained to be done, Garnock housewives of Joyce's set invariably broke off at eleven, for coffee and gossip at a local café. On entering the place, Deborah and Joyce saw Enid Sinclair beckoning to them urgently from a table in a corner. When they joined her, she gave them an effusive welcome.

She told them she was going to lunch with Judith MacInch.

"Just the two of us. I expect it will be I rather a bore." But it was obvious she hoped her close intimacy with the wife of so wealthy a man would impress them. She spoke glibly, airily, as an insider, one in the know, of the local nobility and gentry, the people whose doings were written up in the morning papers. Under her brittle talkativeness ran a current of discontent, the same yearning for things beyond her grasp that had tormented Erica Garvin.

"Bill will be here any minute. He's bringing the car for me." She turned a toothy smile on Deborah. "What's this I hear about you? It's going to be such a thrill for everyone."

"What is?" asked Deborah blankly.

"Why, you playing the lead in the Amateur Dramatic Society's next production. You are going to, aren't you? Oh, I know it will be a comedown for you, darling, acting with amateurs after all your great London triumphs"—the straight face with which she said this accentuated the mockery—"but just think how exciting it will be for the rest of us."

"It's the first I've heard about it. The secretary did phone to ask if I'd care to give them a few pointers but I told him I didn't feel qualified."

"Oh, we'll have you directing and playing the lead as well before you know where you are."

"Are you and Bill taking part this season?" asked Joyce.

"My dear, I don't know. We haven't given it a thought. We're both frantically busy with one thing and another. But I don't suppose they'll let us out of it. I suppose it's flattering, the way they insist they simply can't do without us but this time I think we must hold out for quite small parts. I mean, it's only fair to give someone else a chance. Oh…there's Bill now."

Catching her husband's eyes, she waved gaily and he made his way to them between tables, pausing briefly here and there to pass the time of day. He was very good-looking, very smartly dressed, very dapper, and very well aware of it. He was the appealingly boyish type so many women yearn to mother but Deborah saw through his facile charm all too clearly.

Enid offered him a cheek as smooth as glass to kiss.

"Is the car outside?" she asked.

"Here are the keys." Bill dropped them in her lap. "Do drive carefully."

"I like that! You're the reckless driver in our family, my love."

Bill sat down, ordered coffee, gratifying the waitress with a smile, brought out his cigarette case, and began to tell how he had handled a recalcitrant supplier that morning; what he had said, what the man stammered in reply, and his own crushing comebacks. Deborah took a cigarette. So did Enid.

Bringing out the cigarette lighter she had picked up at Andrew Garvin's home, Deborah sparked it into flame. She offered it to Enid who leaned forward, lifting her cigarette and talking volubly. All of a sudden, the spate of words died on her lips. She glared at the lighter, then at Deborah, then turned to glare at Bill…

Chapter 17

"So, it's started again!" exclaimed Enid Sinclair, glaring at her husband and Deborah.

Bill was taken aback. "What do you mean?" he stammered.

"You know perfectly well, Bill. A pair of slim legs, neat ankles, a pretty face. Simply can't resist them, can you?"

"My dear, I haven't an earthly idea what you're talking about," Bill replied.

"After all your tears and promises. Yes," Enid said viciously, turning to Deborah and Joyce, "he weeps, sheds real tears, when he wants to convince me that he'll reform." Her eyes stabbed her bewildered husband once more. "I am talking about you and Miss Vail."

"My dear girl!" protested Bill, his jaw dropping.

"Well, really," said Joyce indignantly.

"I'd like to know exactly what you mean by that," said Deborah.

Enid's voice, which had risen to a shrill pitch, now became a feline purr. "Don't be too flattered by his attentions, Miss Vail. You needn't think you're the one interest of his life. He'll go running after the next shapely form that comes along. I expect he told you I don't understand him. The truth is, I understand him only too well."

Bill said weakly, "Enid, have you gone mad? Why, it's...it's ridiculous. I've never been alone with Miss Vail for five minutes."

Deborah drew a deep breath. "If you are suggesting that there is something between your husband and me—"

"I'm not suggesting it," said Enid. "I'm saying it right out."

"Then you are mad!" retorted Deborah.

"Is that so? Then how do you explain having this?" Enid

snatched up the cigarette lighter and held it out on her palm. "My husband's lighter. The one I gave him for his birthday."

People were staring, putting heads together; whispering titillating conjectures. They could not catch what was being said but it was all too evident, even to those at the far side of the café that an angry scene was in progress. Enid was too furious to notice the attention being given her or to care what others thought. In any case, to Enid, a violent scene at intervals was almost a physical need, a specific for frayed nerves. It was perversely characteristic of her to throw dignity to the winds when she was annoyed and resentful and had an audience.

If she and Deborah had been alone, she would have questioned the girl, almost sweetly, about the lighter, and left it at that for the present. The scene would come later, when she had an audience. Knowing her well, Bill watched her apprehensively.

"If my husband didn't give it to you," Enid continued, "how did you come into possession of it? Bill, you absolute swine, you told me you'd lost it."

Bill Sinclair's emptily good-looking face looked suddenly guilty and afraid.

"Then it's your husband's lighter?" asked Deborah quietly.

"Yes, dear," purred Enid, "as if you didn't know. If there's nothing between you, why should he give it to you?"

"He didn't," replied Deborah, enunciating very clearly. "I picked it up at Andrew Garvin's house."

"There you are, Enid," said Bill, a shade too quickly. "Another fuss over nothing. It's all very I simple. I must have left it at the Garvins' last time we dropped in on them."

"It's ages since 'we' last dropped in on the Garvins," Enid persisted, "and I only gave you the lighter on the tenth of last month."

In her bitterness she did not realize the significance of what she was saying, the black suspicion she was casting on her husband. If Bill only got the lighter on the tenth and Erica was murdered on the twelfth... The implication was clear to Deborah. And to Joyce, who caught her breath sharply. And to Bill, whose forehead broke out in beads of perspiration. But not to Enid. She was too hurt and jealous to weigh her words.

"You gave me your word of honour that you'd drop Erica, but this proves you didn't. Did she give you a party for your birthday? An intimate little affair for two?"

"Enid," said Bill hoarsely, "for God's sake..."

And then, Enid got it. It was almost ludicrous the way her face changed, crumpling like a burst paper bag. One minute sharp with anger, the next blurred with dismay. She looked as if she were drowning, going under for the third time. If Bill was shaken and afraid. Enid was almost paralyzed.

But Enid was of strong fibre. She never quite lost her wits. With a hand that was almost steady she turned over the lighter, the silver gadget that had become an ominous thing. Surprising them all, she gave a shrill laugh.

"I had you fooled, didn't I? You really thought I was jealous. Of course, I knew all the time that this wasn't your lighter, Bill. It looks a bit like it but the shape is different."

"Oh, q-quite different," stuttered Bill. He essayed a laugh but the result was ghastly.

"You put on quite an act," he said, but the sweat still glistened on his brow.

"I wanted to see what you would say. It was most amusing."

Enid turned effervescently to Deborah.

"My dear, you should have seen your face. You looked positively guilty."

There was an uncomfortable silence, broken by Joyce saying coldly. "As guilty as Bill looks now?" She gathered up handbag and gloves. "We'd better be going, Deborah." She beckoned to the hovering waitress.

"Don't bother about the check, darling," said Enid. "Bill will see to it."

"I'd rather pay," said Joyce firmly.

As she and Deborah came out into welcome fresh air, Joyce said, "The spite of that woman. The high-handed insolence of her! I'll never speak to her again."

"Don't be too hard," said Deborah. "She's sorry now."

"Yes," said Joyce with a shiver, "she's sorry now. Oh, Deborah, I daren't think what I can't help thinking."

"Where would one buy a lighter like this?"

Deborah had picked it up when they left.

"Probably in Edinburgh or Glasgow," Joyce replied. "Though one might find it at Moirs, the big jewellers across the street. They carry quite nice things."

Across the street at Moirs, an elderly shop assistant was courteous and helpful to Deborah. "You found the lighter, miss? And would like us to help you trace the owner, if we can? No trouble at all. I'll gladly look it up in the book."

Shortly he returned to the counter carrying an open ledger with his thumb at an entry.

"Yes, here it is. The purchase was made by Mrs. William Sinclair. A present for her husband, I believe she said at the time."

"You're sure this is the one?"

"Oh, quite sure. There can be no doubt whatever. It has our mark on it. You wouldn't notice it unless you know exactly where to look."

"Oh, Deborah," whispered Joyce. "Not Bill! It would kill Enid."

"But it was all right for it to be Andrew..." Deborah replied.

Chapter 18

The car stopped in front of the house. Deborah said, "There are too many parcels for us. Joyce, I'll send Scobie to help."

She made the suggestion lightly, as if it had only just occurred to her, as if she had not been trying for an hour to devise a way to remove Scobie from the vicinity of the coach-house for a few minutes.

"You can send him," said Joyce, "but he won't come. If he gives you an answer at all it will be that it's not his work."

"We'll see," said Deborah, tightening her lips.

Scobie, in shirt sleeves, was kneeling by the lawnmower, giving it a squirt of oil. He squinted at her dourly when she made the request. He seemed about to give her a caustic and probably profane answer.

"Mrs. Monteith is waiting," said Deborah, assuming a brisk executive tone.

Scobie only gave a grunt before shuffling off to the front of the house. The instant he was out of sight, Deborah ran to the coach-house. The man's jacket hung there from a rusty nail. She tried one of the pockets, making a face when her groping fingers encountered a moist wedge of chewing tobacco. In the other, she found the folded sheet of foolscap on which he had been pasting printed words when she discovered him in the basement. Going further into the gloomy interior of the coach-house, she spread the paper on a dusty work bench.

It was unmistakably a blackmailing note but there was no indication for whom is was intended. The words were of varying sizes and types, clipped from headlines, advertisements, news columns, wherever the man found the one he needed. They were stuck on at uneven angles, making them awkward to read coherently, but Deborah persevered until she made sense of them. White spaces had been left in place of punctuation.

The note ran:

'I have got it You no what Have plenty cash ready Will let you no what it will cost you no good trying to find it I have got it well hid.'

It was signed: 'Never mind who.'

Hearing footsteps grating on gravel, Deborah hastily refolded the paper and replaced it. Before she could slip out of the coach-house, the footsteps had come disconcertingly close. Going to the far wall, she pretended to be looking for something. She heard the man stopping a yard or two behind her and imagined she could feel his foul breath on her neck. It cost her an effort to turn and face him with a bogus air of confidence.

Scobie's liverish eyes were peering at her suspiciously. "Want somethin'?" he asked in an ominous tone.

"I—I thought I dropped a ring last time I parked the car but—but it doesn't seem to be here."

With heart pounding, she hurried past him. When almost hidden by the corner of the house, she ventured a backward glance and, in spite of an inward quailing, could not repress a smile. Scobie was poking about the dusty floor of the coach house in quest of the mythical ring. If she genuinely had dropped one, he would have made certain that she never found it.

She found Joyce in the living room, settling the baby in his crib with his bottle. On the way home neither she nor Deborah had said anything of significance, though both of them knew there was much to thrash out. Joyce took care not to look directly at her cousin; as if afraid that, if she did, something would snap.

"Paddy has learned a new trick," she said. "Look."

She made the Sealyham sit. Kneeling, she held out a biscuit, then solemnly, she laid it on the carpet, just out of his reach.

"On trust," she said sternly. "Mustn't touch."

The Sealyham promptly craned forward and gobbled it up.

"Well, he did it all right last time," she said defensively.

"Perhaps he wasn't hungry then. Joyce…"

Joyce stood up.

"I know," she said miserably. "It's no good trying to put it off. Sooner or later, we've got to have it out."

"You sound exactly like a dentist," said Deborah, hugging her impulsively.

"If only it weren't Bill Sinclair. He's such a likeable, easy-going sort, even if he does fancy himself as a lady-killer. If he killed Erica, it must have been because she drove him past the point of sanity. She must have been holding on to him with tooth and nail, threatening him, refusing to let him go."

"Does that excuse the crime?" asked Deborah.

"No, of course not. But…it's a woman's way to find excuses for a man's weakness."

"It all fits. Bill has a sports car. He wears tweed jackets and slacks. He had an affair with Erica. He only got the lighter on the tenth of last month. Erica was murdered on the twelfth."

"I know, I know. Oh, don't you think I know?" Turning slowly, Joyce looked piteously at Deborah. "But Enid is my friend. There are times when she annoys me beyond endurance, but she's still my friend. And Bill is all she lives for. Without him, she has nothing. Nothing."

"You're thinking of yourself and Ewan."

"Of course I am. It's like that with us. You don't know how it is, Deborah, to find the person who is the other half of you. It's miraculous. It's like being born again. You're not only a complete being at last, you're twice the being you ever were before.

Everything depends on that other person, with whom you fit like fingers in a glove. Take one away and you haven't got even what you had before. All you've got is…is a void. But…that's a woman's argument."

"I am a woman," said Deborah, moved almost to tears.

"Darling, there's more to becoming a woman than being born a girl. When someone means more to you than you do yourself, then you'll be a woman. Well…it's up to you. Can you do it? Can you walk into the police station and tell them what you've found out about Bill? And what you suspect?"

After a moment of doubt and hesitation, Deborah shook her head. "No, I don't think I can," she said. "Funny, I used to think it would be amusing to play detective. It isn't a game when a man's life is at stake. I must tell Andrew, though. Then it will be up to him."

"You said something this morning that stung," said Joyce. "In a way, it was appallingly true. You said, 'It was alright for it to be Andrew'. No…don't interrupt. I want to explain, if I can. You see, we all thought it was Andrew. We were sorry for him, but it was something he'd got himself into. Even if we wanted to, we couldn't get him out. Oh, I know we turned our backs on him—but isn't that only human when someone threatens us all by breaking the basic law, 'Thou shalt not kill'?"

"I didn't mean to hurt you," said Deborah, "but it seemed to me that you were bound and determined it must be Andrew, that there must be no possibility whatever that it could be someone else."

Deborah sensed she saw a glimmer of uneasiness pass through Joyce's eyes.

Chapter 19

"How do you really feel about Andrew Garvin?" asked Joyce, with wide-eyed curiosity.

"I don't know," said Deborah, embarrassed. "After all, I've only seen the man a few times. I met him under circumstances that were bound to make an impression."

"And ever since you've thought of nothing else."

"I'm sorry for him," Deborah said slowly. "I'd like to help him. Is that love?"

"Pity is a part of love…but only a part."

"Don't ask me to explain my feelings. How can I, when I don't understand them myself?"

"He's always been different, somehow, from other folk," said Joyce uneasily. "Perhaps that's the artist in him. No matter how this business comes out, he'll be marked by it, scarred deeply. Don't let sympathy lead you into something you'll regret."

"Alright, Mother, I'll be careful," Deborah rejoined, but the flippancy was jarring and false. "There's something else I've got to tell you," Deborah continued. "I only hope it won't upset you too much. When I came back for Ewan's library book this morning, it was evident that Scobie had been rummaging about the living room. I traced him to the basement. And, a few minutes ago…"

Deborah told her cousin about the blackmailing note in Scobie's pocket. The episode worried and frightened Joyce. She said they would have to get rid of Scobie without delay. They ought not to have employed him in the first place.

"The note said to 'have plenty cash ready.' That suggests that the blackmailee is rich," Deborah pointed out.

"To Scobie, anyone who washed regularly would seem rich," Joyce responded.

"He refers to 'it' in the note. 'I have got it. It is well hid.' Joyce, don't you see! He probably means the missing weapon. Perhaps he recovered it while he was supposed to be helping the police look for it. He must have it now. That's what his blackmail note implies. If only he could be forced to give it up."

"Deborah, don't be a fool! If you've got some crazy idea in your head, you'd better get rid of it. Scobie is no one to trifle with."

"Let's keep to the point, Joyce. Since nothing is missing from the house, the murderer must have brought the weapon with him. That suggests it was premeditated. He went there intending to kill her. Joyce, I wouldn't be surprised if the weapon led straight to the murderer."

Joyce said firmly, "Well, it won't! You're wrong about that."

Deborah was startled. "How can you possibly know?"

"Because I'm almost certain he found it at her bedside."

"B-but the maid," stammered Deborah, "she's sure nothing is missing."

"This is something the maid didn't know about. Something that only reached the house that morning after she left on her errand to Dumfries."

A few days before the murder, Joyce explained reluctantly, she and Erica had been in Glasgow on a shopping expedition. Erica's eye was caught by a statuette of a naked youth, about a foot high, and she bought it, ordering it to be sent. On the morning of her death, Erica had talked to Joyce on the telephone, from her bed, and told her that the statuette had just been delivered.

"After I got over the shock of hearing about the murder," Joyce continued, "it occurred to me that it might be the weapon. It's missing. There's no doubt about that."

"And you were the only one, barring the murderer, who knew of its existence. Oh, Joyce, why didn't you tell the police?"

"None of us told the police any more than we could help," said Joyce wearily. "It was all too...too close to home."

Deborah wondered how many others of the 'nice' people of Garnock were keeping significant facts to themselves. Going to the mirror, she put on a hat.

"I'm going for a walk," she said. "I've got to think."

* * * * *

For an hour or so Deborah walked the cobbled streets, lined with soot-blackened sandstone buildings, in the old part of Garnock that the poet Burns and several generations before him had known.

Then, tired and hungry, she went into a snack bar for a cup of tea and a sandwich. At the next table, two attractive girls in their late teens had their heads together, talking animatedly. When they saw her, one of them nudged the other and then made a hesitant gesture of recognition. It was the pleasant country girl who had been Erica Garvin's maid.

Deborah beckoned encouragingly and the two picked up their half-finished sodas and eagerly joined her.

The one she had seen before said, "This is my girlfriend, Jenny."

"I've tell't ye a hundred times, it's no' Jenny. It's Jennifer."

The girls were openly admiring Deborah's smart appearance.

"Ye're no' a bit like whit I expected," said Jennifer. "When they tell't me there was a lady detective in the town, I thocht—"

"Good heavens," protested Deborah, "I'm nothing of the

sort. I'm afraid I'm—well, perhaps you'd call me a nosy stranger, poking into matters that are none of my concern."

The girls exchanged crestfallen glances.

"It's a bit of a facer," said Margaret, "that you're not what we thought. I had Jenny—I mean, Jennifer, keyed up to come to see you. She's got something on her mind."

"I'm no' just sure I hae the right tae tell ye," temporized Jennifer. "If I tell ye, will ye promise no' to make trouble for Joe MacKay? It's his secret mair than mine."

"Who is Joe MacKay?" asked Deborah.

"He's the farmer's son at Auld Knowe Farm," replied Jennifer, her eyes glowing with fondness for the lad.

"I won't make trouble for him."

"He's fair beside himself wi' worry," said Jennifer. "He disna ken hoo tae make matters richt. Withoot meanin' tae dae it, he made trouble for Mr. Garvin wi' the police. On the day of the murder, Mr. Garvin said he was paintin' a picture in the fields behind Auld Knowe. Joe was pushed into making that seem a lee. But the truth o' the matter is that Joe disna ken whether Mr. Garvin wis there or no'."

"But the boy claimed to have been mending dikes all that day at the very spot," said Deborah.

"Aye," said Jennifer, flushing. "That was the work his faither mapped oot for him. And then his faither went off tae market in Dumfries, to be gone all day. The minute the auld yin's back was turned, Joe nipped off through the fields tae see me. We're... in love, ye ken," she said shyly, "but the auld yin will no' hear of it. He says Joe's got his way in the world to make afore he can think o' courtin'. The aul yin's terrible strict wi' Joe. That's why we hae to meet on the sly."

"How long was Joe gone from his work?" Deborah asked with interest.

"It was nearin' dark afore he left ma," replied Jennifer, her flush flaming brighter. "I'd made up a wee basket o' food, and we went on a picnic. When he got back, his faither was in the yard, talkin' tae twa polismen. They asked him where he had been all day. Before Joe could answer, his faither said: 'He's been mendin' the dikes back there on the hillside.' The polisman looked at Joe and said, 'Hae ye seen Mr. Garvin the day?' By that time, Joe ken't somethin' was wrang but he stuck tae his guns, 'No,' he said, 'I havena seen Mr. Garvin the day'. Ye can believe me, Miss Vail, he'd no' gang intae the witness box and lee. But he's been feart tae speak oot—his faither wid kill him."

Chapter 20

In broad daylight there was nothing sinister about the lines and aspect of Andrew Garvin's old house. It had a solid dignity, concording well with the rolling country it stood in.

There was a touch of wariness about Andrew when he opened the door, until he saw Deborah standing there. Then he looked surprised and stepped aside with a word of welcome. He was thinner than she would have liked to have seen him. He had shaved recently and his clothes were neat, but his cheeks were drawn. There were hollows under his eyes. He had the stamp of a man condemned to loneliness, shunned by his kind and withdrawn from them, given overmuch to solitary introspection.

"Have you come to scold me for making a fool of myself the other night?" he asked. "I've already said much harsher things to myself than you could think of."

"I haven't come to find fault," said Deborah. "I've come to talk."

He ruffled his hair with strong, spatulate fingers. She had an idea that he was wondering how to discourage her without being rude.

"I'm out of the habit of social intercourse," said Andrew, "but come in. There's a fire in the studio. I'll even make coffee, but I warn you, the coffee will be foul. I don't know what I do that's wrong, but the flavour is always beastly."

"Let me make it," Deborah offered.

He stood back, gesturing widely. "The kitchen is all yours." To Deborah, it was good to see him smiling.

She had to scour the percolator before she could use it. She wondered if all women had the pushful streak that she was displaying. Perhaps they acquired it as small girls as a result of being avoided and discouraged by little boys.

After she set the coffee on the stove she found some eggs, butter and bacon, and made an omelette. When she carried it toward Andrew, his eyes lit up and he cleared a space on his cluttered table.

"You're just like every woman. You think if a man is left to himself he'll starve. How about joining me?"

"I've had my lunch. Eat yours while it's hot."

While he ate, Deborah asked permission to look at the canvases that were stacked along one wall, with their faces to it. She knew nothing about the techniques of painting but what she saw impressed her. He had captured on canvas the rustic loveliness of the district. A lonely moor; a brook sparkling in sunlight; winter-dormant fields with hovering gulls; a glimpse of the sea between majestic cliffs...

Wisely, she offered no comment. Obviously, he approved of and was relieved by her respectful silence.

When he had cleaned the plate he lit a pipe, rose, and walked to the canvas on his easel. It was the portrait he was painting of his dead wife. Deborah came to his elbow with a cup of coffee. She saw that the artist's recent touches had been kinder; from the beautiful face looking out at them he had smoothed away some of the lines of discontent that had troubled her before. It was as if, having portrayed her as she was, he was striving to show her as she might have been.

"It's no good," Andrew muttered. "I can't do her justice. You can't imagine how lovely she was."

"That's the way you've painted her. Lovely."

"She was ten times more lovely in life," he said impatiently. "But her beauty was all on the surface. Inside, she was—"

"Don't torture yourself."

"I didn't care what she was. I knew her through and through but I loved her just the same. I had no right to marry her. She needed someone who could give her everything in the world that she wanted. Then, perhaps, she'd have been happy."

"I've got a lot to tell you," Deborah said, changing the subject. "Some of it isn't going to be easy."

She began by telling him that the evidence of the garage attendant, of Old Mrs. Craw and the farmer's son could be set aside quite easily. However black they had made the murder case against him, on examination their stories disintegrated into nothing.

"Don't you see," said Deborah, "if those three lied or were mistaken—"

"Three? There are ten thousand people in Garnock. All of them convinced that I am guilty."

"But if the police can be forced to—"

"The police have not said they have a case against me. They have allowed it to be taken for granted, but they haven't said it. They can't be made to withdraw what they haven't said."

"Are you merely going to wait for justice until the real murderer is found?" She was annoyed at the attitude his tone implied.

"Will that change anything? I hardly think so. Too much mud has been thrown for it ever to wash off. Don't think I'm not grateful for all you've done, all you've tried to do."

"Now I come to the difficult part," said Deborah.

And she told him what she had learned about Bill Sinclair. While she talked, his face became sickly and pale. Suddenly he shook himself, as if to shrug off an intolerable burden.

"No! Not Bill. It couldn't have been Bill! Oh, I don't doubt that Erica dallied with him, as she did with so many others; but—"

"Don't you think he should at least be made to explain?"

Andrew stared at her. "How does one explain away an appearance of guilt? You start with the assumption that, since you're telling the truth, you'll be believed. But there's this point. That point. A doubt here. A doubt there. The more you try to justify yourself, the guiltier you look."

"It's so unfair! I am telling you that a strong case can be made out against another man —and your sympathy is all for him."

"Because I know what suspicion can do," said Andrew. "The lies it breeds. The slanders. The malice. Enough to drive you away from your home, from your life, out of your wits. Bill isn't half strong enough to stand up to it. If I can only help myself by entangling him, I won't do it."

"Because his wife is your sister?"

"You're thinking that I have precious little to thank her for?"

Deborah was silent and he continued vehemently: "I loved Enid when we were children. You don't stop loving people because they let you down. It's the human frailty in them that makes you love them in the first place. And it's the human frailty that lets you down."

"Supposing the murder is never cleared up. Can you bear the weight of suspicion all through your life?"

"It's on my back. I'm in it. I've learned how to live with it. I've no choice. But Deborah"—it was the first time she had heard her name on his lips—"please don't meddle any more. Do you understand? Even if you could set me free, I'd still say the same. What do you think would happen if, by some fluke, you did get close to the murderer?"

"I haven't thought that far."

"Then think," said Andrew forcefully. "A man who has killed one woman won't balk at another murder. Stop poking and prying. It can only lead you into danger."

After she left him. Deborah realized that she had forgotten to tell Andrew about the statuette. But did he have to be told about it?

Chapter 21

On this particular evening, matters were not arranged as Deborah would have preferred them. She felt she was being dragooned into participating in the Amateur Dramatic Society's forthcoming production whether she like it or not. Having promised her cousin's willing services, Joyce brought her to the hall very firmly, as a governess conducts a reluctant child to the dentist. Then, having presented her to the secretary, Joyce proceeded to abandon her, saying that she must run along now. Ewan was up to the ears in midterm examination papers of his students and could not be trusted to listen for the baby. And off Joyce went, nodding blithely to one and another of the scattered groups in the hall with the self-satisfied bearing of one who has seen and done her duty.

"Well," said the secretary breezily, "this is jolly."

He pressed Deborah's fingers in a moist palm, brandishing a sheaf of papers in the other.

"It's going to be such a thrill for all of us, working with a real live actress from London. The first thing is to introduce you to everybody. They'll all be as delighted as I am."

They were not. At least, the reactions to the secretary's fulsome little speech of introduction were mixed, which was not surprising since the way he put it made it seem that Deborah was about to take over the Society lock, stock, and barrel. Deborah saw several faces shaped for resentment. One of them belonged to the doll-like pretty girl who had played the heroine for several seasons and suspected Deborah of plotting to supersede her. Another was that of the wary-eyed spinster, an English teacher at the high school, who 'always' directed the plays and foresaw herself being thrust ruthlessly aside.

Deborah saw Enid Sinclair in the gathering, looking bland and innocent but whispering occasional asides to her neighbours; verbal digs, Deborah imagined, at this interloper from London. As soon as she could, Deborah made a little speech of her own. Mustering all her acting ability, she played the, part of a guileless ingénue, a mere stage tyro, humbly anxious to efface herself and unlikely to step on anyone's toes. She began to see friendly nods of encouragement where hostile glances had been shaping. She sat down with a final smile that made her inwardly sick, to a ripple of applause.

The treasurer gave a forlorn accounting of the Society's finances. None of the three productions undertaken the previous year had paid their expenses. In fact, but for a gratifying donation by Mrs. Hector MacInch, the Society would now be hopelessly in debt. It was all very well preening themselves on their Thespian talents but it was vitally important to get out and sell tickets.

The set designer, a young woman in horn-rimmed spectacles, with frantic hair, who lit each fresh cigarette on the stub of the last, asked to be allowed a word and proceeded to spill over with a thousand. It was no use, this time, expecting her to be designer, carpenter, painter, electrician, stage crew, odd-job man, and every other thing, she declared bitterly. It was always the same, endless promises of help that weren't kept. If they wanted her to do it all on her own again let them say so, here and now, and they could have her resignation without delay.

The president said he entirely sympathized and, this time, a proper work crew must be organized but, after all, this meeting had been called for the purpose of choosing a play. Had anyone a suggestion? Almost everyone had. Shakespeare. Ibsen. Shaw. Someone called out, "'Charley's Aunt'?"

A lively brunette said, "How about 'Night Must Fall'?" She

giggled. "Wouldn't it be wonderful if we could get Mr. Garvin to play the part of the psychopathic killer who carries his victim's head about in a hatbox?"

"Well, at least we'd have packed houses for every performance," said another voice.

Deborah repressed an indignant retort. It was not humanly possible to protest against every crude joke carelessly made about Andrew Garvin. But she knew she would always detest the scoffing brunette.

The treasurer said, "No period plays, please. We simply cannot afford the costume rental."

A Scottish dialect comedy was proposed and Deborah's opinion was sought. She advised against it. Most of the members habitually spoke ordinary English with merely a Scottish intonation. Their attempts to render a manner of speech unusual to them might sound false and patronizing. She suggested a play she knew to be safe for amateurs, one with enough parts to go round. If they would allow her to do so she would hold the prompt book and be ready to give such occasional advice as the director asked for.

She soon discovered that no one wanted the choice of a play to be made simply and reasonably. They wanted to fight over it, to bicker and shout, to break up in irreconcilable antagonism and go homeward in argumentative groups, gesticulating wildly and proclaiming each other blind, daft, and reactionary. It was all in a spirit of fun, with a seasoning of healthy spite; and when she tired of it, she snatched an opportunity to slip out unobserved.

It was pleasant to stroll homeward in the quiet of middle evening through tree-lined streets of modest houses, each in a small garden tended with loving care. Lights were on in all the houses. The folk of Garnock were reading, sewing, chatting, listening to the radio in the tranquil hour before bedtime. It was good to walk alone for a spell with only her thoughts for company.

They were restful thoughts as long as they dwelt on Ewan and Joyce and their baby or on the gathering of human beings she had left, letting off steam in a human way before settling down in earnest to express themselves through a rewarding hobby. It was only when Andrew Garvin came into her mind that the serenity was ruffled. No matter how the fact might chafe, it was impossible to think of Andrew Garvin without also thinking of the murder.

Perhaps Joyce was right. Perhaps she ought to forget the man, relax and make the most of her visit to Garnock. Stop being a busybody. After all, it was only chance that had thrown her together with the artist. He had told her himself to forget him, to stop meddling, to stop poking and prying. He warned her what might happen if she did get close to the murderer. 'A man who has killed one woman won't balk at another murder.' She shivered at the thought of lovely Erica Garvin, battered to death with the beautiful bronze sculpture she had bought for her own delight. No, she could not go on. She had not the kind of reckless courage it takes to walk knowingly into appalling danger.

A man walked by, going the same way, with solid, sure-footed strides. A pace or so beyond her he checked himself and looked back. Halting, he raised his hat. It was Inspector Gray, clad in a civilian suit and a raincoat. He looked strong, confident, healthy; and the world was on his side. The unfairness of it, in contrast to Andrew Garvin's lot, rankled in her mind...

Chapter 22

"Going home, Miss Vail?" David Gray asked.

Deborah said, "Yes," rather stiffly to the police inspector. It would be foolish to go out of her way merely to snub the man, especially since he seemed impervious to snubs. He fell into step with her.

"I hear you've been seeing quite a lot of Andrew Garvin," he said.

"Is that your affair?" Deborah said tartly.

"An artist. An outcast. A combination that might well appeal to a girl's imagination."

Deborah coloured with annoyance. He sounded patronizing.

"You speak as if I were a silly schoolgirl."

"That's not the way I see you."

"I don't care how you see me!" said Deborah angrily.

"It seems we can never meet without clashing. Why is that?"

Deborah said forcefully, "Because you're stubborn, hidebound, blind—"

"Stupid?" he suggested, with a twinkle in his eye.

She could not help laughing. He said approvingly, "That's better."

They strolled along together. The air was still, hushed, as if the night held its breath.

"Who made him an outcast?" Deborah said suddenly.

"You're going to say it was me."

"Well, wasn't it? You're a policeman. You ought not to be blinded by prejudice. You should look for the truth."

"And what is the truth?" asked David Gray amiably.

"I don't know; I'm not sure: but it's there if you dig for it. I'm only a girl, as you pointed out, with neither credentials nor authority to back me up, but already I've found out that at least three of your witnesses against him either lied or are mistaken."

"It's a way witnesses have," said David Gray. "Their eyes or their memories play tricks. Most of them want to tell the truth but what a man calls the truth is generally what he chooses to believe, not what he knows for certain. In my job you have to sift facts from fancy. Often it isn't easy."

Now was the time to tell him all she had found out about Bill Sinclair. Why did she hesitate?

"I could make out as strong a case against several men in Garnock," she said, temporizing, "as you can against Andrew Garvin."

"No doubt. But we police are not quite blind, nor asleep. We've investigated several suspects rather closely. Believe me, we're still at it."

"And then, there's that man, Scobie. He knows something."

"What he knows he won't tell. Scobie's a close-mouthed scoundrel." The police inspector scowled. "I'd give a year's pay to get the goods on him! We've had him before the bench a dozen times. Maiming a sheep to get revenge on a farmer; malicious wounding; breaking and entering; poaching. All sorts of charges. Insufficient evidence every time. It's baffling to a policeman to be up against a crook who has no friends. Most criminals have a few pals with whom they're free and easy, to whom they boast of the clever job they've just pulled off. Time after time, it's the crook who gives himself away because his tongue wags too freely in convivial company. Not Scobie, the man hasn't a friend or casual pal in the world, and what he knows stays bottled up in his ugly skull."

"The whole town knows that you're having Andrew Garvin watched. In the eyes of the town that makes him guilty."

"Do you expect me to announce publicly that I haven't accused him?"

"It's unfair to leave him with the burden of suspicion."

"There may be a reason for that. Perhaps it's to make the real murderer think he's thrown us off the track. Or perhaps we're sure it's Garvin and hoping he'll do something to give himself away. After all, he almost killed his wife once before. It was at a party and she was too interested in another man."

"He probably gave her the good shaking she deserved. Wouldn't you?"

"Perhaps I would," said Inspector Gray.

They walked along in silence for a while.

"Don't go flying off the handle," he said. "I've got a word of advice for you."

"To mind my own business, I expect?"

"That's about it. You know, of course—all the world knows—that British policemen don't carry revolvers."

"It's common knowledge," said Deborah impatiently.

"What isn't so generally known is that a few revolvers are kept at every police station for issue to policemen sent on especially dangerous errands. The regulations are strict; the danger has to be great before a firearm is issued. Well, Miss Vail, I'll tell you this: if I were sending a man to arrest the murderer of Erica Garvin, I'd see that he went armed."

Deborah winced, struck again by the brutality of the murder. "You knew her," she remarked.

David Gray understood what she meant. "I met her several times," he replied.

"Did you like her?"

"It wasn't as simple as that. You didn't just like her or not like her. The impact went deeper. I could say she was beautiful. That wouldn't be the half of it. I couldn't be with her and sum her up dispassionately. No man could, if he had blood in his veins. When you thought of her you got all tangled up emotionally."

"You were in love with her."

"Was I? With another man's wife?"

"The Chief Constable wouldn't have approved?" said Deborah scornfully.

"Blast the Chief Constable," said David Gray. "A man has principles." He eyed her quizzically. "You wouldn't be trying to make me out as a suspect?"

"You have a little sports car. You wear tweed jackets."

"You've been listening to Old Mrs. Craw. An important point to remember about the old lady is that she's asleep at her window as often as she's awake. More than one man could have come to call at the Garvin house while she was dozing. It happens she saw one man. We think it was Garvin."

"You knew Erica," she persisted. "I think you fell for her. And, as Hector MacInch pointed out, you're a presentable bachelor."

"And likely to remain one for long enough. I have my future to think of, Miss Vail."

"You needn't make the point so earnestly. I have no designs on you."

"There's only one answer to that."

He took her in his arms and kissed her. It was a warm, full-lipped, expert kiss. But a wondering expression came into his eyes and he kissed her again, more gently.

Deborah averted her head, turning her lips away.

"Didn't mean much to you, did it?" he said in a tone of pique, releasing her.

"Not much," said Deborah. "Was it supposed to?"

"Funny, it meant a lot more to me than I'd have expected."

For the moment he was not as self-assured as usual but Deborah felt no tolerance for him. How like the man, she thought. How very like him, to grab a girl and kiss her on the confident assumption that she would enjoy it.

Chapter 23

Scobie's brutal sullen face was heavy with rancour as he leaned on the bar in a local pub, nursing a grudge. His red-rimmed eyes were fixed in hatred and resentment on a young man who sat chatting and laughing with friends at a table near the fire. A few minutes before, Scobie's elbow had been jostled by the young man, or so Scobie fancied; and instead of apologizing the offender had looked straight through Scobie as though he did not exist.

Scobie had an idea that he had caught the words "drunken lout" as the young man rejoined his companions.

He was just drunk enough to see an insult in every trifling slight. Besides, he resented the young man's spotless collar, neat blue suit, well-brushed hair, and generally spruce appearance. He resented the white, evenly-spaced teeth the young man kept showing in carefree laughter. He resented the finicking way the young man made a drink last, sipping it and setting it aside, instead of gulping it down and calling for another.

"I'll show him" was the nearest to a coherent thought in Scobie's mind. He felt like breaking his glass, crossing the room in two strides, and jabbing the jagged edges into the laughing young face. Only...you could get two years hard labour for a caper like that.

"Same again," he said, his grimy fingers placing a coin on the bar.

"You've had enough," said the landlord bluntly. "Watch your step. I've got an eye on you. Don't try any of your larks in here."

The landlord was large and solid, with fists like hams. For all his size he could move quickly. Scobie had seen him thrusting up the flap of his counter and coming through ready for action before a man could follow one breath with another. Already Scobie was barred from several pubs in the town; he could not afford to lose this one. Besides, the landlord was always a ready customer for a plump hare or a brace of pheasant if Scobie brought them to the back door.

With an inaudibly snarled oath, he slouched out of the place. It was no good waiting about to take a bash at the young chap when he came out; it would mean taking on his friends as well. Better to wait and give him a going-over one night when he was alone; and if he lost his watch and pocket money at the same time, so much the worse for him.

Scobie would not forget. Scobie never forgot an injury, real or imagined. One of these dark nights he was going to get his revenge on that fancy young woman from London who was visiting the Monteiths. He was sure it was because of Deborah that he had lost his job with the Monteiths. It would be a pleasure to smash her pretty face. He could wait. Nothing was lost by waiting, by mulling over in your mind the indignities and brutalities to be inflicted on the victim.

He was taking his time over that bit of blackmail. Letting the bloke sweat and stew over the notes in printed wording that let him know there was someone who could give him away. He would be all the more ready to pay and pay plenty, when Scobie decided how the money could he transferred without danger to himself.

On his way along Market Street, keeping out of habit to the shadows, he saw a man dismounting from a newish bicycle outside the chemist's shop, crossing the pavement hurriedly, and ringing the night bell. In a minute or so, a light went on in the shop, the door was opened, and the man went in.

As soon as he was out of sight, Scobie crossed the deserted street, whipped a leg over the saddle, and rode off on the bicycle.

While cycling to his hovel on the outskirts of the town he saw only one policeman. The dark was his element and he spotted the uniformed patroller in plenty of time to dodge him with ease. The big black dog chained near his door would have shattered the night's hush with savage barking at the approach of anyone else but he only whined when his master rode up.

Propping the bicycle against a well, Scobie unfastened the chain and the dog ran off silently into the dark to find its own supper. It would come home with the blood of a rabbit warm on its jowl.

Unlocking the padlock that secured his door, Scobie went in and lit an oil lamp hanging by a rope from the rafters of his one-room habitation. He went out again, carried in the bicycle, and stood it on old newspapers where the murky light fell on it. He shut and barred the door, covered the windows with sacking, and went to work on the bicycle as systematically as if it were a routine he followed every day. He stripped the frame, removing all the accessories that might aid identification. Wrapped in oilskin and sacking, they would lie hidden in the crotch of a tree in the woods behind his shack until they could be sold for quick cash, no questions asked to a dealer of his acquaintance.

He burned off the original blue paint with a blowlamp and applied a coat of quick-drying black. He roughed up with sandpaper the new leather of the saddle. He would be in no hurry to sell the bicycle. As it stood, the rightful owner would reject it without a second glance. Until he got the right offer it would serve Scobie on his journeyings to the town, in place of his present one, which was falling apart from ill usage.

Crumpling the paint-spattered newspapers, he stuffed them into the round-bellied stove that smouldered all day in the middle of his shack. While he worked, he heard the dog snuffling at the door. Going out, he welcomed it with a half-hearted kick and refastened the chain to its collar. In the early morning he kicked off laceless boots, threw his hat, muffler, jacket and trousers on a chair, and went to bed in a filthy shirt and underwear.

Almost at once he started to snore. Sleep always came quickly to Scobie. He had nothing on his conscience.

Hours later, sunlight seeping through an unwashed window fell on a tangle of grey hair protruding from a fetid heap of tattered blankets. The morning was half gone but Scobie lay foundered in sleep, breathing stertorously through a gaping mouth.

The sun was directly overhead when he came out of his tumbledown dwelling, pulling his crumpled hat down to shield his eyes. He had a headache and his whole being felt sour. Many people feel sour on rising but Scobie carried his sourness all day. The hat had been an elegant thing with a jaunty feather when he found it, long ago, on the driving-seat of a parked Bentley. In its present state it would have disgraced a scarecrow.

In a muddy enclosure behind his shack, he scattered grain to the hens that scrabbled and pecked about his ankles. They had been acquired, a few at a time, from distant farms on moonless nights and brought home, trussed and sacked, on his bicycle.

From a screening clump of bushes on the side of a hill, Deborah was watching the man's movements through field glasses. She saw him foraging for firewood and returning to his shack with loaded arms. Soon after he came out again, cast a cursory glance all round him and shambled off down the dusty road. Through the field glasses she scanned the rises and bends of the road for his passing. She did not leave her hiding place until he was well out of sight…

Chapter 24

When Deborah Vail approached Scobie's converted shed, his dog raved and snarled at her, straining the chain. It was a huge black beast, part Labrador part mastiff, with an awesome set of teeth. Its hackles were risen and the fierce teeth were bared.

Deborah said, "Good boy," soothingly, but took care to keep out of reach. The animal was not appeased. His objective seemed to be less to frighten her away than to get hold of her and rip her to pieces. It was reassuring to see that the links of the chain were strong. Deborah was carrying a small parcel. Opening it, she took out a piece of liver and threw it to the dog.

She had feared he might have been trained to reject food from strangers but from the way he snapped up the morsel in mid-air and gulped it down she surmised that he welcomed food from any source. She spoke to him again, a seductive crooning that commiserated with his loneliness and offered comfort. He quieted a little but regarded her with an unwinking stare as if speculating on the chances of getting her within reach.

While talking on and on, in a consoling murmur, she kept throwing him scraps of liver. He ate them voraciously and whined for more. When the paper was empty, she made a ball of it, threw it away, and showed the dog her empty hands.

Squatting on her heels, so that their faces were on a level, she said, "Good boy. Poor old boy. Don't be afraid, I shan't hurt you." The words were ridiculous, she was well aware, for if 'good boy' got loose it would be a case of him hurting her, certainly not the other way round. Nevertheless, her sympathetic tone and obvious friendliness began to mollify the animal. He stopped straining. His lips hung down, hiding the fearsome teeth. His stubby tail began to thump against the wooden wall of the shack.

Very slowly, very steadily, Deborah put out a hand until it was close enough for the dog to smell and inspect. Now was the crucial moment. He might bite. If he bit he might hold on. There was no saying what he might do. But Deborah all her life had felt a love of dogs and none of them had ever rejected her.

This one licked her hand. "Good boy," she said again. "Good old Blackie-boy."

She stroked his ears, his skull, his neck; the long black back that had bristled with ferocity only a little while before. He responded to her almost feverishly, out of a long submerged but not yet extinct yearning for love.

It would not yet be safe for her to try the door. Almost certainly he would stop her in spite of their newfound friendship, for that was what he was there to do. You could not overcome training, habit and instinct with a few morsels of liver and a show of affection. In any case, she noticed, the padlock was much too massive to yield to anything less than a sledge hammer.

Rising, she went to a window and peered in. There was nothing much to be seen except the stove, the table with the remains of a meal, the bicycle, a chair or two, the tumbled bed and some orange crates full of tools and other oddments. It would have been difficult for her to say what she had expected to accomplish by this visit, but she was not dissatisfied.

By the time she left the dog had become a friend and whined beseechingly after her.

"I'll be back, Blackie-boy," she told him. "I'll be back one day soon."

The gate was crudely fashioned from odds and ends of lumber. As she pushed on it, she glanced back and noticed a lean-to shed behind the hen run. With the idea that it might repay inspection she made her way to the shed across a waste of ragged grass and weeds. The door was fastened only with a hasp.

When she dragged it open it hung at a tipsy angle from one hinge. Inside, she found a heap of sacks, some bags of feed for the hens, and a few rusty tools hanging from nails driven into the cross-members. In the faint hope that some-thing might be hidden under them she began to turn over the sacks.

She was balancing on her heels, holding the lowermost sack in her hands and examining the bare earthen floor on which it had lain, when a shadow fell across her shoulder. Turning in alarm, she saw the loutish form of Scobie blocking the narrow doorway. He was eyeing her in a way that made her heart pound with fright.

"Ah heard ma dug barkin'." he said slowly, "an' came back as quick as ah could." A glint of humour, of a venomous sort, briefly lit his sullen eyes. "If it's anither ring ye've lost, ye'll no' be findin' it there."

She tried to speak but no words would come. In his hand was a chunky billet of wood which he had picked up as a weapon on his stealthy return through the fields. Noticing her frightened eyes on it, Scobie sniggered.

"Aye," he said tauntingly, "a blow from this wid change that pretty face for ye."

Suddenly she sprang up and threw the sack over his head and shoulders. He flung up his arms to ward off the dusty encumbrance and she hurled herself at the narrow gap between him and the door post. With elbows, shoulders, knees, she thrust, pushed, jabbed and stumbled, bruised and out of breath, into the open air. It took an instant for her to realize that she was free; and then she started running as fast as she could toward the road.

Before she had gone twenty yards the billet of wood, hurled with savage force, struck her between the shoulder blades. Toppling forward, reaching out her hands to break the impact with the ground she felt a stab of pain as her knee hit a stone. Sprawling full length, winded and helpless, she heard the footsteps of Scobie nearing until he stood over her.

Seeing a hobnailed boot drawn hack in readiness to aim a kick, Deborah threw up both arms to protect her head.

That moment of cowering on the ground, waiting to feel the hurt to come, seemed an eternity. In her despair she kept thinking, he daren't kill me, he daren't kill me; but who knew what extreme of suffering he could inflict while still leaving the breath in her body? All her life she had displayed a certain reckless daring but with that façade shattered she felt herself a coward. She was ready to scream with the anguish of expected pain before the pain itself was felt. It was the waiting that was so dreadful, the tensing of flesh and sinew in apprehension of what was coming. She could have cried out to him: "Go on! Go on! Get it over with."

Half dazed by fear, she heard the impact of a blow. But there was no pain to her. There was a hoarse outcry and a scrambling of feet on rocky soil. Raising her head, bracing her tremulous body with numbed arms, she saw Scobie struggling brutally with another man. They broke apart and she saw that the newcomer was Andrew Garvin...

Chapter 25

Deborah Vail felt sick and dizzy, unable to hold up her head. She thought she was going to faint. By the time the vertigo passed and she could see and think again, Scobie was lying on the ground and Andrew Garvin stood over him, livid with fury. Staggering up, Deborah walked unsteadily to Andrew and clutched his arm.

"Take me away!" she begged. "I've got to get away from here."

They could hear the frenzied barking of the black dog chained to Scobie's shack. Andrew glowered at Scobie lying supine at his feet. Deborah was afraid that if he grappled with the brute again, he would not stop short of killing him.

"By God, I ought to—"

"Don't hit him again," said Deborah brokenly. "He hasn't hurt me. I… I'm only frightened."

Looking her up and down, Andrew saw that she could stand no more of this. Putting an arm around her, he led her to where his car stood by the gate he had smashed down in his haste to come to her aid.

He helped her in, climbed in beside her and drove off. But Deborah would not let him drive her home.

"I don't want to frighten Joyce," she said. "My car is not far off down this lane. If you'll take me to it and park there for a little while, and let me smoke a cigarette, I'll get my nerve back. I'll be all right."

"What on earth were you doing at Scobie's place?" asked Andrew. "Didn't I warn you—"

"Do you mind if we don't talk? If I try to explain myself, I'll burst into tears. Tell yourself I'm a stubborn fool and ought to be locked up for my own good. It's perfectly true but please don't say it out loud. All I want to do is sit, breathe, and realize that I'm alive."

"If I hadn't happened to be passing," said Andrew, shaking his head.

Deborah refused to think what might have occurred if he hadn't happened to be passing. It was too dreadful to contemplate. Now that the danger was past, she was thinking that Stobie held the answer to the murder of Andrew's wife. Judging by Scobie's savage resentment of intrusion, the secret he was hiding must be a tremendous one.

Next morning, the Montieths were breakfasting early to enjoy the meal on their own. While fond of their visitor, the pleasure they took in her company somehow added spice to their moments alone. Joyce helped herself to a crisp wafer of bacon from her husband's plate. In her other hand was a triangular wedge of his hot buttered toast. She nibbled alternatively on the two. In theory, she was on a diet and never took anything except coffee in the morning. In practice, she cooked Ewan rather more breakfast than he could eat and saw that none of it was wasted.

"I'm worried about Deborah," said Joyce.

Ewan glanced up from the headlines of his morning newspaper with a humorous lift of an eyebrow.

"You've been worried about her since the day she came."

"I wish she had come some other time," Joyce responded. "Not now. Oh, I know I couldn't wait to see her. I looked forward for weeks to her coming. She isn't a bit of trouble and I do love her. Only..."

There was no need to go on. They both knew what she meant. It worried her to know that her cousin was becoming more and more deeply involved with Andrew Garvin. To her mind it made little difference whether Andrew was tried and convicted, tried and acquitted, or left forever under suspicion.

Whatever happened, she could not see a future in which he could lead a normal life. She felt that involvement with him must spell unhappiness for any woman.

If only Deborah had come on her visit before the murder; or long enough after so that it had ceased to be an avid topic of conversation. If only Deborah hadn't met Andrew on the very first night. Joyce sighed, wishing it were possible to keep Deborah from seeing the man, thinking of him, hearing about him.

But wherever the two of them went they heard him spoken of. Only yesterday over mid-morning coffee at the café, Joyce had sensed Deborah stiffening when they overheard a woman at a nearby table talking volubly to her friend. The other day, she was saying, she had driven over to a local beauty spot, a hillside with a celebrated view and, would you believe it?—there was Andrew Garvin, large as life and bold as brass, with his easel and his paints. You'd think he'd keep out of the way of, decent folk…

Joyce was reminded of something.

"Deborah came in yesterday with a torn stocking," Joyce said to Ewan, reaching for another scrap of bacon.

"Well, you're always saying how quickly they wear out."

"This wasn't a run. It was a gaping hole in the knee. Something had happened but she wouldn't tell me what. It's worrying me."

Her husband offered her no comfort.

"I won't be home for tea," Ewan said, rising and folding the newspaper. "Henderson is ill and I've promised to pop up and see him." He was speaking of a fellow teacher at the school. "I'm borrowing David's car since he won't be using it."

"I wish you wouldn't," said Joyce, in a curiously fretful tone.

Ewan stared at her. "Why not? You know I always drive carefully."

"It isn't that."

"Then what is it?"

"I don't know," said Joyce.

But she knew very well. Lately, she felt disturbed and uneasy every time she saw Ewan, in a tweed jacket and slacks, getting in or out of the M.G.A.

"Nerves, I suppose," she said.

He patted her shoulder, kissed her cheek, gathered up an armful of books, and went out through the back door. Why did her heart sink momentarily, hearing him backing the car out of the coach house and revving it in the drive? It was only an ordinary sports car. There were thousands of them.

Soon afterwards Joyce's cheek was kissed again, this time by Deborah, who came down looking young and fresh, in a grey suit with a flamboyant foulard scarf. A letter postmarked 'Glasgow' lay by her plate.

"From a London friend," she explained after skimming through it. "She's playing second lead in a touring company of 'One More Spring'. She, wants me to come up and see her. I suppose I could go today. We haven't anything on, have we?"

"I hadn't planned anything," said Joyce, pondering briefly whether it would be a good idea for Deborah to go off on her own to Glasgow, and deciding quickly that it would.

"Supposing I take a small case and stay overnight? I'll be back about teatime tomorrow."

Joyce nodded emphatically. It would do Deborah good to get out of Garnock, if only for a day and a night. In Glasgow there would be no nagging reminders of Andrew Garvin, no reason for her to risk getting into trouble.

Chapter 26

On the journey of ninety miles or so to Glasgow, the little car behaved unusually well. In the early afternoon Deborah Vail left it at a garage in Wellington Street and went to the matinee of her friend's play. Afterwards she found her way backstage, waited while her friend changed into street clothes and makeup, and then they went to the Malmaison for an early dinner. It cost more than either of them was accustomed to spending on a meal but they enjoyed the feeling that they were being extravagant.

The friend spoke ruefully of her Hill Street landlady, whose alternative to sausages and mashed potatoes was a 'lovely' kipper. Deborah went one better by recalling a landlady at Worthing who served mutton roast, cold, hashed, en casserole, and curried all in the same week.

It was only a month or so since Deborah's last play closed but already it seemed an age. She was hungry for the small talk of the theatre, the stimulating intimate gossip of a private world. They talked incessantly, both at once, and still revelled in talk while strolling back to the theatre barely in time for the evening performance.

That night Deborah shared her friend's room, sleeping in a camp bed. After they put the lights out, they went on talking. It was only by degrees that the conversation became sporadic and dwindled off in drowsiness.

In the morning Deborah left her friend asleep and went off after breakfast to one of the large shops in Buchanan Street. It did not take her long to find the counter she wanted, although the object she sought was not to be seen.

"A statuette of a naked youth?" repeated the clerk, frowning.

"Yes, I remember the item. I had three of them, I think. I'm afraid they've all been sold."

"Oh."

Seeing Deborah's face falling, the clerk's frown deepened. "Now I come to think of it, I believe there was one we set aside to be called for. Yes, I'm sure there was; and the order was cancelled. If you don't mind waiting, I'll have a look in the stockroom."

On his return he placed in Deborah's hands a replica of the bronze sculpture with which, Joyce believed, Erica Garvin had been killed. A beautiful piece of work with slim, graceful limbs and an exquisite face uplifted in the ecstasy of being strong and young. Deborah paid for the statuette and watched it being parcelled.

Now that she had it, she wondered what she was going to do with it.

* * * * *

A few miles before Garnock, coming from the north, there is a fork where the wrong road can easily be taken if the signpost isn't observed. Deborah was going as fast as her little car allowed and she never did see signposts until she had passed them, so she veered left instead of right and found herself on a bumpy stretch of back-road in the same direction as Garnock, though more circuitous than the main road, Deborah decided it was less trouble to continue on and put up with the bumps than to turn and go back.

Half a minute later she wished she had decided otherwise, for she was forced to pull over to the ditch, park, switch off the engine, and wait while a young man riding a skittish horse persuaded the animal to stop shying and sidling and coaxed it past the car and down the road to a farm gate.

At least, her first impression was that of a young man on a horse. When she looked again, she realized that the rider was a woman with short hair, clad in a tweed jacket and breeches. After horse and rider had passed through the gate and Deborah was free to go on, she continued to sit at the side of the road, gripping the steering wheel and staring unseeingly in front of her. Supposing the person Old Mrs. Craw saw getting out of a sports car at Erica Garvin's gate was not a man at all, but a woman in mannish clothes. A jealous wife. Could the old lady's eyes be trusted to differentiate at such a distance?

Driving on through the gathering dusk, with part of her mind teasing at the question, Deborah rounded a corner and almost ran into Scobie who was lurching down the middle of the road. She jammed on the brakes, narrowly escaping a bumped forehead from the windshield. In his scramble to safety Scobie dropped a dismantled shotgun and a bundle of feathers which, on Deborah's second glance, proved to be a pheasant.

As soon as he had his wits about him, he snatched up the gun and stuffed it under his coat; but he left the poached game lying in the roadway. He was furious and shaken.

"You, you—" he panted, taking a step nearer to the car, "ye could have killed me."

Seeing him still quivering from shock, Deborah lost some of the fear of him that had haunted her since their last encounter. Why, at heart he was a bigger coward than she was! Still, it was comforting to know that a hefty tyre lever lay on the floor at her feet available to be scooped up swiftly if he turned ugly.

Taking a pound note from her handbag, she crumpled it and tossed it to him through the half-open window. He caught it, stowed it away, and eyed the handbag greedily. Deborah stirred the engine to noisy life, reminding the man that she could drive off faster than he could reach her.

"How would you like ten pounds?" she asked, in a voice whose steadiness surprised her.

"Whit wid ah have tae dae for it?" he countered watching her face suspiciously.

"Answer a few questions. I think you know who killed Mrs. Garvin."

His little eyes widened and his blubbery lips let out a startled oath. "Ye're ravin' mad, woman."

"If I told the police that you're concealing evidence—"

"It's a bloody lie," he declared angrily. "And the police dinna frighten me. Ah've broken the head of more than yin copper."

"I think you are frightened," said Deborah, though slightly appalled by her own daring. "Perhaps, you killed her yourself."

"That's enough of that talk," he said. His gesture was threatening but his shifting eyes betrayed his nervousness. "Ye'll get yerself in too deep if ye dinna watch y'r tongue."

He took another step toward the car then paused and glanced warily up and down the road. Seeing a cyclist approaching, he changed his mind and turned to slouch away.

"Don't forget your pheasant," said Deborah.

"Who says it's mine?" he cried, halting and looking back.

"You risked prison for shooting it out of season. You might as well have it."

She drove on. Until the little car bobbed out of sight, Scobie stood watching it with a mingling of mistrust, apprehension and enmity on his unwashed face...

Chapter 27

On an afternoon of bright sunshine, Andrew Garvin sat on a stool placed in a niche on a hillside with a breath-taking view of the sea. He took a long look at the scene, photographing it mentally, then added a series of bold strokes to the canvas set on an easel before him. Of late his technique had become less meticulous, more spare and ruthless; it had also become stronger. He was using colour more challengingly. Those who had not liked his work in the past would like his present work less; but those who had seen promise before might now see fulfilment.

In the fervour of creation, he forgot the hurts and loneliness that had become his lot. Whether he was happy or miserable seemed utterly unimportant compared with the tremendous factor of self-expression. They could do with him as they chose, slight him, spurn him, drive him out, and none of it would matter as long as he could paint. He thought of Van Gogh, accepting confinement in the madhouse, living only for the pictures he produced between attacks of frenzy. The frenzies and the fears were nothing; the exultation of creation was all.

Deborah saw Andrew when she came over the brow of the hill, having plodded through fields with a small wicker basket. So deep in concentration was he that she felt qualms about disturbing him. It seemed unfair to intrude when he so obviously wanted and needed to be alone. After all, but for that garrulous woman in the cafe the other morning, she would not have known where to find him.

Her jaw tightened. She would not turn back now. She was going to have matters out with him, once and for all. That was the decision she had reached after lying awake half the night, thinking, conjecturing, and no qualms were going to make her change her mind.

It was unfair that she should take the risks and bear the burden of exonerating him when he did nothing on his own behalf. He had warned her of the dangers and urged her not to meddle, but he ought to realize that when you have a tiger by the tail you cannot let go.

It surprised her to sum up all she had learned. The pieces were all there. It only remained for a hand to reach out for the odd piece which, set in place, would reveal the murderer. Andrew's hand, not hers. It was time for him to take over.

Deborah was prepared for him to look unwelcoming at first sight of her. She was agreeably surprised to see his face lightening spontaneously. Andrew rose, stretched himself instinctively to relieve cramped muscles, and came to help her with the basket. He did not ask how she had found him. All week he had been plagued by sightseers and picnickers, and they would spread word of his whereabouts all over town.

"Food in the basket?" he asked.

"A cold chicken, rolls, and a bottle of wine."

"Let's start on it now," he said. "I'm ravenous."

"I was in two minds about disturbing you," Deborah said.

"That's all right. I've done all I can. I don't mean that it's finished. I've reached a point where I must wait for fresh insight. No, don't look. It hasn't anything to say yet."

He spread his raincoat to be sat on and they lunched together, enjoying the food, the sunshine and the view in a carefree insistence on the moment that thrust past and future alike into nothingness. They could have been any two people picnicking on a hillside. Instead of the serious discussion she had intended he made her tell him all about herself. She found, to her delight, that he was one of the rare people she could talk to and know her work and aspirations to be understood.

There were so many inevitable gaps and reticences, things

that could only be left unsaid, and it took a sympathetic, comprehending listener to fill them in. Tell most people that you were on the stage and they wanted to know what glamorous stars you had met; but it was the technique of acting, the creative process, that interested Andrew Garvin as it interested her.

Only too well he understood her doubts and misgivings over her own ability; weren't those hesitations and feelings of uncertainty his own as well? And the glorious uplift of knowing that you were doing well what you had been born to do; he had felt that also.

"I must paint you," he told her. "Not now. When I know you better. When I can see you as clearly in my mind when you are absent as I see you with my eyes when you are there, then I'll be able to do you justice."

He was examining her with the eyes of a painter. The eyes that see the bone and sinews under the flesh. Her slim body was beautifully formed. There were lines and curves so perfect that he doubted his ability to impress them on canvas. Her face was interesting, attractive in an intense fashion, rather than beautiful; her hair and skin were exquisite.

"It's not only because you're lovely that I want to paint you. It's rather more than that. There's an indefinable quality about you that intrigues me." He was still studying her. "Your nose is too long did you know?"

"I know my face isn't large enough. Stage stars always have large faces."

"It's a sweet face," said Andrew Garvin, "even if the proportions aren't quite right."

Bending forward, he kissed her. The touch of his lips sent a vibrant tingling through her. She wanted the moment to go on and on. It was of a sweetness such as she had never known. Andrew drew back and she saw his face becoming withdrawn and haunted once more. They had been two ordinary people enjoying a carefree afternoon; but that was only make-believe. He was remembering the curse that was on him, setting him apart from other men.

She wanted him to kiss her again. She wanted to know whether the second kiss would affect her as much, or less, or more.

Suddenly he scrambled up and was staring eastward, toward the summit of a neighbouring hill. Before she could collect herself; he started running in that direction over the uneven ground. Looking after him in bewilderment, Deborah saw Inspector Gray perched high up on the adjacent hill. Perhaps he was spying on them. Deborah could sympathize with Andrew's sudden anger. On a day like this, in a spot like this, it was intolerable to be watched like something under a microscope.

Andrew was now only a few yards from the police inspector. She heard him shouting furiously as he ran, the wrathful challenging shout of one who has been goaded beyond endurance. The inspector came to his feet and awaited Andrew in a stance more aggressive than placatory. Deborah could not catch a word but the men's attitudes and gestures were eloquent.

They were going to fight. It seemed a collision was inevitable.

Chapter 28

It infuriated Andrew Garvin to feel he was spied on at every turn, even in the normal pursuit of his vocation as artist. For weeks he had been tensing to have it out with the police, to demand that they either arrest him or leave him alone. It was galling to glance up from his easel and see a policeman determinedly idling not far off. That he could not even picnic with a girl on a hillside without being watched was the last straw.

For his part, David Gray resented being called a spy. Even professional spies prefer a less odious appellation. He was off duty. He had a book with him. He had planned an afternoon of study. True, he had known for a week that Andrew was painting in this vicinity; but it was not Andrew who brought him here. He had glimpsed Deborah putting a picnic basket into her car and followed her on impulse, knowing of her propensity for getting into trouble.

It was not an explanation he could offer even if he had been in a placatory mood, which he was not. For days he had been smarting from a verbal lashing administered by the Chief Constable, who accused him of bungling the Garvin case; a frustrating experience for an ambitious man. And now here was Andrew charging up with fire in his eyes. He hankered to meet him with a clenched fist.

Behind the inevitable antagonism of policeman and suspect lay a deeper enmity. Since they were small boys in their first school caps, in the same form at the same school, Andrew Garvin and David Gray had been hostile to each other. One an extrovert, the other an introvert, both outstanding and vigorous personalities but as unlike as denizens of different planets, they had rasped on each other like opposing abrasives from infancy to adolescence.

They could not lucidly have explained this tacit dislike. It was simply that when one appeared the other's hackles rose.

One had achieved his early ambition and become an artist. The other, eager to follow in his father's footsteps as a doctor, had been forced by lack of funds to give up that cherished dream and join the police force. Although David had become proud of his calling, it had rankled at first to know that people were joking about him as he paced a beat in uniform. His satisfaction with financial security and promotion was diminished by Andrew's winning a thousand-pound prize and returning from London with a wife who was the most beautiful woman David had ever seen.

Since young manhood they had purposefully kept aloof from each other until now.

They were in no mood to settle their differences with words. Neither of them could have been coherent in argument. The fact that a brawl could cost David his rank meant nothing. Andrew did not think of the consequences to him of a fight with a police inspector.

David was twenty pounds the heavier but the artist had a feline agility and his wrists and forearms were incredibly strong. They were evenly matched, equally angry, and neither cared about being hurt if only he could hurt the other.

It was only by chance that David struck the first blow. Andrew was rushing at him. David put up his fist and hit Andrew on the mouth. It might have been a brush with a feather for all the notice the artist took in his hot anger.

Andrew lashed out swiftly with his right fist, then his left. The blows went through his adversary's guard and landed on his lower ribs and jaw. David staggered back and Andrew followed him with a flurry of swift thrusts that pounded flesh and bone again and again. David went down and Andrew stood panting, waiting with hands clenched for him to rise.

As his back touched the ground, David rolled over and scrambled up. He lunged at Andrew with his head down, taking a smash across the mouth that brought blood, but succeeding in gripping him about the chest with both arms. They struggled and swayed, legs interlocked, feet scrabbling, shoulders jabbing, and went down in a tangle, rolling over and over on the grassy slope.

David emerged from the tangle astride the other man, striving for a grip that would give him control when, with a powerful upthrust of stomach and knees, Andrew threw him off. They sprang simultaneously and drove at each other again, smashing, pounding, each taking as much punishment as he dealt out. Neither cared for anything but getting at the other man.

Deborah had followed Andrew up the incline and now stood helplessly watching the fight. She had never before seen grown men using their fists on each other and had no idea how to stop them. It looked as if they meant to kill each other. She winced with every telling punch that landed and, at last, covered her eyes with her hands unable to bear the sight any longer.

A voice behind her said, "They're really going at it, aren't they?"

Whirling round, uncovering her eyes, she saw Hector MacInch strolling across the grass, clad in grey tweeds and nonchalantly swinging a walking stick. He had the same complacent air she had noticed at his dinner party, as if the world were his own. The twinkling eyes in the ruddy, well-fleshed face were bright with interest. Watching the fight, he was as gleeful as any mischievous urchin.

"Does it thrill you to see them fighting over you?" he asked Deborah.

"Me!" she said astonished. "You're wrong. They're fighting over something entirely different."

"No matter what they imagined their quarrel to be," said

Hector, "they are really fighting over you. Which do you want to win?"

"Don't stand there preening yourself!" Deborah cried furiously. "Can't you do something?"

"What, for instance?"

"Stop them!" she cried more angrily.

"My dear girl, I wouldn't dream of interfering. It's years since I've witnessed anything half so stirring. I find the spectacle enthralling. You wouldn't be willing to make a small wager on the outcome? No, I was afraid you wouldn't. Pity."

The sun racing the clouds cast a pattern of light and shadow that skimmed over the rough grass. A sea gull screamed raucously, hovering in suspended flight. A light wind blew in from the west with the salt of the sea on its breath.

"A grand day for a walk in the country," said Hector, in the jovial tone that rarely varied whether he was being cutting or kind. "I loathe walking, but my doctor insists. Now I'm glad he does, or I should have missed a sight worth a hundred weary miles."

"Men battling like animals?" She was astounded by Hector's indifference to two humans hurting each other.

"My dear Miss Vail, man is an animal. Don't be deceived merely because he drinks tea out of a cup. It is by repressing animal instincts that one gets nervous breakdowns and such disorders. Far better punch an enemy's head or tear at his throat than let hatred brew poison inside of you."

"I think you're loathsome." She looked around wildly for other help in breaking up the fight.

"That's rather a pity, for I think you're charming," Hector responded.

Chapter 29

The adversaries were beginning to tire. Their movements were less deft, their blows less accurate. David was bleeding from the mouth and from a wound over an eye; Andrew from the nose. Their clothes were torn and dusty. But neither of them would yield an inch except under extreme pressure; and if either was forced to recede it was only to return fiercely to the attack.

They were obviously going to fight to the point of exhaustion, until the last strength was drained from bruised, tired muscles, as a matter of masculine pride and perversity.

Deborah saw Andrew driving at David with short, punishing jabs. She saw David retaliate with a punch to the heart that made the artist grunt. Suddenly she clenched her own fists and began to scream in hysteria. She could not stop. It was as if the screams were being torn out of her. She was shocked beyond all self-control.

The men drew apart, looking awkward and guilty. They glared at each other, then Andrew walked unsteadily to Deborah and put a hand on her shoulder. She shook him off, unable to bear his touch after the injuries and hurts that hand had done its best to inflict. The artist rubbed the hand over his face and glanced at the resultant smear of blood. Deborah's screaming quietened to hoarse sobs. David Gray looked from one to the other, then turned and limped away.

Hector MacInch leaned on his stick with the assurance of one awaiting in keen anticipation the second act of an absorbing play.

"It's all over now," said Andrew to Deborah, between gasps for air. "Don't cry."

"You...you were like beasts!"

"I'm sorry you had to see it."

"You're not sorry!" She dabbed her eyes with a handkerchief. "You'd go at each other again without a second thought."

Stumbling, she picked her way between tufts of tall grass, clumps of gorse and outcroppings of rock to the sheltered hollow where they had lunched. Andrew somewhat unsteady on his legs, helped her to gather up the residue of the picnic. Carrying the wicker basket, he walked with her to her car. He stowed the basket in the baggage compartment, opened the door and handed her in to the driving seat.

Feeling the constant tremors that passed through him, she realized how greatly the fight had broached him physically.

"I know you don't take good advice," he said, in the same harsh, breathless voice as before, "but I've got to say this. Keep away from me. Forget about me. I have nothing but shame and misery to offer any woman."

Slamming the car door, he turned and made his way painfully to where his easel stood.

* * * * *

It was to be an informal little party, a gathering of friends who had entertained Deborah, or whom Joyce wanted her to meet, a sprinkling of teachers and their wives from Ewan's school, and some members of the Amateur Dramatic Society. They would help themselves at a makeshift bar to sherry, Madeira or cider. There would be tea and coffee on a side-table. There would be sandwiches made to be eaten in two bites; small sausage rolls; triangles of toast bearing chicken livers wrapped in bacon, fillets of anchovy, chopped egg and toasted cheese, or spread with savoury pastes. And, of course, the fancy cakes the Scots love and are artists at creating. Nothing elaborate. When telephoning the invitations, Joyce said, "From fourish to a bit after seven."

A simple affair, hardly a party at all. No need for fuss. It would run itself. None of it would be the least trouble. Having so decided, Joyce rolled up her sleeves and went to work. For a full day, from morning to early evening, she and Deborah and the house-worker who 'obliged' from time to time scoured, dusted, polished until the house could have stood inspection from cellar to attic.

"Who's going to go looking under beds and behind wardrobes?" asked Deborah, a little wearily.

"You don't know Garnock," replied Joyce, briskly carrying on with the attack on fugitive specks.

Deborah wondered what domestic upheaval would have been necessary had they been giving the sort of affair that does call for a preliminary fuss.

On the day of the party the whole morning and part of the afternoon was spent in preparing food, for Joyce had a card-index memory for every edible curiosity that had graced her friends' parties and was determined to outdo them all. The guests would have arrived to find her still regrouping dishes, polishing glasses that gleamed already and marshalling china in new arrangements, had not Deborah taken her by the shoulders at three and propelled her upstairs to change.

They left their doors open to enable them to talk from room to room without overly raising their voices.

"I wish you hadn't asked the MacInches," called Deborah.

Joyce's reply was only a mumble until she removed a safety pin from between her teeth.

"After the lovely dinner they gave us?"

"She is a dear but I can't stand him. He's such a sadistic beast."

"Well, I do admit he's a bit provoking but, as this isn't their cup of tea, they'll probably come late and leave early. You can stand him for an hour. We couldn't possibly have left them out."

"No, I suppose not."

For a time Joyce did all the talking, which did not discomfit her in the least. As long as she had a listener she would carry on a sporadic monologue for hours. Deborah unpacked the bronze statuette she had bought in Glasgow, admiring again its slim elegance. The fight on the hillside had frustrated her intention of telling Andrew the mass of fact and surmise that was in her mind and leaving it to him to carry on from there. For the present, at least, she could not intrude on him again. He had said vehemently, 'Keep away from me.' True, he was thinking of her safety and happiness; but a rebuff like that could not be ignored.

As she saw it, the case now hinged on the missing murder weapon, the other statuette. Find that, said intuition, and the answer would be plain. She already had a plan for finding the thing; a plan that frightened her when she thought of it. She was not at all sure she would find the courage to carry it through. If only she had been able to pour out her thoughts to Andrew. If only the two men had not behaved like belligerent schoolboys, breaking up what had promised to be a wonderful afternoon.

Meanwhile, here was the replica of the murder weapon; and she had a use for it. As soon as she was dressed, she carried it down and placed it on one of the bookcases in the living room. It was an object to draw the eye: Perhaps one of the guests would betray a consciousness of having seen a similar object before. She would be watchful…

Chapter 30

Deborah's plan was almost cancelled at the outset by Joyce, who came downstairs chattering blithely. The words died abruptly on her lips when she saw the bronze statuette on the bookcase. Ashen-faced, appalled, she stared at Deborah.

"W-where did you get that?"

"It isn't the one the murder was done with," Deborah said quickly. "It's a copy I bought in Glasgow."

"Why didn't you tell me?" Joyce demanded. "And what's it doing there?" All of a sudden, she understood. She was furious. "Deborah, how dare you? You're setting a trap for one of my guests!"

"Erica's statuette stood at her bedside for only a short while before she was murdered. Anyone who saw it there saw it during that brief period."

"And you're hoping one of my guests will look guilty!"

"Not hoping, exactly. I admit I hadn't thought of—"

"Then think now!" Joyce said heatedly. "I won't have you using my party to— Why, it's as if I planned the affair simply as a trap."

The back door slammed and Ewan walked in breezily. He kissed his wife and put a friendly arm round Deborah.

"What's this?" he asked, noticing the statuette. "Something new? I rather like it. Only hope it didn't cost a packet. Well, I'd better dress for the party."

"Put it away, Deborah," Joyce said firmly, as she turned to follow her husband upstairs. "Get the thing out of sight."

Deborah reached out a hand to the bronze figure. She drew it back. The doorbell rang and she went to answer it, leaving the statuette where it stood.

The party had begun.

Within half an hour the living room was thronged. To everyone's surprise, the MacInches made an early appearance. They were usually late everywhere. Judith faded and angular, yet still with an aura of past beauty, in dove grey with a rose-pink hat. Hector genial, assured, impeccably tailored, and good enough to commend Ewan's sherry, sincerely or not.

His eyes, resting on Deborah, had a mocking glint. She flushed slightly and had an uncomfortable feeling that he was going to embarrass her in public by spinning a mischief-making tale out of the episode on the hillside. But he did not allude to it.

"I've got to thank you for doing me a good turn," he said expansively to Ewan, who looked surprised. "By giving that scoundrel Scobie the sack, I mean."

"Well, I certainly packed him off," said Ewan, "but I can't see how that means anything to you."

"Been needing a man to help prune my orchard. Too much work for my gardener to manage alone. You know how the labour situation is. Can't get help for love or money. Didn't think of Scobie until I found the blighter prowling in my grounds. Thought at first he was nosing about in quest of something worth pinching, but he told me he was looking for a job. I put it up to my gardener. If he could manage Scobie, we'd take him on for a few weeks. He said he'd manage the blighter if he had to take a cudgel to him, so that's how it stands. Must say he shows up every morning and does his share of the work—as long as you keep an eye on him."

"When do you go back to Edinburgh, Mr. MacInch?" asked one of the guests with the respect due to a distinguished Queen's Counsel.

"Tomorrow or the next day, I'm afraid. Can't get out of it. We love the country, Judith and I, but duty calls, you know."

Glass in hand, he joined the group round Deborah. Here it comes, she thought. But his first remark was an innocuous one about his work at the Law Courts. He glanced at the statuette. She watched his face covertly for some unusual reaction. There was none.

It was half an hour later when Hector MacInch stopped her for a moment in the hall. "Can you keep a secret?" he asked.

"I think so," Deborah replied.

"I've had a pretty broad hint from an old friend in Edinburgh. Can't reveal his identity but he holds a high official position. I know you'll be interested. Promise you'll keep it to yourself...? They've practically decided to prosecute Andrew Garvin. Whether the evidence is sufficient or not, they feel it's important to clear the matter up. There's to be a meeting in a day or so and then the warrant will be issued."

If he hoped to shock and dismay her, he succeeded. She stared at him, the vivid colour of her lipstick contrasting oddly with the pallor of her quivering face. Though dazed and shaken, she had sufficient wit to wonder why he had told her this.

"You mustn't tell anyone," he said. "Especially not Garvin. It would be all the worse for him if he tried to bolt the country."

"What is he to do? I know he hasn't any money. How is he to defend himself?"

"Leave that to me. I'll undertake his defence. Get him off, too, if it's humanly possible."

"You?"

"I don't want to boast," said Hector complacently, "but I don't yield first place to any advocate in Scotland. Anyone will tell you his defence couldn't be in more capable hands. Besides, I've known the chap all his life. And his father before him.

"Pull yourself together," he said sharply. "We've got to go in and join the others, and the guest of honour must look her best."

Over his shoulder she saw herself in the hall mirror and thought she looked ghastly. Was that why he had given her the distressing piece of information? To shatter her composure and give the guests food for conjecture over the sudden change in her? Considering his malicious sense of humour, it was not unlikely.

Well, she was an actress and now she must play the part of a smiling girl without a care in the world. Turning from him, she ran upstairs to put on a touch of colour.

The Sinclairs arrived in her absence. When she came down Enid gave her a fulsome greeting but Bill only nodded vaguely before wandering off and attaching himself to another group. Since that morning in the café, when Enid exploded over the silver cigarette lighter, Bill had been mistrustful of Deborah. Dropping the tentatively flirtatious approach, he kept himself warily aloof from her.

The evening was drawing in, for which Deborah was thankful. Soon the guests would begin to leave.

She had to remind herself to smile, and go on smiling. Coming face to face with Bill Sinclair, she saw him looking at her suspiciously.

He said, "Nice party," preparing to edge away. His eyes were caught by the statuette on the bookcase and his jaw dropped. The glass fell from his limp fingers. Taking a faltering pace backwards, he stepped on the glass, grinding the splintered fragments into the carpet.

He seemed to be having a stroke.

Chapter 31

Those nearest Bill Sinclair were clustering around him, asking questions and offering suggestions. One more practical than the others went for a glass of water. Deborah would have liked to do something for the stricken man but knew he would flinch from her if she came close.

"It...it's nothing," Bill was saying, speaking very slowly and with a visible effort. "A...a sudden twinge of pain. It caught me here, in the side. Don't worry. I think it's going now."

With wifely intuition, Enid Sinclair knew that he was lying; that it was shock, not a pain that unhinged him. She also knew that, for the time being, she was not likely to get at the truth. When Bill started to lie, he went on lying. Only by remorseless questioning in private would she break him down. And he was afraid. Why? She looked searchingly at Deborah but could find nothing in the girl's face to give her a clue.

"I'd better take you home," Enid said to Bill.

"Home," he stammered, snatching at the suggestion. "Yes, I want to go home."

Enid steadied him as he stood up and gave him the support of her arm in crossing the room. She was abrupt with those who wanted to be of service. In the doorway, she paused for a moment.

"It's been a lovely party," she said acidly, glancing from Deborah to Joyce and Ewan.

The departure of the Sinclairs broke up the party. When the door closed on the final guest, Joyce dropped into a chair.

"Well, that's over!" she exclaimed. "What was all the fuss about? I could see that something was wrong but I was too occupied to grasp what it was."

Deborah did not answer. The shock which the sight of the

statuette had caused Bill was too grave a matter to he discussed offhandedly. She wanted time to think.

"If you'll excuse me," she said, "I'll just run up and powder my nose."

She went out swiftly before Joyce or Ewan could ask any more questions.

* * * * *

Deborah did not suspect Scobie of being the murderer of Erica Garvin, though it should have occurred to her. He obviously was a brute capable of anything if he thought he could get away with it. Unless in panic or passion, he would not risk killing in the cold light of day. But Deborah did not doubt that he knew, or strongly suspected, the identity of the murderer.

Scobie had found temporary employment at the MacInches. Hector had said the man turned up every morning and worked all day at the odd jobs the MacInches had for him to do.

Deborah took the precaution of halting at a secluded place overlooking the MacInch estate before scouting the orchard through field glasses. When she got the range she saw Scobie balanced on a tall ladder, lopping the branches of a tree, while another man, presumably the gardener, steadied the ladder from the ground.

Feeling reasonably safe with the knowledge that Scobie would be occupied for the better part of the day, Deborah drove to his shack.

The huge black dog chained by the door barked menacingly when her car stopped at the sagging gate. When he saw who approached he stopped barking and wagged his tail. He was a menacing-looking beast but he remembered the juicy liver and soothing caresses she brought him last time. The chunk of red meat she threw him before coming close was quickly engulfed by the awesome jaws. Gulping it down without chewing, he wagged his tail again.

"Glad to see me, Blackie-boy?" she murmured, kneeling to fondle his silky ears.

He was delighted. Starved of companionship, he made much of her, wriggling his powerful body in ecstasy, nuzzling her with nose and jowls, making it clear with whines and excited movements how very welcome she was.

Deborah moved slowly round the shack, examining it from all sides. The windows neither opened nor shut. They were single panes, set in rough frames nailed tight to the structure. The only way in, short of smashing a window or ripping down a wall, was through the door. And the padlock and hasps were discouragingly stout.

Naturally, she could not be sure that the missing murder weapon was hidden inside the shack—Scobie might have a dozen ingenious caches for filched property—but the shack seemed the obvious starting place.

Deborah remembered the method used by Sherlock Holmes to find a secret recess in 'A Scandal in Bohemia'. 'When a woman thinks that her house is on fire, her instinct is at once to rush to the thing she values most. It is a perfectly overpowering impulse.'

A man might well do the same thing. A mere whiff of smoke would not make Scobie lose his head, but surely there was a way to trick him into revealing the hiding place. It seemed to Deborah that there was a way, a very simple one...

* * * * *

After dinner that evening, Deborah put on a coat, arranged a scarf lightly on her hair, and went out to post some letters. The mailbox was only a few streets away.

They were dark streets, with long stretches of shadow between the yellow pools of light cast by the lamp posts. Few lights were showing in the houses and there was not a solitary pedestrian, not even a slinking cat, to enliven the deserted pavements. It was so still that the patter of her own footsteps seemed jarringly loud.

Reaching the box, she dropped the letters into the slot. She heard them slithering down, and started back. Before she had gone far, she heard, or fancied she heard, footsteps following behind. Looking back casually, she saw no one. The street appeared as deserted as before. But when she walked on the footsteps behind her started again.

They kept pace, like an echo. When she slowed down, the sounds behind her slowed down; when she quickened, they quickened; when she halted in indecision, they halted. She hardly dared look back again but steeled herself to do so and saw an empty street.

Her fright rose moment by moment at the thought that someone stood, motionless and unseen, waiting for her to go on. She told herself sharply not to be an idiot. The assumption that she was being followed deliberately implied that someone had lain in wait for her; and no one could have known she would come out that evening when she had not known it herself until ten minutes before.

She took a tentative step, then paused and listened. There was no echoing step. Emboldened, she walked on steadily and heard herself being followed again. The sound was unnerving.

Panic-possessed then, she started to run and heard running footsteps in pursuit. No, this was no mistake. The footsteps behind were running like her own. They quickened. They were gaining.

In a dark place overshadowed by the hanging branches of a tree, two gloved hands reached out from behind and grasped her neck...

Chapter 32

Out of a deep unconsciousness Deborah Vail awoke to broad daylight. Fumbling for her watch, she saw that it was almost eleven. She had slept without stirring for nearly twelve hours. The voices that had wakened her could still be heard; the sound of them floated up the stairwell and through her partly open door from the front hall.

Her curiosity aroused, Deborah slipped out of bed, wincing with the pain of a lacerated knee, and crept to the door.

"I wouldn't dream of waking her," Joyce was saying firmly. "After an experience like that, she needs all the sleep she can get."

"I really must talk to her," insisted Enid Sinclair's high-pitched voice.

"I'll tell her when she wakens," said Joyce, "but I hope that won't be for hours."

Wrapping herself in a negligee, Deborah went out and looked over the banister. "I'll be down in a minute." she announced.

There was a pregnant silence.

"Don't bother to come down," Joyce called back quickly. "I'll bring your breakfast up."

Almost simultaneously, and articulating very clearly, Enid said, "I want to talk to you, Miss Vail, but there's no great hurry. I can wait."

"I wouldn't dream of keeping you waiting," replied Deborah, in a clear, sweet voice. To her cousin, she added, "I'm not a bit hungry, Joyce, but I'm dying for some strong black coffee."

"You'll eat a proper breakfast," said Joyce.

While cooking it she made Enid keep her company in the kitchen. She was not going to risk having Enid sneak upstairs.

When Deborah finally appeared, she was dressed and

made-up most becomingly. Though only one plate was set for breakfast, Joyce had put down three coffee cups, which did not in the least please Enid, who wanted to be alone with Deborah. The three of them sat at the table in the breakfast nook. Suddenly realizing that she was hungry, Deborah applied herself with appetite to the food. Enid kept up an impatient scrabbling on the surface of the table with her long scarlet fingernails.

"Don't I hear the baby crying?" she asked.

"No, you don't," replied Joyce, sipping her coffee.

"Joyce," said Deborah, quietly, yet meaningfully.

Joyce rose. "Oh, very well," she said.

Leaving the room, she went upstairs, treading more heavily than usual on each step, to leave them in no doubt that she was departing out of hearing. Enid rose and shut the door. Sitting down again, she leaned forward and stared imperiously at Deborah.

"What are you trying to do to my husband?" she demanded.

Deborah's hand, lifting a cup to her lips, halted in mid-air.

"I don't know what you mean!" she exclaimed. "Perhaps you can explain yourself a little more —deftly."

"You've got him all upset. I don't know what it is, what you're doing to him. I can't get him to tell me what it's all about. But I know Bill. He's worried and edgy. He's drinking too much. And it's all your fault."

"Well, really, Mrs. Sinclair—"

"It's no good trying to put me off. At the Monteiths' party the other afternoon, you were talking to him—I was watching the pair of you—and suddenly he almost fainted. A big healthy man—and he almost fainted. What had you said to him?"

"Nothing that I can remember. Only the ordinary sort of thing one says at parties. Perhaps"—Deborah hesitated—"perhaps it was something he saw."

"If something he saw upset him, you know what it was. And you had better tell me."

"I can't do that." said Deborah. "No, I shan't tell you what it was. I have an idea the fewer people who know about it the better. I'll tell you this; it was something that would have significance to the person who killed Erica Garvin."

Enid drew in her breath. "So that's it! Still trying to involve my husband."

"If he's involved, he involved himself. There's nothing I could do—"

"You tried it before. There was that ridiculous cigarette lighter you made out to be his."

"If you'll trouble to remember, it was you who claimed it was his. And, it is his. We both know that."

"But Bill didn't do it!" Enid's voice had lost its brittle sophistication and was strained and hoarse.

"Do you hear me?" she went on. "He didn't do it! Oh, there are a number of things I might as well admit. The lighter you had is his; it's the one I gave him. And I suppose he did leave it at her house. I knew he was having an affair with her. I tried to pretend I didn't know. I even tried to fool myself that I was mistaken. No matter how many kinds of an idiot he makes of himself, he's my idiot. I love him and I'll never give him up."

Deborah could find nothing to say.

"Perhaps he was with her on the morning of the day she died," Enid continued earnestly, "but she was alive when he left her. I can vouch for that. That morning, I went to his office to talk to him about something. Bill was out and my first thought was that he might be with Erica. I phoned her and she answered. While we were talking on the phone, Bill walked into the office.

"Don't you see? She was alive, talking to me, and he was at my side. Afterwards, Bill took me out to lunch. It must have been three o'clock—a couple of hours after the murder—when I dropped him at the office. He had been in my company continuously since twelve."

Deborah said thoughtfully, "But you'd lie for him, if need be, wouldn't you?"

"Of course, I'd lie. Any woman worth her salt will lie like a trooper for her man. But what I've told you is the truth."

Deborah looked down at her hands. There was something she wanted to know but she was hesitant over putting the question. Considering the implications of it, it seemed a dreadful question to ask a woman about her husband.

Suddenly resolving herself, she raised her head and looked Enid full in the face. "Where was Bill at ten o'clock last night?"

"At ten," said Enid, moistening her lips. "I see what you mean. That was the time you were attacked."

Somehow, she managed a return to her normal tone of frothiness and spontaneity.

"My dear, it's too ridiculous. If you knew Bill, you'd never think such a thing of him. He's the gentlest soul in the world. When we catch a mouse I'm the one who has to dispose of it. Besides, he was at home with me."

Deborah had not the slightest idea whether the woman was lying or not.

"If Andrew did not kill Erica," Enid continued, "I can tell you who did. There's no need to look further than Hector MacInch. Hector was the one she really cared about. And Hector has a ruthless way with an old flame when he tires of her. I ought to know..."

Chapter 33

The Monteiths and their guest went up to bed early. After a last word on the landing with Joyce, Deborah entered her room, shut the door, and undressed. She did not take up the nightdress that lay on the bed. Instead, she put on a tailored suit of dark material, her one pair of woollen stockings, and a pair of rubber-soled shoes. She put a flashlight in her pocket.

While changing clothes with a minimum of sound and movement, she kept hearing the bland voice of Hector MacInch: 'They've practically decided to prosecute Garvin…meeting in a day or two…a warrant will be issued…' If Enid Sinclair was right and Hector was guilty, it would suit him admirably to have Andrew put on trial. Oh, yes, he would defend him without a fee. He would defend him right into prison.

Deborah put out the light and sat down to wait for the half hour to pass that would see the rest of the household soundly asleep.

Stealthily raising the window, she leaned out and touched a stout branch of an elm tree that stood near the house. As she had thought, it was near enough to be grasped. Before climbing through the window, she dropped out a knobby walking stick of Ewan's and heard it hit the ground.

The bark of the tree chafed her hands, but she swung nimbly from branch to branch and reached earth safely and silently. That afternoon she had taken her car to a nearby garage for a minor adjustment and asked the mechanic to leave it in the lane behind the place to be called for later. Picking up the stick she stole down the drive. As soon as she was out of earshot of the house she started to walk briskly.

There was no moon. Her nerves were on edge. It was in this quiet street that she had been attacked the previous evening.

She parked her car in a disused cart track leading into the woods from a country lane some miles from the town. When she switched off the lights, darkness closed in. She stepped out, reached back for the stick, then changed her mind and left it on the driving seat.

With caution she made her way through the night-blackened fields and coppices toward Scobie's hovel. It was now about eleven but a light still showed in the shack. When she came within a hundred yards of it, the chained dog sensed her proximity and started whining. The door opened and Scobie's warped figure appeared on the threshold. He glowered out into the darkness, stood listening for a time, then cursed the dog and went back in.

Deborah crept nearer, pausing every few paces. Some instinct gave her warning. She chanced using her flashlight for an instant and saw that one more step would have toppled her into a ditch. Jumping down, she took cover in it.

One of her pockets contained a folded sheet of foolscap and a length of twine. Groping in the dirt with her fingers, she found a large stone and tied the paper securely to it. Standing up, she took careful aim.

The stone flew with a crash through one of Scobie's windows.

In an instant the door was flung back on its hinges and the man ran out. Releasing the huge black dog, he shouted an angry order to it as it sped into the dark. Scobie withdrew into the shack and reappeared with a shotgun.

The dog found Deborah without delay and jumped down into the ditch, whining with pleasure. She petted him and gripped his collar. "Good boy. Good Blackie-boy. Quiet, boy."

She fondled his ears, fervently hoping that her attentions would keep him from barking and giving her away. Hearing his master's hoarse exhorting shouts, the dog whimpered and dithered, torn between duty and inclination.

Scobie was tramping through fields and thickets with the shotgun, too wrathful for caution or stealth. His harsh shouts were becoming querulous and bewildered.

Deborah released the dog with a final pat. "Go, boy. Go!"

When the dog came to him through the dark, Scobie greeted it with a kick. "Lost him, did ye? What good are ye?"

After a further period of fruitless searching. Scobie returned to his dwelling, leaving the dog free but admonishing it: "Stay there, dung you! Don't go wanderin' off." When the door closed on him Deborah risked stretching her painfully cramped muscles and sinews. Now came the really dangerous part of the venture. She was glad the flashlight was solid enough to make an effective weapon if she needed one in a hurry.

On tiptoe, hardly daring to breathe, she moved nearer to the shack. The black dog came silently to meet her, staring up at her in distressful uncertainty. A poor baffled creature, unsure of himself for the first time in his life. Inside the shack, Scobie rummaged about until he found the stone. He had concluded that the smashing of his window had been a loutish prank and that the perpetrator, probably a young farm labourer, had made off on a bicycle. Otherwise, why hadn't the dog found him?

His mental processes were sluggish, and finding a paper tied to the stone disconcerted him. He glared at it mistrustfully, uncertain what to make of it. At last, he cut the string and spread the paper on his table in the light cast by the dangling lamp.

An incredulous oath burst from his lips. He stared at the paper as much aghast as if it had fangs. Pasted on it were printed words clipped from a newspaper, in imitation of the blackmailing notes he himself had concocted. His lips moved forming the words, as he read it:

'What one can hide another can find.'

Puzzled and perturbed, he dashed outside again. He cursed

the whimpering dog that cringed at his feet. He cast about him suspiciously, not expecting to find an intruder, since the dog had not found one, but reluctant to admit himself beaten. A few steps further in one direction and he could have touched Deborah by stretching out a hand. Finally, he went into the shack, muttering and swearing.

Shifting the table aside, he levered up a floorboard, uncovering a rectangular space from which he took an object wrapped in sacking. He cast a furtive glance over his shoulder, half expecting to see a silent watcher in the far corner.

For a while he stood holding the rough parcel in brooding uncertainty. Going out, he hovered at his door, peering about him and cocking his head to catch any stray sound. At last, he kicked the door shut and, skirting the hen-run, walked toward the woods.

Occasionally he halted to listen again. He moved among the trees like an animal, with scarcely rustling to betray his presence. Reaching a tree with a trunk thicker than a man's chest, he stood still under it, eyes and ears alert. Hearing no sound, detecting no stirring, he raised himself on his toes and slipped the wrapped object into a hollow as high among the branches as his hands could reach...

Chapter 34

On his way back from the hiding place in the tree, Scobie passed within a yard of where Deborah crouched behind another tree. She turned her head cautiously to peer after him but before he had taken six paces the murky gloom swallowed up his shapeless form. She decided to count to a hundred before venturing a move. Even though she stood in darkness, shrouded in shadow, she felt as if a thousand eyes were intent upon her.

"Ninety-four, ninety-five, ninety-six..." To be on the safe side, Deborah counted another hundred before stealing out and thrusting warily through the undergrowth to the tree with the hollow cache high in its trunk.

To reach the hollow she had to pull herself up by the lowermost branch. It cost her a broken fingernail and a bruised shin, but she found and withdrew the wrapped object, manipulating it gingerly lest she smudge the fingerprints that might be on it. Cradling it in her arms, she hesitated in the shadow of a tree, unwilling to retrace her footsteps past Scobie's shack, but unsure which rough track would lead nearest to her car.

Deborah decided to go to the edge of the woods, then keep to the left, skirting Scobie's piece of land. She dared not show a glimmer of light but must depend on instinct to guide her between bushes and sapling growth and over rocky, uneven ground. Without the slightest warning, Scobie suddenly stepped out of hiding and grabbed at her. Uttering a wild scream, she ran in the opposite direction but tripped on a root and sprawled on the earth.

Scobie stood over her, clubbing a stout branch which he brought down savagely at her head. Deborah rolled over frantically and the blow missed her, striking the ground with a thud.

One of her clawing hands touched the sacking-wrapped bundle which had dropped when she fell. She grasped it tightly, scrambled to her feet, and ran on again, with Scobie at her heels. She heard him, barely a pace behind, shouting furiously to his dog.

Her courage almost failed. At any instant she must feel his hands on her throat and, this time, there would be no escape.

Off to the right, a bulky form was crashing through the undergrowth at an angle to her flight. It was Scobie's dog. The tangle of brush and trees ahead seemed impenetrable; she was running into a trap.

Scobie let out a triumphant yell. "Get her!" he called to the dog. "Sic her, bring her down!"

And then his triumph turned to bewilderment and chagrin. There was a confusion of sounds behind Deborah; a snarling, a rending of cloth, a thrashing about of heavy bodies, the hoarse cursing of Scobie.

Daring a backward glance, Deborah glimpsed a tangled, heaving mass, half-animal, half-human, on the ground. Instead of springing on the girl, the dog had gripped his master's trousers and brought him down heavily.

There was no time to waste. She found a narrow way through the undergrowth and scurried down it. Somewhere in headlong flight she had dropped the flashlight but in her arms she tightly held the object for which she had come.

She gave up all expectation of finding her car. That was too much to hope for. Her one obsession was to come upon an open space where there was nothing to trip her.

When, at last, she reached the cart track that cut through the woods, she was at first too harried to recognize it. She kept on going, across the deeply-rutted grassy path, and was starting into the woods on the other side when a spark of intelligence checked her. Turning back dizzily, she looked right and left. There was no moon. It was too dark to see anything clearly; but the track was like a grey ribbon on a black dress. She turned right and, after a hundred yards or so, came upon her car.

Before giving any thought to herself, she laid carefully on the driving seat the crude bundle for which she had risked so much. She did not unwrap it but, by a gentle touch here and there, identified the object swaddled in sacking. It was the statuette, the bronze youth with which Erica Garvin had fallen in love when she saw it on a counter in a Glasgow shop. Deborah had not the slightest doubt that it would lead police to Erica's murderer.

Oddly, she felt no elation, no triumph. She was too spent and worn for emotion. A cigarette might have been soothing but she was not sure she could light one. Her fingers were trembling too much. Far better to lie back and do nothing until the taxed muscles were more at ease. There was still so much to do when she found the strength to stir again.

It was the thought of Scobie's dog that roused her. In her defence it had turned upon its master. What would Scobie do to it? The thought was dreadful to contemplate. It made her sit up straight, start the car, and back it out onto the road.

A mile or so away she found a telephone box at a crossroads. Dropping coins in the slot, she dialled the number of the local police station. A solid voice, a little bored, answered her.

"There's a man killing a dog," she said jerkily. "You've got to send a car—a patrol car—at once."

"Who is this speaking, ma'am?"

"Never mind that. It's not important. The important thing is you've got to hurry. It's Scobie. You know who Scobie is, don't you? You know where he lives? I'm afraid he'll kill his dog. Do you understand? He'll kill it!"

"If you're making a complaint, ma'am, you'll have to give me your name."

"It's Miss Vail. Deborah Vail. Now will you please hurry?"

The desperate urgency in her tone impressed him. "I'll have a car out there in a matter of minutes, miss. In fact, if you'll hold the wire, I'll start it off now." A few moments later the voice, no longer stolid but brisk and inquisitive, spoke in her ear again. "The car's on its way, miss. And now, there are one or two particulars I must ask you to give me."

"Can't that wait? I'll come to the police station in the morning. Won't that do?" Now that she had done her best for the dog she felt it was urgent to turn over the statuette without delay to someone qualified to deal with it. "Is Inspector Gray there? May I speak to him?"

"Inspector Gray went to Edinburgh this afternoon, miss. We're expecting him back at any moment."

"Oh. Then I'll call him later."

Hanging up, she found more coins and looked up Andrew Garvin's number in the directory. After she had dialled it fruitlessly several times, the operator cut in and told her that service to that line had been discontinued.

Deborah hung up. Coming out of the booth, she climbed into the car and started the engine. Why hadn't she gone straight to Andrew, instead of losing time on the telephone? Between them, they would decide how the piece of evidence could be used most effectively...

Chapter 35

Andrew Garvin's house was dark except for the one room in which he painted, ate, and brooded away long dragging days of loneliness. On that wild night, weeks ago, the light in that room had suddenly gone out when Deborah knocked on the door. She remembered how rebuffed and bewildered she had felt at the time. Well, from now on Andrew Garvin would be able to open his door with confidence at any hour. He would no longer be a target for idle tongues and eyes.

This time, while Deborah's knock still echoed, a curtain was drawn back from one of the lighted windows and the artist stood there, outlined. Deborah moved back from the door to let the light fall on her, to let him see who it was that came knocking at this hour. He let the curtain drop. In a few seconds the hall light went on, she heard footsteps approaching, and then the door swung open. Andrew stood looking out at her. His frowning eyes travelled over her from head to toe. He stared into the darkness beyond, as if expecting to see someone in the background.

"Deborah! My God, what's happened to you? You look as if you'd been in the wars!"

"Are you going to let me in?" she asked weakly. "Or must I faint again on your doorstep?"

"Come in, of course," he said quickly, pushing the door wider.

It was all she could do to take the two steps that brought her over the threshold into the house. After that, Andrew supported her, with an arm about her waist, through the hall, into the lighted living room, and eased her into a chair in front of the fire. He said something about fetching brandy but she shook her head.

"I'll be all right in a minute. I've been through a lot tonight. Now it's up to you. You've got to—"

The warmth of the fire, the comfort of the chair, brought a drowsy lassitude stealing over her senses, stilling her tongue, making her head nod, making it difficult Ito think, far less speak.

"Yes?" said Andrew, after a little while. He regarded her curiously. "What were you going to say? What have I got to do?"

"You've got to stand up for yourself. It's up to you to prove your innocence."

"How can I?"

His eyes were fixed keenly on her face. They shifted for a second to the crude parcel in her arms.

"I've found it," she said dizzily. In another moment she was going to let her head drop, she was going to pass out.

"Found what?" he asked. "Deborah, can you hear me? What have you found?"

"Of course I can hear you," she said, rousing herself with difficulty. "I've found what the police searched for so long in vain. I've found the missing weapon."

He was silent. She looked up and saw him turning away, going slowly to the mantelpiece and resting an arm on it, letting his head drop until it rested on the arm.

"Don't you see what that means?" she said. "There may be fingerprints."

"So there may," he said quietly, without looking at her.

It was a strain to force herself to be fully awake but she made the effort. There was so much to tell him. About the obviously blackmailing note that first caused her to suspect that Scobie had the weapon. About her visits to his shack to spy out the land and make friends with the watchdog. About the nocturnal adventure that almost ended in disaster.

"And that's it?" he asked, raising his head.

"Yes."

"Let me see."

"It ought not to be handled until the police test it in their laboratory. I don't know much about fingerprints but surely there's a danger of smudging them."

"Give me the statuette," he said compellingly, reaching out a hand.

Deborah stared at him. His lean, haggard face looked sickly. "What did you say?"

"My dear girl," he said, controlling himself by a visible effort, "there's no need to look so startled. I only asked to be permitted to examine your prize, whatever it is."

"You said 'the statuette.' How did you know it's a statuette? Even the police don't know that. It only stood at your wife's bedside for a short time before she was murdered."

"Did I say 'statuette'? I suppose that's how you described it when you were telling me."

"I didn't describe it. I said 'the weapon'."

She had risen unsteadily to her feet. Now she started edging toward the door. He was there before her. He put his back to it. His expression was odd, as if he felt overwhelmingly sorry for her.

"You're exhausted and nervous," he said gently. "You've been through so much, it's no wonder your mind is ready to snatch at any strange fancy. Go back and sit down. You need rest. Just relax. Close your eyes. Try to get a little sleep."

His tone was soothingly hypnotic but she knew she must not be swayed by it.

"If I'm as tired as all that," she said, trying desperately to speak lightly, "I'd better go home. Come and see me in the morning. We'll talk things over then, when I'm more myself."

"Don't be a little fool," said Andrew Garvin, quite calmly. "You know quite well I can't let you walk out of here. Put the statuette down over there, on the table, and stand back from it."

A shaky laugh came out of Deborah without her volition; she

could not help it. "And I believed in you! I thought it dreadful that an innocent man should be persecuted."

"Do you think persecution is the worst of it? How little you know. When a man destroys the thing he values most the rest of his days are spent regretting it."

"Please don't tell me you're sorry you killed her!" said Deborah angrily. "That would be a little too much."

"It doesn't matter whether you believe it or not. No matter what she was—and no one knew better than I what she was—I loved her. If I'd been given time to think she'd be alive today. My God, I didn't want to kill her. And I begged you, for your own good, to stop playing detective."

"It was you, following me, the other night," said Deborah.

"I could have killed you then. A little more pressure on your throat, and that would have been the end of you. I hoped a fright would be enough." In a pitying tone, he added, "You see, I didn't want to kill you."

A shiver passed through her slim body but she said almost boldly:

"You didn't want to kill your wife…but you did."

"As long as I live—and, believe me, I intend to live—I'll regret it. It wouldn't have happened if she hadn't driven me out of my wits with anger. For a few seconds I went mad, only a few seconds, but then it was too late to control myself. Now I see her face wherever I turn and I know I'll never kiss her mouth again, never hold her in my arms again. If there's a hell it can't be worse than the hell I've made for myself…"

Chapter 36

Andrew Garvin rocked to and fro on heels and toes. His facial muscles twitched slightly as he talked to Deborah.

"I told the truth, or part of it, when I said I was painting at Old Knowe Farm the day I killed Erica. I ran out of yellow and had to come back for a fresh tube. It's the little things that affect our destiny. If there hadn't been a golden haze on the hillside; if it had been a purple sort of day, Erica would still be alive. As I passed the crossroads, I saw Hector MacInch driving down the other road, toward his house. It was no news to me that he was one of Erica's lovers. It was one of the humiliations I had to swallow if I wanted to keep Erica...and I did.

"When I went into the house, she was surprised to see me home but not upset or in the least afraid. She knew I must have seen Hector driving away but that didn't bother her. She said, 'I'm sick and tired of being poor, Andrew. Aren't you? But we're not going to be poor any longer. Hector is filthy rich. I think he must be made to share with us.'

"Erica had a plan to trap him. She had it all worked out."

Wearily, he passed a hand over his forehead.

"Her idea was that we should be partners in blackmailing Hector and go on living together on his money. Did you ever hear anything so disgusting?

"When I came in I had picked up the trashy bronze figurine that stood by her bed. Something new. She was forever buying something new. I was holding it in my hand while she talked. Suddenly I was hitting her, utterly unable to stop. I had heard people speaking of blind rage but I had never understood how blind, savage and crazy a rage could be."

He took a step forward and Deborah retreated, bumping

into the table. She sidled around it and he faced her across the littered surface.

"When I saw what I had done my first impulse was to call the police and give myself up. With Erica dead, why should I want to live? But there was my work. You don't know what that means to me; you'd have to be a painter yourself to understand.

"My life wasn't my own. Do you understand that? It belonged to my work. I had no right to surrender it. It was only after I left the house and was getting into the car that I realized I still carried the statuette; a revolting thing, clotted with blood and hair. I didn't think about fingerprints. I only wanted to be rid of it. I flung it away as far as I could. Going back to Old Knowe Farm, I spent the rest of the day there, forcing myself to go through the motions of painting. When I came home at dusk the house was swarming with police. All I could do was brazen it out; protest my innocence; trust that they'd never be able to find conclusive proof against me. It would have been all up with me if they had found the statuette. But…they didn't find it.

"I knew it was Scobie who was sending me these menacing notes in printed wording. I was as sure of it as if the idiot had signed them. Given time, I could have dealt with Scobie. But now…now I've got to deal with you…"

Deborah stammered, "If you gave yourself up, if you told your story as you've told it to me, they wouldn't hang you. They'd know you weren't in your right mind at the time. Oh, God, Andrew! You're not in your right mind now!"

"Would they let me paint in a criminal lunatic asylum? Not bloody likely. And what would it mean to be alive if I couldn't express myself in colour?"

He made a sudden lunge at her. Dodging, she barked her ankle on the camp bed. "This is not anything I want to do," he said. "It's something I've got to do."

For a desperate period, they played cat-and-mouse about the crowded room. Suddenly he made a dart and his powerful hands closed on her throat.

"It won't hurt," he muttered, "if you don't struggle."

She kicked, fought, clawed in his grasp. With the fading remnant of consciousness she heard a crashing of glass. And then there was no more fight in her. She was being drawn down, down, down, into a whirlpool of oblivion.

* * * * *

Inspector David Gray was being driven back to Garnock from Edinburgh through the dark with a warrant for the arrest of Andrew Garvin in his pocket. Tired, he sat slouched beside the driver with his hat pulled down over his eyes.

When they neared the artist's house David uttered a startled exclamation and leaned forward to peer through the windshield. When he was sure that he was not mistaken, that it really was Deborah's small car that stood in the road by the gate, he started to swear. The moment the car stopped he flung open the door, scrambled out, and ran up the stone path toward the house.

He rang the ball and pounded on the knocker but was too impatient to wait for an answer. Peering through a gap in a curtained window, he saw Andrew's arched back, his taunt arms; and Deborah's lolling head.

David turned swiftly to the driver, who had hurried close to his heels. "Got your truncheon?"

"Yes, sir."

Snatching the compact club, David smashed at the window-pane, breaking a hole in the glass large enough for his head and shoulders to pass through. He shoved both arms into the hole and struggled to thrust his body alter them. The man behind him put a shoulder under his hips and boosted him through. He landed in a heap on the floor of the room.

Over the girl's dangling head, Andrew Garvin stared at the police inspector with suddenly demented eyes. Dropping her like a lifeless puppet, he darted to his littered table and snatched up a knife. When David flung himself forward, the artist moved aside but made a swinging pass with the knife that slashed through the policeman's waistcoat and raked his ribs.

David lashed out with a foot, kicking the other man below the kneecap. As Garvin toppled forward David rocked him with a punch to the jaw and jabbed a bleeding fist into his stomach. The knife dropped from the artist's numbed fingers and clattered to the floor.

* * * * *

As if in a dream, Deborah found herself cradled in strong arms. Opening her eyes dizzily, she looked up into David's anxious face. In a weak voice she said something so silly that he doubted whether he had heard correctly. After all, one does not expect a girl who has narrowly escaped dying to come out with a foolish joke.

"I can't be in heaven," she said feebly, "for what would you be doing there?"

He kissed her—gently—and she roused herself sufficiently to say, "Not on the forehead, silly."

And then she started to weep.

"It's all right, darling," said David. "You're safe now. Don't cry."

"I'm crying for him," said Deborah huskily. "Is that very silly of me? You see, he loved her."

THE END

www.ingramcontent.com/pod-product-compliance
Lightning Source LLC
LaVergne TN
LVHW011756060526
838200LV00053B/3607